THE LAST BATTLE OF ATLANTIS

FIRST CHRONICLE
THE STORY OF DAYGUN

THOMAS D. TURNER

authorHOUSE®

AuthorHouse™
1663 Liberty Drive
Bloomington, IN 47403
www.authorhouse.com
Phone: 1-800-839-8640

Published by AuthorHouse 12/19/2012

ISBN: 978-1-4772-9851-0 (sc)
ISBN: 978-1-4772-9850-3 (hc)
ISBN: 978-1-4772-9849-7 (e)

Library of Congress Control Number: 2012923408

The book is dedicated to my father
Donald Ray Turner

If I can be half the father my father is to me, I will be a great dad.

Thomas D. Turner

CONTENTS

FOREWORD/AUTHOR'S NOTE

To some, it seems mankind goes through similar circles of learning the same lesson. History can be ten minutes or twelve thousand years. In the scheme of humanity, it makes no difference. In the past, empires have self-destructed or nations have gone too far in politics and war to only be destroyed.

Through recorded history, people have known mankind's triumphs and defeats. What could have been before written history? Societies all over the world have heard rumors and tales of a great society, but there is no concrete evidence of a once great race that was lost in time.

Like in our society, individuals must accept or disregard what mankind learns through trial and error. As individuals, people's learning experiences can be very painful. In being human, we need to know pain to know happiness. Individuals need history and pain to make us who we are. A person can integrate their past in order to improve their future, or choose to self-destruct. Every person makes these decisions every day.

The evolution of man and the evolution of earth bare many similarities. Many scientists suggest something struck the Earth in its beginnings. When the impact was over, it created what we know today as the Earth and the moon. The moon circles our planet every day and reminds us of what happened in one moment in time. There is no written history of what really happened with the two heavenly bodies, but we all know it is there, and the theory makes sense. The moon is part of the history of mankind's existence. It moves the tides of life one day to the next in every direction.

CHAPTER 1
THE FINDING
({PRESENT DAY})

"Two months of digging, and still nothing," Duncan murmurs.

"That's because there is nothing here," Kyle responds. "We only have two more weeks, and then we will go to the next adventure."

Duncan looks at the sky. He feels he has failed his fellow archeologists. It is dreary, and the clouds are thick and gray. Touches of blue can be seen peeking through the heavens. The mountains of Spain, with their magical sprinkles of snow, make Duncan feel as though everything is a dream. There is hardly a breeze at the dig site.

Duncan, who is forty-two years old, with brown hair, blue eyes, and in shape for his age, scans the mountainside and sees scattered groups of his teams working through their assigned areas. The only people around are his teams of archeologists. The closest town is eighty miles away through rough terrain. He and his team have been commissioned to dig all over the world, but only in rare cases has Duncan's team failed to find anything. Because the expedition has gone on for over three weeks with little success, the archeologists start to feel they are wasting their time.

"Go check the sites. Make sure everyone is alright. We still have two more weeks," Duncan says wearily to Kyle.

Kyle nods, and walks down the trail. He makes his rounds of the sites to see if there is anything that his coworkers have missed. It is getting very frustrating to Duncan's teams.

Duncan promised his investors the mountain region should be a refuge for a society. It was the investor's idea to come to Spain.

1

Duncan's gut instinct tells him that the region was once rich with a past society. There are traces of fertile soil, rivers, creeks, and stone. Because of the remoteness of the region, the area has not been excavated in detail from anyone else before. In Duncan's past, he has had success with places like this. The site is driving him crazy.

About four o'clock in the afternoon, Kyle, who is twenty-seven, with sandy brown hair, and brown eyes, steps under the canopy of a dig site and asks Raymond, a student on internship, if they have found anything of interest.

"Nothing," Raymond replies. "I have gone through everything in great detail, and I can't find anything."

Kyle bends down and filters through the stones. One catches his attention. He lifts it up and breaks off a section of hardened clay. He sees it is a stone carving of a horse with reins. All the archeologists look at the stone carving with confusion. The archeologists will have no way of telling where or when it was made until it goes to a lab for testing.

Kyle grabs his global phone and calls Duncan immediately and tells him of the find.

"Find out exactly where you found the stone and get our crews to that location. Don't stop digging until you find something else," Duncan orders.

Kyle says, "Because the crew has had little sleep, everyone is exhausted. This artifact could have been dropped in passing. The crews have pushed themselves to the limit. Because it's getting close to the end of the expedition and our supplies are limited, we need to wait until daybreak."

"I don't care," Duncan interrupts with anger. He tries to regroup his thoughts and says in a direct voice, "Get the supplies and crew there now. I don't want excuses!"

By nine thirty at night, the crew has completed its setup with equipment and digging tools. It is really starting to get cold. There is a full moon, which will help the excavators. They start excavating close to the rocky mountainside where they found the artifact. The archeologists start to move stones and rocks; they work until two thirty in the morning. By this time, most of the crews are working like zombies. Some cannot feel their hands because of the weather. Duncan sees their exhaustion and rethinks his decision to work through the night. He wants everyone to push themselves, but he knows he cannot destroy his crews physically.

About a hundred yards from where they found the artifact the tides are turning for the archeologists.

Rachel, who has worked at Duncan's side on many projects, shouts towards where her boss is excavating, "I found something!"

She has found a line of stones underneath rubble of rock, six feet high leading up the mountain side. The entire crew runs towards the new discovery. Everyone's heart starts pounding when they hear Rachael yelling of her discovery.

Duncan and Kyle run quickly towards Rachel. During their hasty run, the archeologists slip and fall at the same time trying to climb the hill. Duncan scrapes his hands and Kyle hits his knee hard. The two archeologists get up like nothing ever happened.

When Duncan and Kyle arrive at Rachel's site, she says, "You're both bleeding."

Duncan takes a bandana and wraps his hand tightly to stop the bleeding. He responds, "I can't feel anything."

Rachel shows Duncan the line of stones going towards the mountain. To the archeologists, it seems completely unnatural. Because there is a full moon and the lamps they brought are not sufficient, they all feel it could be the two lights playing tricks on their eyes.

Rachel says to Duncan, "I didn't know what we were uncovering until I brought more light up here. It just dawned on me. It was in front of our faces the whole time."

Duncan calls out to the crew, "This site is where we'll concentrate all of our resources. Move everything up here right now!" Duncan smiles at Rachel and says, "You are the most beautiful woman in the world."

Kyle says, "The light from the moon can play tricks, but if you put the light at the right place, it can put things in a different prospective."

After digging into the formation of rocks, they see the top of what appears to be a stone door blocked by carved stone. Duncan knows it is a doorway to the past that has not yet been discovered. Every crew member is on the site working. With the new discovery, everyone pushes themselves harder. Later into the night, they cannot go anymore. They all have to stop and rest.

Finally, after a few days of urgently digging away at the rock to uncover the entire door, they realize the true magnitude of the entrance. The stone door is almost ten inches thick, sixteen feet wide, and twelve feet high. The outer part of the door has spectacular carvings and writing in a language Duncan has never seen before. It reminds him of Egyptian hieroglyphics, yet quite different. The writing is in vertical lines, rather than horizontal, and is faded from time.

On the third morning, as the sun is about to peek out from the darkness of the night, the archeologists connect chains from their jeeps to the stone door. The excavators try to pull the huge stones and boulders away from the mountain. Slowly, the ancient entrance is pulled from the mountain. Because the weight of the stone is so great, the jeeps and trucks start to lose traction. Finally, a small piece of the entrance breaks off, and Duncan shouts for the drivers to stop. At the top of the door, the entrance is almost wide enough for one person to be lowered into the chamber. The archeologists cannot pull the door out anymore without destroying it.

Everyone is ashamed of what just happened. The archeologists take the chains and ropes off the doorway. No one says a word to one another. Because of haste, a piece of history has been destroyed.

Duncan humbly walks over to Kyle, and says, "We always talk about how tomb robbers destroyed history. We just did the same thing with the entrance, and it happened here under my supervision."

"They only cared about money and riches," Kyle replies back to Duncan. "We stand for more than that. We are uncovering something no one has ever seen so we can share it with the world."

Duncan says, "Still, we did this out of haste, and we didn't respect history or preserve it."

Kyle responds, "It already happened, and the only thing we can do is to keep going forward."

Duncan and Kyle go to the breach and can feel a draft of cool air coming from the top of the entrance. Stale air comes from the opening. Duncan takes a flashlight and looks through the chipped barrier. The crews are silent. They are still stunned about their discovery. Duncan looks inside the mountain and cannot see an end into the darkness. Finally, he backs out of the entrance and instructs his crews to go back to the original camp so they can bring more supplies to the new site. Many of the archeologists have not slept for over twenty-six hours. Some of the team members have forgotten what sleep feels like. The leadership of Duncan, and good discipline, is the only thing keeping the archeologists going.

Duncan and Kyle sit on a rock close to the entrance and look at each other and laugh. They know this may be their biggest discovery yet.

Duncan says to Kyle, "This will never be topped until we find the Ark of the Covenant."

"What do you expect we'll find inside?" Kyle asked.

Duncan replies, "Great things, Kyle, great things."

Chapter II
A Labyrinth of History

The next morning, all of the supplies have been moved from the old sites and everyone rests but Kyle. While Duncan sleeps, Kyle pries open the entrance just wide enough to send someone through the dark chamber. Kyle wakes up Duncan and tells him the structure is ready to be breached. Duncan gets up and smiles at his right hand man. He puts on his boots and jacket and they jog toward the site. Rachel is already waiting on the edge of the entrance with ropes and climbing equipment. Kyle and Duncan both climb to the opening.

"Ready?" she asks, shaken with joy.

"Ready as I'll ever be," Duncan replies as he fastens his harness to his belt.

He and Kyle are ready to descend down the opening with their ropes.

Duncan jokingly tells Kyle, "I'll go in first. I may need you to save me."

Kyle responds, "Well you are forty-two. You may break your legs touching the floor. Don't go in too fast."

Rachel starts to lower Duncan into the mountain. He clicks on his flashlight and stares in amazement at what he sees as he twirls with the rope going down. The full descent is almost sixteen feet to the floor inside.

"What do you see?" Kyle calls down.

Duncan yells, "I don't know; my eyes are failing me because of my age. Lower Kyle in here. Rachel, you come too. There are things in here only God can answer."

After a couple of minutes, the three are on solid ground inside the mouth of the mountain. All of them look in different directions with their flashlights.

Kyle says to Duncan and Rachel while he goes forward with his flashlight deeper in the mountain cavity, "If this is the entrance, where does it end?" It is hard to see. All they can hear inside is wind, echoes from talking, and the footsteps as they walk.

Duncan, Rachel, and Kyle take their flashlights and shine light upon every structure. Halls and walkways splinter off in every direction with no end in sight. The archeologists are shocked at what they see. They do not know what to think at this point. They go in different cavities and see buildings, bridges, and statues. It is a miniature city.

"A civilization this large should not be here," Duncan says in awe.

Kyle points out holes in the stone wall with metal plated hangers used for torches, and ventilation shafts right above them. They all feel the draft coming from the holes inside the walls where the smoke could ventilate outside the chambers.

"There's just enough wind sucking through these holes to not extinguish the torches. It must be for lighting. This is a very complex system. This would take years to produce such a system," Duncan says.

Duncan pokes his head inside one of the holes and shines his light into the darkness. He can see the past society used the ventilation system for escaping smoke. As he puts his head deeper inside the hole, Duncan's hair is wind blown. Because of the air rushing from the ventilation shaft, he has to put his hair back into place. When he looks back at his colleagues, Kyle and Rachael start to laugh but hold it back.

"This society doesn't meet the profile of any of the surrounding cultures in this area. If this place is as old as I think it is, they were way more advanced than any society in this region," Duncan says.

Kyle goes back to the mouth of the doorway and yells to the crew above, "Bring down the small generators, lights, and surveying tools."

Meanwhile, Rachel notices the writing on the walls does not match the writing outside the doorway.

Kyle looks at the writing. "It doesn't make sense," he says. "The symbols in the writing outside are vertical. These are horizontal and look totally different all together. Why would a society have different styles of writing?"

"Maybe they had two different languages," Duncan guesses.

Before noon, Duncan tells the survey crews to come down and measure the main room. He instructs everyone to stay in the light until more people are lowered down from the surface. He does not want his crews to get lost because their safety is his responsibility. Even though Duncan wants to go forward himself, he does not want to be a bad influence. The team begins to lower generators, lights, and digging equipment. They eventually turn on the lights, but it is not enough to penetrate the darkness more than forty feet.

Duncan calls up to a team member named Julie, "Go to the nearest town and buy new generators, lights, lamps, and supplies. Buy everything they have."

Julie says, "By the time I get down the mountain and come back, it may take two and half days."

"We need as many supplies as we can get until our investor sends in the heavy gear," Duncan says while Julie gathers her things. "Mr. Callaway was phoned this morning, but I don't know when the supplies will arrive. Time is our enemy right now. I need fast solutions."

Duncan, Rachel, and Kyle take their flashlights and start to venture deeper into the mountain structure. For safety purposes, each of the three takes teams with them, and they all go in different directions. Because it is their first time, no one goes more than two hundred meters in any direction. There is a labyrinth of openings leading into larger rooms and some of the hallways are sixty feet across. The ceilings are one hundred and twenty feet high in some areas. Inside the mountain there are buildings three stories high. All structures are different colors with many different pictures painted on each wall, particularly with the image of a bull. Duncan sees no resemblance to the Romans, Greeks, Egyptians, or Eastern cultures. The buildings inside are like nothing Duncan has ever seen or read about.

Two days later, close to nightfall, Mr. Callaway, the main investor of the excavation, arrives with three helicopters full of food, water, generators, tools, and lights for further exploration. The millionaire comes to Duncan and asks to see what he has found. Duncan gives

Callaway the stoned carved horses and asks to get it carbon dated when he gets back to civilization. After telling the tycoon about the site, Duncan gives him a list of supplies. Right away, Callaway orders helicopters to bring more materials. Because of the season, the temperatures are cold at night and hot during the day. Calloway wants to see more of what Duncan has found.

Mr. Callaway is in his fifties, but in good shape for his age. He climbs to the cavity in the mountain and asks to be lowered into the underground city. Duncan cannot refuse. He needs the tycoon's funds and influence to continue the dig. Callaway has already invested tens of thousands into this project, and he has gotten nothing in return until now. Duncan knows Callaway has more resources he can invest and help speed the project along. The government of Spain could become involved and stop the excavation. Time is the enemy here. Callaway is lowered with Duncan.

After Calloway investigates the find, he calls several sources for more men and supplies and uses his ability to expedite more resources to the site. He stays at the site for another hour and is amazed. After a couple of hours, Callaway flies off in his helicopter to get more supplies.

While Duncan and Kyle watch the helicopters fly into the distance, they realize they will have everything needed to realize their dream. All necessary equipment and supplies are now at their fingertips.

After Calloway leaves, a smart kid named Lucas yells from the entrance of the city, "I need Duncan to come down here right now. I found something astonishing."

Duncan and Kyle both run towards Lucas inside the entrance. Lucas takes the two archeologists three hundred yards from the entrance where no one has ventured yet.

"Look at this over here," Lucas says with excitement.

They follow Lucas sixty more yards into another small hallway. Duncan shines his flashlight on a set of armor in the middle of the room. It is made of tarnished silver, but has not eroded. There is writing engraved into the armor across the breastplate. In the center of the body armor is a symbol with a bull. It seems to be the crest of the once great society. There is a skeleton inside the armor.

"I am wondering who this could have been," Duncan says. He

shakes his head and studies the warrior which apparently died on this spot.

"Do you have any thoughts about the time period?" Kyle asks out of astonishment. "I am trying to fit this together, but I don't know where to begin."

Duncan looks around and says, "Look here at this sword. It looks like it is made of steel. This could be revolutionary. We need to find out what metals make up this artifact."

The archeologists take the skeleton, sword, and armor to the surface. They conclude the sword is made of steel. The crest on the armor is unlike anything they have seen before. Duncan will instruct Calloway to get the armor and body to be carbon dated on the next supply run. The crews take the breastplate and sword to a tent and start to study the objects more carefully.

"The carbon dating will give us a clearer picture of when this took place," Duncan says, as he paces back and forth.

In the meantime, Rachel's crew brings up different artifacts from the mountain city to the surface. The teams find gold and silver. The crews know this is only a fraction of what is inside the mountain. Many places have not yet been excavated because of cave-ins.

Duncan, Kyle, and Rachel decide to go forward with more exploration. They want to push deeper inside the mountain. Duncan fears a cave-in and knows the chances of them getting lost are great. Even though the city has been here for centuries, the walls and ceilings look as if they could cave-in at anytime in certain areas. Just in case of being trapped, they take food and water for a day's journey. During their excavations, they see barracks and defensive bridges which have not been walked on for thousands of years. They look and see small communities of buildings and market places.

In one of their adventures inside the mountain, the archeologists find a large chamber. They see what they think are two temples for worship. The room is about the size of a modern day city block. In the middle of the large assembly room, they see a statue which towers sixty feet towards the ceiling. The face of the statue is a man with a beard and long hair. With one hand in the air and an olive branch in the other, the statue seems to be a symbol of peace. It is made of concrete and tarnished with metals. At the foot of the huge sculpture, the crews look up with bewilderment.

"Look at the two temples; both are pyramid shaped. The temples' architecture looks as if they are between Greek and Egyptian. It looks as if a timeline is between two thousand years to a thousand years B.C.," Rachel says while she walks around the structure and studies it.

Duncan interrupts and says, "It looks as if there was only one God in their civilization. They might have been monotheistic. Look around. There are no other statues to worship. Considering the history of man, this also doesn't make sense. Except in the last two thousand years most cultures in the past believed in multiple gods. The timetable is off. There is great deal of unanswered questions here. This culture is totally on its own."

Kyle says, "Rachel take pictures. We can get more of an understanding at the surface. There is very little light here, but the flash from the camera will help us see what is in the shadows."

After about three days, Callaway comes back with supplies and equipment. The tycoon lands five helicopters three hundred yards away from the mouth of the entrance. The millionaire has an army of men and women to help excavate the site. The tycoon's army is at Duncan's disposal. Callaway has also brought a small bulldozer carried by one of his huge helicopters. Duncan immediately informs him of the chest plate. Callaway orders it to be taken directly to be carbon dated.

Callaway tries to yell over the helicopters, "I have wonderful news as well. Is there anywhere private that we can talk?"

Away from the others, Kyle and Duncan walk with Calloway towards a tent. The tycoon says, "This is a private matter. Kyle can you give us a moment?"

Duncan looks at Kyle and gives him a face of reassurance that everything is okay.

Kyle walks away mad, but with his head tall.

"What is so important that I can't have my best archeologist here by my side?" Duncan asks.

Callaway says, "He needs to hear this from you. You may need to sit down."

"What is going on?" Duncan asks.

Callaway says, "The carbon dating came back from the stone horse, and it is a lot older than you and I ever thought."

"How old is this place?" Duncan asks, pacing around. The archeologist cannot take the anticipation of the answer.

The tycoon looks away for a moment and looks intently into Duncan's eyes.

Calloway says, "It looks as if it is about ten thousand years before Christ. We need more artifacts to be sure."

Duncan sits and leans against a small and unstable portable table. He can barely keep it together and replies, "That can't be true Mr. Callaway, but maybe you're right. In the last three decades, archeologists have found cities dating back during that era. With this city, it will change the way we have seen mankind before written history. Look at the ancient site close to Dwaraka in India. It is believed to be over twelve thousand years old. The city is submerged a hundred and twenty feet under water inside the Gulf of Cambay. After the ice melted during the Ice Age, it is predicted the oceans rose over four hundred feet. With what I know, mankind flourished after the Ice Age and something destroyed it. It could have been disease, climate change, or mankind killing itself. We are lucky to find this site. It has written history before the Egyptians and Samarians."

Callaway shrugs and says, "The artifact I brought back confirms the dating. I think it is a part of the lost civilization of Atlantis."

"We can't put that out of the question," Duncan replies. "But if this is the lost civilization of Atlantis, a new story will be told. Looking here, Atlantis may not be a myth, but until we find out what the ancient writing is saying, we will never know. I am putting Rachel in charge of the project. She can break the text."

The millionaire walks toward the door and Duncan follows him. Callaway points at the opening of the cave where everyone is working double time and says, "The answer is in that doorway. If you think Rachel can figure it out, I have complete confidence in her. But, she is only twenty-seven years old. I thought you hired her because of her looks."

Duncan responds, "She is one of the most intelligent people I know."

The next morning, the tycoon's crews help Duncan's team to clear the doorway. The two teams work side by side and are able to excavate the site faster and with greater efficiency. Duncan is still in control of the excavation. Callaway does not get in the way. The millionaire knows this is too important for a hasty treasure hunt.

The crews are finally able to get equipment and trucks into the mouth of the city, and begin exploring further into the mountain. They find more statues, artifacts, and buildings deeper inside the mountain. The archeologists find the city has a sewer system and baths like the ancient Roman society. They find marvelous monuments and jewelry made of gold and silver. It becomes clear the expedition will make everyone rich.

Duncan and Callaway do not want any media or government interference until some answers are found. The government of Spain could stop the excavation. The tycoon reinforces that this expedition must stay a secret. Everyone agrees. In this part of Spain, there are very few people that venture this deep into the mountain regions. It is far from any large populations. Callaway orders a perimeter to be built around the site to keep out hikers and mountain climbers. The millionaire has a great deal of pull with the Spanish government. If something does not go in his favor, he could cash in some favors with the Spanish administration.

Three weeks after finding the city. Duncan and Kyle begin to establish a map of what they found so far. The teams find skeletons and weapons deeper inside the entrance. Duncan has concluded that there must have been a major battle toward the end of the civilization, and the silver plated warrior was protecting the city from their attackers. The teams find other soldiers that were also probably killed in the same conflict. Duncan concludes the enemy of the city was not as advanced as the inhabitants of the mountain. The archeologists find other weapons which were only made of bronze, and the other enemy warriors were more primitively armored.

Duncan says to Kyle, "The other army must have been overwhelming to take the defensive positions of the city. The population here had swords made of steel. No one had this kind of technology for centuries to come. The placements and devices here were centuries ahead of its time. Look at Göbekli Tepe found in Turkey not long ago. The site was built twelve thousand years ago. The technology there to move ten ton stones is unbelievable. But yet, they did it. The way we look at mankind before written history is starting to change."

Looking around inside the mountain, they find another

chamber. Duncan and Kyle find large lanterns hanging from the ceiling. The lanterns are made of metal and glass. Duncan and his crew are completely surprised.

Kyle says, "In this mountain, history will have to be rewritten. Everything thought to this point in history has to be revised."

Days later, Duncan and Callaway find out the lanterns were filled with whale oil. To do this, the society had to have good boating and hunting skills. The ships, which hunted whales, had to be very large to do so.

On the twenty-fourth day, Duncan, Callaway, Kyle, and Rachel wait for the opportunity to enter through another cave-in. A cavern was discovered with thirty feet of rubble blocking the entrance to a new pathway. Large boulders keep them from entering, and the crews try to dig a path around the obstruction.

"I have a feeling this will be a key to unlock the answers to these people's lives," Duncan says to Callaway.

Diggers finally announce they have broken through the hallway. It is still dangerous to enter, but they venture in the chamber anyway. Duncan, Callaway, Rachel, and Kyle start to climb through the entrance of the ancient room. They flash their lights into the cavity and crawl into the next chamber. They slide off an obstruction and hit the floor. The four look all around and immediately understand the fate of the city's inhabitants. Callaway and the archeologists find thousands of skeletal remains in the large room. The grand hall still has burned scars on the walls.

"They were burned alive," Duncan says to Callaway. "There must be tens of thousands of them, and I don't see any weapons. These must have been the citizens."

Callaway replies, "But why would any army burn the civilians? They have no weapons. There was not a fight here."

With tears on her face Rachel says, "I don't see any children's remains."

Duncan wants to believe that the children were spared, and says, "Most likely they were put into slavery by their attackers."

Kyle walks gently over the remains like it was a giant grave and asks, "Why not kill everyone? Why eradicate only adults?"

"Children can be incorporated into other cultures. Adults are too dangerous; they can rebel," Duncan replies.

Callaway, who is only thinking of money, says, "Let's start

excavating for more artifacts. I will leave this to you. I will be leaving tomorrow."

Duncan starts to breathe heavily and replies to the group, "This was a massacre. It reminds me of Nazi concentration camps of World War II."

During the thirty-first day of the excavation, Duncan's health is failing; he has lost fifteen pounds in the last month, and he has kidney stones. Callaway brought antibiotics and pain medicine to help him, but Duncan starts to dehydrate from the side effects of the kidney stones. Around noon, Duncan, in considerable discomfort, is looking over some artifacts in his tent.

Rachel comes in the tent. She is out of breath and says, "The crew has just broken into another room. You need to see this."

In the excitement of the new find, Duncan starts to get weaker and grabs his stomach; he begins to cramp badly. Even though Duncan is in pain, he runs with Rachel, and they grab Kyle on the way. They all jump into a golf cart, and go towards the site. On the cart, Duncan can feel every bump they hit, but he says nothing to Kyle or Rachel about his pain.

They arrive at the site. Duncan can barely think straight. With all of the enthusiasm, Kyle and Rachel do not sense Duncan's pain. They move in and break through the chamber. The three archeologists flash their lights all around, and they put a stationary light in the large room.

Duncan says, "This is what we've been searching for."

Kyle points his flashlight to the walls and says, "Look at the carving and metal objects that surround this room."

Duncan picks up an object off a stone table and says, "It looks like a crossbow. It's in remarkable condition. The cave-in must have kept most of the moisture out. The wood is in remarkable shape for its age. Crossbows were not invented for thousands of years after the Ice Age."

Kyle studies the wood in detail and asks, "What kind of wood is this?" He puts it down and says, "I have never seen this kind of wood in this region or anywhere for that matter."

Rachel picks up an artifact and looks at Duncan and says, "The society appears to have taken great pride in farming and family. Look at this carved stone. It is a little boy farming with an ox."

Kyle looks at a wall with shelves carved out of the mountain and says, "There are thousands of tablets that tell their story. It's going to take a long time to decipher this text. Rachel, you have your work cut out for you. Mr. Callaway will send you people to help."

Kyle notices a glimmer in a corner and shines his light on the artifact. He yells, "Oh my!"

Duncan runs to Kyle as he grabs his stomach in pain and asks, "What is it?"

"Look at this sword. I think it's made of pure gold and it is engraved with writing. It must have belonged to royalty of this city. The sword is very heavy but thin."

Duncan shines his flashlight at the object while he trembles with excitement and says, "This should not be here."

Duncan takes the sword and leans against a stone desk. The pain from his cramps intensifies. The archeologist looks at the sword in wonderment, but as he holds the artifact firmly, he falls to the ground holding his stomach and the sword. He starts to feel weaker and fades in and out of consciousness. He cannot stand the pain any longer.

In great pain, Duncan grabs Kyle and says, "I feel as if a thousand ants are crawling all over my body."

Kyle and Rachel try to help their mentor, but Duncan starts to go unconscious. As if in a daydream, Duncan is totally aware of his surroundings, but his soul is being stripped away from his body to a different world. The unconscious archeologist drifts like a lost soul going back in time, and he sees the destruction of a great city. He sees the conflict which took place in the city of the mountain. Duncan floats like a feather to the chamber where tens of thousands of the city dwellers were burned alive. He can see in his mind how the inhabitants were killed. The sensation seems to take him back in time. In Duncan's mind, he sees the citizens being massacred. As if he were there, the burning flesh inside the chamber engulfs him, and his involuntary mind floats to the outside of the mountain city. He sees thousands of children taken by force to a new world of slavery.

After seconds of floating, Duncan is swept away again. As if he is going a hundred times the speed of sound into darkness, the archeologist can smell the ocean. In his state of mind, it is very vivid as if he were there. All of a sudden, he rises swiftly to the surface and sees waves from the ocean.

Because Duncan feels in control, he feels he can wake up or continue his journey. He chooses to go forward with his travels. He feels an earthquake and sees a beautiful city being destroyed with the shaking of the earth and going into the sea. At the same time, the city looks like as if it was deserted for hundreds of years. With such exquisite buildings and stone pyramids, the archeologist does not understand why it was uninhabited. Duncan floats in the air again and feels as if he is slipping backwards in time. He looks around again and sees a great civilization prospering and learning. Duncan sees children playing and people walking in a great city close to the shore, and he can feel what the culture is feeling. The passion coming from the society is nothing but honor, family, and the search of making mankind better.

Then the unconscious archeologist is swept away again to another land where he knows the beginning of the end takes place of this great culture. Duncan sees the sun passing in front of his face hundreds of times in a matter of seconds.

Time stops and Duncan sees the army of a great civilization prepared to engage in a battle. He floats like a balloon and sees armies getting ready to fight one another.

CHAPTER III
THE BIRTH OF A GREAT WARRIOR

The day is ripe with the fear and pride of warriors. It is dawn. Eighty miles northwest of the western border of the Empire of Atlantis, the Atlantean scouts spy on the vast army of the Valtear Kingdom which is approaching them from their north. The Atlantean generals will know every aspect of the Valtear Army before the battle even begins.

A little later, the dust flies upward towards the sun. The day is getting warmer. It is spring and getting closer to summer. From the large Valtearean Army, the earth trembles with a hundred and thirty thousand men and beasts riding and marching towards the Atlanteans.

King Tulless, ruler of Valtear, leads his men onto the battlefield. His family has ruled the Valteareans for over three generations. He has been a strong leader and will defend his lands to the death. The Valtearean Army is composed of many different factions and tribes from throughout their kingdom. They have all come together from all across their lands to fight alongside their king.

King Tulless' army is not as well trained as the Atlanteans, but the number of warriors brought to the battlefield is astonishing. The Valteareans have brought hundreds of mammoths and elephants to fight their aggressors. Tulless' heavy cavalry is trained to work in the fields and mines, but has little training in warfare. On the other hand, the Valtear warriors have been trained to fight, but not to the extent of the Atlantean military. Each tribe fights differently, which Tulless knows will not be in his favor on the battlefield.

The Atlantean division in Valtear is the elite of their military. The division consists of fifteen thousand infantry, three thousand cavalry horseman, or light cavalry, five hundred heavy cavalry, including elephants and mammoths, five thousand archers, and fifteen hundred artillery personnel who are the best fighters of the empire.

The Atlantean Army's defensive perimeter is heavily fortified and is on a hill with valleys below. They have brought their highest technological weapons to the battlefield. The Atlantean soldiers are outnumbered more than six to one, but they have the confidence in their weaponry, tactics, and generals to defeat Tulless' army.

For hundreds of years, the Atlantean Empire has traded with the Valtearean people. Tulless' kingdom's main export to the Atlantean Empire is iron ore. Iron ore is the backbone of the war machine of the Atlanteans. The mining of this precious resource started the economy of the Valtearean civilization. Before, the Valteareans were only nomadic and had no formidable governments. The ore helped build cities and develop a new society in Tulless' realm. Lately, the Valteareans have fallen short in their mining output to keep the Atlanteans at full production in making military weapons. Because Atlantean technology is becoming more dependent in using steel for their weapons, their empire needs more resources to help protect their borders.

The main threat to the Atlanteans is the Kayout Empire. Kayout is outside the Atlantean peninsula to the east side of the Alber Mountains. The Atlanteans have gone to war with this civilization more than once since the beginning of their society, and Atlantis is getting fearful of another war.

The Kayout culture is greatly different than the Atlanteans. The two empires have two totally different religious and cultural beliefs. The majority of the people on the main continent believe in more than one deity. Only the inhabitants of the Atlantean peninsula believe in one God.

Atlantis has decided to conquer Valtear before someone takes it first. If Atlantis tries to bring a peaceful takeover with Valtear, the Kayout Empire will see the inhabitants of the peninsula as being weak. Because of world politics, Atlantis has to become a bully just to keep the other empires on the continent from attacking their own homeland.

If the inhabitants of the peninsula take Valtear, it will make the Kayout Empire think twice before attempting to attack Atlantis.

The Atlantean generals in Valtear need to win a swift battle to gain the respect of other potential enemies. This is why there is only one Atlantean division attacking the Valteareans. If the peninsula loses, the Kayouts will see the Atlanteans having only one division. If the peninsula wins, they will be seen as undefeatable.

To the Atlanteans, Tulless' people are very prideful of their heritage and warriors, but they are still in the early stages of being a centralized government. If the Valteareans were more organized in politics, the tribes could come together and become just as powerful as the Atlanteans. The Valtear Kingdom would be a true economic and military power. However, bad politics from factions and religion is hampering their progress.

Emperor Aten, the ruler of Atlantis, has no choice but to take the Valtear people under occupation to reconstruct their neighboring kingdom. If Atlantis does not occupy Valtear, Tulless' resources will be stripped away from neighboring empires and be used for their own war machine. Atlantis' Military Council and Senate see the future occupation as beneficial to both societies.

Part of the reason to take Valtear under occupation is to make it stronger and destroy the corrupt factions. In doing so, Tulless, who is thirty-three, with a beard, and long blond hair, has a better opportunity to have a more centralized government. The corrupt Valtearean groups do not want occupation because of their own greed and power. With the world in so much turmoil, Atlantis cannot take the chance of Tulless falling out of power. Plus, Valtear is the main producer of natural resources to Atlantis. Aten cannot let Valtear fall in the hands of any other empire.

If Aten takes Tulless' kingdom, he will occupy Valtear for two years. The Atlantean's main goal is to help their neighboring kingdom to become stronger. In doing so, the west of the Alber Mountains will be safer from any future attack by other empires. Valtear also borders Mearth, Gambut, Kayout, and Kanis. All of these empires are strong, but since half of the population of Valtear believes in the same gods as their neighbors, there is little hostility.

On the eve of battle, Daygun, son of the Atlantean Emperor, assembles his generals for the battle. Prince Daygun, Quentoris, and Laptos, are all twenty-four years old and have grown up together. Because Quentoris is the same age, they all went to the same elite military school. In prior military engagements, they all know each other's weaknesses and strengths on a battlefield.

Daygun, who is six feet, two inches tall, with dark hair, and blue eyes, is the natural leader and has no fear of death. The Atlantean Prince understands only too well the necessity of resources in Valtear, and he knows it is a matter of time before the East comes knocking on the Atlantean door in conquest. In two years, the Kayout Empire could reorganize and attack Atlantis. At this moment, the Kayouts are having trouble with their Northern states and a great deal of their military is there to keep it under control.

For the last five hundred years, Atlantis has been an empire. In the Atlantean past, war has broken out with powerful empires on the continent, and the only way to ward off their enemies was to bring all of the peninsula's kingdoms together. A great leader named Atlandreous was the first to unite the kingdoms. Aten is a descendent of the first Emperor of Atlantis.

On the Atlantean peninsula there are four city-states, or kingdoms, which have come together to make one centralized government. Each of the city-states has at least a million people in population within their city walls except one. Each has brought their culture, resources, and technologies together to become the most powerful empire in the world.

An important city to the Atlantean Empire is the City of God. The city of Halotropolis has brought the gift of the sword and infantry to their empire. Halotropolis' sword engineers are the finest in the world. The technology and technique in making the swords has made the Atlantean Empire what it is today. The reason their infantry is so strong is good discipline and practice. Everyday, the people of Halotropolis spar with one another. The apprentices must spar with each other every week in the presence of a council. After each match, they move up in rank until they are masters of the art.

The city is the center point of the Atlantean religion. It was Halotropolis which brought God to the rest of the peninsula five hundred years prior. There are more lavish temples inside Halotropolis than any other city-state. People come from all across the peninsula to pray in the beautiful temples.

Masaba is the city of trade and commerce for the Atlantean Empire. The city mostly trades animals for war and farming. The city trains and domesticates elephants, mammoths, and horses. With good irrigated farmlands, the people of Masaba learned to feed the entire empire. The city is closest to the Great West Wall of the Atlantean Empire. Because Masaba is closest to Valtear, Aten has four military divisions stationed at the city-state to back up Daygun's conquest. They are there to reinforce the Great West Wall in case of an invasion from the Gambut or Valteareans.

The largest Atlantean seaport is Vasic where Aten's navy is built. The population of the harboring city is only a quarter of a million and is the smallest of the four city-states. But a great deal of sea-trade goes through Vasic and is one of the richest cities on the peninsula.

Inside Vasic's harbors are the Atlantean destroyers. Each ship is one hundred yards long and twenty-five yards across. Vasic has just built twelve large battlecruisers that reach almost a hundred and fifty yards long and forty yards across. The massive battlecruisers hold over six hundred oarsmen and support large catapults and giant crossbows. With the latest technology, the Atlanteans have put turrets on the new ships to utilize their artillery. With using turrets, these ships can concentrate their firepower on any ship they encounter. No other navy in the world has this kind of technology. It is simple, but very effective.

At the same time, the Atlanteans have also completed two heavy battlecruisers as flagships. The two ships are two hundred yards long and seventy yards across. The Atlantean heavy battlecruisers require over a thousand oarsmen. These massive ships resemble two parallel giant canoes with a large deck going across them both. It has the largest platform on water. With the Atlantean technologies striving so quickly, they are very optimistic about keeping their sea power. With this power, their sea trade will strive and keep the Atlantean's economy strong.

The capital city of Aten's empire is Atlantis. The city is the center of knowledge and technology. The city is full of universities, libraries, and military schools. Orchards outside the gates of Atlantis produce the molless tree. The wood is used to produce the best bows in the world. The bow can shoot almost sixty-five yards farther than that of any enemy. In turn, the Atlanteans have the best archers. At the age of six, each child in the capital is trained with the bow.

Daygun, Quentoris, and Laptos have had twelve years of

training at the elite military school in the city of Atlantis. All three generals have specialized skills, and their division marvel at their ability. The loyalty of their soldiers comes from victories of past battles. The Atlantean trusts their generals enough to die for them. As the battle is about to begin, Laptos approaches his fraternal twin brother. Daygun examines the battlefield in full attentiveness of his adversary.

Laptos asks, "What is the best way to defend our position? Moreover, how do we counter their attack?"

Laptos admires his brother and wonders if he will ever be as great of a leader. Daygun has always been a people person and has helped with his father's military politics. Even though the two twins look similar, they are different in their personalities. Daygun has a great deal of common sense and personality. He can picture a battlefield and make things happen to his advantage. Laptos, on the other hand, has been sheltered because of Daygun's accomplishments.

Daygun replies, "You can always have an idea of how to attack and how to defend, but until it happens you will never really know." The Atlantean Prince points at their rival and says, "A good general has hundreds of ways to defeat a challenger before the battle begins. Those hundred ways may not do the trick. A good general will always make the enemy come to him on his own terms. Life and death is a chance. If an army doesn't take a chance, the army can't win. The discipline to die is the heart and soul of our army. If a general can take out the fear of dying on the battlefield, courage will take over and destroy any adversary. You may be emperor one day, brother. One day, I might not be on the battlefield with you. You will be the one to lead our men into battle and victories."

The enemy has come to the Atlanteans as anticipated. Daygun is fearful for his army, but not for himself. The Atlantean Prince would rather die here than retreat to his father. Daygun looks up to Aten and wishes he could be half the father that his father is to him. He knows he is about to conquer a kingdom for Atlantis, but he knows it is only for the survival of his people. Daygun thinks about the enemy soldiers that are about to oppose him, and he knows they have families as well.

For the most part, Daygun was opposed to the war, but he knows there is no choice. Kayout is growing stronger, and the

Atlantean Empire needs the ore to produce their weapons to defend themselves in case the Kayout attacks.

Daygun stands behind his artillery with Laptos and Quentoris looking at the battlefield. He sees the Valteareans lining up to attack. As Daygun looks, he sees five hundred Valtearean heavy cavalry lining up to his right, and three hundred mammoths and elephants lining up to his left. In the middle are Tulless' main infantry, archers, and light cavalry. Over seventy thousand Valteareans are about to attack dead center of the Atlantean fortification.

Daygun says to Quentoris, "Order our twenty-five giant crossbows to fire our projectiles to our right and order the catapults to fire at our enemy to our left." Then Daygun looks at his brother and says, "Order three thousand archers to take out the threat to our center and take a thousand archers on each side to reinforce our artillery."

Each giant crossbow projectile is filled with a flammable liquid in its warhead. The projectile's base is made of hollowed thin steel and the head of the projectiles are made of pottery. In the air, the projectiles are stable and can withstand the thrust from the power of the large crossbow. Once the projectile hits the ground, the warhead bursts into flames.

As his enemy gets closer and every piece of artillery is in position, Daygun orders, "Fire!"

Horns blow from the Atlanteans for their infantry and archers get in position to defend against what is coming. Every Atlantean warrior runs into formation and stands ready.

In minutes, one quarter of the battlefield is blazing from the giant crossbow projectiles on Daygun's right. Many Valtearean cavalry are on fire or crushed by the boulders from the Atlantean catapults on the first round of the Atlantean artillery. Daygun's archers are able to keep the first round of Valtearean cavalry from breaching into their formation.

After the first round from the Atlantean artillery, the Atlantean crossbows are reloaded with the krample projectiles. The krample is a projectile full of spikes. When the krample explodes on the battlefield, it throws hundreds of spikes that can go through the hooves of enemy horses and heavy cavalry. Daygun's catapults and giant crossbows load the krample.

At the last possible moment Daygun yells at his artillery, "Fire!"

When the krample hits the battlefield, hundreds of Valtearean light and heavy cavalry fall to the ground. The men riding on their beasts are injured or killed by being thrown off at high speeds. After just ten minutes in rushing towards the Atlanteans, the Valtearean cavalry are starting to get depleted.

On the other side of the battlefield the Valtearean and Atlantean infantry become engaged in Daygun's center. The Valtearean archers in the rear of their infantry are getting closer to the Atlantean fortification.

Out of desperation, Tulless looks at his archer commander and yells, "Fire!"

Tulless' archers fire their arrows and they fall short of the Atlantean defensive parameter.

Daygun can see his plan is working except his center. At the Atlantean center, his infantry and archers are losing ground. The Atlantean's left and right engagements are stabilized, but Daygun's infantry and archers in his center are in trouble.

Daygun says to Quentoris, "Take our light infantry and go around to divert their attention. After engaging, I need twenty minutes." Daygun looks at his brother and says, "You want glory. Here it is. Take our heavy cavalry and hit their center. You lead the charge. I will command our military resources here, and together we will accomplish our goal within thirty minutes."

With most of the Valtearean heavy cavalry destroyed. Daygun's archers are ordered to concentrate on Tulless' light cavalry. The Atlantean infantry holds on but still is in trouble from the overwhelming numbers of Valtearean infantry.

Tulless gets closer to the Atlantean fortification and feels he is about to make a breakthrough.

The King of Valtear looks at his archer commander and orders, "Fire!"

Being closer to the Atlantean perimeter, the Valtearean archers start to hit their mark. The Atlantean infantry and archers are hit, and Daygun's main army has to fall back giving Tulless the momentum.

Daygun looks at his artillery commander and yells, "Fire at will. Give them everything we have!"

Quentoris, who is strong and heavy set, goes around the battlefield and engages the Valtearean's rear flank. With his light cavalry, he confuses the Valtearean Army. Daygun has Tulless somewhat surrounded.

When the Atlantean center is losing badly, Laptos' heavy cavalry explodes through the ranks of the Valtearean center. The momentum on the battlefield changes in minutes. Laptos has no competition on the battlefield except the Valtearean archers.

Because Quentoris' light cavalry is swift, the enemy has a hard time using their archers to counter Daygun's diversion. Plus the Atlanteans have a better range because of their superior bows. The Atlantean light cavalry confronts the Valteareans on two fronts and brings confusion to the Atlantean enemy even more.

Because of the constant bombardment from the Atlanteans archers and Quentoris' light cavalry, Laptos' heavy cavalry breaks the ranks of the Valtearean infantry. At this point, the Valtearean warriors are doomed. The battle is over. The Atlantean captains can handle the rest with ease.

After Daygun sees his center taking back the ground they lost, a white flag comes from the Valtearean side of the battlefield and Daygun orders a ceasefire. Tens of thousands of men back off to have a summit between the two leaders.

While only ten percent of the Atlantean soldiers are dead or wounded, the Valtearean Army is destroyed. The prince knows the battle was ultimately for the greater good of the two societies. Daygun will go home as a hero, but feels guilty about the death of his soldiers.

CHAPTER IV
DIPLOMACY TO A CONQUERED KINGDOM

Two hours later, King Tulless sends a messenger to Daygun, and asks what needs to be done to save his people. The Atlantean Prince tells Tulless' messenger that he will speak with the King of Valtear in the morning and to carry his wounded from the battlefield. Daygun assures the Valtearean messenger that they will not be harmed. The Atlantean Prince offers to take the badly wounded Valteareans to the Atlantean treatment centers. The Atlantean medical teams will help the wounded of their enemy. Because of Atlantean technology, the Valtearean soldiers will have a better chance of survival. Daygun uses this act of goodwill to aide in the occupation of Valtear. It is the policy of the Atlanteans to preserve life after a war.

The next day, King Tulless officially surrenders to Daygun. Blood soaks the battlefield. The Valtearean wounded and dead are still being taken off the combat zone. There are still cries of warriors on both sides pleading for help. The King of Valtear sees his own defeated warriors and must swallow his pride for the good of his people. Tulless goes to Daygun's tent. Inside, Tulless looks toward the ground around Daygun's feet.

Tulless asks, "How is your father?"

Daygun accepts him with open arms.

The Atlantean Prince salutes in the Valtearean military protocol and says, "My father is in good health and good standing with our people. I salute you in your military tradition. You are in command here. We are here to help your kingdom."

Tulless looks at him in puzzlement and relief. He replies, "What do the people of Atlantis want with our land? There has been peace and trade with our great societies for hundreds of years. We have traded with your empire without greed. I thought we were partners in this world."

"We must take your land for both of our sakes," Daygun says directly. "Kayout is getting stronger and they have many strong allies. We have to make the mining of your iron ore more efficient to make our war machine stronger. Our steel production will protect your country as well as ours. Atlantis has no desire to take your kingdom. We want to rebuild it to make it better. In the long run, it will be in both of our interests. Tulless, you are the king of this country. If the mining of iron ore remains inefficient, both societies will fail. We have attempted to get what we need from your lands, but you want to mine your natural resources in outdated ways. We have asked you to change, and you have refused or been unable. If you could have mined with our techniques, your production would have quadrupled and the situation wouldn't have come to this."

"The way the Atlanteans asked us how to mine is much different than what we are accustomed to," Tulless replies with a shaken voice. "My people don't understand. We are simple people and hard workers. Our ways are different than yours. We have mined the same way for centuries. What do I need to do?"

Daygun relaxes a little, and Tulless does the same.

Daygun says, "During the occupation of your land, I will have my people help produce more iron ore. Our occupation will only last until the supply of iron ore is more sufficient. During this time, we will protect your borders from foreign invaders and help rebuild your country to make it more prosperous. I will help you have a more centralized government and you will be its king. Our people believe in you."

Tulless raises his brow and asks, "Why should my people believe in you?"

Daygun looks at Tulless and shakes his head back and forth and replies, "You can't afford not to believe in me. There is too much happening in world politics. Your people can rebel, and make it more difficult for us. I would rather you be the leader of your kingdom than someone else. It's your choice."

Tulless bends as if he is about to bow to the Atlantean Prince and says, "Whatever you need, My Lord."

Daygun replies in a reassuring voice, "I don't want to be known as your lord, but an ally in desperate times. You are a weaker kingdom than your neighboring empires. If we don't take Valtear under our arms, the Kayout Empire will attack your borders within two years. Atlantis wants to take you first to protect your kingdom. The dead men you see on the battlefield now will be nothing compared to a full attack from the East. Your four neighboring empires have no mercy. The East will kill every adult in your kingdom and they will take your children into slavery. We are not taking your country. Atlantis is saving it."

With a puzzled look, Tulless asks, "What do I call you?"

"You can call me a friend, or Prince Daygun, just like you did a year ago. I will address you as King Tulless," Daygun responds in a reassuring voice.

After the battle, the Atlantean reinforcements from Masaba show up to relieve the veterans on the battlefield. The Atlanteans who fought on the battlefield will be able to return home to their families. Daygun takes out a map and creates future military posts to protect the country that he has just conquered. After Tulless leaves with his men, there is discussion in the tent between the Atlantean generals. Daygun wants to make a very clear point about the relationship between the Valteareans and Atlanteans, and he slams his fist on a table.

"Generals, if there is any wrong doing by our soldiers, they will be mining the Valtearean mines and expelled from the Atlantean Empire," Daygun says in a stern voice. He stops to get his composure and says, "We are here to help these people and share our technologies with them. Atlantis will not to take advantage of a conquered kingdom. Twenty years down the road, the Valteareans will be a formidable force. I am hoping one day they will be an ally to our empire and not an enemy. I want construction of hospitals and libraries in their capital. I need teachers to teach the advanced ways of our civilization. I will acquire engineers and farmers from our lands to help these people grow crops. These people will never go hungry again."

Two weeks into the occupation, Daygun receives a message from his father to come to the Atlantean capital. It is a twelve day journey to the city of Atlantis. That night, Daygun tells his generals and captains to join him for dinner and wine to inform them of what needs be done in his absence.

Two hours after nightfall, the Atlanteans feast to their victory. Daygun invites King Tulless and his generals to the feast, but it is short-lived. Tulless and his generals come to eat with the Daygun out of respect. After an uncomfortable engagement, the two leaders of the two governments go towards a military tent. Prince Daygun starts to talk about the politics in helping reconstruct the new occupied territory.

Daygun goes towards Tulless and stands at a distance but talks very direct and says, "Tulless, I am leaving my best generals here for your protection. They will take over all military decisions if you are attacked by your neighboring empires. Other than that, they are at your disposal. If there is any rebellion in your nation, the Atlantean Army will help keep your people in order. You have a complete division of Atlantis' best men to help reconstruct your kingdom."

Tulless responds, "Thank you, Prince."

"Here is something from my father to show good faith," Daygun says. The Atlantean Prince points at a large chest filled with gold and silver. Daygun says, "Emperor Aten gives you a home in Atlantis and this treasure box. If you want, you can have a seat in the Atlantean Senate and be a part of our politics. To our Senate, you will be a kingdom of a potential state of our empire."

Tulless replies, "I thank you again for keeping me as my country's leader. I will get back with you on your offer about the seat on your Senate. My whole life has just changed and I need time to evaluate my new situation."

Daygun bows his head and says, "The treasures don't make up for your dead soldiers, but it does show that we are not your enemy. Quentoris will take half of the Atlantean Army stationed here and protect your borders."

Quentoris respectfully says, "What if we are attacked from foreign invaders or attacked by rebels of the Valtearean Army?"

Daygun says, "Destroy them. We will treat this country like a city-state, and we will begin mining for the benefit of our two governments."

Tulless asks, "How long will the occupation be in effect?"

With a reassuring voice, Daygun replies, "At the most, two

years. Your military will be strong enough to threaten the Atlantean Empire in the near future. I would rather your kingdom be an ally in the years to come than our enemy. We must ensure the production of iron ore to produce a formidable military to keep the East from attacking your land and ours. I will leave Laptos to protect your capital. My brother will be your right hand in the reconstruction of your kingdom."

After the congregation of the two governments, Daygun and Laptos go to Daygun's tent and talk as brothers. They talk about their childhood and becoming masters of the arts of war. Daygun is a natural leader. Laptos has always looked up to his fraternal twin brother. Despite Daygun's accomplishments, Laptos has never been envious, and he is very proud to be a part of his brother's life. The two brothers sit around and drink wine. They say little to each other and enjoy each others company.

Laptos breaks the silence and asks, "When will you return?"

"I will return in two months." Daygun replies. While Daygun makes final preparations for his departure he says, "Our father will have peace talks with the Kayout Empire. Our father wants me to be by his side in the negotiations. He trusts you to take care of the occupation. As emperor, he has great faith in you. You're becoming a good leader."

"It is because of your guidance, my brother," Laptos says with great pride.

"No!" Daygun replies with a smile. "It is you. At this rate, you will make a better leader than I could ever be."

"I don't want to succeed you," Laptos says. "I respect you, and I could never be the warrior or leader you are."

Daygun comments, "Never is an extreme word, a powerful word, a negative word. You have strengths that are hard for me to compete with. The word never gets a person nowhere."

Laptos looks at him in puzzlement and asks, "What strengths do I have that are hard for you to compete with?"

Daygun replies, "Another time will come to tell you. We will sit down when I get back and have a very good conversation."

Laptos laughs and wants to ask the question that he has been contemplating for sometime. Laptos pauses and finally asks, "Will you marry Kaydence when you return to Atlantis?"

"Yes, I will marry her," Daygun replies.

Laptos jokingly asks, "How can you marry the most stubborn woman in our empire?"

Daygun, in a protective voice, responds, "Watch it."

Laptos looks straight at Daygun and with more puzzlement says, "I don't see it."

Daygun replies, "I have courted quite a few women in my lifetime. I have seen all types. I could have gone down the easier path with others, but I don't have to worry about Kaydence. Do you remember Mayla?"

"Yes!" Laptos replies. "She is beautiful, smart, and she was very loyal to you."

Daygun says, "When we went to battle with the Krosh Army, I was worried about leaving Mayla and dying in combat. I was considering marrying her. She didn't want me to leave. Mayla feared I would die. She built her life around me. It was nice to have that feeling for a little while. However, I soon grew scared of dying in battle. I knew thinking of dying would make me hesitate with my sword, and sooner or later it would have killed me. Kaydence is proud I am a warrior. If I marry her, our children will be taken care of. She is stubborn and wouldn't fail our family. If I pass over to the next life I will know my children are in safe hands. Therefore, I will not have any hesitations with my sword to destroy our enemy, nor will I have fear of dying. It is nice to have the company of such a strong woman."

The next morning, Daygun leaves for Atlantis. As the prince travels, he thinks of Kaydence and his father. He imagines every street and building of his homeland. The prince misses his native soil and his people. Daygun rides with his garrison. During the journey, every conversation has to do with Atlantis and them returning back to the comforts of their civilization.

In the first couple of days, Daygun and his garrison make good time. Even though it has been raining hard, Daygun compensates with less rest. His garrison is the strongest of the Atlantean Empire and they have been under Daygun's command for several years. The warriors have been in many battles with the prince. The garrison takes great pride in protecting Daygun and the ideals of Atlantis.

On the third day, they reach a river that cannot be forded. The river current is too strong for their horses to swim across. Daygun will have to decide to take a chance of going through the

Kayout territories, though he knows it is forbidden by both sides. If the prince decides to cross the Kayout border, their journey will be reduced by two days, and he can arrive at the summit on time. Daygun is concerned. If they cross into the Kayout realm it will be interpreted as an act of war. Because of past negotiations, the two empires cannot step into each others territories, except in designated areas concerning trade.

Daygun decides to cross through the Kayout Empire anyway. After entering into the Kayout Empire, the prince sends scouts ahead. Daygun travels a mile away from the river into the thick forest, just in case a Kayout outpost can spots them on the banks of the river. After a day's journey, the garrison rides to higher ground and finds a place to cross the river back into Atlantis.

On the horizon, Daygun sees a scout racing towards him and his garrison. The scout, Jivan, approaches the prince and is out of breath. The scout has a look of fear.

Jivan yells, "Sir, you must follow me!"

Daygun knows this scout would not come to him in such urgency if it were not a serious situation.

"What did you see?" Daygun asks.

Jivan starts to recover his breath, and responds, "A large army three miles away from here."

"Who is it?" Daygun asks the scout.

"I don't know, sir," Jivan replies.

Daygun looks at his garrison's commander and he says, "Granin, I want the garrison to stay here and wait until I come back."

"I can't let you go without adequate protection, My Lord. You are too important to lose if something goes wrong," Granin says to Daygun in stern voice.

Daygun orders, "If you don't hear from me in three hours, I want you to return safety into the Valtear Kingdom. I want you all to tell my brother what you've seen here and to warn my father."

The prince and Jivan rush away on horseback. The garrison waits, and they are uneasy of what can happen. Daygun and Jivan draw close to the grand army. About two miles before Daygun and the scout reach the unknown army's camp, they tie up their horses. The prince and the scout creep up on foot to the camp and spy on the potential enemy. The two Atlanteans see a vast army of cavalry, hundreds of mammoths, and thirty thousand infantry men from the Kayout Empire. It looks as if the Kayout military is running drills. The Kayout Army here would present a formidable force against any Atlantean division.

Jivan says, "This part of territory has no strategic value."

Daygun replies, "I agree. I don't trust this."

Jivan asks, "Why do the Kayouts have such a large army so close to our borders?"

"I don't know," Daygun replies. The prince points to the left of the Kayout camp and says, "It looks as if there are more Kayout infantrymen in the horizon."

The two Atlanteans run back towards their horses. When they get close, they see that their horses have been seen by a Kayout scouting party. There are six Kayout warriors and they are searching the Atlantean horses' packs. The Kayouts' scouts try to find out anything about their invaders and where the horses came from.

Daygun orders Jivan to run back to their garrison. The prince goes towards the Kayouts scouting party and removes one of the six daggers strapped to his belt. At close quarters the prince throws the dagger and hits the first Kayout warrior in the face. The Kayout scout is killed instantly and the warrior falls to the ground. Before the first soldier hits the dirt, Daygun throws another dagger and hits an additional Kayout warrior right in the heart. The other four Kayouts grab their axes and swords to attack Daygun. The prince takes his sword and starts to fight them one by one.

Against Daygun's orders and out of nowhere, Jivan throws a dagger at one of the remaining Kayout's scouting party. The Atlanteans fight sword to sword with the Kayout warriors. In seconds, the battle is over. Because the Kayouts were no match for the two Atlanteans, they are not even short of breath. The two Atlanteans take their daggers and wipe the blood off the steal. They put their weapons back in their holsters and makes sure there is nothing left behind. If the Kayouts see something from the Atlanteans here where their comrades were killed, it could lead to a war between the two empires.

Daygun looks at Jivan and smiles.

"I gave you an order to stay out of the fight," Daygun says to the scout, as the Atlantean Prince puts his last dagger into his holster.

Jivan looks at Daygun with great pride and replies, "I also took an oath to protect my commander. If I had watched you die, and I did nothing, I could never look at your father again."

"I would have done the same for you," Daygun replies, as he smiles at Jivan.

They rush back to the Atlantean garrison to tell them what has occurred. The Atlanteans cannot be seen here, especially while there are dead Kayouts in the area. They finally arrive back to the camp and Daygun climbs off his horse.

"There is something going on here. The Kayouts are conducting drills near our border. I need one third of you to rush back and tell my brother what is happening here. I need another third to go through Valtear and find another route to get past this river. It may take a week to get through, but it must be done. The other third will come with me and we will go around the army to get to Atlantis. I have to warn my father," Daygun orders in a very unyielding voice.

Granin looks at Daygun with a pleading voice and says, "If we split our warriors, we might be attacked, and you told us that there is safety in numbers."

Daygun replies, "This is not the survival of Atlantean warriors. This is the survival of our race. We must split up, and it will insure that one of us will get to Atlantis before an army can conquer our lands."

A warrior asks Daygun, "What if the Kayout Army always uses this area for drills?"

"It isn't normal for any army to be here. They are so far away from their supply lines. This is too far out to keep supply lines running smoothly. I saw the formations of men and beasts. Being so close to our border, we can't take a chance," Daygun replies in a confident voice.

Granin nods his head up and down and says, "I agree, but if we start to strengthen our borders, it may start a war."

The garrison goes forward with the Daygun's orders. The prince goes towards his horse, and Granin follows to have a private word with him before he goes. Daygun notices that someone is approaching him, and he turns and looks at his great warrior.

"I agree with what you said back there. This could be normal protocol for the Kayouts, but I do not trust what I saw. Go back the long way and try to ford the river," Daygun says.

"Thank you for your leadership. If I don't make it back to Atlantis, it was good serving with you," Granin responds with a pride.

The Atlanteans go in different directions. Daygun and his group go around the Kayout Army. After not sleeping for two days, Daygun arrives at the border of his fatherland. When the prince reaches a safe distance, he camps with his protectors and rests for a couple of hours.

At their camp, the Atlantean warriors ask Daygun what he thinks will happen. Because the prince does not want them to think the worst, he tells them nothing. Even though there is a chance of war, he also knows he will reach his father first and tell the Atlantean Emperor the news. If the Kayouts do attack the Great East or West Gates to Atlantis, Daygun wonders what will happen to his fatherland. The only thing Daygun can do is tell his father.

CHAPTER V
FAÇADE OF TWO NATIONS

It is early morning. The children of Atlantis are playing on the shores of their capital. In the horizon, the gathered Atlantean soldiers see three Kayout ships about to slip into their massive harbor.

Each Kayout battlecruiser is slow but thickly armored, painted black with gold trim. The Eastern Empire's ships have high sails, but are slightly smaller in length than the Atlantean battlecruisers. They are in no way superior to the Atlantean Navy, but a large fleet of these new Kayout ships could challenge the Atlantean fleet.

The main exports of the Kayout Empire are wood and leather, and their craftsmanship is renowned throughout the world. A grave concern between the Atlanteans and Kayouts is the trade of these goods.

The Atlanteans are expecting the Kayout Emperor. No Atlantean knows what Emperor Melercertis looks like because previous negotiations were done through a third party. Many Atlantean citizens walk close to the shores to see the massive Kayout battlecruisers. The Atlanteans are amazed at the leaps of Kayout technology coming into their harbor. For centuries, the Atlanteans have been able to rule the seas without any fear. No other country had this kind of technology in ship building until now.

The Atlantean horns blow. A small group of Atlantean tower guards run up the colossal lighthouses to light the fires that will welcome the Kayout Emperor into their homeland. The two hundred foot pillars light up a blaze of fire that can be seen for twenty miles off the harbor shore of Atlantis.

When the Atlantean bells ring, it is relayed throughout the entire empire. Aten's civilization uses bells to signify any big event.

It is a form of communication that helps bring news between city-states on the peninsula. There are different bells with different pitches from high to low. Each sound is translated into words. When Melercertis arrives, everyone in the Atlantean Empire knows within thirty minutes.

The meeting between the two empires has been planned for months. For the last three months, the negotiations have brought the two superpowers to this spot. This is the first talk between the two empires in over twenty-six years.

Emperor Melercertis is six feet three inches tall, forty-eight years old and very strong for his age. On this day, he is wearing a black leather chest plate, black cloak, and a sword made from bronze hanging from his side. The coat of arms sketched on the Kayout Emperor's chest plate is an elephant and a horse. The two animals are facing each other on their hind legs as if they are about to stomp on each other. The cavalrymen on the beasts are holding a sword ready to strike their adversary.

Melercertis looks out from the bow of his ship. He did not imagine the Atlantean capital to be so beautiful or this large. Melercertis began his political career through trade with the Atlanteans. Because it is forbidden for people on the continent to enter Aten's realm, very few people have seen inside Atlantis. Melercertis does have spies, but the true magnitude of what he sees is nothing like what he expected. He never dreamed the Atlanteans would have this kind of technology and the architectural skills necessary to build such structures.

Emperor Aten is six feet tall and is forty-six years old. The Atlantean Emperor is also in excellent physical condition for his age. He is clean-shaven and is wearing a gold and silver chest plate with a bull engraved in the metal for this ceremony. The bull is the coat of arms for the Atlanteans.

Aten became emperor at the age of twenty when his father was killed in battle. Twenty-six years prior, Akakios, Aten's father, started the quest to conquer the continent on the east side of the Alber Mountains. The kingdoms, which became Kayout and Gambut, beat back the Atlanteans. Treaties were made, and Kayout started to thrive after the Atlanteans were defeated. Melercertis was a major general during the confrontation. After the war, Melercertis went to trade than politics. At the age of thirty-four, Melercertis became the Kayout Emperor.

The great Kayout ships enter the harbor and prepare to dock. The Atlanteans crowd towards Melercertis' ships. The Atlantean military stands down to make the Kayout captains feel less threatened and more welcomed.

The Atlantean harbor has over three hundred docks for trade and military ships. While the Kayout ships are about to be pulled by ropes into the dock, Melercertis looks into the harbor and sees that there are exactly six hundred statues. Each stone figure is ten feet high. The sculptures are soldiers that have given their lives for Atlantis. The images are a tribute to their bravery. There are two warrior statues for every dock. Each of the statues is holding a lamp in their hand. At night, they light up the entire harbor.

Close to the harbor, there is a centralized building connected by bridges. It is called the Central Trading Building. The harbor and buildings took the Atlanteans decades to build. The harbor required tens of thousands of laborers working on it every day to bring it to completion. The Central Trading Building is five stories tall with statues of bulls along the walls of the building. It is the most detailed building in the capital and the most beautiful building in the Atlantean Empire. All trade between friendly nations and states are held inside the Central Trading Building.

Melercertis admires the handiwork of the Atlantean people and says to his captain "It is incredible what Atlantis has accomplished. This city will stand beyond the time of mankind."

It takes several minutes to finally dock the Kayout battlecruisers. The Atlantean dock masters do not know how to secure the small Kayout fleet into their dock. The width of Melercertis' ships is larger than most Atlanteans' vessels.

Back in the ready room of the Central Trading Building, Aten contemplates his opening conversation with Melercertis. Because of the religious and cultural differences, Aten is uncertain of how to welcome the Kayout Emperor. In the back of his mind, Aten knows he must maintain the peace until Atlantis is strong enough to make the inevitable battle against the Kayouts a decisive one. Aten feels the Atlanteans can protect their borders, but are not yet able to go on the offensive. Even though Atlantis has superiority in training of their soldiers and higher technological weapons, the Atlantean military is outmatched in numbers by the Kayout Empire. Aten's empire has close to one million available soldiers to fight against four million men of Melercertis' military.

Despite being outmatched in numbers, the Atlanteans can keep at bay any empire at their Great East or West Gate defenses. Aten also knows the Kayout people are at a large disadvantage. The Eastern Empire cannot make a full scale attack on Atlantis. There is too much political turmoil inside Melercertis' empire. The Kayout military will have to keep at least half of their warriors in its borders to keep a rebellion from rising. Melercertis' military is the only thing keeping his empire together.

The Kayout Empire is vast and was without good leadership until he came into power. He knows it will take decades of a strong centralized government to have the resources to take Atlantis. Melercertis' empire has taken many countries to their north. Their newly conquered territories are hard to maintain because of rebel fighting. Unlike Atlantis, it lacks the strength of government and politics to hold their outlying states in secure subservience. The only way the Kayouts can conquer Atlantis is to take the Gambut Empire, which has until now actively sought to maintain their neutrality.

The Gambut's main export is stone and granite, which is of great value to the Atlanteans. Wealth has made the Gambut Empire more powerful, and thus far held Kayout ambitions at bay. The Gambut Empire profits far too well from their trade with the Atlanteans.

In the last couple of years, the Gambut people have sensed a threat from the Kayouts. The Eastern Superpower has a small corridor of land that borders the Atlantean trading post. The Gambuts are more technologically advanced than the Kayout Empire, and they have almost three million men to defend their borders. Aten also trades technological advancements to the Gambuts. The Kayout Empire would have to take the Gambut Empire first to even threaten Aten's empire. There are vital supply lines the Kayouts can use for a full-scale campaign against Atlantis which are in Gambut. Because there are mountains and rough terrain outside Aten's empire, it would be hard for any one kingdom to transport sufficient supplies and men to the Atlantean Great East and West Gates.

The best Atlantean defense is their natural defenses. Atlantis has a bottleneck peninsula that is covered sea to sea by mountains.

The mountain range creates a natural barrier which keeps Atlantis safe from invaders. It would be very difficult to attack and conquer Atlantis from land. The Atlantean Great East and West Gates are on high ground and defended with five gates and walls just in case one is overtaken. Aten's military can regroup and counter if a gate falls.

The Great East Wall protects against the borders of the Kayout and Gambut Empires. The Great West Wall is on the side of Valtear. These two gates are the only way in or out of Atlantis, other than climbing very high mountain ranges. The Atlantean walls are constantly maintained and built up. At the gates, Aten has massive artillery to ward off any enemy. Four elite Atlantean divisions are at the Great East Wall, and two more are in reserve at the city of Halotropolis, which is the closest city to the Eastern Gate.

The continent and Atlantis both trade in their own self-interest. If it were not for greed, the world would destroy Atlantis because of its faith. The Atlantean Emperor does not want to start a war with anyone, but he wants to build up his military to avoid one. Aten knows military technology is the key to the future of his empire. To the Atlantean military, this is the only way to keep their way of life.

With each of the Atlantean cities contributing their technologies and skills to make Atlantis better, they feed off one another to produce better weapons and tools. Although Aten wants peace, he knows that the next generation of his empire may have conflicts with the Kayouts, therefore the technology advancements of his people are the primary empirical concern.

The Atlantean military advisors urge a Kayout invasion before their military grows too strong. Aten has evaluated a preemptive strike, but the Kayout Empire is too vast. Even though the Atlanteans know they are the strongest military in the world, the numbers of the Kayout Empire hold their conquest, and keeping that large of an empire under control would be impossible.

Aten sought the wisdom of his cabinet. Asking for their honest advice as men and citizens, he received only contradicting speculations. At the heart of the matter, there is little knowledge of the Kayouts. The Atlantean council has no concept of Kayout politics or culture. A military cannot fight an enemy they do not know. Aten cannot afford to fall into the council's trap of pride and self-interest. It is up to Aten to create the door to peace for the future of his people.

In the meantime, Emperor Aten looks at the large Kayout ships that are securely tied to his docks. It is hard to believe that the Kayout people want to speak to the Atlanteans. The two superpowers have totally different cultures and economic standards. There has been silence between the nobles of both empires for twenty-six years. Why would the Kayouts now seek diplomacy? The whole Atlantean Empire wonders what will come out of this summit. Will it be peace or even greater disagreements between the two large empires? Aten debates whether the war between the Atlanteans and Valteareans have anything to do with the assembly that is about to take place. No matter what, Aten is playing through every scenario in the back of his head. He questions if he has what it takes to make this happen.

While the Kayouts step off the ships, Emperor Aten asks his awaiting councils to step aside. Aten wants to stand alone to represent the people of his empire. Aten's protectors are the only defense protecting him if anything goes wrong. Even the Atlantean grandmasters stand back, which are never to leave his side.

When Emperor Melercertis steps off the ship, he also stands alone with his armed escort standing in the background.

The two emperors stand thirty feet from each other, and there is no one around for another hundred feet. The two most powerful men in the world stand tall and look at one another. As host, Aten makes the first gesture of peace. Aten walks towards the Kayout Emperor very gracefully, and he smiles and holds out his hand to greet his guest. In return, Melercertis mirrors the gesticulation.

The two emperors shake hands and Aten says, "It is a great honor to meet you. Our two societies have been incredulous to one another for over twenty years. I am glad you are here in my capital. Let us relish this moment and just be two men from two different cultures wanting peace."

Melercertis replies, "It has been a long journey. Politics is the last thing on my mind. I would love to see your city. I have heard rumors in my empire, but looking at Atlantis, the rumors cannot give justification to what I see here today."

They both smile, and the Atlantean people cheer in the background. The crowd knows this is a monumental moment, and this will never be forgotten by the spectators. The crowd feels as if they no longer have anything to fear. Now, the Atlantean crowd sees a man rather than an unknown face. The cheering amongst the audience grows louder as the two emperors walk towards the Atlantean capital. Melercertis and Aten walk on a massive bridge over the harbor. The first contact with the East is accomplished. A beginning of trade and peace has started on this day.

Melercertis walks slowly and elegantly with Aten through the entrance of the city. The Kayout advisors and generals follow and say nothing. The Kayout Emperor glances at buildings of marble colored with brown, white, and black. It is a culture shock to Melercertis and his men.

The Atlanteans' wide economic power has led it to all ends of the world in search of marble and other precious stones. Every building in Atlantis is at least two stories tall. The Kayout Emperor sees things he could only dream of seeing in his own kingdom. The two emperors discuss the politics and culture of one another's empire. Melercertis speaks the Atlantean language fluently, and he can understand without misinterpretation. The two emperors know they are similar in greed, love, and power. They also know that they love their empire and they would defend her to the death. They see each other as equals. The more they talk; the more they become at ease with one another.

On their journey to Aten's palace, Melercertis sees a great pyramid with a great deal of smoke coming from the top. It is massive. The pyramid is a hundred feet tall and the base covers an entire acre.

The Kayout Emperor keeps staring at the pyramid and Aten asks, "What is on your mind?"

Melercertis responds, "I see so much. It is overwhelming."

Aten says, "You have come to us in peace. The building you are looking at is where we produce our steel. I see you as no longer a potential enemy. I will take you to the building. There has been so much mistrust between our societies, and I will not hide anything inside my city from you. If you want to know something, I will gladly tell you."

Melercertis replies, "Agreed. I wish our two empires did not have to go to war twenty-six years ago. We could have learned a great deal from one another. I want you to come to my city so you can understand my culture."

Aten says, "One day that will happen."

Aten takes the Kayout Emperor inside the pyramid to show how they make steel. The two emperors take a quick tour and walk toward the palace. Melercertis is almost inundated by the capital of Atlantis.

While they walk, Melercertis sees statues and writing everywhere. He cannot read. Only about five percent of the Kayout Empire population can read or write. Because the Kayouts are going the same direction as Atlantis, they too are moving toward one written language.

On the other hand, the Atlantean population is much different. Their society has had one language for the last four hundred years, and the skill is learned in the home and in schools. Less than three percent of the Atlantean population is without at least some level of literacy.

With different societies inside each city-state on the peninsula, some sects of the cultures did not give up their writing and language heritage. The religious writings are still written in the old Atlantean text. In turn, the Atlanteans have two written languages. The well-educated Atlanteans are taught both ways. The other writings have disappeared over the centuries or been rewritten in the new text. The libraries inside Aten's capital still have the ancient writings, and some scholars can still translate them all.

The Kayouts and Atlanteans speak a totally different language. Emperor Melercertis learned the main stream Atlantean language through trade after the war between Atlantis and his people. Because of the Kayout Emperor's accomplishments in trade, he was appointed by the Kayout nobles to bring the empire together, and he formed his empire into what it is today.

That night inside the Atlantean palace, Melercertis and Aten dine alone without generals and advisors interrupting. They sit across from each other and servants attend to them.

Aten says, "I took the liberty of choosing our first feast together."

Melercetis responds, "I always wondered how and what your people eat. I hope my manners are up to your standards."

Aten finally asks, "I am astonished how your empire grew so quickly?"

Melercertis responds, "Thank you, we have had our own troubles like any other government. I know you can relate. The Kayout citizens are given a job to last for the rest of their lives. Everyone in my empire starts at the bottom and works their way up. Young people are sent into an apprenticeship at the age of twelve based on their physicality, talents, and interest. It has brought success and helped my empire grow quickly. Before this, other empires considered the Kayout nation nothing but a wasteland. Before I became emperor, my people were very nomadic. Each community fought each other and gained nothing but temporary territorial rights. I brought order and civility to the tribes of his lands. After a short time, the country started to prosper. Because I was so good at selling, I sold my philosophies to what is now the Kayout Empire. I was lucky. My empire was ready for change and had grown tired of tribal disputes. The whole empire knew they were self-destructing and wanted to emulate the Atlanteans. But our religion moves us to be different than your culture."

Aten asks, "What makes your people want to strive?"

Melercertis responds, "In the Kayout Empire, everything is given by their government. If a Kayout citizen does well, the person will receive luxury goods that come though trade with other empires. The Kayout government appoints the amount of tokens to trade for specific items at their markets. If a person does not do what is demanded, the citizen does not receive sufficient tokens as their punishment."

Melercertis asks, "May I ask a question?"

Aten says, "Yes, this is the reason you and I are here alone. As leaders of our people, we need time alone to understand one another."

Melercertis asks, "How does your society work?"

Aten says, "The citizens of Atlantis do things differently. Starting at the age of six, every child goes to school until the age of fifteen. Atlanteans are taught the basics of Atlantean technology, reading, and writing. Everyone learns the ways of the sciences. If an Atlantean has a gift in science, the Atlantean child may desire to join a science university and learn to advance Atlantean technology. If an Atlantean can produce a better product or weapons, the government assures royalties. Because of the chance of compensation, a citizen has the potential to become wealthy."

Melercertis asks, "So, the people in your empire have choices to do as they please."

Aten responds, "More or less. After the age of fifteen, all but the gifted join the military. Males and females have the choice of a compulsory five years military service or joining the military schools. If they choose to attend military school, they will have higher ranking and learn all the arts of war to become officers. Because the warriors are giving fifteen years of their life, it is at high cost, but much more rewarding. After fifteen years of military service, the Atlantean is considered a true citizen. The citizen can vote and pursue what he or she pleases. If they decide to stay after their full fifteen years of service, the officers can stay in the lands they conquered and become nobles. Officers become government officials and are given taxes from the new state."

Melercertis asks, "How did you build your empire so exquisite?"

Aten responds, "Apart from the military, the Atlanteans have to serve their empire to become a citizen. At the age of twenty, Atlanteans work in their community on construction of buildings for another five years. Except for the gifted or the ones who went to military school, everyone helps build homes, temples, roads, and anything needed to make the Atlantean Empire more efficient. After the last year of public service, the construction workers work together in building a new home for the ones who gave five years of service. After the Atlantean's fifth year, the home is given to the individual. After the Atlanteans give a large part of their lives to the empire, they are considered citizens."

After Aten and Melercertis finish dinner and go to their quarters, they each realize how different their lands truly are, and wonder if the differences can ever be overcome.

The next day, the two emperors walk towards the Atlantean Senate Chamber Hall. The super structure is the largest pure granite building in the capital. The structure is fourteen thousand square feet with one hundred and forty-four supporting columns and fifty foot ceilings. In the middle of the massive structure, there is a dome that transmits natural light from the sun during the day.

While inside, Aten gives Melercertis a sword that once belonged to his father, but does so out of the public's eye. It is a gold sword and has great meaning to the Atlantean Emperor.

Aten says, "I want to give this sword to you as a peaceful gesture. It belonged to my father who attacked your society. Most generals give a sword as a way to say they surrender. I am giving this sword to show there will be no more hostilities between us. This sword is important to me, but our friendship means more than this sword."

Melercertis says, "I will earn your trust in order to gain peace and trade with your empire. Thank you for this sword. In return, I will give it to your first male grandson when he reaches manhood in the decades to come."

With that, Emperor Aten knows the man is genuine. With a little small talk, they both agree they want to do more trading along the borders and by sea on a larger scale. The talks are going better than either expected.

Because Aten wants Melercertis to see Atlantis' military might, he leads the Eastern Emperor to the main citadel where the best Atlantean archers are practicing. The Atlantean Emperor wants to show off a little. When they get to the archer workshop, there are two hundred craftsmen who are building the bows. Each bow takes three months to build. Every bow has intricate designs and is a work of art. The bow uses pulleys to give the bow more recoil. Steel is used to reinforce and streamline the bows. After completion, it is tested and retested until it is perfect.

After the tour of the factory, Aten and Melercertis go towards the archery firing range. There, Melercertis sees the rigorous training of the Atlantean military. At the training site, Melercertis sees three hundred archers firing one hundred yards towards a circle that only has a diameter of fifteen yards. When fired, only forty Atlantean archers missed their mark. Repetitious practice is demanded until the skill is perfected. If any Atlantean archer does not attain perfection, he or she is dishonored. Each individual strives to be perfect in every aspect of their lives. Determination and perfection is drilled into the children in Atlantean schools. Everyone acts as bees in a hive to protect the masses, not the individual. Honor is instilled through schools, temples, and the home. Melercertis' country has similar fundamentals, but the means are quite foreign.

The next day, the real talks begin. Military officials and

councilmen gather from both empires at the Central Trading Building. At first, they talk about helping each other economically. The Kayouts want Atlantis to use their technologies to help produce more goods and resources in their empire. For advising and how to best to use the Atlantean knowledge, the Kayouts will give a great deal of natural resources in trade. Melercertis is trying to boost trade with the rest of the continent. It would be a partnership which will make Atlantis very prosperous. About midday, the talk between the two empires switches toward conquest. In the middle of the economic talks, Melercertis looks at Aten.

Melercertis says, "So far, we have spoken about utilizing technology and resources to make our two societies better. The only thing we haven't talked about is the Gambut Empire. In the last two years, the Gambut Empire has destroyed outposts on our borders. With a great deal of my men in my Northern territories, it is putting a military strain on my empire, Gambut is probing our weakness. This is one of the reasons I came here. Twenty-six years ago, the west side of Gambut was an Atlantean territory. It was stripped away after the Great War with your people. What if you can have back your lands?"

Aten replies in an angry voice, "Twenty-six years ago, about a quarter of the population of what is now Gambut believed in God. That has changed. The society is closer to your belief in gods. Their military rules the empire now. The Gambut Empire is lost to us."

Melercertis says, "I understand. My military advisors have asked me to consider war with your people. I am sure your advisors have done the same. We can stop this now. I don't want a war with you. I respect you and your people, but there is much to gain from a military alliance. With our two militaries working together, we will win a swift victory against the Gambuts. The military campaign will not cost many lives on either side. I know our cultures are different, but the friendship between our two empires will prevail for our children, and our children's children. With our alliance, Gambut will fall quickly. I know your empire has problems with the Gambuts and so have we. The resources you had twenty-six years ago can be yours again."

Aten shakes his head in a negative manner and replies, "The world as we knew twenty-six years ago has changed. There are very few people in the Gambut Empire that will willingly want to be a part of Atlantis."

Melercertis walks toward him with open arms and says, "Together, we can change it. Atlantis has the best military in the world. I have over four million men if needed to defend or attack an empire. Your empire has one million capable warriors. My advisors say we would lose if we had to fight the Atlanteans. If we take Gambut together, Kanis and Mearth will stay out of the takeover. Even if they do decide to enter the war, our empires will destroy and take the world together."

Aten goes in deep thought and says, "You are a good salesman. Atlantis will consider this. I too want to be the one who brings the world together. I have to talk with my advisors and my people. But now, I don't want to talk of conquest or politics anymore. Let us celebrate the meeting of our two empires for the first time in over twenty-six years."

With a concerned voice Melercertis says, "With our negotiations, I thought your son would have joined our conference."

Aten replies, "I am vexed about my son. He should have been here a couple of days ago, yet, I am confident of his well being."

The two emperors return to their chambers after their talks. They take baths and indulge in the luxuries that go with being an emperor.

That night, the Atlantean politicians hear about the possibility of Kayout and Atlantis going on the conquest together. Some of the senators remember when Gambut was an Atlantean territory. When the Great War was over, the Atlanteans lost provinces on the continent. Now, there is a chance to get that land back through Melercertis.

The next morning, Aten orders his personal council to his palace to talk about the summit. After an hour of discussion, the majority of Aten's council believes Melercetis' plan is the right thing to do, but they are very apprehensive. One of Aten's servants brings a message to him from his Senate. Aten angrily crumbles the note in his hand, and he is very troubled. He orders his chariot to the front of his palace. Aten rushes to the Senate Chamber Hall and goes directly to the doorway. Glasor, who is the head of the council, meets Aten at the entrance. The council is in the background speaking loudly in the background about the alliance with Kayout.

Glasor says, "Your son will be here in three hours, and he asked you be here with us when he arrives."

"Did he say what it is about?" Aten asks him with puzzlement.

Glasor replies, "No, the messenger had little contact with Prince Daygun."

The Atlantean Emperor says with confidence, "There must be problems in Valtear."

Glasor then says, "After your son arrives, the economic council would also like to speak with you. Ellious, speaker of the Economic Council, will be here in an hour."

Aten says slowly, "I understand your concerns. Until I know what my son has to say, there is nothing to act upon. I don't want to be troubled until Daygun arrives."

Glasor replies, "Sir, everyone wants to know about this alliance with Melercertis. Is it going to happen?"

Aten looks at him without emotion. Glasor lowers his head and says, "I am sorry, My Lord."

Aten puts his hand on Glaser's shoulder and replies, "You are a leader of this council, and I expect you to act accordingly. You're in charge until I return. I will not do anything in haste. We need to take one step at a time. Let us hear what my son has to say first."

Glasor looks up to him and says with a smile, "I understand."

This is something Aten does not want to deal with. The talk with the Kayout Empire is putting stress on the Atlantean Emperor. He sees his council as being greedy. Melercertis has put ideas into his political circles. Aten likes the idea of having the lost territory back in the Atlantean Empire, but he wonders what cost it will have.

The Atlantean Emperor goes for a walk. In the back of Aten's mind, he knows something has to be wrong for giving a specific message. The talks between the Kayouts and Atlantis have already taken place. There is much uncertainty in the political circles of Aten's council. All Aten knows is that his council is in disarray. Knowledge is the key to power, and Aten has no power until his son returns to the Atlantean council.

Chapter VI
Politics and Trust

As soon as Daygun is seen entering the Atlantean Senate Chamber Hall, a servant runs to retrieve Emperor Aten. The prince waits, and will say nothing to the council until his father returns. Everyone in the room wants answers, but the prince knows he needs his father to help control the Atlantean Senate. Daygun also realizes he does not have the right to make speculations on what he saw in the Kayout Empire without his father's presence.

The Atlantean Emperor has regrouped his thoughts and takes a deep breath before entering the Atlantean Senate Chamber Hall. A servant opens the door and two grandmasters walk in alongside Aten. The councilmen rise to their feet as the emperor enters. There is stillness in the room. The Atlantean Emperor moves towards his son. Daygun stands at attention in military protocol and salutes his father.

"What is so important to bring the Senate and councils together?" Aten asked.

Everyone waits for Daygun's response. The Atlantean Prince has a worried look on his face. He cannot wait to say what has been troubling him.

Daygun says urgently, "With the flooding rains, I had no choice but to go through the Kayout Empire to make the summit. I had to make good time to make the meeting between you and Melercertis. My garrison came across an army twenty miles from our borders and twenty miles inside the Gambut Empire near the Crayloran River. It is obvious the Kayouts are exercising their military. I fear they are preparing for an invasion of either Atlantis or Gambut."

Aten replies in a reassuring voice, "Melercertis is asking us for a joint effort to take the Gambut Empire. There have been at least a dozen border skirmishes between the two, and the Kayouts are making their presence more known."

Daygun answers, "In my opinion, we can't trust the Kayout Empire. What are Melercertis' full intentions? It can be a trick or diversion."

Aten says, "The Kayouts want the east side of the Alber Mountains, and they will give us the west. The land is exactly what Atlantis had before the Great War. If we take the Gambut Empire together, it will be one less empire Atlantis will have to worry about."

With respect, Daygun asks his father, "If everything is in our favor, why would the Kayouts not want more? This all seems too easy."

Aten thinks for a second and replies, "It is a part of the negotiations. True leaders don't jump at the first talks. It will take many more negotiations before our empires really work together for each other's benefit. The Kayout Emperor is giving us an incentive to take this conquest. They need the resources in Gambut. At the same time, they want our advisement and technologies so they produce their trade more efficiently."

With great emotion, Daygun says, "I do understand. Melercertis is giving too much too soon. Before he was an emperor, he was a tradesman. A former tradesman would have strived for a better bargain first before giving it all away in the first talks."

Aten nods, takes a deep breath, and replies, "I agree. Daygun, you will be a great leader to this empire one day."

Daygun stands at full attention and says, "Thank you, My Lord."

The rest of the council is silent. Aten turns to Glasor and asks, "Glasor, do you have anything to add to this?"

Glasor strolls to the middle of the room, and bellows in a loud voice, "Yes, My Lord. Our council is evaluating every aspect of this conquest to strengthen our empire. If we do take Gambut, it will benefit our society. Like Prince Daygun mentioned, we can't trust the Kayout Empire. If Melercertis is overthrown in the near future, we may not have this chance again. Gambut is growing at a considerable rate."

Emperor Aten walks to the head of the table. He starts to say something, but stops to regroup his thoughts. He wants someone to oppose the idea of an alliance with the Kayout Empire. He listens and tries to make out what the Senate is mumbling under their breath. The councils are still arguing quietly back and forth about the results of such a conquest.

Aten finally says, "So, the best thing to do is to bring an alliance with Melercertis. I think it is a mistake on our part if we do not take this opportunity. After the Great War, our nation was demoralized by the rest of the world. It took our empire ten years to lick our wounds. This is a good opportunity to bring pride back to our people."

Throwing a map on the table near Aten, Gavis, one of the main Atlantean generals, says, "The bulk of the Gambut military is on the east side of the Alber Mountains. The Kayouts will absorb the majority of fatalities. In turn, the Kayout military will take years to recover. Just in case the Kayouts decide to betray us in the future, it will give us the advantage."

Aten replies, "I agree. And I have no indications of betrayal from Melercertis."

The Atlantean Emperor looks at Ryelyne, one of his best young generals, and asks, "Ryelyne, what are your thoughts?"

Ryelyne, who is very strong, with black hair, and tall, does not know what to say at first. He studies the map for a moment and says, "Life is nothing but a gamble. Many Atlantean soldiers will die. At the same time, future sons and daughters will have the opportunity to grow. If this is what the Kayout people want, we should accept the agreement. In the last five years, Atlantis has been concerned with the Kayout and Gambut Empires. We have to assume that they are as concerned of us as we are of them. The potential for a war with the Gambut people has escalated for years. This is a good opportunity for our empire to attack. The alliance will remove one of our threats. In the future, we can concentrate our military on the Kayouts if it comes down to it."

With a reassuring voice, Aten replies, "I understand, but it is as you said before. We must take a chance now before it is too late. This is an opportunity which we can't ignore."

"What do you think my son?" Aten asks Daygun.

Daygun replies, "I do not trust the Kayout Emperor, but I will agree to anything you decide. You are my father and Emperor. I am a servant to protect our people. If it is taking out an empire for our future, I will accept the responsibilities."

Aten shakes his head and says, "I do not believe in Melercertis' cause either, but for our children's sake, we must take this opportunity. I will discuss the alliance more with Melercetis. He is staying for Daygun's wedding. He also wants to see the games. Other than that, Daygun, you are up for grandmaster in two days. In little over a week, we will also have a new member in our family. Kaydence has captured my heart. I feel lucky she will be a part of our family."

With a scared look on his face, Daygun says, "Yes, my life is about to change. I am ready. I have gone into battle many times, but I think I am more scared of being married than dying. In the games to come, I have learned a great deal from last year's competition."

Aten looks at Daygun and says proudly, "You were born ready. You are my son. Take one step at a time. With the games, winning is good, but losing is sometimes better. In marriage, you will lose all the time, but that is a part of being a man."

Daygun looks puzzled and replies, "I don't understand."

Aten tries to show he is a father, as well as an emperor, and says, "Losing battles is a part of the game. As long as you live and learn from it, you win from losing."

Daygun is embarrassed, and replies, "Father, I shall retire for the day. Can I do anything else for you?"

Aten smiles and says, "No. With the competition coming up, I hope you dream of swords, but always remember, you're a man whether you win or lose."

"Ryelyne, are you also going for the grandmaster?" Aten asks while he glances at Ryelyne.

Ryelyne stands at attention and replies, "Yes sir."

"I have two of my best swordsmen here with me. Ryelyne, you have a great deal of discipline and talent. Your division says good things about you. You're a true leader." Aten says with pride.

The next day in the palace gardens, Daygun and Ryelyne practice the art of sword fighting. In the Atlantean Empire, nothing is more important than being a grandmaster. The two friends are in good condition and spar for hours. Afterwards, they eat and think of the people they will spar against at daybreak. They talk about getting to the top eight fighters at the games as if they were still teenagers.

CHAPTER VII
THE SPORTING ARENA

An hour before dawn, just beneath the amphitheater, Daygun and Ryelyne are in the grandmasters' hall. Only the elite can enter the hall. It is restricted to the one hundred best fighters of Atlantis. The two have earned the right to be at the hall because of their previous performance. The hall is lined with statues and the coat of arms of the Atlanteans. The two contenders are nervous and excited at the same time.

Five percent of Atlantean's top grade granite went into the grand stadium. It took ten years to complete and tens of thousands of craftsmen and sculptures to build such a stadium. The sports ground is in the center of the capital. Each Atlantean child dreams of sparring in the arena, but only the best get to spar in the games.

The amphitheater is the pride of Aten's society. Because the arena can only hold fifty-five thousand spectators, the privilege of attendance is bought at a high price. Only the richest and those with greatest stature have a chance to see the games. The masses of spectators are diverse, and they represent numerous cultures in the Atlantean Empire. At the main gate, the grandmasters' names are engraved on a stone wall from generations past. Daygun and Ryelyne are hoping to get their name on the stone.

During the early morning, Daygun and Ryelyne prepare for the fight of their lives. They both have been here before. Neither had previously reached to the top eight fighters who fight the grandmasters.

The two Atlantean generals enter the stadium together. They both come from royal blood. Ryelyne is the son of the Masabaian King, the home of cavalry. Even though Daygun's primary education is archery, Daygun has a very strong hand with the sword, and it is his favorite weapon.

Crowds of spectators are at the stadium to see the sparring matches of the summer. Thousands of spectators wait outside the arena to hear the outcome. Aten and every king of the empire are there to see the games. Aten and Mantis, Ryelyne's father, are there to support their sons. Melercertis is there to learn the games. He has similar games back in his empire, but nothing like this. He is overwhelmed with Atlantean pride for their traditions and sport. Aten introduces the Kayout Emperor as a friend of the empire. It is good public relations for the two emperors to be seen together if they decide to be allies.

It is early morning, right before sunrise. The sparring games begin right when the sun peaks over the horizon on the longest day of the year. Torches are still blazing to give light. Right when the sun starts to peak the stadium goes dark. All torches are put out, and the horns blow. Everyone starts to cheer, even the kings and nobles. The crowd gets louder as day becomes brighter. All one thousand twenty-four combatants are in the arena ready to spar simultaneously. Five hundred and twelve sparring matches go on at the same time, and there is a judge for each fight to declare a winner. It is very crowded on the stadium floor.

When the warriors are thinned out to sixty-four, only two warriors fight at a time in the arena for the climax of the games. At the end of the day, the eight combatants fight a grandmaster one at a time. Each competitor gets a chance of a lifetime. Defeating a grandmaster is almost impossible. The grandmasters do not have to fight until it is time to fight the final eight. This gives the grandmasters the advantage.

The sparring begins. Daygun and Ryelyne both fight different opponents. Each of the two wins their first battle with ease. The second level of competition will start in forty-five minutes. In doing so, it gives athletes time to rest, and also gives the crowd time for trading and to converse about politics and religion. Now, only half of the warriors are on the ground to fight to the next level.

The games go on to the second and then third level. On the third match, Ryelyne's competitor is good and it takes him almost ten minutes to win the third match. Daygun, on the other hand, wins his competition pretty easily. The crowd goes crazy as the spectators start to speculate who will reach the final eight.

About noon after the forth level, Daygun and Ryelyne take out the competitors almost at the same time. They both look at each other and smile across the sparring field. They will go the fifth level. At this level, there are only sixty-four competitors left. Aten and Mantis are proud to see their sons make it this far. Even though Aten and Mantis are of royal blood, they take pride in each other's son like any other father. By the afternoon, Daygun and Ryelyne have won all of their fights. They win all seven matches.

There are different reasons Ryelyne and Daygun have gotten this far. Ryelyne comes from a stern and judgmental family, and he had to learn to adapt in the social arts. Ryelyne wanted to learn the arts of war to protect himself from his uncompromising family. The Masabaian King's son built a comedic defense in his youth to protect himself from the familial harshness he suffered, and he uses it to mask his deep seeded indecisiveness. On the field of battle, Ryelyne has no fear. He is pure in concentration. He has nothing to live for except the roar of the crowd and his brothers in arms.

Daygun's rearing was quite different. His father taught him to make decisions on his own. Aten knew his son might make mistakes, and he was always there to help guide the boy. Aten talked to his son about the consequences of decisions. In doing so, Daygun became pure at heart in his up bringing. Because Aten's son grew up thinking of nothing but honor and family, he has no fear of death. Daygun's life is given to the Atlantean Empire. Only the survival of Atlantis insures the protection of his family and way of life. Life has not been given to Daygun.

Daygun and Ryelyne reach the objective which they failed to reach the year before. They advance to the finals to fight the grandmasters. Because they have fought seven matches already, the two friends are very exhausted. They wish each other luck and concentrate on what is about to occur.

It starts to get late in the evening. Daygun and Ryelyne are the last to fight. The other six contenders have lost very quickly to the grandmasters. They are the only two that can win against the best of the best. The grandmasters have not lost a fight in the stadium for some time. The crowd is ready to see a new name on the grandmaster's stone.

Ryelyne fights first. He approaches the grandmaster and he is nervous, but confident. The swords fly. Mantis' son uses a defensive approach to the fight. Ryelyne wears out quickly, but he knows he must bring the grandmaster to his level of exhaustion. In conserving energy, he uses no offensive advances until the time is right, and he makes sure that the grandmaster is overconfident. The crowd is booing at the underdog. Ryelyne shows weaknesses on purpose. He remembers the grandmaster's movements where he showed his Achilles' heel. Ryelyne replays the same scenario to make his opponent retry where he could have succeeded. The grandmaster tries the same offensive move. Mantis' son counters the moves and he goes on his own offensive. The grandmaster falters and loses his stability. Ryelyne pins the grandmaster down with his sword. The crowd goes wild.

Mantis meets his son on the grounds and congratulates him. No one has beaten a grandmaster in two years. Ryelyne and his father bow to one another as with tradition. If a warrior wins in the top eight, it is expected for the father of the warrior to bow to his son. It is a sort of pride for the father to enter the arena to his son's victory. In the games, a fighter is a fighter regardless of his father's stature. Ryelyne falls to his knees before his king as a servant of Atlantis. A warrior has no stature on the stadium grounds. It is the code of honor that is taught from childhood in the Atlantean Empire.

Daygun comes up next, and he has had twenty minutes more rest time than Ryelyne. Aten's son enters the grounds. Right before the match, the setting sun hits Daygun's face. The grandmaster deliberated on this before the match. The grandmaster enters the gate that shadows his face to Daygun. It is intimidating to the prince.

The swords start to fly. Daygun is on the defensive right from the beginning. The prince tries to move the grandmaster to his advantage, but the grandmaster counters and stays on the offensive. The grandmaster tries to keep Daygun's face in the sunlight. The prince has brief moments of relief from the sun, but the grandmaster is too good. The swords hit one another over and over again. Daygun counters every measure of his opponent, but he is at a huge disadvantage. The prince musters a short offensive and then the grandmaster puts him right back on the defensive. They both grow tired. There are split seconds that Daygun does not see where the grandmaster's attack is coming from. Aten's son is still blinded by the sun. The prince has only thirty percent visibility. Daygun attempts a final offensive, but the grandmaster counterstrikes, and the grandmaster pins him down.

Daygun is defeated. There is no shame here. Aten goes to the grounds and says he is proud of his son. The prince is very angry at his defeat as any true leader should be. Daygun also falls to his knees in front of the emperor. The crowd goes wild. The masses have seen the best fight in the last five years. Daygun has fought with the best of the best but has lost. The prince bows to his father, but Aten does not bow back because of Atlantean tradition. The loser does not receive a bow from the father. The games are over. Ryelyne is the victor. Daygun and Ryelyne leave the arena in different mind sets.

After the games, Aten asks to see Daygun. The beaten warrior approaches his father in the emperor's chamber. They walk out to the gardens which consist of plants from all around the world. The grounds are well kept by caretakers.

Aten walks slowly with his son and says, "What have you learned from this my son?"

Daygun sits down and looks up to his father. He laughs and says, "Not to fight blind."

Smiling at Daygun, Aten replies, "No! You are beating yourself up with this. I can tell that you can't see the whole picture. Your mind is clouded with disappointment and ego. I will not accept your answer."

Daygun takes a deep breath. The prince knows it is not Aten that is disappointed, but himself. Daygun can feel the love coming from the Atlantean Emperor. It is a soothing voice that a son can only hear from his father. The prince feels ashamed and wonders how his army will look at him. Daygun knows he faulted for stupid reasons and wishes he could fight the grandmaster again, but he has to wait another year.

Aten looks at the garden and says, "What is the real reason that you think you didn't accomplish your goal at the games?"

Aten can tell from Daygun's expression that the reason is simple.

Daygun replies, "I lost because my mind wasn't clear. I was thinking of my army I left behind. I am getting married and I don't trust Melercertis. All of these thoughts have been racing through my mind since I returned back from Valtear. I can't shake it. I didn't expect what I saw in Kayout and it has plagued my mind. I let my surroundings govern my objective to succeed."

Aten sits next to his son and says, "There are times when I can't get outside the realm of my own mind. I sometimes feel trapped and confined. Everyday I feel this way. I have to leave to find myself again. A true leader has to leave an unclear solution to regroup his thoughts and come back to overcome their tribulation. It happens in fighting, love, and politics every day. If a person can govern their emotions at the right time, they will succeed at anything. A lesson in life is to not let the environment govern you."

Daygun is happy his father is there with him and it shows on his face. Daygun loves his father. The prince hopes he can make his future son feel the same way when his children have faltered.

"Yes sir, I didn't have a clear mind. It will never happen again," Daygun says, this time with a more positive attitude.

Aten stands up and replies, "I want you to remember this. I don't have all the answers all the time. To me, fighting and politics are the same. You have to regroup your thoughts and then fight. If you don't, people will see your weaknesses and take advantage of you. As a leader, you can't let them. Advice is good, but you have to trust your own instincts. The only reason Ryelyne won at the arena is because he had no other obstacle in his way. The grandmaster thought too hard on Ryelyne's harsh attack. Ryelyne did something simple that the grandmaster overlooked, and the grandmaster was defeated."

"I understand what you're saying. I saw this," Daygun says as he stands up. His father can tell that Daygun is feeling better and clearer minded than before.

Aten grabs Daygun's shoulder and replies in a stern voice, "If you can see other people's faults, look at yours first. Govern your emotions first, and then you can help other people with their own fears. This is the only way to become a true leader. If people see you taking charge of your own life, they will follow your example."

"I understand. It will be done," Daygun says with a smile.

On the other hand, Mantis gives praise about the games and Ryelyne becoming a grandmaster, but his father forgets to nurture what Ryelyne really needs from a father. He forgets to teach his son to be humble and conservative about his triumph. The King of Masaba sees Ryelyne as a trophy.

At Halotropolis' market place, Mantis is with some of the city's politicians. He is proud of his son and speaks only about Ryelyne's victory of beating a grandmaster. It makes Ryelyne feel uncomfortable. Mantis' son knows his father is only promoting his win for his own personal gain.

At the marketplace, while Ryelyne and his father are alone, Mantis says, "There is nothing I can teach you. I have taught you everything I know. I have brought you up right. The rest of your life you will have to learn lessons the hard way; the way my father taught me. A lot of what I say may not contribute to your mindset. Seek the people you trust and follow your gut instinct."

"I don't understand," Ryelyne replies with a puzzled look on his face.

Mantis looks in his son's eyes with pride and says, "I have been hard on you. I regret some of the things I have done as a father, but I can't take it back. You need to find your inner-self to find your own way."

Feeling uncomfortable, Ryelyne says, "I will not let you down or let myself down."

A week later, Daygun is at Halotropolis to be married. Aten and his advisors are there to brief the Atlantean Military Council on what is to transpire between the alliance of the Kayouts and the Atlanteans. Melercertis is there to see the wedding as a gesture to a new ally and to go over the alliance.

Even though Aten has full right to wage war on the Gambuts, he still consults with the kings of the city-states and the council of the empire. The Atlantean Emperor can overturn any king, but he fears it will cause resentment. Still, an emperor must have full or partial support of his councils according to Atlantean law. In the back of Aten's mind he wishes there was a different system of government. Aten knows his empire rests on his shoulders. The Atlantean Emperor knows in any political situation his reputation is on the line. Aten's father was killed in the last war between the peninsula and the continent. Even though Atlantis has a strong ally, he is still apprehensive to go on a conquest.

Before the wedding, Mantis goes to Vasic where the Atlantean battlecruisers are getting their final touches. The battlecruisers have steel plating and Mantis is there to inspect the work. Most of the steel is made in Masaba. Mantis goes to Aten and pleads for more steel.

The Atlantean nobles work together as one to make their empire better. The kings and politicians act as one. In the Atlantean Empire, royalty and officials have full jurisdiction inside the peninsula. All kings act as brothers with a common goal to make their civilization better.

Aten is with the council waiting on Mantis. The Atlantean Emperor speaks to Melercertis before he leaves to go back to his homeland. Both military councils are working on how to fight the Gambuts.

Mantis comes in to the council meeting and says, "My Lord, I need more steel to build our military. The iron ore coming out of Valtear isn't good quality. It is very difficult to make our swords with Valtear's substandard ore. Two days ago we learned that the Valtear Kingdom is trading with the Mareth Empire. The natural resources to produce good steel are coming from Mareth, not our new occupied territory. The Valteareans have been trading iron ore for salt and other minerals. King Tulless has lied to our empire."

Aten takes a step back and replies, "Tulless has done nothing wrong. He has been playing the middleman. There is nothing wrong with fair trade between empires and kingdoms. His honor has not been damaged. Atlantis has done worse in trades to gain the advantage. Tulless did the same and took advantage of his own resources for his own kingdom."

Mantis says, "We are about to take the Gambut Empire and destroy it. We will merge the Gambuts with our own empire. Our culture and God will replace theirs. It is not right to push religion. I am having second thoughts about this alliance."

Aten answers, "Our world is full of different nations and cultures. If we make it all the same, there would not be any fears or any way to make man more competitive. The different societies and traditions help keep man strong. There can be no other way. Man's independence is the only freedom of life. Taking Gambut is wrong, but we will let the people of Gambut decide if they want to live in our culture or under the Kayouts. Eighty percent of the Gambut population lives on the east side of the Alber Mountains where most of the culture is similar to the Kayouts. We will not destroy their traditions, but we must have the Gambuts natural borders for our empire's future. Since Melercertis has arrived, I have wondered if we are doing the right thing. We will not push religion on the Gambut society after we take it. As the Atlantean Emperor, I choose our way of life over the Gambuts. If the Gambut Emperor had to make the same decision, I am sure he would do the same."

In what Mantis said, it starts to make others reconsider their thoughts of conquest.

Haylos, King of Halotropolis, says, "I understand, but taking half of the Gambut Empire will make them hate us. They will rebel. I also don't trust Melercertis. There is so much uncertainty. Why should we take a chance of taking on so much? Yes, we are a world power. However, if this becomes a world conflict, we will lose."

Aten looks straight into Haylos' eyes and says, "To protect ourselves in the future, we must go forward. This reasoning is for the future of our children and grandchildren."

Haylos says in a pleading voice, "The relocated Gambuts will be under one rule under Melercertis and they will become Kayouts. In the future, the refugees will want to destroy us because we did the same to them. The hate from the Gambuts will destroy Atlantis. Revenge is a good reason to start a war."

Aten replies, "We have to think of the long term advantage. Atlantean technology is coming forth. In twenty years, there will be no empire that can take on our military. In the future, if we have to, we could wage war against the Kayouts at acceptable losses. In fifty years, Atlantis will be able to change the world to better mankind. This has nothing to do with our time, but our children's time. The new treaty between the Kayout Empire and Atlantis will help our cultures grow. This alliance is a stepping stone for mankind. The one true God will be known across the world. We will become the fathers of our faith. I know in my heart God wants are people to do this."

Mantis says, "I understand. I will fight for God and my government. God is to thank for our success, and he will protect us. All of my soldiers are with you."

Aten looks straight at Mantis and replies, "There are many other obstacles to sift through, but I need you, Mantis. You and I see eye to eye on most occasions. Your city is second only to Atlantis in artillery. The army you have is the strongest in our empire. It comes from the leadership of their king. I have great respect for you and your warriors."

Mantis says, "You have my allegiance. I gave you an oath, and I will keep it the rest of my life."

The meeting is over. Daygun and Kaydence are marrying the same day. The kings and the two emperors all show up for the wedding. Everyone of stature is invited to the wedding of the decade. The Halotropolean Grand Hall is the center point of the special ceremony. The structure can house close to five thousand people. Daygun and Kaydence are nervous of what is about to transpire. Their whole world is about to change.

CHAPTER VIII
LOVE AND FAMILY

Kaydence and Daygun stand on the altar with a high priest. The two have to say their own vows. If the vows do not make the audience agree on the validity of the marriage, the crowd has every right to vote against the couple going forward with the wedding. This is the tradition of the Atlantean Empire.

Even though there are twenty thousand people in and around the Halotropolean Grand Hall, it is silent. The Atlantean citizens give the utmost respect. It is a special day for the Atlantean society to see the future emperor and his wife.

In the traditions of Atlantean society, it is customary to bring prior relationships to the wedding and let them be a part of the ceremony. It is a way to signify to the community that the ones getting married have let go of their past. It is to show their past cannot hurt the future of the marriage. If a person does not have former relationships, they cannot marry. The Atlanteans believe a person has to learn from past relationships to have a good marriage. Family and honor is what makes Atlantis a well built society. The lessons of life help bring honor and wisdom to their culture.

Kaydence, in tradition, stands within a circle amongst family and friends. Tasteral, one of Kaydence's past relationships is present at the ceremony. They were together for two years, and he wants to be the one to give Kaydence away. Even though the relationship fell apart, he is still there as a friend. They stand in the circle together with Daygun.

Kaydence says with great pride, "I am here. This is the most important day of my life. I have learned a great deal from my past. Tasteral, I would like to start with you."

She holds his hand and says, "You were my first love. I was very young. I knew I was in love with you. You gave me independence to grow. It was me who pulled away from our relationship. If I hurt you, it was not my intention. You will be in my heart forever, but Daygun has my heart and soul even into the afterlife."

Kaydence is still good friends with Tasteral, but she knows their friendship will change. In tradition, the prior relationship has to leave the building and walk away. Tasteral does so and gives his blessing for Kaydence to marry Daygun. Tasteral is seen by twenty thousand spectators walking away from the building. The only two remaining in the circle are Kaydence and Daygun and the high priest.

It is Daygun's turn. He goes to the front of the crowd and grabs Shana's hand and brings her into the circle. Daygun and Shana courted for two years.

Daygun says, "You are my first love as well. You have given me more than I could ever imagine. The timing of our lives was never right. I take full blame. I was too ambitious to think of anyone but myself. I was very selfish, but I have gained in wisdom over the years, and am now able to marry. I had to grow and find myself first. I did some thinking on the battlefield at Valtear. Before a shot was fired, the only person I could think about was Kaydence. If I died on the battlefield that day, I knew that I had lived well because of Kaydence's friendship. Friendship is why I am marrying Kaydence today. I need her for her understanding and love. She is honestly my best friend."

Shana bows her head and also leaves the building in accordance with tradition. Kaydence and Daygun go outside the circle as they blend in with the community of Atlantis. The circle is bare. The priest goes inside the circle. He stands alone and looks around the crowd. Kaydence and Daygun go back inside the circle as in accordance to tradition, and they both take the hand of the priest.

The priest asks the crowd, "Can anyone think of any reason for this marriage not to take place?" The whole hall goes silent and the priest says, "In the eyes of God, I see your love towards one another. Go on your way. Start your lives as one. Bring up your children with the same morals and love you have for your empire."

The whole crowd cheers and the two go to the feast of the joining. Daygun looks at Kaydence and is very happy. The prince is proud to have her as his wife. During the ceremony, it felt like a blur to both of them. Because it is so overwhelming, the prince almost goes into a daze at the feast. To them, it is almost like being reborn. Daygun wants to remember every detail, but his emotions are very high. The prince thinks he has the same love that his mother and father have in their marriage. Kaydence sees her husband and trembles with joy.

Aten grabs Kaydence in the middle of mingling with guests and says, "I can see the love you have for my son. I remember my wedding day, and it makes me love my wife even more. I thank you for being a part of our family. Over the years, a person sometimes forgets what is important in their life. A man has to be reminded what he has. I love you as a daughter. Please go to him."

Daygun is far away talking to guests. Aten smiles as she goes toward her husband. With this smile between Kaydence and Aten, they both know this moment in time will be one they remember the rest of their lives.

The party goes on for a while. Aten goes to Daygun and wants to ask him a question. Aten says nothing. The prince knows there is something wrong with his father. The Atlantean Emperor seems like he is about to say something, but looks away for a while. After a couple of minutes, Aten looks at his son again without a smile.

The Atlantean Prince goes to his father and asks, "What is it, Father?"

Because Aten is silent, Daygun knows something is bothering him.

Aten, with a concerned voice, says, "I will not ask anything from you on your wedding day."

Daygun tries to comfort his father and replies, "I would rather know now than to think of the thoughts which are passing though your head. Your thoughts need to escape. I understand you Father, so please don't do this to me."

Aten says, "Okay, when the time is right for you, come to the room on the second floor to the right."

Daygun takes his father's hand and replies, "If something is bothering you this badly on your son's wedding day, I must know. We are family, and Kaydence is a part of that. She'll understand."

After about twenty minutes, Daygun goes to the room his father asked him to go to. Because Aten would not ask of something on such an important day, Daygun is really concerned. The prince knows his father, and speculates the concern has something to do with the alliance with the Kayout Empire.

"What is it my Father?" Daygun asks as he goes into the room.

Aten sits down and says, "I have made a decision. The Kayout people can't be trusted. I am sending Ryelyne to the Kayout Empire to train their men and to keep an eye on their full intentions. After the war with the Gambuts, I want to know the Kayouts' strengths and weaknesses. They can be an enemy in the future. I want to train the Kayout's military the way we fight. They will accept it as a token of peace, and we will use this to our advantage. If the Kayouts learn our tactics in war, they can't be a threat to us in the future. I will send our best people to train the Kayout military in the Atlantean ways of war. I want the war with the Gambuts to be swift. Hopefully, the Kayouts and Atlanteans will start a clean slate. I also found out today the Valtear Kingdom has poor iron ore deposits. They have been trading with the Mareth Empire for their rich iron ore. We have been trading with the Valtear Kingdom thinking the ore was coming from them. It isn't true. The Mareth Empire has the iron ore we seek. We should have gone after the Mareth Empire to get what we needed. The Valteareans haven't been as promising as we have thought. They do have other minerals to help produce our steel. It isn't a total loss, and the Kayouts can't have Valtear."

Daygun replies, "The Mareth Empire isn't as weak as the Valteareans, but we can take them. We must send troops into the Mareth Empire and do what we did with the Valtear Kingdom. There is only a small window to do this. After taking the Mareth and Gambuts, the whole world may hate us."

Aten says, "I agree. I am sending Laptos to attack Mareth. I am also sending Dareous with five divisions to help. He is the most qualified other than you. Dareous has moved up the ranks quickly, and I have confidence in him. We need the iron ore to deter our future enemies. Our new navy depends on it, and so does our infantry. The time has come for Laptos to have his victory; he has matured over the last three years. Daygun, you have trained him well. Do you think that Laptos can do it?"

Daygun responds, "Laptos is still a little unsure of himself, but it's time to give him a chance to do something on his own. My brother has good generals to help him with his decisions, but we are still taking a chance. Sending in Dareous is a good idea. He is a good leader. Quentoris and Dareous compliment each other on the battlefield."

Aten looks at Daygun. "You were also inexperienced at one time like your twin brother. I have put political stress on you and you succeeded. One day, I hope I can leave the Atlantean Empire to both of you. Our empire was expanding before my father's rule. Times have changed. Our mathematics, astronomy, buildings, and military weapons have changed in the last twenty-six years. Your brother is knowledgeable in the new way of fighting and uses our technology to his advantage. Three days from now I will assemble the Senate and military advisors in the Atlantean Military Grand Hall. I will make an executive decision to wage war on the Mareth people. I will tell Melercertis of our intentions. I have asked him to stay another week. He will accept my proposal because of his own imperialistic nature."

Aten tells Melercertis the plan and he agrees. The Arber Mountains will be the line drawn between the Kayout and Atlantean Empire. Melercertis will not go to war with Mearth or Kanis. The Kayout Empire will take the bulk of the Gambuts' defenses. In the negotiations, the Kayout Emperor cannot help take Mearth because their Northern territories are still fragile.

Three days later, Daygun, Ryelyne, Dareous, and The Military Council gather around the Atlantean Military Grand Hall in Aten's capital.

Emperor Aten declares to his Military Council, "There will be a new beginning to our people. Melercertis has come to us in peace. He wants us to make a never-ending alliance with the Kayout people. Even though we are small in numbers, we have the technology to protect our borders. The Valteareans have deceived us, but their iron ore isn't what our empire needs. We will honor our forefathers' wishes to never destroy another society or enslave our foes. We need resources from Mareth. Nextear is the most powerful man in Mareth, and he is killing innocent people who don't agree with him. We must protect these people from his military. The Atlanteans and Kayouts will conquer the Gambut Empire together. We will take back what we had twenty-six years ago."

Dareous stands up and says, "To take on two empires, we must train new soldiers. We need more weapons and manpower."

Aten responds, "You are right. We need the next harvest of the molless tree which will be next month. It will take us six months to build our bows for our new army. A months before the longest day of the year, we will attack Mearth. After we take their empire, we will put our military might on the border with Gambut on two fronts. On the longest day of the year, we will attack. The future new territory, which we know as Mearth, will be our spearhead into Gambut. The Gambuts will think Atlantis will attack on two fronts. In doing so, our military tactics will spread out their military. A month later after we have reorganized inside Mearth, Kayout and our armies will march into Gambut."

Ryelyne says, "Nexter is a strong leader, and he is getting stronger by the day. Nexter's men will be harder to take."

Aten says to his generals and Military Council, "I will send Dareous with five divisions to help Laptos. That will give us seven divisions inside the Valtearean Empire. Ryelyne, I need you to take a division to teach the Kayout generals how to fight in our arts of war. We have to show the Kayouts that Atlantis wants peace. If we teach our ways of war to Melercertis' military, we will show them that we do not want them to lose their warriors in the Gambut Campaign. Kayout is not strong enough to help us with Mearth. In eight months, we can train four more divisions to reinforce our Great East and West Walls. I want Ryelyne to lead the fight into Gambut on the Kayout side. I will take at least ten Atlantean divisions to attack the Gambut Empire myself. I want this to be swift. Daygun, our empire needs you to stay here to protect our capital and make our military machine more powerful. It is time for you to lead the other side of warfare. Take our manpower to produce more weapons and train our men for battle. Keep twenty divisions in reserve for reinforcements. You will be in-charge while I am gone. It is time for you to take leadership. Our armies believe in you and so do I. My father took the pride out of Atlantis. It is up to me to bring it back."

Daygun is shocked, and says, "I can't take your place as emperor. I want to lead the attack against the Gambut Empire."

Aten replies, "I will not let Kaydence hate me for the rest of her life. Your mother already wishes I was dead."

The whole council laughs. Eventually, the men in the Atlantean Grand Hall agree. The council debates what is going happen in their near future. Ryelyne is overwhelmed by what Aten is asking of him, but Ryelyne knows this campaign will put him in tales that will be told in generations to come.

Aten goes to Melercertis about his plan. The Kayout Emperor said he will not interfere. Melercertis will get the bread basket of Gambut, and Aten will take the iron oar of Mareth. The two empires will get what they need to evolve to their next stage of development.

As Ryelyne is starting to walk on the dock to go to his ship, Daygun runs up to him and says, "I heard about your mission. I came to say good luck and to say congratulations about becoming a grandmaster."

Ryelyne responds, "I think winning at the game put me in this position. I don't want to leave Atlantis. Now, I wish I never won at the games."

Daygun says, "No matter the circumstance, I will miss you. It will be more than a year before I see you again. I love you as a brother."

Ryelyne responds, "Your father has been there for me. I see you as family. One day we will look at this and smile." They hug as brothers and walk away from each other and do not look back.

Later, Ryelyne steps on a Kayout battlecruiser with his generals and advisors. Melercertis is on board and welcomes him onto the Kayout ship. When the ship sets sail, Ryelyne looks at the shores of Atlantis and knows his life is about to change. The Kayout officers will march with Ryelyne's division to the Kayout capital. Going into the Kayout Empire, Ryelyne knows his division could be attacked by the nomadic tribes. The Kayout officers will protect them.

Dareous is a promoted to Major General, and he sets out with five divisions to implement Aten's wishes to occupy Mareth and to reinforce the Valtear Empire. Aten has seen Dareous' leadership skills and he has done well in other campaigns. Aten trusts Dareous to help take the two divisions already in Valtear to attack the Mareth Empire.

The whole weight of the future of mankind is on the line. Daygun goes to the temple and prays for his people. The prince does not know what is to come, and he knows of only honor and family. He obeys his father and stands down as the Atlantean Supreme Commander. Daygun wants to fight the Gambuts, but he knows his time will come. Ryelyne and Dareous go on separate missions to accomplish one goal. In these two campaigns, there will be Atlantean wives who will not see their husbands again. Daygun knows there will be a new beginning for mankind, but many Atlanteans will not live to see the changes. The only thing the dead Atlanteans will see on the road to the afterlife is a vision of their emperor.

CHAPTER IX
A DIFFERENT WORLD –
A DIFFERENT TIME

Two days have passed. Ryelyne stands at the rear of the Kayout battlecruiser, looking in the direction of Atlantis. He wonders if the Atlantean Navy will one day fight the ship upon which he is aboard. As a warrior, Ryelyne looks for any weaknesses the ship may have. He notices different ways the Kayout ship can be destroyed in battle. The main strength of the Kayout battlecruiser is that it has a very thick hull. The Atlantean destroyers would have a very hard time penetrating the warships by ramming. If the Kayout ship is rammed with an Atlantean destroyer, it would take a great deal of speed to break through the hull. However, the Atlantean destroyers are very fast, and speed is their main strength. Because of the dexterity of the Atlantean ships, their weakness is a thin hull. If an Atlantean destroyer were rammed by a Kayout battlecruiser, it would almost cut the Atlantean destroyer in half.

On the third day towards Kayout, Melercertis is not speaking much about the implications of the alliance between the Atlantean and Kayout people.

The Kayout Emperor tries to win the affections of Ryelyne and his council. The past three days have been nothing but feasting, drinking, and learning about each other's culture. Melercertis and his people mainly speak the Kayout language on board their ship. Only the Kayout council and generals knows the Atlantean language.

On the third night, Ryelyne asks Melercertis to help teach him the Kayout language. If Ryelyne is to help the Kayouts, he must learn their basic language. After eating and drinking, the two talk. With an almost full moon behind them on deck, they discuss the language and the Kayout culture.

Melercertis starts off and says, "Our way of life is very simple. Our empire is still in its infancy. We are one with the earth. Every tree and plant is replanted, and we don't kill more than we can eat. Everyone goes to an assembly every night to talk about the next day and what can be done to please our gods. If I may ask, why do the Atlanteans believe in one god? To me, there are too many elements in life for one god to control."

"You have a god for love?" Ryelyne asks.

Melercertis says, "Yes, Ka-Taina; she is the mother of our people. If it weren't for her, we wouldn't be here. To me, I can't understand your god. How can one god take on all the love in the world and also protect the oceans? I do not mean to disrespect your god or your culture, but true love is almost too much for even one god to handle. We are a different society. To be allies, we have to understand one another. Do you agree?"

Ryelyne scratches his head in puzzlement. He sips on some water and tries to piece Melercertis' arguments together.

Ryelyne replies, "I do agree. I know there are questions you may have. I will answer every question to the best of my ability. The answer is simple. The way Atlanteans think is that there can only be one emperor, and he controls every aspect in the life of our empire. Only one god could exist because each god would destroy one another until there was only one. If there wasn't such a thing as our emperor, there would be too much confusion and greed. It is simple, only one god and only one emperor could exist."

Melercertis says, "So, Atlanteans think there can only be one emperor on earth."

Ryelyne responds quickly, "No. I only speak for Atlantis. Aten said there has to be different cultures and religions to make mankind better. He doesn't want to destroy any society. In our beliefs, different cultures are here on earth for a reason. Man is different, and our God is beyond our comprehension. We seek technology to please God, and fulfill His vision for mankind. He made man with a mind. I'm sure that He wants us to use it. We want to make God's world prosper for future generations. Forty years ago, we developed a device to see what is too small to be seen by the human eye. A person can look through a lens and see a new world. Atlantean scientists are able to see tiny organisms. Our scientists believe the small organisms can enter a wound, take over the body, and destroy it. We have learned to kill those organisms. Technology is linked to our theology. God wants us to improve ourselves. God helps us every day in our lives, and my empire wants to help the rest of the world to become better."

Melercertis glares at Ryelyne and replies, "Atlanteans have found a way to play God."

Ryelyne says, "Our God shares our way of thinking. He wants us to use our brains to better life and to better humanity."

Melercertis redirects his voice and says, "I understand, but many people fear the Atlantean technologies. People who are not from Atlantis don't understand your mysticism. Man should not be able to control nature, but life should control itself."

Ryelyne says quickly, "Right now, we are riding over the water on a ship, created by man."

Melercertis argues, "But there is a limit to what man should do."

Ryelyne says, "Tell that to the people that have never seen a boat before. Technology has its advantages."

Melercertis fears he has lost the conversation. He replies curtly, "Many countries are scared of the Atlanteans using technologies to destroy societies."

Ryelyne asks, "Why is this? Because we use technology to produce more than we need and we give to different societies in need."

Melercertis says, "But the Atlanteans are decades ahead of the rest of the world. In less then fifty years, Atlantis will be able to take over the world with ease. The Eastern countries seek out the Kayout Empire for protection. The fear of Atlantis is making Kayout stronger. If you were a leader of a primitive nation, wouldn't you do the same?"

Ryelyne replies, "If we take a country, the country has a right to be independent again. We only occupy up to two years. A country can become a state of Atlantis or return to its traditional standing, and we still give assistance to that country. We give royalties to the nobles, and they govern themselves. Atlantis honors their heritage and way of life. We don't destroy it. On the other hand, Kayouts conquer and strip the culture away."

Melercertis says with frustration, "It is not true." He places his hand on Ryelyne's shoulder. "The countries we take are usually in turmoil. Tribes fight one another and never advance. The Kayout Empire goes in and takes that turmoil away. If we didn't do this, the country would destroy itself, and its resources would be squandered. In your history books, what country has the Kayouts taken that was not going through political turmoil? Plus, Atlantis still takes a nation away for two years, and corrupts the nation's nobles into the Atlanteans' way of thinking."

Ryelyne replies, "Our books say the Kayouts take countries and destroy cultures. It doesn't say much about the countries' politics."

Melercertis asks, "Who writes those books?"

Ryelyne replies, "Our historians."

Melercertis takes a second and says, "We have the same historians. Each culture has major differences, yes, but people are people. Man has the same emotions. Propaganda, on both sides, has made our civilizations wary of each other. We believe in different religions that are taught by our fathers and mothers. How can I say that your God is the right one, or is it our gods? Religious leaders use fear to sway people towards their politics. Religion is a tool for politicians. A normal person doesn't want to kill or destroy anything, but misguided religion can kill millions. If outside people look at our two religions, they will see they are basically the same. Yet, if religious leaders say kill in the name of God or gods, it's done. Most people don't blink an eye if they kill for their god."

Ryelyne feels uncomfortable and replies, "Sir, you have to excuse me. I am tired. I have had too much wine."

Melercertis says back, "Thank you for talking to me. I must retire as well. I will talk to you tomorrow. We have a couple of more days before we dock. I hope you're enjoying the voyage to a new world."

Ryelyne sees the world a little bit differently after the conversation. The Atlantean General is true to the ways of the Atlanteans' beliefs. Ryelyne would never betray his empire, and he is highly patriotic for his fatherland. He has risen up in the ranks to become a grandmaster and is the son of the Masabaian

King. Ryelyne has earned respect from his people in the Atlantean Empire. People heed his advice and guidance. Most Atlantean men wish they had the stature as Ryelyne. He retires to his chamber and lies to sleep. He thinks of the battles of his past and what Melercertis said. The Atlantean General only wants simplicity in life. Even the way Ryelyne fights is very simplistic. Every move of an opponent's sword has a counter move. He understands people cannot learn the sword through a book. He wants a simplistic life, but he knows all too well that is an impossible task because Atlantis is not a simple empire.

The next morning, the seagulls are flying around and the sun rises over the horizon. There are clouds all around, and it is raining at a distance. Ryelyne sits up and stretches his arms to the sky. The Atlantean General prays to God and goes on deck. Melercertis stands at the front of the ship, anticipating his return home. The Kayout Emperor misses his family and empire.

Ryelyne meets Melercertis at the front of the ship. There is a very strong breeze in the air. The Atlantean General looks at the Kayout Emperor and senses he has something heavy on his mind. Ryelyne wants to know what he is about to experience in his life. The Atlantean General is curious and fascinated by the land that he is about to see. No Atlantean has seen into the Kayout Empire this far without the fear of death. The Atlantean planters, or spies, have seen almost everything, but Ryelyne is about to see it first hand, openly. In the past, the Atlantean General has learned to hate Melercertis because it was taught to him in schools, but now Ryelyne sees the Kayout Emperor in a new light. Even though they are from two different worlds, it seems the cultural barrier is breaking.

Ryelyne looks at Melercertis and asks, "What is so heavy on your mind?"

Melercertis does not know what to say, and he does not want to show any weakness. After a moment, Melercertis turns to Ryelyne and says, "An emperor has a lot on his mind all the time."

Melercertis turns and walks away from the Atlantean General.

"I can't imagine," Ryelyne replies, and follows the Kayout Emperor.

Melercertis says, "It never stops. I can only imagine what is going on back in my home. In life, everyone wants power. I have to resist my political counterparts. I know I will have to put them back into their place when I return. Because all the young bucks think they can handle an empire, I don't have the luxury of wasting any time. I know exactly what Aten goes through every day. I have great respect for him. Because Atlantis has more stability than my empire, I can honestly say Aten has it a little bit easier."

"Aten has taken me in as a son. I am a very close friend with Daygun. Aten has picked up the slack as a father because my father is too stern and close-minded. I listen to Aten's guidance, and he is a good father to Daygun. Aten treats me as a father should," Ryelyne replies.

Melercertis asks, "If I may ask, what is your relationship with your father?"

Ryelyne looks at the seagulls like he is distracted and replies, "My father has too much on his mind to think of me. I am one son of one million who live under his rule. Masaba is the third largest city of our empire. There is pressure in being a king. A son can't look bad in the public's eye. I have made mistakes, but I have learned from them. My father seems to be embarrassed by my mistakes. I think I am an outlet for his frustrations. I can never please my father. I can't do enough. Just a week ago, I was given title of Grandmaster, and my father said I should make my own mistakes and learn from them, and that I was already a man. When I make a wrong choice in life, I need my father's guidance to understand why I took the wrong path. Daygun seems to get his guidance from his father."

Melercertis looks at the seagulls and says, "I understand. I wish my father was still alive to help me. I know I have made some mistakes here and there, but I know I wouldn't have listened to him anyway. When people are young, they never listen. It seems like they have to go through the emotions even if it is unpleasant. I see your point, but I see your father's as well. I would like to get together and talk with you and your council. I need to know what you require from my empire to make this transition easier. You and your generals will be in Kayout for a while. Let's meet after the midday feast. We only have one more day before we reach our capital."

They look at each other and smile. Ryelyne feels like he can relate to Melercertis. Ryelyne senses he can trust him a little more. The emotional defenses between Melercertis and the Atlantean

General are almost gone. Ryelyne is ready to begin the campaign. The past days of sailing have felt like a vacation to him. Even though Ryelyne has spoken to his council a little, his work has not yet begun. He needs direction from Melercertis. Ryelyne has no idea what to think of the Kayout Army and he does not yet know the strengths and weaknesses of those he is going to train. Because of insufficient reports from Atlantean planters, the Atlantean General does not know what he is headed into.

During the midday feast, Ryelyne does not eat much. When they all finish, they go to the ship's military formal room which is cramped due to the twelve men from both empires.

Melercertis starts the meeting and says, "Let me begin by saying thank you. I have taken you away from your lands to save lives for a new alliance between our two civilizations. The world will change for the better. I would like to give you some of my thoughts. I would love to hear yours in return. I hope that we can compromise. I am a good warrior, but nothing like the Atlanteans. Your battle tactics are far superior to ours. We have won many battles, but at a high cost. I need you to help save my countrymen. I would love to learn your battle tactics, but ours have succeeded as well. My generals will not want to change. We have almost two million warriors ready for battle separated in over eighty divisions. We have seven thousand mammoths, three thousand elephants, and over fifty thousand horse cavalry to overcome our weaknesses. I have taken every mammoth and elephant in our empire to help in the Gambut Campaign. We need the resources of the Gambut Empire for our societies to advance. I need the Atlanteans' help. If not, we can't win this war."

Ryelyne asks, "Do you see any other problems with our alliance?"

Melercertis says, "The only problem I can see is the Kanis Empire getting involved. Borealeous, the Kanis Emperor, has a strong military. I am in good standings with their emperor, and he will stand down in your conquest to take Mearth. The Kanis Emperor hates Nexter. Atlantis is doing the world a favor by taking out Mearth. They have a corrupt military. We cannot help you take Mearth because we are using our military resources on the east side of Gambut."

Melercertis backs up and gives the floor to the Atlantean

General. Ryelyne stands. The Kayout Emperor is putting a great deal of confidence in Ryelyne.

Ryelyne stands tall and says. "The world needs differences in cultures. If not, the world will become stagnant. Humanity will stay the same. The only way the world is able to move forward in the future is to have different beliefs and religions. We will be allies with the Kayouts for generations to come. I will use my influence for the future between our two empires. Our two empires need each other to go forward. We will help in making Kayout more efficient. If we combine our technologies together, mankind will become better. Atlanteans can learn from your way of life, and I think your people can learn from us as well."

Melercertis stands up from his seat, and Ryelyne sits down.

Melercertis says, "When we arrive in Madera, you will see our accomplishments in war technology, and also what we have done for our people. Ryelyne has made me understand the Atlantean people a little better. Now, let's get to the matter at hand. We must take the Gambut Empire. If we don't, we will not be able to feed our population. We need their land for food. We could have traded with the Gambut Empire, but they will not use the land to their advantage for trade. The land goes to waste. The Kayout Empire is growing at a considerable rate, as is Atlantis. Gambut resources are the only way for us not to suffer in the future. Gambut has land to farm and natural water sources. In this quest, I wish for Ryelyne to become Supreme Commander of my forces while Atlantis and the Kayouts are in this alliance. I want Aten to know that we trust him and his generals. Every Kayout soldier is at your disposal. What do you think Ryelyne?"

Ryelyne stands upright and replies, "I don't know what to think. Thank you. I will take command to help your warriors. When this is done, I will return to my homeland and protect her."

Melercertis announces, "This meeting is over. There is nothing else to talk about until we get back to Madera. Every warrior we can spare will be near our capital next week. I will send my council to my capital. They are to be hand picked by me. I have enemies in my political circle. I don't trust politics or any man in it. There is too much greed in most politicians' souls. But if I die, there will not be a Kayout Empire. The country can't govern itself. Because of their own greed, the politicians will tear apart my empire."

Melercertis excuses his council, and the meeting disperses. All of his council leaves the war room except for Ryelyne and Melercertis. The Kayout Emperor asks the Atlantean General to stay. Ryelyne's council goes to their quarters and prepare for the last feast aboard the Kayout battlecruiser. This night, Melercertis is giving the best feast of the voyage. The Kayout Emperor has asked all generals and council to dress up into their best clothes and not to bring their swords. Melercertis has something planned for them. They will reach Madera in the late afternoon the next day.

In a complementary voice Ryelyne says, "I thank you for this opportunity. I will not let Atlantis or Kayout down."

Melercertis replies, "I believe in you, Ryelyne. This dinner will be very symbolic. We will all eat looking towards Atlantis out of respect for your empire. I ask for your council to believe in me. I know it is hard to do so."

Ryelyne cocks his head and says, "I don't trust you completely, but I am more at ease in your presence."

Melercertis smiles at Ryelyne and replies, "I don't expect you to. The silence between our two nations has put too much mistrust between our empires. It will take decades to overcome the mistrust with one another. I suspect religion will hamper our alliance in the future. On the Atlantean's side, there are extremists. We also have the same religious extremists. I respect your beliefs, but I know the majority of our people don't. I ask you to not speak about religion anymore. You can speak it with me, but please only in private. When we reach Madera, it will be better to keep your beliefs to yourself. I'm leaving you with the best interpreter I have. She is my daughter. I need you to not say anything to your council of who she is. My daughter is the best thing in my life. I trust her. She is a good politician. I am asking you to help keep my daughter safe from anything that might go wrong. She is family, and family comes first over everything else in my life. I'm going to trust you. With this, I don't know if I'm going mad or I'm trying to trust my instincts. A real man trusts his instincts, and he goes with it even if it drives him mad."

Ryelyne says, "You can trust me. Aten trusts me. I will be the bridge that connects our two empires together. You have your politics, and I have mine. I will play by your rules in Madera."

Melercertis replies, "Politics is always the same. Greed comes first, and then they serve the masses, but only if the masses can give them something in return."

Ryelyne leaves the room. He has much to think about. He does not speak to his advisors, and returns to his quarters.

Hours go by and the sun starts to go down. The feast begins. Melercertis servants are taking care of all the Atlanteans' needs. About thirty minutes after the Atlanteans have already started to drink wine, the Kayout advisors and generals come up to the deck at the same time. No general or advisor is carrying a sword. Because Melercertis has not joined them yet, there is some tension. Ten minutes after the Kayout generals and advisors arrive on deck; Melercertis comes on deck slowly and quietly. All of the Kayout generals and advisors greet and salute him in their custom. The Atlanteans do the same out of respect. Aten told them to respect the Eastern culture and their customs. Ryelyne's officers are at Melercertis' disposal and under his command.

The tables on deck are facing the rear of the ship looking towards the horizon of Atlantis.

Ryelyne is dressed very nicely, as are all of his generals and advisors. The Atlanteans are dressed in military protocol with silver breastplates with a bull symbolizing their coat of arms. The rest of the attire is in brown leather. Over the Atlantean armor, they all wear a blood red cloak, and the cloaks are flying in the wind.

All the Kayout warriors and generals wear bronze and black leather with a black cloak. One of the main exports of Kayouts is leather. The Eastern Empire has very good craftsmen in the art of leather goods. They are sought throughout the world. The Kayout generals wear polished bronze breastplates engraved with a horse and elephant on their hind legs facing each other. The riders of the beasts hold swords as if they are going to strike one another in battle. The decorative clothing of the Atlantean and Kayout warriors took months to make.

The Kayouts and Atlanteans eat, and the sun is almost down for the day. There is silence between the Kayouts and Atlanteans like most feasts on any occasion. Then Melercertis speaks as a leader.

Melercertis says, "I consider the Atlanteans as friends. For me, trust is never given. It is earned. As tradition in your empire, generals are given taxes from the lands that they conquer. For the rest of your natural lives, you will reap the benefits of the Gambut

Empire. It is only right for me to give you what you deserve. All of you are considered nobles in my land. Even though you will return to Atlantis after this campaign, I will give you lands in the new country that we are about to conquer. You will be lords of the land. I will give you some of the lands on the east side of the Alber Mountains. The Kayout divisions that are helping take the Gambut Empire will stay there to occupy the land and govern it for you. I will be the caretaker of the new county, but you will be richly rewarded. I can't take this county without Aten. The earning of trust is beginning."

Melercertis raises his cup in the air and stands. The rest of the Atlanteans and Kayout warriors do the same. The wind is increasing and the Atlantean cloaks are waving in the wind. There is a storm brewing in the distance.

Ryelyne looks at the storm and says, "It seems you have control of the weather as well, Melercertis. You made the wind blow and made us all look heroic when you spoke."

Both sides laugh at Ryelyne's joke. The conversation between the two empires becomes easier. The Atlanteans and Kayouts talk about children and women. Ryelyne knows why Melercertis did not talk of the conquest so much at the beginning. Before talking of conquest, the Kayout Emperor had to bring down the tensions between the two empires. After the feast, the Atlanteans go to sleep with little fear. The voyage has helped bring the two sides together.

The next morning, Ryelyne wakes up and eats breakfast with Melercertis. Both of them are anxious to dock at Madera. Because they say little, they both go on deck. Melercertis goes to the bridge and speaks with the ship's captain. Ryelyne goes to the front of the ship and stays there alone. Some of the Atlanteans' advisors try to talk to Ryelyne, but the Atlantean General answers their questions with short, pointed answers. He feels pressure on his shoulders, and wishes he had his father to guide him in his adventures. Even if Mantis were here, he would not give what Ryelyne requires from a father. Ryelyne's father is not personal with him, and he treats him almost like a servant of the empire. Melercertis treats the Atlantean General more like a son than Mantis does. Ryelyne knows his next sight of land will change the rest of his life, and he is drawn to a country he knows very little about. He feels as if the breeze is coming from the seas of Atlantis, and he wants to take in every breath he can. Once in Madera Harbor, he knows life will change. The Atlantean General stays at the front of the Kayout ship for hours until the Kayout capital is in sight.

In hours, everyone on board the Kayout ships sees their destination. Madera is getting closer and there is not much traffic coming in or out of the harbor. The few merchant ships are primitive compared to Ryelyne's home port. The ship's sails are not crafted as the sails of the Atlantean Empire. As the Kayout ships sail closer to the docks, there is a crowd gathering to meet Melercertis. Ryelyne can tell that the Kayout people love and respect their emperor. Cheers echo through the harbor. Ryelyne backs away from the front of the ship and lets Melercertis take the front.

Melercertis feels he's finally home, and his advisors can see the emotion coming from their emperor's face. The Kayout Emperor trembles with the anticipation of touching Kayout soil again.

The Kayout battlecruisers finally tie up, and the Atlanteans see a massive ceremonial line of warriors in the road from the dock. A mammoth with ceremonial attire is waiting to carry their emperor throughout the city. The Kayout Emperor's best guards are there to escort him. He knows this is a good sign. Some of his own fears about rebellion are abated.

Ryelyne waits to step off the ship last. It is customary for the Atlantean generals and advisors to be the last ones off a ship in war or ceremonies, while Kayout generals are the first off the ship. The Atlanteans stick to their traditions in military code. Ryelyne knows he has to learn all the customs of the Kayout Empire to intertwine with their culture. He knows his life is about to change drastically.

CHAPTER X
THE BEGINNING OF THE END

The Kayout children play around the docks, just as any child would throughout the world. The children are ignorant to what is going on in politics and war. Everyone other than the children are standing in the harbor, watching their emperor mount the ceremonial mammoth. The animal is trained very well. The mammoth kneels when Melercertis goes towards the beast. The Kayout Emperor climbs onto the animal, and everyone on the dock of Madera cheers as the mammoth rises on all fours.

Ryelyne is the last to exit the Kayout battlecruiser, and the crowd cheers as he steps onto the dock. The cheering makes him feel welcomed, but he realizes the strangeness of the moment. Four months prior, the crowd would have tried to kill the Atlanteans if they sailed into their harbor. The emotion of the crowd is not what Ryelyne is prepared for. He goes to the nearest patch of ground and takes off his shoes to show he is embracing the Kayout Empire.

Every Kayout warrior lines the street from the harbor saluting Ryelyne as he enters the city. The Atlantean General cannot shake off the emotional uneasiness, but he stands tall. He salutes the Kayout warriors in their own tradition. The Kayout Emperor instructs Ryelyne and his generals to mount the mammoths which are waiting for them at the end of the harbor street. The Atlanteans and Kayouts will ride with each other to display their alliance.

The Atlanteans follow Melercertis' orders because of the confusion of mannerisms. The visitors are afraid of doing something that can be interpreted as rude. Melercertis is in his own world and the Atlanteans are on his turf. The Kayout Emperor glows with confidence as he sees the Atlanteans' uneasiness, but he does not exploit it.

The mammoths with the Kayout Emperor, generals, and advisors parade though the streets of Madera. For miles, the street seems to have no end. Melercertis sits up straight and looks forward. He has to look strong in front of his people. Melercertis wonders about the state of his empire. He feels confident about his people, but he wonders what is going on with his high officials.

Ryelyne sizes up the Kayout warriors and he cannot see a single warrior without good discipline. Discipline is the key to any good army. The Kayout warriors salute their new Supreme Commander without hesitation. They salute Ryelyne in the Atlantean tradition. With this kind of discipline from these warriors, he wonders why Melercertis needs Atlantis. The Kayout warriors look strong and are uniformed in impeccable military protocol. Ryelyne was not expecting to see an army like this. He expected an untrained army, unable to defeat the Gambuts without high casualties.

Ryelyne looks at the city of Madera. He admires the Kayout buildings made of brick. Other structures are made of wood with very good craftsmanship. Madera has lush forest outside its city, and the best craftsmen of the empire live in the Kayout capital. The buildings are less impressive than those in Atlantis, but Ryelyne can tell the Kayout craftsmen spent many man hours building each structure with high detail. Each building can stand for centuries, barring a natural disaster. The wood is sealed with a stain. Atlantis does not have the chemical composition to make this kind of tarnish. Ryelyne ponders that the Kayouts are not without their own technological advantages. This is nothing he had ever imagined when he entered the city.

The Atlantean spies did not reveal such details. They only reported the city was well kept, and their buildings were not like a modern city of Atlantis. The Atlantean planters also talked about how substandard the Kayouts cities were in comparison to Atlantis. Ryelyne is not so sure, but he knows the Kayout Empire could not prosper without technology. When he returns to Atlantis, he will talk to the Atlantean Military Council and Aten.

Right now, Ryelyne considers asking Aten for a preemptive strike against the Kayout Empire after the Gambut Campaign. He knows Melercertis' empire will only grow stronger in the next decade, and the Eastern superpower will never be able to be conquered if Atlantis does not do something quickly. With the confusion after the Gambut Campaign, the Kayout military will be thinly spread out. An Atlantean spearhead through the Kayout Empire will ensure victory to Aten's military conquest.

Ryelyne is a warrior, and it has been built into his nature from military school and Atlantean tradition to make Atlantis more powerful. Even though Ryelyne is dignified in culture, he always has conquest on his mind. Yet, he trusts Melercertis as an individual. Ryelyne wants to talk to Melercertis more to find out why he feels this way. The Kayout Emperor has accepted Ryelyne into his circle, and the two of them have faith in this new alliance. On the other hand, the word 'trust' could simply be another word. The Kayout Empire could still be holding on to hate towards the Atlanteans' society from the Great War.

After thirty minutes of riding the mammoths, the paraded caravan reaches the end of the road. Ryelyne has so much on his mind, and he almost goes into a trance. At the end of the trip; he only remembers the cheering of the crowd and the discipline of the Kayout warriors.

Melercertis and the Atlanteans reach the gates of the Kayout Emperor's palace. When they reach the last gate, the gate opens. Inside, the Atlanteans see a building made of nothing but wood from the largest trees in the Kayout Empire. It is Melercertis' home. It is a sight that no Atlantean has seen until now. Aten's spies have never penetrated this far because of security around the palace. The palace has four gates and four walls. The palace itself is sitting on thirty- two acres. Close to five hundred men protect the palace, and each of them has their own barracks and is treated well. It is an honor to be one of the royal guards of the Kayout Emperor. They are the premier warriors of the Kayout military. The longer the Kayouts are a guard for their emperor the more tokens are given throughout their lives. If a Kayout warrior guards their emperor for ten years, they are rewarded well enough to have a family and not work for the rest of their lives.

The Atlanteans and Kayouts go inside the palace. The guards salute every step the Atlanteans take towards the palace door. Melercertis is still looking straight ahead. In the Kayout culture, the emperor is treated almost as a god.

The Kayout servants run to Melercertis. Ryelyne can tell that the servants have missed him. The Kayout Emperor talks to them one by one as he goes inside the palace. The façade of sternness he had going through the Kayout capital is completely changed. The Atlanteans feel they can relax now. Even though Melercertis is an emperor, his leadership skills towards his servants are unbelievable. He treats them like family.

The Atlanteans and Kayouts enter the main hall of the palace, and the servants have prepared a feast. The servants have cooked their emperor his favorite foods, as well as Atlantean cuisine. The Atlanteans eat less spicy food than the Kayouts. Thousands of candles light the hall. The chamber is made of mud brick and it is very cool inside for this time of the year. There are close to thirty servants waiting hand and foot on their guests from the peninsula. Most of the servants are young woman and beautiful. Melercertis wants to make a good impression on Ryelyne's officers and advisors, and he is succeeding. Melercertis starts the meal with a toast.

The Kayout Emperor speaks as if he is kind of embarrassed and says, "I had many volunteers to serve you this afternoon. I hope you all don't mind. I told my council this kind of show would not be appropriate, but even an emperor has to do what the main majority of the Senate wants. I thought about it a little bit more, and I wanted to show off the beauty of our land."

Ryelyne is sitting down and says to Melercertis, "We thank you for your hospitality."

Melercertis looks back at Ryelyne and replies, "I need your help, Ryelyne."

As he is served by a beautiful young girl, Melercertis says, "I have been waiting for this for weeks." Melercertis pauses for a moment, and says, "I don't think you will want this assignment. Let's just say I have a little problem with my men, and you are the only person who can solve my dilemma."

Ryelyne replies, "If I am not mistaken, I am here for that."

Melercertis says, "In my realm, I have good warriors. They believe they are capable of leading the attack against the Gambut Empire without your empire. At the same time, your warriors are feeling the same way. There is a pissing contest between our two militaries. Everyone thinks their fighting skills are better than the other. My warriors have trained for war all their lives. I need to shut them up. I need you to spar against my best warrior and prove your standing. The only way they will respect and listen to you is if you beat them at their own game. I saw you fight in the stadium. You are good, but my warriors are not bad themselves. My best general Tito wants to face you. If you beat him quickly, the others will bow down to you. Tito has never been beaten in combat. He is a feared fighter throughout my empire."

Ryelyne takes a drink out of his cup and says, "Give me a few days to regroup my thoughts and to get situated to my new environment. On the third day, I will spar against your best warrior."

Melercertis replies in relief, "I will inform Tito that he will have his chance. After the fight, I will assemble my Military Council to finalize our plans. Everyone needs a good kick in the teeth every once in a while. I hope for the sake of our alliance that you win. I wish I could stage this, but Tito is an honorable man and my best fighter."

The next couple of days, Ryelyne use his advisors and generals to help prepare for the fight. Ryelyne practices the first day for eight hours. The next day he practices for four. Later on the second day, the Atlantean General stands alone imagining attacks and counterattacks. Ryelyne remembers the sparring match with the grandmaster at the sparring games, but he knows how Atlanteans fight. He has no idea how the Kayouts fight sword to sword.

The night before the fight, Ryelyne's generals come up to his room. Ryelyne's generals know the alliance lies on their commander's shoulders. Acteon is Ryelyne's highest-ranking general. Acteon is twenty-seven, and five feet, ten inches tall. He is thin and athletic. He has been under Ryelyne's command for three years. His father died in the Great War twenty-six year prior.

Acteon asks, "How can Melercertis ask this of you?"

Ryelyne responds, "He is testing me. He wants to know right now if I am the one for the task. Melercertis knows I am out of my element and he needs to know if I can handle the pressure. These men are no different than we are. Atlanteans would have done the same thing if the situation were reversed. It's like a pack of wolves. The wolves have to fight until they have a top dog. I have no choice."

Acteon proudly says, "Let me fight Tito first. Then you can see how he fights."

Ryelyne stops Acteon and replies, "Melercertis said that Tito is an honorable man. I should do the same. If you fight first, it will give me the advantage. I don't know how the Kayouts fight, but maybe it is what Melercertis wants to see. He may want to see how each empire can fight man to man."

Acteon pushes a little more and says, "Maybe Melercertis wants to see if you will go into a battle blindly. You and I both know from military school that a fighter must know their opponent first before they can conquer them."

Ryelyne nods his head and says, "You may be right. I will discuss what you have said with Melercertis. I will also give you credit for your idea."

Acteon says, "If you take the Kayout warriors blindly into battle, the casualties could be high because of your misjudgment. I think this is a test. Melercertis will respect you more if you make me fight first or make up new rules before you fight. Let's say that the best Kayout warriors fight our best warriors. There has to be more Kayouts that want to play with us on the sparring field. If you see how they fight, you will have an idea how to fight Tito."

Ryelyne responds, "I agree with you. I will go to Melercertis and ask for his best to come forward, and we will fight one on one. Tito and I will fight last. Well done Acteon."

Ryelyne goes to the Melercertis and he asks him about the sparring match to be conducted in accordance to Acteon's advisement. The Kayout Emperor is at the end of his day, and the last of his council has just left. Besides talking with the Atlanteans, Melercertis has been very busy with the politics of his own lands. Because it is very taxing, Melercertis is tired and Ryelyne can see it on his face. Melercertis agrees to the new terms of the sparring match. After a brief discussion, the Atlantean General slips quietly out of emperor's chamber.

The next morning, the sparring begins. The eight best Kayout warriors fight against the eight best generals and captains of the Atlanteans. Tito and Ryelyne both fight the first round against other men who they defeat pretty quickly. The Atlanteans place their weakest fighter against Tito. During the second round, the fighting becomes a little tougher. The spectators are enjoying the games. The audience sees both sides have lost two men. The Kayout's thought of the Atlanteans being undefeatable have changed.

The sparring goes on, until only four men remain. The men are Tito, Kryless, who is a high ranking general of the Kayout Empire, Acteon, and Ryelyne. Kryless fights Ryelyne next.

Ryelyne and Kryless look at each other and bow, and immediately the swords start to fly in the hands of the combatants. They spar for several minutes, and then Ryelyne finds a weakness and almost pins down his opponent. Both of the fighters are out of breath. The Kayout spectators become very silent. At this point, Ryelyne knows he is winning the respect of the soldiers and civilians in the Kayout Empire. Sparring at this altitude is making the fighters very exhausted. Ryelyne saves his energy and takes advantage of Kryless' fatigue. The Atlantean General finds another weakness and strikes his opponent on the ground. The new appointed Supreme Commander wins.

It comes time for Acteon to fight Tito. Acteon thinks back to all the sparring and fighting he has done in his lifetime. He is not afraid to fight Tito.

The fighting begins. The crowd goes wild for Tito. Right away, Tito knocks Acteon to the ground with a harsh blow. Acteon stands up and is not discouraged. He attacks with his own sword to only be countered by Tito. After about thirty seconds of blows and counterblows, Tito goes on the offensive. Fifteen seconds into the offensive, Acteon is worn down and does not have a clear mind and is defeated with one easy move by Tito.

After the fight, Acteon goes to Ryelyne and tells of his encounter with the best fighter of the Kayout Empire. Acteon has helped the Atlantean General in understanding the way Kayouts fight. Their offensive moves are much different, but he understands it now.

It all comes down to Tito and Ryelyne. The pride of the Atlantean Empire lies with their general. The alliance and respect of the Kayout Empire will rely on this sparring match. Ryelyne goes into this with a clear head. The Atlanteans are desperate for Ryelyne to win. The Atlantean General and Tito look eye to eye for almost a minute before sparring. Neither of them wants to throw the first blow.

Ryelyne decides to take the first charge. After a quick offensive move, he purposefully goes on the defensive. The appointed Supreme Commander wants Tito to wear himself out. The Kayout warrior has strength, but no comparison to Ryelyne. Tito's strength is his ability to block any move without giving way. Tito's sword blows are constant. The appointed Supreme Commander has no idea when Tito will become tired. Ryelyne's adversary shows no sign of breathing heavy whatsoever. Ryelyne is showing signs of fatigue, and Tito capitalizes on it. With blows going on both sides, Ryelyne thinks back to the time when Daygun fought the grandmaster and lost. He decides to use the same tactic the grandmaster used to defeat Daygun. Ryelyne turns Tito's face to the sun and continues to counter every blow. The trick starts to have an effect. Tito becomes confused about what to do next. Ryelyne takes full advantage and pins Tito down. The audience falls silent. Their best fighter has been defeated. A simple move won the sparring match for the Atlanteans.

After the fight, Ryelyne's pride soars. He has always wondered how the Kayouts would muster in battle. Even though it was a long match, Ryelyne's confidence is high because he just beat the best warrior in the Kayout Empire, but the Atlantean General also has a new respect for the Kayout military.

With the Kayouts' numbers and discipline, they could conquer the Atlantean Empire even with the Great East and West Wall. After the match, Melercertis walks to the sparring grounds. Ryelyne and Tito see Melercertis coming and they congratulate each other. The Atlantean General shakes Tito's hand and salutes him in the Kayout fashion. Ryelyne does this to show there is no barrier between the Atlantean Army and the Kayouts.

Ryelyne says, "You are the best I've ever fought. You would give our grandmasters a run. Your sword skills are unbelievable."

Tito looks at the Atlantean General with enthusiasm and says, "I have great respect for you. That was the best rush of my life, thank you."

Ryelyne laughs and replies, "It was a lot of luck."

Tito says, "My father fought in the Great War and I grew up hating the Atlanteans. I was a skeptic about this alliance. I have helped to make the Kayout Army great. You will make it better. I am at your command. My loyalty is to Melercertis and you. There is a gathering tonight with my generals. They will come from all over the Kayout Empire. I will introduce you as the Supreme Commander of our empire. We have ten months to prepare for this campaign together and fight as one. You will be in command on the battlefield against the Gambut Empire. Your army will arrive in three days. Our scouts say they are making good time. We have two divisions escorting them through our realm. They are the elite of our soldiers. With my colors escorting them through my empire, they will face no threat."

Ryelyne says gratefully, "Thank you. My men are important to me. I know our civilizations haven't seen eye to eye. It concerns me a Kayout faction can ambush my men. They can take care of themselves, but it can start a war between our two empires."

Tito replies, "We do have some factions, but they aren't strong enough to fight against your elite division. It wouldn't be in the best interest of any Kayout faction. Melercertis and I have complete control of our empire."

Ryelyne says, "I have confidence in our alliance."

Melercertis arrives and salutes Ryelyne in the Atlantean fashion. Ryelyne acknowledges with a Kayout salute. The audience screams with joy. Cheers are heard a mile away. The Atlantean General feels like a hero.

The rest of the day, Tito and Ryelyne are in conversations about the Kayout Army. They talk of the weaknesses and strength, and what resources they have. Tito tells Ryelyne that Palexus, Melercertis' daughter, will be there at the gathering. Like any man, Ryelyne wonders what she looks like. At the same time, he knows he has a mission to accomplish.

After nightfall, families gather and have dinner all over the Kayout Empire. This is a custom throughout the east of the Alber Mountains. It is family, then organizing and thoughts of the next day. The gatherings help make the Kayouts strive harder to make the empire stronger and to bond themselves to family and friends. Every once in a while in the gatherings an idea is discussed which changes the ideas of millions.

After dinner, the Atlanteans and Kayout military and advisors go into the Kayout Military Grand Hall. The building is more distinguished in scale than the Atlanteans and it is made of wood, and brick. The ceilings are twenty feet high and full of chandeliers which use candles for light. All of the Kayout advisors and generals are dressed in their best. Ryelyne feels like he is at home, except for the language barrier. In the Kayout Military Grand Hall, about half of the Kayout generals have a good grasp of the Atlantean language. Ryelyne is a little concerned about how his gestures will be received. Even though the Atlantean General has beaten Tito in sparring, he has not won the approval of the Kayout masses. The Atlantean General goes into the political realm blindly. All of a sudden in the middle of introducing Ryelyne, he is invited to give a speech to the Kayout elite. Tito introduces him as the Supreme Commander of the Kayout Empire. Everyone's eyes are on the Atlantean General.

Ryelyne says, "I have been sent here from the Atlantean Emperor. In the past, I have learned to hate your civilization. The Great War has made my empire humble. Every history book in the Atlantean Empire paints you in a negative light. The unknowing has become fear, and the fear has become hate. Those Atlanteans are not here to see what I see now. I have seen nothing but a good civilization. I see children playing just like the children in Atlantis. I see a culture full of future and dedication to family and values. I can see your people wanting your grandchildren to not have the same hardships as you do. Melercertis is a good leader and I see him as a friend. The emperor has helped me see you as people who are motivated to make mankind better. I don't see you now as I saw you in the Atlantean classrooms. It will be an honor to train your military."

Everyone claps for their new Supreme Commander. Ryelyne walks away from the spotlight. He returns to the table and starts to talk to the Kayout generals about the training process that needs to be completed in the next nine months. Ryelyne tells the Kayout generals his officers will have a large role in organization and supplies.

The Atlantean General wants to train the Kayout military in segments. With the expertise of Atlantean archers, cavalry, and heavy cavalry, training one to one is the most effective way. In the last months of training, Ryelyne will bring all segments of the Kayout Army together to make up divisions in the Atlantean fashion. This is where the Atlanteans are strongest. Each Atlantean military segment has a role on the battlefield, but Ryelyne does not yet know the strengths of the Kayouts. He only knows they have a very large cavalry at his disposal to attack the Gambuts.

When Ryelyne, Tito, Kryless, and top Kayout advisors sit down, a beautiful woman walks in. She is wearing a blue dress. Because all the servants are all wearing white, the Atlantean General knows she is not a servant. The beautiful woman in blue stands out in the room. The servants come to her first before anyone else.

Ryelyne leans toward Tito and asks, "Who is that beautiful woman? She was not here earlier."

Tito chooses his words carefully, "She is your assistant. The servants and generals won't reveal who she really is. I know Melercertis told you that she is his daughter. She can never be revealed to any Kayout outside these walls or to your people. Any person telling who she is will be put to death. Only a few know of her existence. She is known as an advisor and translator only. I hope you understand."

Ryelyne replies, "I gave Melercertis my word."

Tito says, "She will be around you every day until we start the Gambut Campaign."

Ryelyne replies, "I am honored for Melercertis to give me this kind of trust. I still don't understand why. I am a person who was hated only months ago."

Ryelyne thinks back into his past. He has never seen such a beautiful woman in Atlantis. Palexus' hair is charcoal black and she has long eyelashes. The Kayout Emperor's daughter has freckled cheeks, olive skin, slender and is five foot eleven. Ryelyne believes that God must have used the sun to kiss her cheeks a hundred times. He glances at Palexus, and she glances back several times during the gathering. The Atlantean General does not know how to approach the beautiful woman in blue, and he wishes his emotions would subside. He wants to meet her, but he stays his distance. Ryelyne tries to distract himself and begins conversations with the Kayout generals about the resources for the Gambut Campaign.

Acteon recognizes something different about his commander. He has never seen Ryelyne act this way. The Atlantean General is acting like a schoolboy with his first crush and Acteon fears it will be seen as a weakness. He quickly pulls Ryelyne to the side to acquire knowledge of his actions.

Acteon, like most men, says, "Sir, I can see the Kayout Empire has its attributes."

Ryelyne admires Palexus across the room and replies, "Yes, they do. I have never seen such beauty. I'm only distracted modestly, but I know my mission."

Acteon asks, "Who is she?"

Ryelyne responds, "She is going to be my Kayout interpreter. She is fluent in our language. She is one of Melercertis advisors from their Northern states."

With a concerned voice Acteon says, "I know there isn't a chance of anything happening, but remember the law of our land. We can only marry inside our realm. Even though we are here, we can't get too close to these people or their culture emotionally. We may have to fight them one day. Ryelyne, you are the leader of the Atlantean Army here and now the Supreme Commander of this joint effort. These people look to you for guidance. If they see you pursuing young Kayout ladies, their respect for you will be destroyed."

Ryelyne responds, "You know these feelings usually fade pretty quickly. She is a Kayout. Her beliefs are totally different than ours. I know it could never happen, even if I wanted it."

Acteon says jokingly, "If so, try not to stare at her like you are a thirteen year old boy. It makes you look weak."

They both laugh about their awkward conversation. Ryelyne knows Acteon is right. The Atlantean General goes back to the gathering. He dares not to look at Palexus again, but in the corner of his eye, he notices that Melercertis' daughter is still staring at him. Ryelyne makes sure there is no eye contact between the two.

In the middle of arbitration, Tito spreads a map over the table, and the generals fall into silence.

Tito says, "Melercertis will be joining us in a couple of minutes. He has had joint sessions with his council and our nobles."

Acteon is at the table with Ryelyne going over ideas and maps. Ryelyne is glad Acteon is there with him. The other advisors from both sides are going over preparations for war. The Atlantean advisors are discussing food, supplies, logistics, and weather in the region which would benefit the Kayouts in battle against the Gambuts. Each of the Atlantean advisors has a Kayout interpreter and they go back and forth deciphering what is said in the gathering.

A couple of minutes go by, and Melercertis walks to the table with Palexus by his side. Ryelyne does a double take and tries to focus on the matter at hand. He stands to his feet when the Kayout Emperor gets close. He stands at attention. Acteon does the same, and both men salute the Kayout Emperor in their military fashion.

Melercertis takes his daughter toward Ryelyne, and he starts to almost blush.

Melercertis says, "I would like to introduce you to your aide, Ryelyne. This is Palexus."

Ryelyne takes Palexus' hand in a gentlemanly manner and replies, "I have heard only good things about you. Melercertis is very proud of your accomplishments."

Ryelyne and Palexus stare at one another, and then quickly turn away.

Melercertis transitions his demeanor into a protective father's tone, and says, "I want the two of you to get to know one another tonight. There is much to do in the next couple of days. It is important you two to spend time together and act as a team. Acteon, I also want you to come to my chambers in an hour, and I will introduce you to your aide as well. She is very good in the arts of war, and she knows your language. It may be a long night for the both of you, but it's very important."

Acteon looks at Melercertis and asks, "May I ask her name?"

Melercertis says, "Her name is Carissa. I have found out that our women are quicker to learn the Atlantean language than men."

Acteon replies, "I will be there tonight after the gathering. Thank you, sir."

Melercertis stands on a table and yells into the crowded room, "Let us all retire for the night. I don't want this war to become an obsession. We have less than ten months to prepare. My troops will be here in Madera tomorrow, and the Atlantean division will be here the day after. I want to meet here tomorrow mid-day."

Everyone leaves the Kayout military council room. Acteon tells Ryelyne he would like to freshen up before he meets his new aide. Ryelyne gives him permission to do so. Palexus and Ryelyne cannot stop looking at one another. Right before Acteon leaves, he goes to his general.

Acteon says to Ryelyne, "Stay focused, sir."

Ryelyne replies, "You do the same."

Ryelyne escorts Palexus outside, and Acteon goes to his quarters. The Atlantean General is unsure of what to say to his new aide. Ryelyne and Palexus walk out of the military council room in silence and they walk side by side in a close manner going down the hall. Palexus suggests going towards the market place in the middle of the capital. Ryelyne has no objection. The two decide to walk rather than ride horses. It takes them forty-five minutes to walk to the market place.

Even though it is night, Madera's market place is still alive. The trade in the Kayout capital goes on twenty-four hours a day. The Kayout capital has numerous people along the streets, and laughter can be heard from open windows as Ryelyne and Palexus walk by. The population of Madera is young. All the luxuries of the Kayout capital are here. There are taverns and food establishments. In the middle of the walk, Palexus stops Ryelyne.

Palexus asks, "Are you hungry?"

Ryelyne replies, "A little. What is there to eat here?"

Palexus answers, "Nothing you are accustomed to eating, but the food is better. This isn't the ship or my father's palace. My father makes sure you eat as you do in Atlantis."

Palexus takes him into a restaurant. They sit down but they do not know what to say to one another. People inside the tavern know the two are different than the typical patrons of the restaurant. Ryelyne is wearing his Atlantean military attire, and no one really gives him a negative gesture. They sit where they can talk in private.

Ryelyne decides to speak first and says, "I know I haven't said much. I don't want to be rude. I don't know where to start."

Palexus starts to giggle and says, "I don't either. I always wondered what it would be like to talk to a grandmaster. I have been taught in the arts of war. Based on what I have learned, grandmasters are legends in your society and my empire. We have heard many stories about them from our borders between Kayout and Atlantis."

Ryelyne says shamefully, "My family is royalty, but I am just a man. I am no different than anyone here. I have a question for you. How can you walk down the streets without anyone knowing who you are?"

Palexus responds, "For several reasons: First, I am wearing a blue dress, which is typically only worn by middle class women. Also, I have been at our Northern states taking care of my father's affairs. I haven't been in Madera since I was a young teenager. While I was away, I had time to learn war, languages and politics. When I returned for the first time in twelve years, very few people knew of my identity. This is for my protection. I can speak to the senators in masses at the palace, but they can't talk to me anywhere else. My father asks my advice about politics because I haven't been corrupted by our Senate. He wants me to be emperor, but in our society it will not be possible. It was me who started the summit between our two empires. My father would have never thought to go to Atlantis for help. For the last twenty years, women have been seen as second-class citizens. My father is trying to change the old traditions. But many Kayouts are still use to the old ways. We have reached a turning point in our civilization, but with any major change, there is resistance."

Ryelyne says, "I can see similarities in your people and mine. People are the same all over the world."

After eating, they go on talking and asking questions about each other's culture. They spend hours together. The conversation seems like they have known each other since childhood. Ryelyne asks if he can see her again other than in the Kayout Military Grand Hall, and she says yes.

The next morning, horns blow throughout the Kayout capital. Palexus informs Ryelyne that his division has come early. The Atlantean warriors did not stop to camp the night before. Ryelyne's army marched for thirty-six straight hours to be reunited with their general.

The Atlantean General missed his men. Ryelyne and Palexus rush to the palace. He goes to Melercertis and asks to be able to see his army. The Kayout Emperor tells him they are marching to the military outpost where they will be stationed there until the Gambut Campaign. Melercertis tells Ryelyne that he will meet him there after they get situated. The Atlantean General and Palexus mount their horses, and rush to the military outpost west of Madera. Ryelyne speaks little to Palexus on the way to his men.

The Atlantean General has been around the Kayouts too long. The Kayout people have been very good to their new Supreme Commander, but he has almost forgotten about his homeland. Ryelyne just wants to have a conversation with someone who speaks his own language. The Kayout accent is difficult to understand when they speak his language. Now, Ryelyne can have a good conversation without elucidation.

Palexus and Ryelyne finally reach the grounds. The Atlantean

General knows war and he knows his men. He has a mission, and he wants it to be over with. He thinks of the food and the entertainment of his homeland. He realizes how much he misses the comforts of Atlantis.

In a short amount of time, Melercertis has built a compound for the Atlanteans. When Ryelyne enters the gate of the military grounds, he salutes his men, and they salute back. The Atlantean General's division has sorely missed their commander. Ryelyne is respected by his division and his warriors are willing to die for him.

Ryelyne and Palexus dismount their horses, and the Atlantean General goes towards Miro, Ryelyne's captain. He is the one who brought the division into Kayout. The Atlantean captain stands at attention until Ryelyne gives him the sign to stand down. The whole Atlantean division cheers for their general. The pride of Atlantis has come to Kayout. Acteon also comes to the military barracks and is saluted by his men. The Atlantean division looks up to their leaders as heroes. Ryelyne and Acteon say some choice words to encourage their army. They cannot hide their smiles at the familiar faces of their warriors. This is a happy day for the two generals. Palexus, knowing of military protocol, stands back and waits until Ryelyne returns to his horse. The Atlantean General sees Palexus and asks her to come and meet his captains, and he properly introduces her as his interpreter and advisor. Ryelyne is keeping his word to Melercertis and will not break it.

CHAPTER XI
THE WAR BETWEEN THE GODS

A couple of hours go by and Ryelyne is helping his men get situated with their accommodations. A messenger informs him Melercertis is coming towards the military compound. He prepares his men for an inspection. Aten gave specific orders to treat Melercertis as they would their Atlantean Emperor. It may not be in the Kayout military protocol, but Ryelyne does it anyway.

Melercertis rides inside the newly constructed Atlantean complex standing tall with an escort. He jumps off his horse and goes to Ryelyne. The Atlantean General introduces Miro, his highest-ranking captain, to the Kayout Emperor. Miro salutes Melercertis in the Atlantean fashion. All of the Atlanteans stand at attention in columns in front of the Kayout Emperor.

As Melercertis looks at Miro, he jokingly says to Ryelyne, "He is a very devoted Atlantean isn't he? I can say one thing about him. He has discipline."

Ryelyne replies, "Miro is my best captain. He saved my life. He risked his own life to save mine. On the other continent, my battalion was in serious trouble. He fought against all odds and stabilized the battlefield. I owe him everything."

Melercertis says, "Well, your captains are here. I will be at the gathering tonight. I would like to meet some of Atlantis' best officers. I want to know how to integrate the Kayouts and Atlanteans to fight with one another as a team. I have some suggestions. I know my men."

That night, Melercertis is at the Military Grand Hall to help converge the two armies together. Beforehand, the Kayout Emperor has let his generals and advisors share their opinions. Many ideas are being shared. The whole room brainstorms in ways to defeat the Gambut Empire. Dozens of interpreters are there to help with the language barrier. Palexus is very helpful to Ryelyne. She is good at filtering out what is and is not important. Melercertis finally stands on top of a side table and speaks.

Melercertis says, "I have heard all the different ideas. I am leaning towards the ideas presented by Ryelyne and Acteon. We have eighty military divisions for the Gambut Campaign. Some of these divisions are at the borders of my empire. Sixty divisions are within three hundred miles of Madera. I have to use other cities to feed my warriors. It will be too taxing to hold two million men inside the capital. I suggest the Atlantean division should split up eighty ways. This will give three hundred of the finest Atlantean warriors to train each and every division. I also suggest that some Atlantean officers and high-ranking warriors stay here and train my generals. We have less than nine months to prepare our alliance. We will attack Gambut on the longest day of the year."

The next day, most of the high-ranking Atlanteans stay in Madera for a couple of days. Acteon, second in command of the Atlanteans, makes the preparations with the Kayout generals and sends Atlantean warriors on their way to train. Some of them go to the far reaches of the Kayout Empire. It will take weeks to reach their destination. All of the Atlanteans yearn for their homes and wish they were not in Kayout. However, most dream of the day when they will be able to tell their grandchildren stories of how they went to Kayout and made a difference in the world.

Two months go by; the Atlantean warriors are treated well. Most of the military reports are showing good progress in training. The Atlanteans are treated like heroes. Some Kayout factions still view the Atlanteans as their enemy.

In the city, the Kayout women giggle like teenagers when the Atlanteans cross their paths. The Atlanteans are taller and in better physical shape due to their rigorous training. Their attire makes them stand out amongst the crowds of the Kayout masses. The Atlantean silver plated breastplates and red cloaks are not what the Kayout people are accustomed to seeing. Because the Atlanteans cannot speak the Kayout language very well, they are clouded with mystery. Ryelyne's division can see their surroundings, but the language barrier is keeping them from seeing the whole picture of the world they are in.

In the middle of the third month in Madera, Ryelyne is sparring with some of the Kayout warriors with Palexus. On this day, the Atlantean General decides to push the envelope, and he puts himself in the middle of a circle of Kayout warriors. Ryelyne is trying to show off his skills. The Kayout warriors come at him with their swords. Even though it is sparring, the swords fly pretty quickly. The Atlantean General blocks every sword on the first wave of attacks. On the second attack, Ryelyne blocks a sword and counters towards one of his opponents. In doing so, he thrusts forward and another Kayout sword catches him under his armpit where there is no protection from his armor. The Kayout warrior pulls back as fast as he can. But the sword slices Ryelyne, and he is bleeding pretty badly. The Atlantean General stands tall and walks towards his horse. Palexus runs to Ryelyne and helps him. Before Palexus can put him in the saddle, she puts her hand where the wound is bleeding. Her hand is covered in blood. She goes into panic and throws Ryelyne on his saddle. Palexus then mounts her own horse and guides him to the Kayout treatment center.

On the way, Ryelyne tries to stand tall, but he goes into shock. He becomes very dehydrated, and he is barley able to stay awake. The Atlantean General just wants to rest. Palexus tells him to stop. She dismounts her horse and climbs into the saddle with Ryelyne to hasten their journey to the treatment center. After they arrive, she has difficulty in removing the wounded general off the horse. The Atlantean General almost falls to the ground, and he cannot stand on his own. Because the wound is so fresh, Ryelyne is not yet in extreme pain. He tries to walk tall into the treatment center, but he stumbles a couple of times trying to walk through the door. Palexus gets a physician, and the doctors put him on the first available table. He lies there uncomfortably, and the pain is starting to hit. Palexus asks a servant to alert Melercertis. Ryelyne looks at Palexus and shakes his head no.

Ryelyne says, "Don't bother the emperor because of this. I'll be fine in a couple of days."

Palexus replies, "Melercertis has a lot of respect for your work and you are the most important man in our kingdom right now. My father needs to know. He can abate the accident to our people."

The servant runs to the palace. In less than an hour, the doctor is sewing up the last stitch in the wound. The Kayout Emperor goes to Ryelyne to see what he can do. Melercertis stands there quietly.

Melercertis says, "Are you going to be okay? How bad is it?"

Ryelyne replies, "The sword blow cut some bone and a couple of veins. I am going to be okay. I'm going to be sore for a week. I will be at the gathering tonight. I will be able to hide my injury from advisors from both sides."

Melercertis says, "I do not think it is a good idea for you to come tonight. My generals see you as unbeatable. You have beaten the best warrior in my empire. If they hear of you being hurt, the invincibility is gone. Your sparring partners have been told not to say anything about the accident, and they have been sent on missions where they can't say anything to jeopardize our campaign here. I want you to rest for a couple of days. I will cover for you at the gatherings."

Ryelyne notices that Melercertis is genuinely concerned about his health. Ryelyne wonders if his own father would be so concerned. The Atlantean General feels more love from Melercertis than his own father.

The next couple of days inside the treatment center, Palexus and Ryelyne discuss life and personal matters. They have no choice. The Atlantean General cannot be seen in public. Palexus will not leave Ryelyne's side. He really feels good about Palexus. In the back of his mind, he wishes she were pure Atlantean. He knows he cannot marry her without betraying his own empire, but he feels like she would make a good wife. Ryelyne will not betray his beliefs. He becomes stubborn about the idea of courting Palexus, but he has strong feeling for her. It is very apparent Palexus has strong feeling for Ryelyne as well.

In the weeks to come, it becomes obvious to Melercertis that Palexus is falling in love with Ryelyne. Like any father, this is a huge concern for him. Every father is protective of his daughter in some form or fashion. The Kayout Emperor knows Ryelyne is an honorable man. Melercertis is concerned Palexus will get hurt, but he puts his emotions to the side because of the Gambut Campaign.

Six months in training in Madera. Ryelyne is starting to speak the Kayout language a little better everyday, and he starts to understand the environment and the Kayout culture. The Atlantean General can understand what is said at the gatherings. Palexus is a good teacher to the Atlantean General. Ryelyne starts to teach Palexus the written language of the Atlanteans. They spend every day together. Even though they do not have to, they make excuses to see each other.

The military gatherings are becoming successful in strengthening Melercertis' army. The Eastern Army is learning tactics they did not know before. The Kayouts have built an overwhelming force. With heavy cavalry as their greatest strength, Ryelyne can capitalize on their attributes. The Kayout military has more elephants and mammoths than the Atlanteans. The Gambuts will not be able to stop Atlantis and Kayout on two fronts.

Melercertis' generals consider Ryelyne as one of them. The Atlantean General has mastered diplomacy in the Kayout Empire. In the middle of the sixth month, Ryelyne and Acteon go to the marketplace for a change of scenery. They walk and talk, and Acteon stops Ryelyne in the middle of a street.

Acteon says, "I am feeling funny about my interpreter. I am starting to have strong feelings for Carissa. She's a beautiful Kayout woman, but she's not Atlantean. I start to see these people as our equals. Before I came here, I was very prejudiced of the East. They are not like what we learned in school. Their technology is not like ours, but their lives are similar. I will miss this place soon after we return to our fatherland."

Ryelyne replies, "As you already know, I am feeling the same way about Palexus. I don't know what to do. I have never had strong feelings like this towards anyone. Melercertis acts like a father to me. I think totally different than when I first came to Madera. When I first stepped off the Kayout ship, I wanted to go back to Atlantis. But now, I am very content here. Their ways with nature and how they see things have opened my eyes to a whole different world. It's not just Atlantis or Kayout, but humanity in general. I see the world in a bigger picture. It is not empire to empire or culture to culture. It is man to man."

At the gatherings, the Kayout generals speak to Ryelyne as their leader. The Atlantean General is starting to take pride in what he is creating out of the Kayout military, and he cannot wait to fight alongside Melercertis' warriors against the Gambut Empire.

During the ninth month inside the Kayout Empire, and less than two months from invading Gambut, Melercertis goes to Ryelyne's chambers. The Kayout Emperor wants to talk to the Atlantean General. It is two hours before mid-night and Ryelyne just got out of his bath. He is clothed and in his bed attire. Melercertis enters the door and catches the Atlantean General off guard. Ryelyne does not flinch as he stares at Melercertis. The Atlantean General can tell this is not going to be a good conversation.

Ryelyne asks, "What can I do for you, My Lord?"

Melercertis breaks down and says, "I have to ask you about a few things. I have seen you become a great leader to my people. In our culture, the Eastern world cannot see a woman being strong enough to rule an empire. Palexus is strong enough to be the first, but it will take another half century before our culture can accept it. I am getting old. My health is failing me. I don't feel bad, but my physicians say I may only live for another five years at the most. No one knows of this except you and my doctors. My hands shake without any assistance. I have little control of my body. I have to hold something to keep my hands from shaking in public. The ailment will only progress in the future. I need someone strong to take my place. Most of my generals are strong enough, but they don't know how to play politics correctly to hold an empire together. You have a good military mind, and you're strong enough to challenge my Senate. You have what it takes to replace me when I die. I don't expect you to take care of my daughter, but if you do love her, take her hand."

Ryelyne cannot believe the offer. He takes a moment, and responds, "I feel very important here in your empire. I feel like I am making a difference for mankind. Everything I have learned in my life brought me to this point. I am in love with your daughter, and I feel like you're a father to me, but my religion is different than the Kayout culture. If I take your place, everyone will say my politics are done in the name of my God, and not for your gods. I will not surrender to any other theology."

Melercertis says, "I understand what you're saying. If you marry my daughter, we can stage that you had to convert to our religion to become a Kayout."

Ryelyne responds, "You see me as an honorable man. A mendacious act of religion is iniquitous. How could you ask me to lie?"

Melercertis says, "We have another problem. You know the Atlanteans are about to start a war with Mareth a month before our Gambut Campaign. Borealeous, the Kanis Emperor, has found out from his spies about Atlantis' conquest. Nextear and Borealeous are forming an agreement to take out Atlantis."

Ryelyne says, "From our intelligence, the Mearth armies are scattered. Aten is not expecting to fight the whole empire. Dareous and Aten's son are getting ready to attack Nextear's forces of seven hundred and fifty thousand. They are only expecting to fight one army at a time. Our military stationed in Valtear does not have the manpower to take on Mearth's full military strengths at once."

Melercertis responds, "On the continent twenty-seven years ago, the Great War saw the Atlanteans as a world threat. The Kanis Empire is thinking of helping the Mareth Empire, and they will declare war on Atlantis. We are allies with Kanis. I will have no choice but to back them. Our two empires are very close in culture. Kanis is also speaking with Gambut to form an agreement to completely destroy your empire. What I warned you about on the ship is beginning. Your empire has made too many enemies. Atlantis is a very imperialistic. Mearth is trying to turn this into a Holy War, and they're succeeding. Your men are not safe here anymore, and they have to return to Atlantis. If I can't resolve this with Kanis, I will have to do the unthinkable. Because we believe in the same religion as Kanis and Mareth, our people will want to follow the rest of the world. I can't go against our gods, even if it doesn't have anything to do with religion. Your division is honorable and should be able to fight for your land. I want them to die a soldier's death. I will honor them like they have honored me. The war is becoming a war between the gods. Atlantis can't win. I am trapped. If I fight with your empire and we lose, my empire will be destroyed as well. If Kanis, Gambut, and Mareth come together after beating your civilization, the empires will be in position to finish my empire effortlessly. If I decide to stay neutral and not fight, it will make us look weak, and they will try to take my land. My Northern states are still fragile. I can't win against all three empires even with Atlantis."

Ryelyne responds, "You asked me those questions about Palexus to see where I stand. We are allies now. Our two empires know how to fight with one another. Our two empires can take on the world."

Melercertis says, "Even if Atlantis and the Kayout Empire come together, we cannot win against the world. With all three empires combined, there are close to eight million warriors against one million fighting men of your empire and four million with mine. Our land is too vast and we border all three empires. They will destroy my armies one by one. If my empire has to fight with the three, there will be twelve million warriors against Atlantis. If Kayout doesn't come together with the three other empires, we will be known as a traitor to our own gods. I will convince Borealeous to delay the inevitable. I want your men to leave before anything occurs. The world is about to change, but not like Aten and I wanted. I wanted to make peace with Atlantis. I think both civilizations could have benefited if we came together. Man is not ready for Atlantis. I'm coming to you in honor. I am expecting you to do the same. I need you here to help me to take care of my empire, but there is a thought our alliance may not happen. I am telling you this because I respect you."

Ryelyne replies, "I don't understand. Do you want me to fight against my own people? It doesn't make sense. I can't."

Melercertis replies, "It is over for Atlantis, Ryelyne. Atlantis will be destroyed. I have my own gods to answer to. I can't go against my religion. Even though I don't think this is a Holy War, it will be fought as such. I am giving you a choice, Ryelyne. I will leave it up to you. You can leave with your men to die in honor. The Kanis diplomats will meet me in two days about their alliance. I will delay it so your division will be able to leave in honor. The Kanis Empire will not strike until I talk to them. They haven't declared war on Atlantis yet. Only a handful of people in the world even know about this idea. I want you to tell Aten I do respect him, but I may not have a choice. I will have six divisions to escort your men to Atlantis. They will be safe. You have my word no harm will come to your men."

Ryelyne says, "If I stay?"

Melercertis replies, "You will be known as the prince and an heir to my thrown. If we do have to go against Atlantis, you will have to lead my men to battle. You will have to marry my daughter. My men will not believe in you if you don't. To my generals, you are either an Atlantean or a Kayout. If you marry my daughter, it would help my generals believe in you which they already do. They will die for you and stand behind you. The majority of Kayouts believe in love. It is what makes us strong. Marrying Palexus will prove your love to her and my people. I need your decision after the talks with Kanis. My generals and advisors know nothing of this matter. A messenger from Kanis came to me in secret an hour ago. I haven't even told Palexus. I will have no choice but to tell my generals tomorrow afternoon. My spies will be here early morning or mid-day tomorrow to tell me what is going on in Kanis."

After Melercertis leaves, Ryelyne is shocked. He sits at the edge of his bed wondering what just happened. He can't believe the offer he has been presented with. In his mind, everything the Atlantean General has done to this point has gone to waste, and his teachings of military tactics can kill his own people.

Ryelyne goes to Palexus' chambers. Melercertis has not said anything yet to her, and she is ignorant to what is about to happen. He knocks on her door and a servant answers. Palexus goes to the door after hearing Ryelyne's voice.

Ryelyne says, "I may have to leave here in a couple of days and go back to my empire. Your father came to me with grave news. The Atlanteans are about to take Mareth, but Kanis and Gambut may ally with Mareth to fight against my homeland. I don't know what to do. I respect this empire, and I'm in love with you."

Palexus' heart jumps like a rock skipping across a pond. Tears fill her eyes. She stands there in silence and says nothing to the man she loves with all of her heart. Palexus tries to say something, but she keeps her head down. She cannot look at the Atlantean General. This is the first time Ryelyne sees Palexus being fragile. He is surprised. The Atlantean General cannot hold back his feelings any longer. He takes her in his arms and holds her as if he is never going to see her again. In the back of his mind, he feels like a traitor to his own people.

Ryelyne looks at Palexus, and he asks, "What if you marry me and come to Atlantis?"

Palexus responds, "It can't happen. I belong here with my people, and you belong to yours. The only way Atlantis can defend herself is if you are there to do so. Your laws say you can't marry outside the Atlantean borders. I wouldn't even be a citizen in accordance to your laws."

Ryelyne says, "I have enough pull to make it happen. You will be the first."

Palexus responds, "My father will not let me go. Atlantis is doomed. If Kayout enters the war, I will die, and so will you if we go back to Atlantis. I will not live in Atlantis as a potential enemy to your empire."

Ryelyne says in desperation, "I will go to your father and ask him to reconsider an alliance with Atlantis. Together, our militaries can take on the three empires."

Palexus says, "It will not happen. Kayout is on the verge of collapse. Even though we have a strong military, our politics is corrupted. If we don't fight, the other empires will try to take us next. Our empire is still in its infancy stage. Our religion will destroy us if we fight the rest of the world with the Atlanteans. The Kayout Empire has no choice but to take out Atlantis with the rest of the world. There has already been a loose alliance between the Kanis and the Mareth Empires. Gambut has always stood on its own. If the Gambuts are considering alliances with Kanis and Mareth, our two empires could not stop them."

Ryelyne says, "What if I stay here?"

Palexus angrily responds, "I can't live the rest of my life thinking you didn't protect your fatherland just to stay here with me."

Ryelyne says, "I will stay and ask Melercertis if I can be the one to take Atlantis. Then, I will become its governor after it's been taken."

Palexus replies, "How does my father know your true intentions?"

Ryelyne says, "Love is truth, and I love you. It doesn't matter what is going on in the rest of the world. I believe in you."

It is one hour after mid-night; Ryelyne leaves Palexus' chambers and shuts the door behind him, and he mounts his horse. Ryelyne goes to Melercertis.

Ryelyne is escorted to his main chamber, and he asks, "Can I speak, sir?"

Melercertis replies, "After I spoke with you at your chambers, three of my spies reported from the three empires telling me the same thing. There will be war against Atlantis. I will have no choice but to join them. You and your men are set free. Your division is going to take a different route to reach the Atlantean border faster. I will not kill them. Your warriors will die like they should in battle to protect Atlantis. I may have to fight them later. Your generals are here. I am sending them home on my ships. I have told them the plans have changed and your division is to fight with Aten."

Ryelyne replies, "I want to accept your offer, but only on one condition. After the war, I want to govern my people after the take over."

Melercertis says with sadness, "You will be killing your own people to accomplish your goal."

Ryelyne says with great emotion, "If you want to be a great leader, you have to see the whole picture. If I go in and take my empire, I will let the women and children live. They may become slaves, but they will still be alive. If the other three empires are the main aggressors, they will kill everyone inside my empire. I have a small chance to save the lives of my people. I can go back to my fatherland and fight against the world, but why? It is a lost cause. The whole world is against what happened twenty-seven years ago, and I can't do anything about it. I can go and warn my empire, but that isn't enough to hold off all four empires. I understand your politics. If I fight for you, I will know the strengths and weaknesses of my land. I will be saving millions of lives. If you help me Melercertis, I will take your place when you die."

Melercertis replies, "I have one question for you. Do you really love my daughter?"

Ryelyne says, "I love her more than my homeland. This is the reason I'm here."

Melercertis replies, "To make my empire strong, I need you to become a prince and marry my daughter. Within a week, everyone will know what side you're on. The war against Atlantis will happen a month prior to the longest day of the year. All of the empires on the continent are coming together. Every warrior in the world will be at the gates of Atlantis."

Ryelyne desperately says, "I will protect this empire and your daughter."

Melercertis asks, "What about Acteon? Is he leaving or staying? I know he is very loyal to you."

Ryelyne replies, "I will find out, My Lord."

Melercertis says, "Come to me when you know. Get your generals out of here before this gets out of hand."

Two hours after mid-night Ryelyne goes to Acteon's chambers, and knocks on the door. Acteon is loyal in his discipline and he wakes and stands up almost at attention. Ryelyne asks Acteon to sit down. Acteon is wondering why the Atlantean General is coming to his chambers so late.

Ryelyne sits down beside Acteon and says, "Listen to me very carefully, old friend. There is going to be a full-scale attack on our fatherland. Close to twelve million men will attack our empire. Even with our reserves, it is almost a twelve to one ratio. We cannot defend ourselves with that enormity. Our empire is well defended by our natural borders, but we cannot withstand what is about to happen. The walls of Atlantis give our people a huge advantage, but we don't have enough warriors to repel such magnitude of combatants. The world will destroy Atlantis. I have spoken with Melercertis. The only way you and I can save our homeland is to take the side of the Kayouts. If Gambut or Kanis take our homeland first, they will exterminate the Atlantean race. If we fight for the Kayouts, we will occupy our country, and our race will survive. We can lead the attack and conquer Atlantis. If we don't take our lands in this attack, everyone in Atlantis will die. I have decided to stay in Kayout, but our officers will leave for Atlantis tomorrow."

Acteon is shocked and replies, "I can't do it. I can't go against my own civilization. I would rather die. I will go back with the generals tomorrow."

Ryelyne starts to go out the door and says, "I understand. I hope I don't have to fight you. The Kayout ships will be sunk on the spot if our navy catches wind of this. It will take you two weeks to return to Atlantis. I have to inform Melercertis of your decision. Respect my decision, and I will respect yours."

Just before Ryelyne exits, Acteon yells, "Wait! I can't leave you, sir. I believe in you. I will stay. I think God sent us here to save what is left of our empire."

Ryelyne replies, "Then I will see you in the morning. I will tell Melercertis that you are here as a Kayout. The Kayout generals have great respect for us. You will be second in command of the Kayout Empire, under me. Plus I need a best man. I am marrying Palexus in three days."

Acteon asks, "Why in three days?"

Ryelyne responds, "I don't know. Palexus doesn't even know yet. I just decided."

The next couple of days are very chaotic. Ryelyne and Acteon get prepared for war. The other Atlantean generals are on their way back to Atlantis. Ryelyne's division was told their generals were being sent to Valtear in preparations to fight the Mareth. No Atlantean warrior knows of the plan being formed against their homeland. Ryelyne works with the Kayout generals to reveal the weaknesses and strengths of the Atlantean Great East Wall defenses. Acteon and Ryelyne stay in the palace to keep Atlantean planters in the dark of what is about to take place.

In the meantime, Ryelyne asks Palexus to marry him, and she says yes. Acteon asks Carissa to marry him as well. It is good politics. If the two Atlantean generals are to be trusted, they have to have a reason to stay. They are marrying for love and to be trusted by the Kayout Empire. If the Kayouts win, they will become heroes. On the other hand, if the Kayouts lose, the two Atlanteans will be known as traitors to their fatherland. Either which way, they both will make history.

On the third day, Ryelyne is at the palace to be married. The citizens of Kayout have been told Palexus is Melercertis' daughter. The Kayout citizens accept the idea of an Atlantean marrying a Kayout woman. Tens of thousands of people come to see the wedding.

At the ceremony, Melercertis escorts Palexus down the path to Ryelyne to give her away. One hundred Kayout officers and generals line the path of their emperor and his daughter towards the groom. Ryelyne is waiting on his future wife as she walks with Melercertis towards him. The military officials salute their emperor in a ceremonial process as they walk past. The saluting is to honor the marriage and their emperor. Palexus' bridesmaids are right behind, and they hug every Kayout general one by one to show compassion to the ones who protect their empire. The emperor, Action and Ryelyne line up in tradition towards the priest. Ryelyne and Palexus hold hands in front of the cleric. After the walk of life, as the Kayouts call it, the priest starts to conduct the marriage.

The priest says in a loud voice to the crowd, "This is a good day for the Kayout Empire. The best general in the world is here to marry the Princess of the Kayout Empire. Ryelyne sees the beauty of our land and culture, and he believes in the gods and has taken them into his soul. The gods said a leader from a far away land will one day rule Kayout. The gods sent Ryelyne to us as a blessing. Thank the gods!"

The whole crowd cheers. The entire speech was staged on Ryelyne's behalf. Melercertis knows how to conduct political stages.

Even though Ryelyne is disappointed in himself for betraying Atlantis and God, he feels that he is doing the right thing. Palexus and Ryelyne say their vows and walk down the path of the generals. The emperor stays with the priest, and every Kayout general salutes the new married couple as they walk past.

The next day, Acteon marries Carissa. The thought of the two Atlantean generals possibly having to kill their own soldiers to save lives makes them sick. They wonder if they will have to destroy their own division.

A couple of days after the weddings, Acteon and Ryelyne go on horseback after they sparred. This is the only way they can talk without being heard by the Kayout people. The question always comes up in their conversation. Are Ryelyne and Acteon going to be heroes or traitors in the centuries to come?

Acteon and Ryelyne both seek the Kayout Military Council to make preparations to attack their own homeland. A large force of Kayout warriors are camped at the gates of the Kayout capital. At this point, the Kayout Empire does not trust Mareth, Kanis, or Gambut. The Kayout borders to the Kanis, Mareth and Gambut are saturated with Melercertis' military. The whole world is full of mistrust.

Three days after the wedding ceremony, a messenger comes from the Gambut Empire. The message is rushed to Melercertis. After the Kayout Emperor reads the message, the horns blow for the Kayout Military Council to come together.

Once everyone is gathered, Melercertis stands from his chair and says to Ryelyne and Acteon, "Kanis, Mareth and Gambut are combining forces. It is official. I can't postpone this any longer. It is becoming a Holy War against Atlantis. We can't stay neutral. Most of the Kayout people want your God destroyed because it interferes with the rest of the world's beliefs. The world sees technology as the backbone of your god, and they are scared of it. If it were ten years later, the circumstances could have been different. My empire would have been strong enough to take on the world with Atlantis. But I can't control the world's fears. Atlantis will be conquered."

Ryelyne asks, "Is their anything else we can do?"

Melercertis replies, "It is a done deal. I can't go against my religion. It will destroy me politically. Religion is the core of any civilization. In negotiating my empire to enter the war, Atlantis will be under my rule. The other three empires want Atlantis' military completely destroyed and not a threat anymore. Because the three empires think the peninsula is evil, they don't want territorial rights to your lands."

Ryelyne says, "I never knew the world hated Atlantis this badly. If I take my empire, I will put it under my rule and save my culture. Atlantis will be reformed to the rest of the world, but I know that is the only way to save my culture from complete destruction. Thank you, Melercertis."

Ryelyne starts to think of every scenario that can save his fatherland from total destruction. He can't return to Atlantis and fight for her. The Atlantean General has made a commitment to Palexus and the Kayout Empire. Ryelyne and Acteon have married outside the boundaries of their homeland. They are no longer citizens in accordance to Atlantean laws. Even though they are trying to do the right thing for humanity, they are helpless and sickened with the known world hating the Atlanteans' civilization this intensely.

Ryelyne and Acteon try to look strong, but know they are falling apart inside. They believed there was a great future for Atlantis, but now every empire wants to destroy their homeland. Either general could have been an asset for Atlantis in the upcoming war, but they have reached the point of no return.

For Ryelyne and Acteon there is no turning back. It is very difficult for them to overcome, but they have no choice. They will lead the attack against their own empire hoping to save what culture is left after the war. It is a simple answer to a hard situation.

Chapter XII
The Beginning of
a New World

Five weeks before the longest day of the year in Valtear, the Atlantean divisions are ready to take on Nextear of Mearth. Laptos' army is close to the Valtearean border. Dareous is very confident in the military campaign. Almost a hundred and twenty-five thousand Atlantean soldiers are ready to take the Mearth armies one by one.

In Sidra, the Valtearean capital, Quentoris has done well in swaying the Valteareans to become a state of Atlantis. The Valtearean Senate will vote on the issue of annexation next year. Even though it has only been less than a year of occupation, the Valteareans can see progress and are preparing for the transition to statehood. No one has gone hungry or died of an epidemic in Valtear since the Atlantean occupation. The Atlanteans have irrigated farmland, and Tulless' empire now has a surplus of food. Quentoris respects the Valtearean nobles and has become good friends with many of them. He has also helped build a military force out of the Valtearean Army, and he has trained over five hundred thousand warriors ready for battle. The Valtearean Army is still using crude weapons, but they are trained in the Atlantean fashion. Tulless' empire is growing stronger. The nobles of Valtear are becoming heroes and leaders to their people.

Some Valteareans, however, still do not want to convert, and they want their empire to return to its state prior to Atlantean occupation. The Valteareans who had good trade the old way have now been cut out of the loop. The leadership of the Atlanteans is making Valtear more economically and socially stable. Even though there are drastic changes in Valtear, the masses want statehood with Atlantis.

In the last two months, Nextear has proclaimed himself Emperor of the Mareth people. The new Mearth Emperor has brought together communities all across his lands. In doing so, he has gathered two million able bodied men. His army is not trained as well as the Atlanteans, but his army has grown stronger every day. Mearth's military technology is primitive compared to the Atlanteans.

Atlantis has to conquer Mareth to claim the resources to develop a sufficient amount of steel. The Valteareans have been trading iron ore to Mareth in exchange for other natural resources. The Atlanteans did not know the iron ore of Valtear was really coming from Mareth. Aten's empire took Valtear thinking the iron ore was coming from them.

To the Atlantean intelligence, Nextear's main military force is only thirty miles from the Valtearean border. If Laptos provokes a fight with the proclaimed emperor first, they can destroy his army and take out the rest of the Mearth's leaders one by one. Even though the Atlanteans are outnumbered, they are confident of a victory. When the Atlanteans enter the Mareth Empire, they will pick the battlefield so it can be on their own terms.

According to the Atlantean spies, Nextear has enemies in his own country and many of the tribes will not join the fight against Atlantis. The tribes are wrapped up in their own small affairs to worry. Some of the Mareth tribes want the Atlanteans to come in and dethrone Nextear. The Mareth Emperor is using propaganda to make the Atlanteans think it is going to be easy. To the Atlantean generals, other than Nextear's military, Mearth armies are spread out to control areas of their empire. Atlantean spies have said only Nextear's seven hundred and fifty thousand men will put up a strong resistance to Laptos' invasion. On the other hand, Mearth is making sure the Atlanteans do not know their full strengths and alliances.

In Valtear, Dareous is second in command of the Mareth Campaign. Laptos, son of the Atlantean Emperor and brother to Daygun, has been appointed Supreme Commander of the Valtearean territory. Laptos has decided to leave twenty thousand Atlantean infantry out of the battle to protect the assets of Valtear just in case of an attack from the Gambut or Kanis Empires. There have been some hostilities on Valtear's borders, but only small skirmishes.

The twenty thousand Atlanteans left behind to take positions at the Kanis borders is led by Captain Presus. They are stationed there to protect the Valteareans from an invasion from the Northeast. Quentoris' small infantry legion is close to the Valtearean capital. If anything happens to Dareous and Laptos, he will take command of the Valtearean Army. The Alber Mountains are a good natural border between the Gambuts and Valtear, and there is little the Atlanteans have to protect. There are small specks of land which connect Gambut to Valtear, but the Valtearean military reserves are stationed there in case of an invasion.

The border between the Kanis Empire and Valtear is broad. There is a thin line of Atlantean men to protect it. Presus' twenty thousand men, in five different points, are on the Kanis and Valtearean border. Atlantean scouts go back and forth along the border of Kanis in intervals. If something happens, the Atlanteans will know about it quickly, but all of the main Atlantean artillery and heavy cavalry are getting ready to march inside where the Atlanteans want to fight Nextear.

For days, the Kanis borders do not look as if they are preparing for an invasion. The atmosphere on the border is relaxed. The Atlantean warriors play in the fields and think nothing of the day. Presus is prepared for battle, but there is no one to fight. Most of the Atlantean warriors wish they were in Mareth fighting with their comrades. Presus' scouts ride back and forth, but see nothing out of the ordinary. The Atlantean infantry predicts they will be called in for reserves at the Mareth front.

In Atlantean military politics, Dareous' army is loyal to him, and they do not see Laptos as the same kind of leader as his brother, Daygun. Laptos has not yet proven himself in battle on his own. Because Laptos is the emperor's son, it has worked to his disadvantage. Aten and Daygun are the strongest leaders of the Atlantean Empire. No one sees Laptos as a strong enough leader to lead the invasion of Mareth. Even though he has some strong points, his inexperience is hard to overlook.

One month before the longest day of the year, the stage is set in Mearth, and Aten's son takes the high ground close to Nextear.

When Dareous reaches Laptos, they both salute one another. The Atlantean Army has come together ten miles inside the border of the Mareth Empire. According to the Atlantean scouts, they will have the advantage.

Dareous makes sure Laptos is in command. He gives Aten's son military advice for the battle to come, but leaves the commanding to him.

The Mareth generals are hesitant to make the first move. Nextear thinks back to when the Valteareans attacked the Atlantean defensive position almost a year prior. Some of his Mareth spies were present during the battle. Nextear fears the same scenario. The Mareth warriors have also traveled a long way. Nextear's army wants to fight, and they are very eager to make the first move. Their code is to fight to the last man, and they do not care if they die in defense of their empire.

Laptos, the Supreme Commander of the Mearth Campaign, sees close to seven hundred and fifty thousand Mareth soldiers on the battlefield's horizon. It is the same number he was told to expect. Dareous and Laptos gaze over the hill down to the valley below. Laptos looks through a looking glass towards his enemy. He can see the strength and weakness of the Mareth formations. This battle is the first chance to show his father he can take on a difficult task. However, the sun is about to set, and Mareth will not fight this day. It is in the interest of both empires to wait until daybreak.

The next morning more Mareth and Kanis warriors show up on the valley below the Atlantean fortification. They have deceived the Atlantean spies into thinking they had a smaller force. Because of this deception, the Atlanteans do not know what is about to come at them.

Nextear has a total of three million men from Kanis and Mearth to attack Laptos. The Mareth Empire has close to three thousand mammoths and twenty thousand light cavalry, but they have no artillery. Nextear knows he can win this campaign with overwhelming manpower.

The Mareth soldiers carry bronze swords and wooden shields to fight the Atlanteans. The Mareth wear brown leather, but it is too thin to protect them from the thrust of an Atlantean sword. Nextear's military has thick and heavy swords to keep them from breaking in battle. The Atlantean infantry is outnumbered twenty-five to one against the Mareth and Kanis. Nextear has brought every tribe together in his empire. The newly proclaimed Mearth Emperor has made this into a Holy War. His men will not only fight for him, but also for their gods.

Dawn breaks and the Atlanteans are looking at the vast army. They are not surrounded yet, but in the next three hours there will be no way to retreat. Laptos' artillery is moved to the front lines. The Atlantean heavy cavalry moves to the top of the hill. Laptos has over one hundred giant crossbows and one hundred catapults at his disposal. The Atlantean artillery is formed into a star shape and pointed in every direction. It will be hard for the Mareth soldiers to penetrate the Atlantean defenses, even with the overwhelming forces. If the Mareth launches a frontal assault, the Atlantean rear crossbows and catapults can be turned around for a close attack.

Right before the battle, an Atlantean scout finds Laptos and Dareous and tells them most of their reconnaissance patrols have not reported in. Laptos looks over the battleground and begins to feel uneasy about the situation.

Dareous says, "There is something wrong here. I feel like this is a trap."

Laptos replies, "I agree. But this battle has already begun. I cannot tell my father we had to regroup because of fear of the unknown. Call for Presus' and Quentoris' men to regroup with us. We can take them on two fronts. The Valtearean warriors can protect us from the Kanis Empire if they get involved. Nextear wants us, and we will fight here."

The bells sound to alert the Atlanteans in Valtear the battle is about to begin, but the Kanis military had already shut down the Atlantean bell post to stop the lines of communication.

Dareous goes to Laptos and says, "There is no relay coming back from our communication station. We cannot get reinforcements. We are alone here."

Laptos responds, "We will stand here. We will not retreat because of the unknown."

In Valtear, right before Laptos tries to ring the bells; the first line of attack comes from the borders of Kanis. Over a million warriors come forward to engage Presus. Another million Kanis warriors have been sent to fight with the Mareth. There are over four million men about to take on the Atlantean divisions sent to

Valtear and Mearth. The first objective of the Kanis and Mearth warriors is to engage Presus and to outflank the Atlantean supply lines. Presus' men stay at their post until they know there is no way they can hold their position.

Nextear looks at the Laptos' fortification and knows he will lose thousands of men, but he also knows he must win this battle no matter what the cost. The Mearth Emperor leads his three million men to fight against Laptos' main fortification. Nextear has no artillery, but he has three thousand mammoths, and twenty thousand horsemen.

The only advantage the Atlanteans have at the fortification is their archers and artillery. Laptos and Dareous have over thirty thousand archers on the battlefield to protect their infantry. Every giant crossbow has thirty projectiles. The Atlanteans have found every rock in the region to use in this battle for their catapults. With these advantages, the Atlanteans still believe they can take on their enemy.

Laptos and Dareous look over the hill. They can see a large army coming towards their fortification, but do not know how many men. Ahead of the Mareth and Kanis infantry is the cavalry and mammoths. There seems to be no end of men or beasts coming toward Laptos. He feels the whole world is here. The Atlantean commanders can see the colors of the Kanis Empire. Dareous and Laptos look at each other in astonishment.

Dareous says in shock, "It seems the Kanis and Mareth have formed an alliance. We can't win here."

Laptos stubbornly replies, "We can't lose this battle. The whole Atlantean Empire depends on this day and this battle. If we can cripple the Mareth and Kanis here, it will make them think twice to fight beyond their borders and enter our fatherland. We will win from losing."

Dareous says with concern, "The odds are heavily against us."

Laptos says with pride, "This will put us in the history books. Everyone will know what happened here at Mareth. If we live, I'll be happy. If I die, I won't care."

Dareous replies, "This is a matter of the survival of our civilization. We must call on Tulless for reinforcements. Atlantis is too far."

Laptos says, "I agree. We have been training the Valtear warriors for months. They have over five hundred thousand warriors to help in this war. Send Captain Balaris to get Tulless' men to the secondary position. I want you to secure every bit of military equipment left in the Valtearean capital and move it to Bardia. Tell everyone to leave their city and find refuge. If we have to regroup, we will regroup there. Atlanteans and Valteareans can't fight divided, but we can fight as one."

Dareous says, "Should we save the Valtearean capital?"

Laptos responds, "No, Sidra has no natural defenses. They will take the city. I want them seeing us retreating, and we will counter when we have the advantage."

Balaris, with a small garrison, rides to Sidra, and he is barely able to beat the Mearth and Kanis which are surrounding Laptos' fortification. Balaris rides for hours to get to the Valtearean capital.

Balaris finally arrives at Sidra and goes straight to Quentoris and says, "Kanis and Mearth have formed an alliance. They have more men than we have expected. Laptos will hold off the enemy so the Valtearean civilians can have time to evacuate."

Quentoris responds, "Presus needs to retreat so we can regroup. We will leave a Valtearean division here to get the civilians out of here."

Every military personnel in Sidra rush to their duties. Quentoris goes on full alert, and he sounds the bells inside the Valtearean capital. Because the bells of the Valtearean capital are so powerful, they are able to communicate their message to Presus. It is a one sided communication, but Presus, in his retreat, receives the message to regroup at Bardia.

Back in Mearth, Nextear's army moves closer to the fortification where Laptos is giving orders. It takes thirty minutes before the Mareth and Kanis are within range of the Atlantean archers and artillery. The Atlantean warriors are a little fearful, but their training and discipline holds them together. Laptos and Dareous will use their artillery to destroy as many of their enemy as they can, and try to fall back to regroup.

In the middle of the day, the battle begins. The Kanis and Mareth have completely surrounded the Atlanteans. The Mearth movement of men and beasts change to confuse their enemy. Instead of a full frontal assault, the Mareth and Kanis concentrate all of the heavy and light cavalry on the Atlantean's left flank. The Atlantean central artillery turns and fires their main assault against them. The Atlantean artillery commander gives the order to fire. The Atlantean artillery explodes on the Mearth and Kanis assault. On the battlefield, thousands of the Atlantean's enemy lose their lives. The Atlanteans hold their position on the first wave of attacks without suffering any casualties.

In the ranks of Laptos' fortification, communication between officers and generals is impossible because of the cries of their enemy. The Atlantean artillery and cavalry prepare for the inevitable attack. All of the Atlantean soldiers stand ready. Laptos and Dareous can see their warriors are pure at heart on this battlefield.

The second assault begins on the Laptos' fortification. Close to a million men run towards the Atlanteans. The Atlantean crossbows and catapults scream back at their enemy. The boulders roll through the Kanis and Mareth lines. Hundreds of projectiles are fired from the Atlantean artillery and destroy entire formations of their attackers. Half of the Atlantean projectiles are fired on a concentrated area at the same time, and the technique stops a break through from Nextear's spearhead. When the enemy marches into the range of the Atlantean archers, they use their arrows to ward off the invaders from their fortification. The Mearth and Kanis archers are nowhere close to hitting their mark.

In a counteroffensive, the Atlanteans send in their infantry under the cover of their archers. The Kanis and Mareth fall back to regroup. Almost seventy thousand enemy men die on the second wave of their attack, with thousands more injured.

The Kanis and Mareth wait to attack again. After a while, there is nothing to burn on the battlefield from the Atlantean artillery and the land is totally barren. The Atlanteans have waited to use the full extent of their archer, and have used their artillery sparingly. The enemy is not as daunting as it was on the first attacks.

Three hours after the first attack, the Mearth start the third wave of their attack. The Atlanteans blaze the battlefield again, but this time there is noting to burn except what is in their warheads. The Mareth and Kanis charge towards the hill to simultaneously attack all sides of the Atlantean fortification. The Mareth and Kanis mammoths and cavalry come from all sides. The Atlanteans can no longer hold their position.

Laptos yells, "Fire the last bit of projectiles and dismantle our artillery!"

Dareous yells to his captains, "Form a barrier with our mammoths, and I need ten thousand archers firing every arrow towards the south side to make a hole. We are falling back, but we need time!"

Laptos yells, "All light cavalry to the south side! We are going to punch our way out of here!"

At the Atlantean stronghold, the fighting becomes more intense and the enemy is advancing closer to the core of the Atlantean fortification. There is death all around. The Atlantean infantry is holding on, but they are becoming tired. The Atlanteans were killing ten to one at the beginning. But the ratio is becoming more even as time goes by. A huge concentration of Atlantean mammoths is ready to burst through the enemy lines.

Laptos orders to the heavy cavalry commander, "Now, Now, Now!"

Dareous yells at the ten thousand Atlantean archers, "Fire!"

All the archers fire their arrows in a spearhead shape. The Atlantean mammoths go right between the spearhead formations of their firing archers and they burst through the endless sea of enemy soldiers. The Atlantean infantry protects their archers and forms a barrier. The Atlantean archers protect their heavy cavalry. Right in front of the cavalry, Laptos' artillery fire to give cover and punches a bigger hole through their enemy. The Atlantean mammoths run over the enemy. Laptos' infantry follows behind fighting backwards. The Atlanteans have fought so well that they have made a barrier with dead enemy soldiers. The Atlantean explosion of men from the fortification stuns the Kanis and Mareth. It is hard for them to regroup.

After the breakout, forty thousand Atlantean infantry, nine thousand light cavalry, twenty thousand archers, and seven hundred heavy cavalry make it out alive. The Atlantean wounded have to stay to die. The ones who were saved were very fast in fighting and their adrenaline pulled them through. Other Atlanteans were saved because of their cavalry taking the wounded comrades aboard their beasts.

The Atlanteans are on the run. The Kanis and Mareth concentrate all their might on the original Atlantean fortification.

The Atlanteans who stayed will not to return to Atlantis. The remaining Atlanteans are destroyed without a formidable number of archers and artillery. There were too many men from Kanis and Mareth to withstand that kind of punishment. The Atlantean warriors stayed behind to allow the rest of the Atlanteans to retreat. They gave up their lives for their brothers at arms.

Back in the Valtearean capital, Tulless goes to Quentoris and says, "We are being attacked. The Atlanteans took my kingdom. I hated them for that. I saw a little girl on the side of the road two months ago and I could tell she had been fed. Two years ago the same girl would have been starving. I have seen what the Atlanteans have given to my kingdom, and I stand behind your empire and so do my men. We are here with you. I need your military to help protect the future Atlantean state. I have to know right now if you will retreat or stand to fight in my capital."

Quentoris replies, "We are Atlanteans and stand behind Aten. We can't win here. We must go to Atlantis to regroup and take back your lands later. We have to get these civilians out of Sidra."

Two hours after midnight, almost every man, woman, and child is evacuated out of the Valtearean capital. The civilians are rushed to port cities to leave by boat, and the Valtearean military goes toward the secondary location.

When the Kanis and Mareth arrive the next morning at the Valtearean capital, Sidra is almost completely abandoned. Nextear has won the first battle.

Tulless' capital is on fire. The fires are still burning, and all of the women and children are gone except for a few who refused to leave their homes. The Valtearean Army has burned everything, so the Kanis and Mareth will have to use their own supplies. Nextear is angry; he was hoping he could use the city for supplies so it would be easier to keep pursuing his enemy.

Nextear goes to an old man inside the city and asks, "Where did they all go?"

The old man replies, "They all fled to the sea port of Clarion. The ships are taking them to Atlantis."

Nextear asks, "Where is the Valtearean Army?"

The old man replies, "They went to reinforce the Atlanteans at Bardia."

Nextear shouts, "Bardia!"

The Mareth Emperor kills the man on the spot. Every Valtearean citizen sees the killing and walks away. The Valteareans are hoping he does not come to them and do the same. Nextear orders a scouting party to find the Valtearean and Atlantean military. The Mareth Emperor is determined to destroy the Atlanteans.

CHAPTER XIII
THE FEAR OF DARKNESS

The next morning, a Kanis scouts goes to Nextear with news that the Atlanteans and Valteareans are, in fact, on their way to Bardia.

The main question the Mareth generals ask is, "Why Bardia?" Nextear knows the Atlanteans have no artillery there. Without artillery, he knows the Mareth and Kanis can destroy his enemy.

The next day, the rest of the Atlanteans reach Bardia. The Atlanteans and Valtearean make a defense perimeter on the mountain side of the Albers. Laptos can only be attacked in three different directions. The Atlantean Army will hold the high ground. Dareous knows they have to deplete the enemy supply lines to allow Atlantis to develop their defenses. Because the Valteareans and Atlanteans torched Sidra, their enemy has to get supplies from their homeland.

Laptos, Quentoris, Tulless, Balaris, and Dareous go over their objectives. They are all preparing for battle. They must make a stand. The Atlanteans have sent scouts to the bell outpost and found that half of the lines have been broken. The Atlantean Empire has no clue what is happening in the Mareth Campaign. Laptos is stuck without any reinforcements from their fatherland.

Laptos says inside the tent, "We must seek assistance from our neighbors to the West."

Dareous replies, "The Hamma and Maktar are small city-states of the Empire. They have only a hundred thousand men to fight with us. We must bring them to this battlefield."

Quentoris says, "They are too far away to reach us in time. The battle will not be won here at Bardia. We must lure our enemy to the borders of Atlantis to fight there. The Kanis and Mareth have too many warriors. We must punch them in the face and withdraw. The only way we can win is with reinforcements from our fatherland. We need cavalry and artillery from Atlantis."

Tulless says with pride, "All of my soldiers are with you. We will fight to the death with your empire."

Quentoris replies, "I will fight and protect them with my life."

Tulless says back in a humble way, "I don't mean the past kingdom of Valtear. I mean the new state of Atlantis. The Kanis and Mareth will destroy our way of life. The Atlanteans have proven they will preserve our culture and make it better. We are yours. I hope we will take out our enemy and redevelop Valtear in the Atlantean fashion. I know Aten will fight for my kingdom with everything he has."

Dareous says with urgency, "Laptos, you have your father's influence with the Maktar city-state. Quentoris, Hamma has your first division from your first command. If you both use your influence in this desperate time, you can organize them to fight for us. Balaris, you must go to Atlantis and tell them what is happing here. If the Gambuts are involved, Atlantis can't take on three empires, even if the Kayout Empire stays neutral or fights with our empire."

Laptos says, "I agree. Quentoris, you and I may not make it, but our empire depends on our influence. It is a two day's journey to the two small states. I will meet you at the border of Atlantis in five days. There are two Atlantean divisions at the Great West Wall, but our walls will not be able to withstand a full-scale attack from our enemies. The Mareth and Kanis are too strong. We must weaken them and deplete their supply lines before they reach our borders so, our fatherland can reorganize and counter. Dareous, I am putting you in harms way. You will be in charge of Bardia. Fight here and get to our walls."

Quentoris says, "Before the invasion of Sidra, I already sent a messenger to Maktar and Hamma to be ready. If we don't come together as one force, we all will be picked off one by one. There will not be a Valtear, Hamma, Maktar, or Atlantis if we don't come together. We must bring all military resources on this side to the gates of Atlantis. Dareous, your men must engage the Kanis and Mareth here at Bardia. Our enemy will not split their troops until

Bardia is taken. Nextear will want Bardia too badly. Laptos, you will be safe until you reach the border of Atlantis."

Dareous says, "I will fight here at Bardia to buy Laptos time. It is my duty to protect the royal blood which started our civilization. Even though it is buying time, I gave my oath as an Atlantean warrior to obey orders. In Atlantean military code, we gave our word to protect our states and Valtear."

Quentoris replies, "I agree. The battle at Bardia will make or break our empire. We must slow Nextear down so our empire can regroup."

Laptos throws a map down on a table and points at the destination and says, "Quentoris, my father has confidence in you, and I do as well. Meet me at the border of Atlantis, twenty miles northwest of the Great West Wall, in five days."

They all go their separate ways. Balaris rides to the fatherland. Quentoris and Laptos mount their horses and take a small task force for protection. The two men go on their journeys to the Atlantean city-states to gather the few men who are there. They ride quickly and do not sleep until they reach their destination.

Dareous and Tulless must stay and fight, but they must retreat at the same time. The two must set a line of defense. Every bridge was set afire as the Atlanteans and Valteareans retreated from Sidra. Their enemy will have to go around rivers until they find a bridge to cross. Just because of the lay of the land, Dareous thinks the enemy will attack from the northwest side of the Bardia region.

Burning the bridges will give the Valtearean and Atlanteans a couple of days to prepare for battle. The Atlanteans use every tree they can find and carve stakes that will help defend Bardia from charging cavalry. The Atlantean and Valtearean archers have made tens of thousands of crude arrows from the surrounding area. Dareous' men have time to rest. The Kanis and Mareth are marching with little sleep, and it is becoming harder to feed such a vast army.

On the third day of marching, the Kanis and Mareth are nearby, and have close to three and a half million men ready to take the defenses of Bardia. The Atlantean patrols see the massive army, and are afraid of what is about to occur.

Laptos and Quentoris finally reach their destinations. The Maktar and Hamma city-states agree to fight alongside the

Atlanteans and Valteareans. A ship is launching to Atlantis to warn of the invasion, but it will take three days to arrive in Vasic. The two small city-states have hastily mustered about four divisions. One of the divisions is from Atlantis. Quentoris is glad to see his men. It is one of the elite divisions from the fatherland. The Atlantean division is honored to see Quentoris and is ready to die for their empire. The Maktar and Hamma artillery divisions are sent by ship to meet up with Dareous outside the Atlantean Great West Wall. Hamma and Maktar ships are evacuating their citizens by sea. They are going across the sea where the enemy cannot reach them. In the meantime, the two Atlantean states burn and destroy anything their enemy can use in their campaign against Atlantis.

Laptos marches his armies close to the sea towards Atlantis. Laptos is proud of the men that he has mustered. The two Atlantean city-states have reserve munitions. Their armies take every bow and sword in their arsenal. It will take three days to reach their destination. Because Laptos is exhausted, he tries to sleep in a carriage while traveling. It has been very taxing on his soul for the last couple of days.

Back on the battlefield at Bardia, Dareous sends most of his heavy and light cavalry to the south side of Bardia. Because the Valteareans do not have the same range of the Atlantean archers, they have to move up closer to their enemy. The two armies are spaced correctly to concentrate and maximize their firepower. The Atlanteans will catch the enemy in a defensive crossfire. Dareous' infantry is dead center and is put in reserve. Because the Atlanteans are stronger in battle, the Valtearean infantry is on the left and right flanks.

The Mareth and Kanis decide to attack during mid-afternoon. The battle begins. The Mareth attack the north and west side of the Alber Mountains. The battle to the west lasts for two hours. The Atlantean archers and infantry work hand and hand, and they repel their enemy. Dareous counterattacks, and slaughters many of Nextear's infantry. The Mareth and Kanis have too many casualties to regroup. Tulless has taken charge at the front, and he orders his captains to capitalize on the Mareth and Kanis weakness.

At dusk, the Valteareans and Atlanteans start to lose ground on the north side of Bardia. The Valteareans fight well, but they are few in numbers and start to tire and lose ground. When the sun starts to set, the Atlanteans catch a break. The Kanis and Mareth retreat back to their camp, but still have the Atlanteans and Valteareans completely surrounded. Before nightfall, a Mareth messenger comes to the Atlantean fortification to speak with the commander at hand. The messenger goes to Dareous.

The Mareth messenger stands in pride and says, "Allow our wounded to die in peace. The sun will set in thirty minutes. Allow our warriors to die in the light of the sun so they can go to the heavens and their forefathers."

Dareous is stunned and says, "You may take the wounded off the field, and I will not attack your men during your retraction."

The messenger runs off and relays the message to Nextear. Thousands of Kanis and Mareth go towards their mortally wounded and put their faces towards the last rays of sun and kill them on the spot. In the Mareth and Kanis religion, this is the only way they can go to the afterlife to be with their gods. Light is the key to go into their heaven. When the sun goes down completely, the Atlanteans hear cries from the battlefield and thousands of torches are stabbed in the ground. The dying warriors face the light of the torch and are killed.

Dareous watches this and comes up with a plan, and he gathers the captains together. He waits until everyone is in the tent. After about twenty minutes he speaks to the Atlantean and Valtearean captains.

Dareous says, "The people of Kanis and Mareth can't fight efficiently in the dark. We must break out of here tonight. The religion of our enemy dictates that they can't die without the sun or the torches of light. Our enemy will fear to die this night. They feel they won't be able to go to the afterlife. This is the only way we are going to safely get back to our homeland. If we wait until daybreak, we will not survive."

An Atlantean captain says, "Not everyone in Mareth or Kanis believes in that faith."

Dareous replies, "Religion is religion. Even if everyone doesn't believe in the light to go to heaven, who is going to chance it this night? It is imbedded in their culture. It is our time to go on our last offensive in Valtear. I hope Laptos and Quentoris have secured our reinforcements. Many of our men will die tonight."

Dareous' orders are carried out. The Mareth and Kanis are

only two miles away on all three sides. The Atlantean warriors charge with their light and heavy cavalry, and their archers follow closely behind. The Atlanteans and Valteareans fire in the darkness, hopefully hitting their enemy. The Mareth and Kanis are caught off guard. Tens of thousands of Nextear's army are killed in seconds. The Atlanteans rush towards the torches of their enemy alongside the Alber Mountains. The Atlanteans use their heavy cavalry to spearhead through the enemy lines in total darkness. After about an hour, the Atlanteans are outside their enemies' pocket and retreat before sunrise. The Mareth and Kanis do not follow in fear of dying in the dark.

During the night offensive, the Mareth and Kanis lost over six hundred and seventy thousand men, and they are too weak to follow the Atlantean force. The Atlanteans have found the weakness of their enemy. Some Kanis and Mareth retreated because of their fears of the full moon. The light of the full moon leads the dead to their hell. The religion of the enemy has saved the Atlanteans, and they have put a huge dent in the opposing military.

At sunrise, the Atlanteans and Valteareans escape with only two hundred thousand men. Close to four hundred thousand Atlanteans and Valteareans died at Bardia. It was a long fight all night. Neither side completely knows the death toll. After daybreak, the Mearth Emperor wants revenge. In Nextear's eyes, the Atlanteans disrespected his gods, ensuring to his warriors it is a Holy War.

The Kanis and Mareth do try to attack the Atlanteans with their cavalry as the days go by, but the Atlanteans ward them off. In turn, the Atlanteans weaken the Mareth and Kanis a little more. The Atlantean cavalry is the best in the world. Dareous' archers are down to twenty good arrows a piece. The Atlanteans cannot repel another attack like Bardia. A great deal of Atlantean men are cut or hurt in some way. The only thing keeping the Atlanteans going is the idea of making it to their homeland.

Because of the medicines of the Atlanteans, no one is dying of infections. The Atlanteans and Valteareans stop and have funeral services for the ones who did not make it out alive from Bardia. Life and culture has changed since the Atlanteans went to Valtear. Dareous has never seen so much death. In less than a week, hundreds and thousands of soldiers and civilians have died on both sides. Dareous wonders if trying to take Mareth was worth all of this.

He wonders what will happen with the world. He was there to take Mareth. Did he destroy Atlantis with conquest?

In the Atlantean retreat, the Mareth and Kanis light cavalry attack the Atlanteans and Valteareans again, but they too are repelled. The whole countryside of Valtear has a trail of blood running toward Atlantis. After a long march, the Atlanteans and Valteareans finally reach where they should meet Laptos and Quentoris. They send scouts and a messenger to the destination. Dareous is where he should be. That morning, the reinforcements from Maktar and Hamma finally arrive. Dareous is relieved when he sees Laptos leading the corroboration.

Laptos and Quentoris have brought back four divisions. The Atlantean scouts run toward the communication post to try to warn their fatherland, but the posts have been destroyed. The only way the Atlanteans can communicate with their own is through messengers. Tulless, Laptos, Quentoris, and Dareous meet in Akco, the bordering outpost of Atlantis, and make plans for that afternoon. Since they are outnumbered, they need to fall back into the borders inside the Great West Wall and get reinforcements from the Atlanteans. They talk about battle strategies and transporting artillery from the ships from Maktar. They are weary of going towards the Great West Wall. The enemy can be in the mountains ready to attack them.

Then, Balaris rides his horse up to Dareous.

Balaris is out of breath and says, "I can't get to our gates. The Atlanteans are fighting someone. Thousands of men are fighting at the first barrier into our empire."

Dareous asks, "How many men do you think? We were right not going towards the Great West Wall alone. The Kanis and Mareth have a stronghold there, and I think the Gambuts may be a part of this."

Catching his breath, Balaris says, "I say about four to five hundred thousand enemy warriors are at our gates."

Laptos says to Dareous, "Do you think the Kanis and Mareth split up?"

Dareous replies, "No! Why would they split up and try to take the Great West Wall of Atlantis with a small army? This is a diversion. Our fortification is too strong. An enemy will know five hundred thousand men are not enough. We have a half days march to get there. I think the whole world is against Atlantis. The whole world is on our doorstep."

The next morning, Dareous and a few scouts look upon the Atlantean Great West Wall to see what is going on. Dareous sees about five hundred thousand men from the Gambut Empire attacking his empire. Over three million more of Nextear's soldiers are not even a day's march away.

Dareous rides back to camp in haste, but he can only think of how he is going to die for honor of his empire.

CHAPTER XIV
THE BETRAYAL

One month before the longest day of the year, Emperor Aten is at the Atlantean Great East Wall training eight of his divisions. He has one more month to prepare his men to invade Gambut with the Kayout Empire. Four elite Atlantean divisions are already fortifying the Great East Wall. This gives Aten a total of twelve divisions, with over three hundred thousand soldiers. With this kind of force and weapon technology, Aten is confident his empire is safe from any invasion.

If Atlantis is attacked, the entrance of the Great East Wall will force an enemy into a bottleneck. There is only a mile and a half of width between the two mountain ranges. Right in the center is the Atlantean gate. The space is too small for a major attack from an enemy. With the weapons of Atlantis, the whole battlefield can be destroyed within twenty minutes. There are also five gates and walls between the Atlanteans and the outside world. The fortification has the best artillery and men in the world to protect it.

At the Great East Wall, there are three hundred giant crossbows and four hundred catapults. Because of the high elevation of Aten's artillery, the enemy's artillery cannot come close to the gates without being destroyed. The Atlantean artillery personnel have been trained to hit with great accuracy anything that comes close to the wall.

Because of Atlantean pride, the Atlantean Great East Wall has been carved with intricate designs over the past hundred years. Former Atlantean warriors have been memorialized into the stone of the mountain so they will never be forgotten. There are two towers outside the first gate, just like in the Atlantean Harbor. The fires coming from the two pillars have burned continuously for the last five hundred years. It is said, from generations past, as long as the towers are burning, the culture of Atlantis is safe from the rest of the world.

To the Atlantean civilization, it is a great honor to work on the fortified monuments of the wall. It is said throughout the Atlantean Empire that as long as the Atlantean walls are standing, God will be in the hearts of the Atlanteans forever. Because of their devotion to religion, every Atlantean citizen works on the gate for one year of their lives.

On each side of the gate, there are two statues of God alongside the pillars. Each statue is a hundred and fifty feet tall and facing towards the continent. Carved from the mountains, the effigies were built to honor war and peace. It required thousands of laborers, and took decades to complete. The statue on the right side of the gate is holding an olive branch. The other statue is holding a bow and arrow and a sword to its side. The bow is aimed towards the heavens. Anyone that comes close to the statues can tell it is the true Atlantean God. Between the two monuments, stands the hundred foot gate made of wood and steel.

Two hundred yards in front of the gate are three pyramids. All three are sixty feet tall and made of black marble. The marble came from the outermost part of the Atlantean Empire. On top of each pyramid there are glass light towers. From a distance on a pitch-black night, the fire coming from the pyramids seems to float in air. At night, the light from the pyramids shines directly on the statues of God.

Another Atlantean barrier into the peninsula is the mountain range. Beyond the gates, the mountain range is too steep for any enemy invader to climb and enter Atlantis. Aten's civilization has found the perfect natural barrier on earth to defend their civilization from the rest of the world. Spies from other empires tell their superiors the Atlantean gates are impossible to breach.

The only other way into Atlantis is through the Great West Wall near the Valtearean border. This gate does not have as many natural defenses, but more manmade ones. The mountain region is there, but it is more open for attack. The Great West Wall on the border between Valtear and Atlantis was built at the same time as the East, but it has not been upgraded yet to the impenetrable degree. Both the Valtear and Gambut entrances have three miles of corridor and five gates. The Great West Wall has one hundred giant crossbows and one hundred and fifty catapults at their disposal. Only two Atlantean divisions are stationed at the Great West Wall to protect against an invasion by the Kanis or Mareth Empires. Because of the mountain range, it is impossible to invade Atlantis except through the two gates.

Emperor Aten's family has been ruling since the beginning of the Atlantean society. He considers what his father told him, and his forefathers had told them. Aten remembers being a small child; his forefathers were irrigation builders, and began to develop buildings and built monuments for God and their land.

The first Atlantean Emperor was named Atlandreous. He was the first person who brought order to the peninsula. Tess, his wife, started the beginning of exploring science for the sake of mankind's progression. Atlandreous focused on the art of irrigation. The engineers started using machines to manipulate the land; this was the first way of controlling nature. After developing irrigation, the Atlanteans started to go beyond the art of farming. Atlandreous brought the word of God to his civilization, and everyone in the kingdom converted to one religion. He united the city-states, but left them with individual leaders. Because of this, there are still kings in each of the great cities of Atlantis.

Aten looks at the walls and does not want to let his forefathers down. He takes tremendous pride in his army. The Atlantean Emperor trains with his men like a true leader. He is on the field with the army every day. His warriors feel honored by their emperor's presence.

Aten knows he has his armies divided in Valtear and Mareth. He knows he has the strongest army in the world, but if they are divided, his empire could be in jeopardy. The Atlantean Emperor does not like the idea of engaging on two fronts, but at this point, he has no choice.

During the early hours of that morning, the emperor is interrupted.

A servant yells, "A messenger is coming toward us, My Lord!"

The scout is approaching on horseback, with panic in his eyes. Two grandmasters follow Aten to meet the scout. The Atlantean

Emperor stands tall, and he can see the issue must be very important.

The scout yells, "The Gambuts are at our doorstep!"

Aten turns to his grandmasters and says in a direct voice, "Sound the bells for a full alert. Send another messenger to my son, and tell him what is transpiring here!"

Aten mounts his horse and goes to the front gate. The bells ring throughout the Atlantean Empire. Aten knows the Gambuts cannot win this battle by themselves. The whole Atlantean Army goes on full alert. Men are running all over the gate's fortification to take their positions.

Back in Atlantis, the message from the bells reaches the ears of Daygun. The emperor's son is with Kaydence in their new home. He hastily mounts a horse in his garden. In this kind of alarm, all high-ranking generals are to report to the Military Council Hall immediately.

Kaydence runs out to the garden and yells, "Wait Daygun!"

Right when she yells, Daygun is turning his horse around abruptly and does not see her. He pulls on the reins of the horse and turns towards her. This is the first time Kaydence has seen Daygun so scared and angry at the same time. She strokes the horse's head to calm the beast down.

She looks at Daygun and asks, "What is happening? Are the Gambuts at war with us?"

Daygun says, "I don't know. I must assemble the Military Council. The Gambuts are at the Great East Wall. I know my father sent a messenger. It will be four hours before we know what is going on in full detail. I must get to the Council and set up our reserves and send our fleets out to sea for scouting. If it is only the Gambuts, we will defeat them. A million men can't break through our Eastern defenses. We have over three hundred thousand warriors stationed there."

Daygun assembles his Military Council and orders all Atlantean ships to go to sea in search of enemy ships. The prince orders his captains to prepare the military reserves, and he tells another captain to find out where all the Atlantean divisions are located.

About four hours later, the messenger from Aten's army arrives to inform Daygun and the Atlantean Military Council of the situation.

The messenger marches quickly to Daygun and salutes.

The messenger says, "The whole Gambut Army is standing out of firing range at the Great East Wall. They wait for us to engage them in combat. Your father wants you to know we have twelve divisions at our Eastern defense. He wants you to pull the archer youth reserves to the Great West Wall at the border of Valtear. He told me to tell you to get two divisions to Vasic to protect our military port. There could be an amphibious landing."

Daygun says, "It must be more desperate than I thought if he wants us to pull our archers, which are no older than sixteen, to defend our empire. If the Mareth or Kanis are allies with the Gambut, they can take the Great West Wall. If that happens, I want our divisions to retreat back into the gates of Masaba. The city has a very good fortification to withstand an attack. I want twelve divisions in reserve in Atlantis. This will be our last stronghold. From here, we can send reserves to Masaba or Halotropolis, if the need arises. I will need the rest of our reserves in Vasic. The Vasic King will not give up his ships if we don't give him something in return. Since Halotropolis is so close to the Great East Wall, I want eight divisions to reinforce and protect God's city. At this point, Masaba is not in danger. If the Gambuts take out our Great East Wall, they will have to go through two major cities before they can attack our capital. The enemy cannot go straight to Atlantis without being attacked on two fronts."

A general says, "The Senate from Halotropolis will not think eight divisions will be enough to protect the City of God."

Daygun replies, "I will send Kaydence to Halotropolis. She is of royal blood. The Senate there will compose itself with her presence. Now, believe in my command, and let it be done."

At the Atlantean doorstep, Melercertis, Borealeous, and Origenes, the Gambut Emperor, look at the Great East Wall.

Borealeous says, "With the Atlantean Army divided, and Laptos on the run, we can take their defenses here."

Origenes says, "I want my warriors to be the first to attack the walls of Atlantis."

Ryelyne asks, "With the agreement, we do all agree Kayout will govern the peninsula after the war."

Origenes says, "We all see the Atlantean lands as evil. To our civilization, Atlantis is tainted. After this war, the conquered civilization will be hard to keep under control. Yes, the agreement stands."

Borealeous responds, "We will keep the pact. Atlantis cannot become a military power as it was twenty-seven years ago. Right now, we cannot ignore their imperialistic nature. The Atlantean Empire has gone against the treaty set forth after the Great War to attack another empire. They had no right to wage war on Mearth."

Ryelyne responds, "This is the reason I am here amongst you. They did go against the agreement. For the few that survive, I will keep them from becoming a threat to the rest of the world. What I am doing right now shows honor to you and my people."

Origenes says, "I do understand your grief and despair. It must be hard to take control of your civilization. The world will change on this day."

Ryelyne says, "I will help bring this war to an end quickly. The world will have enough bloodshed."

The first attack starts on the Atlantean Great East Wall. Over five hundred thousand Gambut warriors attack the Atlantean fortification. The bells ring throughout the Atlantean Empire. If Ryelyne does this right, Atlantis will send most of their reserve soldiers to the Great East Wall. Ryelyne knows Aten has enough men to keep at least a million soldiers from taking the gate, but the Great West Wall is not as well fortified. So, Ryelyne expects the Atlanteans will try to reinforce the Great West Wall, leaving the East susceptible.

The Gambut and half of Kanis' military start their attack on the Atlantean Great West Wall hours after attacking the East. The bells ring from the Great West Wall telling Daygun of the attack. The Atlanteans hold off their attackers on both fronts on the first day. Mareth and Kanis have destroyed every communication post between Valtear and Atlantis. Because Laptos' army is so far away, they will not know their homeland is being attacked. When Nextear attacked the Atlanteans in Mareth, Ryelyne decided to attack his homeland. The new Kayout Supreme Commander knew Atlantis could not hold in Mearth. The first attack is to confuse the Atlanteans. At the end of the day, the Kayouts and Gambuts lose very few men.

On the second day, Ryelyne sees there is a storm coming.

Ryelyne waits until it rains, which will be a disadvantage for the Atlanteans. The Atlantean crossbow projectiles are less effective in the wet weather. After hours of fighting, the Kayouts have to back off right before nightfall. Even though the giant crossbows were not as effective, the Atlanteans beat off the attackers easily. The Atlantean walls are still strong.

Two hours before sunrise on the third day, Aten waits at the Atlantean Great East Wall war chamber. The Atlantean Emperor can see every aspect of the battlefield. There are so many torches a mile away from his gates it seems like daylight. Right before sunrise, the Gambuts and Kanis attack the Great East Wall again. Even though the Gambut and Kayout believe in more than one god, they do not share the same beliefs of the Kanis and Mareth. They do not require the sun in their death rituals. Another half million Kayout warriors, under the Gambut flag, attack the Atlantean main gate. If the Continental Alliance continues to attack both walls, the Atlanteans will not know where to send reinforcements. Ryelyne does not want the Atlantean Army to concentrate only on the Great East Wall. He wants the Atlanteans to keep on guessing where to send their reinforcements.

Minutes before sunrise on the fourth day of the war, forty thousand Atlantean infantrymen are standing outside the Great East Wall waiting to fight their enemy. They are inside the lights of the pyramids. As long as the Atlanteans are in the light of the pyramids, they are protected by the Atlantean archers and artillery. Tens of thousand torches come towards the Atlantean infantry. The sun peaks through the mountains, and most of the Atlanteans think this will be their last sunrise. Aten's infantry is told to stay in the boundaries of the pyramids and not go on an offensive.

The Gambuts march closer, and the Atlantean archers are ordered to fire. Sixty thousand Atlantean arrows hit the battlefield killing thousands of Gambut warriors. The Gambuts rush towards the Atlantean gate. Aten's warriors and his enemy go head to head. The second wave of Atlantean arrows kills Gambuts reinforcements, but half of Ryelyne's assault makes it through. The Gambut and Atlantean infantry fight and brutally kill one another.

From a tower on the Atlantean side, Aten sees the heavy Gambut cavalry coming to attack the right formation of his infantry outside his gates. The Atlanteans counter fire with all their artillery at the enemy's heavy and light cavalry. The Atlantean catapults fire at will, killing hundreds of enemy beasts. Some of the enemy's light and heavy cavalry make it through the Atlantean bombardment and push towards the unknowing Atlantean infantry. Aten orders out his light and heavy cavalry to counter his enemy. The Atlantean infantry moves out of the way and their cavalry punches a hole through their attackers.

Within ten minutes, the tide of power changes back to the Atlantean advantage. Aten's heavy cavalry starts to devastate the Gambut Army and moves outside the protection of their archers and artillery. Drawing closer to Ryelyne's trap, the Atlantean cavalry keeps fighting deeper into their enemy's ranks.

Ryelyne looks at the battlefield and yells, "Fire!"

The Kayouts use their heavy artillery and fire on the Atlantean heavy cavalry killing a quarter of Aten's cavalry in minutes. It is a fast and divesting blow to the Atlanteans. The Kayout artillery is out of range of the Atlantean artillery. It is a brilliant move by Ryelyne, and the Atlantean heavy cavalry have to retreat back through their gate.

Ryelyne looks over the battlefield and looks at Tito and Melercertis.

Ryelyne says, "The Atlanteans will not let that happen again. They will stay on the defensive for the duration of this campaign. It is time to go forward to the next stage of this campaign."

Tito asks, "How can you be so sure they will not counterattack and go on the offensive?"

Ryelyne replies, "We just defeated their cavalry, and the people of the continent aren't as injudicious as they thought. They will be second guessing themselves every step of this campaign."

The Atlanteans ring the bells and tell Halotropolis to send more reinforcements and ammunition to the front. The Atlanteans' supplies are quickly being depleted. The giant crossbow projectiles take five days to produce. Every Atlantean ammunition factory has gone into full production twenty-four hours a day, since the Gambuts came to their doorstep.

Three days go by and there is no clear victor on either side. The fighting starts and ends every day. Many men from both sides have lost their lives. Ryelyne is waiting for Nextear to reinforce the

Great West Wall, and Aten is wondering if it is only the Gambut attacking his empire.

On the seventh day, five hundred thousand men are sent forth from the Kayout camp. Because the Kayouts and Gambuts have similar clothing, the Atlanteans are not sure who is attacking. The Kayouts use the Gambut flag to confuse the Atlanteans. At this point, Ryelyne uses the elite Kayout warriors all under Tito's command. They charge into battle, but the Atlanteans counter and hold them back. The Kayout warriors kill quite a few Atlantean infantry because the Atlanteans are growing fatigued. The ratio to Atlanteans goes down to ten to one. It is still a defeat to the Atlanteans.

The Continental Alliance is still waiting for Nextear's warriors to help reinforce their attack on the Great West Wall to make a full-scale attack on the East. With Laptos destroying the bridges and holding at Bardia, it is putting the Mearth Emperor behind schedule. The Atlanteans still think the Gambuts are the only ones attacking. Atlantis knows the numbers of the Borealeous' empire. Aten thinks Gambut can only fight for another couple of days before they too will have to retreat back and sue for peace.

Ryelyne and Melercertis are apprehensive at the thought of losing so many men after the gates have been taken. The main Atlantean forces are still stationed at Masaba, Halotropolis and the capital city of Atlantis. The enemy will have to take three cites to conquer the Atlantean Empire. The kings of the Atlantean cities will not let their armies leave their walls. Daygun has to comply with his kings. The Atlantean Prince cannot deplete the cities' defenses to where they can be easily conquered. For now, all three Atlantean cities think they are safe with their fortifications, weaponry, and armies.

After the eighth day, the hardest day of fighting, the Continental Alliance starts to retire for the day. The Gambuts send a messenger to Aten to see if they can remove their dead and wounded off the battlefield. Atlantis asks to go first, because they have the medical knowledge needed to save their men. The Atlanteans are given two hours to complete the retraction, and the Gambuts have the same amount of time to gather their fallen men and beasts off the battlefield. When the dead are removed, Aten looks out from the emperor's chambers and sees nothing but a field of blood. The battlefield is not a light brown, but a dark chocolate color because of blood and dirt. The blood is so thick on the battlefield; it looks as if every man, woman, and child, on earth have given every ounce of blood and spilled it at the gates of Atlantis. Aten knows the dust will not fly in the air as it did on the first attack from his enemy.

That night, the Atlantean wounded warriors fill the beds of the hospital inside their mountain fortification. Screams ring throughout the mountain fortress. Because the mountains are hollow, the screams seem as if ghosts are shouting from inside the mountain. The Atlantean physicians cannot see each patient in time to treat and save their lives. Many Atlantean men lose their lives because of the shortages of medical attention. Aten sounds the bells to send more physicians to the Great East Wall.

After the Atlantean Emperor leaves the beds of his injured warriors, he goes to his generals in the military chamber.

Aten says, "We are losing the Great East Wall. I do not know if it is only the Gambuts or the whole mainland. My gut instinct tells me every empire on the continent is a part of this war. If it is the only Gambut, our enemy will not be able to keep fighting. We can't ask for anymore reinforcements from our cities. If it is the whole continent, we all must die here as warriors for our homeland."

The general replies, "If it is the continent, they can't keep losing this many men. They also have politics to play with in their own homeland."

Aten says, "There has been so much hate towards or civilization for decades. I truly feel Gambut is not the only empire outside our gates."

Late night after the hardest day of fighting, there is a silence across the battlefield. Both sides gave it their all. The Atlanteans won a moral victory by holding back such a force. On the other hand, the Gambut generals tell their army they need just one more thrust, and the Atlanteans will be exhausted, confused, and defeated. Both sides call it their victory.

About midday of the ninth day at the Great East Wall, the Atlanteans have almost exhausted their giant crossbow projectiles. Nextear has arrived at the Great West Wall. The Gambuts see this and take action on the battlefield. They see the Atlantean infantry reorganizing. The Gambut generals see the Atlantean infantry filtering in and out of the gate. To the Gambuts, this is the perfect time for attack. Even though the Gambuts are not ready for a full scale attack, it is ordered out of haste.

The Gambuts cross the battlefield. The Atlantean archers and artillery fire repeatedly at their attackers, killing about one third of the soldiers coming towards their infantry. Thousands of Gambuts and the Kanis burst through, and the full Atlantean infantry runs to meet them on the battlefield. The Gambut and Kanis heavy cavalry charge dead center of the Atlantean's infantry. Aten sees his infantry is in considerable danger and opens the gates. Every Atlantean light and heavy cavalry charges out the gate to challenge the enemy. The Atlantean archers and artillery concentrate all their firepower towards the Gambut light cavalry and heavy cavalry. It is not enough.

The Gambut break through and destroy the center of the Atlanteans infantry, and they are forced to fall back. From the center of the Atlantean infantry come three hundred Atlantean mammoths and elephants, in a spearhead which explodes like a volcano, through their enemy. They charge the Gambut heavy cavalry dead on. The Atlantean cavalry have been trained better and are able to make good ground. With the help of the Atlantean archers and artillery, the Atlanteans' beasts break through the Gambut and Kanis lines. The Atlantean infantry counters forward, and reclaims the ground they lost within hours. The Atlantean infantry does not go beyond the range of their archers and artillery range.

The Gambuts are having trouble retreating through their own dead. The Gambut horses stumble as they gallop back to safety. Gambut horses trip over the lifeless bodies. The Atlantean archers take advantage of their confusion. The Atlantean's giant crossbows fire their Krample projectiles with spikes that scatter on the battlefield. It gives time for the Atlantean infantry to reorganize and take on the enemy.

Ryelyne goes to Melercertis and Tito.

Ryelyne says, "It is time. The Atlanteans are tired, and it is time to completely catch them off guard."

Tito replies, "If I think what you're thinking. I agree. We need a moral victory soon."

Melercertis says, "I trust you like I said back in my capital. If you say it's time, it is time. I am losing face to our allies. If I don't produce quickly, we will not be the dominate empire here. The only way we can save Atlantis after the war is to take complete control of this war. We will retire for the day. We will ask to take off the dead on the battlefield for the next step in our military campaign."

CHAPTER XV
THE TIGHTUS

Ryelyne orders the new weapon of the Kayout Empire, which has been a secret until now, to be introduced to the battlefield. Ryelyne waited to use the new weapon until the Atlantean artillery was weakened. The Kayout engineers have worked for a decade on a weapon to breach the walls of the Atlantean fortifications.

The Eastern Empire has thousands of mammoths at their deposal, and the Kayouts are very good craftsman. The military introduced the idea of the tightus, which is an enormous, covered chariot. The tightus is a hundred feet high and seventy-five feet wide. The mobile structure has fourteen wheels which are over eight feet high.

The tightus has eight levels, which are powered by four mammoths. The Kayout beasts are protected under the first story of their war machine. The second story has very powerful crossbows, which can shoot projectiles and is able to inflict serious damage on the Atlantean defenses. On the third level there is a ram, which can damage an Atlantean gate. The fourth level holds forty archers. The top four levels hold hundreds of warriors. When the men jump out from the top of the tightus, they are level with the top of the Atlantean wall. It is the most powerful machine of its day. The Kayout are going to use seventy-five tightuses to take the Great East Wall.

In the tightuses, the Kayout crossbow technology was copied from the Atlanteans. Kayout spies took the idea ten years prior, and the weapon went into production. The tightuses' projectiles explode with fire upon impact.

The horns blow from the Kayout military, and the tightus goes forward towards the Atlantean's Great East Wall. The Atlantean artillery fires their krample projectiles. The Atlantean spikes are cleared by Kayout warriors before they can hurt the mammoths running to power the chariot. Even though the tightuses are one of the largest wooden structures in the world, they can move almost three miles an hour on the battlefield.

The horns blow a second time from the Atlantean enemy, and the Kayout and Gambut infantry charge at full speed.

From within the gates, the Atlanteans brace for what is about the come. The Atlanteans are well disciplined, and wait for orders to fire on the charging enemy. Aten orders the counter measures and blows the Atlantean horns. The horns echo throughout the mountains. The Atlantean's giant crossbows fire and hit the tightus, but the majority of the projectiles glide off the sides of the Kayout war machines. Because of the curved sides and metal plating of the tightus, it was built to ward off artillery.

On the first wave of Atlantean artillery fire, only one tightus is disabled and the others go at slower speeds. All Atlantean's giant crossbows focus their fire on the tightus, and ignore the Gambut and Kayout light and heavy cavalry coming to their right of the Atlantean gate.

Aten orders all of his own light and heavy cavalry to counter and engage the Gambut's cavalry to protect his infantry outside. The Atlantean archers rain arrows on the Gambut infantry. Tens of thousands of Gambut warriors are pierced by Atlantean arrows and fall where they stand. The tightuses are keeping the morale of the Gambut infantry going forward. The Kayouts and Gambuts all know the walls will be taken if they maintain their momentum.

The Kayout covered chariots are moving closer to the Great East Wall. Because of the speed of the tightuses, the giant Atlantean crossbows are having difficulty hitting their target. It is very hard to move the Atlantean crossbows in haste.

Aten orders another wave of crossbow artillery to be fired. The Atlantean artillery reconfigures their firing solution to fire at the base of the tightuses. Over twelve are destroyed and six more disabled. The Atlantean artillery commanders give the order to fire at will. Aten's infantry run out of the gate and go under the tightuses and kill the mammoths, stopping them at a standstill. The Atlantean's giant crossbows hit and destroy more on their third wave of firing, but forty-seven tightuses are still running towards the Atlantean Great East Wall. For the first time, Aten is scared for his people. The Atlantean Emperor will not reveal his fear to his men, but his warriors can see the hesitancy in his eyes as he gives orders to regroup.

The Atlantean archers are raining havoc on the battlefield, and eighty-five thousand Gambut warriors are dead or wounded. Then Aten orders his men to regroup to push his enemy back.

In response, Ryelyne orders the Gambut warriors to climb the mountain on both sides of the gate with ropes. Twenty thousand Gambut warriors climbing the mountain give up their lives for their cause, empire, and gods. The main purpose for trying to climb the mountainside is to draw the Atlantean archers' attention, so the tightus can get to the walls.

Thirty-eight tightuses reach the gate and fire their projectiles at the Atlantean fortifications. The Kayout and Gambut projectiles hit their target and inflict damage on the Great East Wall. Aten's wooden gates are on fire. In some areas, Aten's men have to fall back. The Atlantean catapults fire, but also have little effect on the Kayout tightus. The catapults' boulders skip off like a person throwing a stone across a river.

The Atlanteans archers are accurate, and hitting the holes of the tightus, and they kill hundreds of enemy archers inside. As the enemy draws closer to the Great East Wall, the Atlantean archers hit every area of the giant covered chariots. Because so many arrows fired against the tightus, the Kayout covered chariots look like giant porcupines going across the battlefield. The second wave of the tightuses reaches the gates and fires their projectiles and rams the gate. The Atlantean barrier is weakening in the onslaught. All tightuses reverse to build speed and ram the Atlantean gate again.

The Atlantean Great East Wall finally gives in. The Gambut warriors run fast and infest the inside of the first Atlantean barrier. The arms of the Atlanteans archers are getting tired, and they are becoming less effective. The battleground is covered in arrows. On the top of the mountain, it looks like a field of grass with so many arrows implanted in the ground. It is a battlefield of death.

Due to their overwhelming manpower, the Gambut archers put enough cover fire for the Gambut mammoths to go forward. The Atlanteans hit the enemy mammoths with their arrows and artillery, but the only way to stop the Gambut mammoths is to hit directly in front of the enemy beasts with the Atlantean artillery projectiles. There is nothing to catch a flame on the battlefield. Because the soil is comprised of blood and earth, it is like a dark mud. The Atlantean projectiles are almost useless.

Aten orders a full retreat to the second defensive gate; he orders a division to stay at the first line of defense and protect his men in their retreat. The Gambuts and Kayouts start to tear away the damaged first gate with their mammoths to have better access. Ryelyne orders to destroy the statues of God and burning pillars. What took the Atlanteans decades to create is being destroyed in hours. The Gambut's and Kayout's mammoths pull with their ropes, and they eventually pull down everything at the front entrance of the Atlantean Empire.

The enemy stops at the first gate and stays out of range of the Atlantean firing solution from the second Atlantean fortification. The Gambuts and Kayouts know they have to regroup, and they are hesitant to push forward.

At the secondary gate, the Atlantean artillery personnel are realizing they do not have enough ammunition. The rest of the remaining four walls only have forty giant crossbows and forty catapults each. There is a width of a half mile to protect. Most of the remaining projectiles were in the first gate's munitions deposit and destroyed by the Atlanteans in their retreat. The Atlanteans have to rush to the third gate to retrieve more military supplies, but it is almost a half mile away. There are fewer men to transport artillery to the battlefront, and the second gate is not as well defended.

The Gambuts and Kayouts attack. Aten tries to evacuate as many warriors as possible before his first line of defense is completely destroyed. Atlantean men fight to save their fellow warriors. It gets to the point Aten has to order the second gate to be closed. Twelve thousand Atlanteans are trapped between the first and second gate. Aten cannot open the gate.

Aten looks at the trapped warriors as they fight their enemy. They fight for thirty minutes and kill their enemy and hold them off. Then the trapped archers run out of arrows. The twelve thousand Atlantean warriors fight valiantly. The archers pick up swords and daggers from their fallen comrades and fight to the death. The last two thousand Atlanteans at the first wall regroup in one final formation. Even though the Atlantean archers at the second wall give protection, the Gambuts and Kayouts push forward.

The last Atlantean commanding officer from the first wall stands between his men and his enemy.

He yells, "They want to take our God from our children and our culture. We are dead already. It is time to fight for God!"

The Atlantean infantry rushes to meet their enemy, knowing this is their last moment on earth. Aten watches from the second defensive position, and he has never been more proud and devastated at the same time as he watches his men die for honor and God. The emperor knows his civilization will never surrender so long as one man is still standing.

Emperor Aten swells with national pride and vengeance, and he now believes this is a Holy War. The Atlantean archers and artillery fire at the Kayouts and Gambuts as they march closer. Using God as their source of strength, the fearful and exhausted Atlanteans fight as if they have had the best sleep of their lives. Even though the Atlanteans have killed hundreds of thousands of men, there are still millions of enemy warriors to hold off. Aten has lost almost half of his men already.

Hours later, the Kayouts bring out the tightuses to fight to attack the Atlantean's second gate. Since the first gate is a half-mile away from Aten's second defense, the tightuses regroup and form a wall with their covered chariots.

Aten knows he will die here, and he blames himself for this attack. He feels as if he betrayed his fatherland. When he was twenty years old, he became Atlantean Emperor. He remembers the Great War almost twenty-seven years ago. His father was very imperialistic, and the rest of the world hated Atlantis for it. He feels he has let his people down. He wishes he had all of his warriors from Valtear and Mareth here to fight, and he wishes he had not tried to conquer Mareth.

Aten turns to General Playtarous, a general from the Atlantean capital, and says, "Go to my son and protect our capital. Tell him exactly what is happening here. I will not let you die with me today. Ride to meet my son, and serve him. I need good generals to help protect the empire when the enemy takes the last gate. You have seen how our enemy fights. Your knowledge and experience here will be beneficial in the battles to come."

It is almost nightfall, and the second gate is in jeopardy of being destroyed. The wall is being pounded with Gambut catapults. Projectile from the Atlantean artillery are not having much effect on the Kayout towers. Under Ryelyne's leadership, the Gambuts and Kayouts are well organized, but the Atlanteans are scrambling to put up a counteroffensive.

Aten orders the second gate to be abandoned, and the soldiers to retreat to defend the third gate. The tightuses destroy the second Atlantean defense. Some of the Atlantean infantrymen do not escape and are left behind to die to the last man, without fearing death. Even the Kayouts are proud to fight against such a noble military.

Aten fears the word of God and his culture will be destroyed. There are too many people against Atlantis and too few allies. The weight of the world is at Aten's doorstep. He thinks of his wife, and the soldiers that have fallen for him. Aten imagines his sons and his grandchildren to come. If only he had foreseen this war, he could have prevented it from happening. But he cannot change what is done. The Atlantean Emperor knows he needs to fight to the last man to give time for whatever his son may plan for the future. Even if it is Aten's last days on earth, he knows his warriors are behind him, and God will give him strength.

After the third gate cannot be held, Aten orders a retreat to the fourth gate where he regroups his men, and where the supply lines are shorter. Emperor Aten chooses to forfeit the third defensive gate, because he believes it will give them time to organize and put up a stronger fight at the fourth gate. The Atlantean men take every artillery piece and fall back.

Ryelyne watches the movement of the Atlantean soldiers and wonders why Aten is giving up the line of defense so quickly. The Gambut and Kayout Armies are slowed for a few hours because they have to take down the third gates.

Aten has won precious time. The Atlantean Emperor has decided not to leave the Great East Wall alive; he will lead his men and kill as many of his enemies as he can. If he puts up a strong fight, it will give the Atlantean cities more time to prepare a more formidable defense.

Aten's forefathers made Atlantis into the greatest empire on earth, and he fears he may be the one to let it be destroyed. The bells ring again. The Atlantean civilians are beginning to panic in their cities. The Atlantean armies inside the three main cities are preparing for the inevitable.

Even though Aten has lost two thirds of his men, he fights the attackers with vigorous force and determination. It takes almost twelve hours for the enemy to take the fourth line of the Atlantean defense. Before Aten is forced back to the fifth and final gate; the bells ring and tell the rest of his empire what is transpiring.

Daygun assembles his generals together to develop a strategy to protect the cities. Atlantean messengers come back and forth from the Great East Wall and the capital. Daygun has heard nothing from his army in Valtear or Mearth. The communication has been broken. The prince has no idea if his brother is dead or alive.

At the fifth Gate, Aten's remaining men hold off the invaders for another two days. The walls are fortified and well armed. It is the final stronghold. The dead of the enemy piles up as the Atlantean archers rain arrows upon them. Aten looks at the battlefield and sees his enemy has no end. The Atlantean dead at the fourth gate are cast aside and trampled by their enemy. Hundreds of thousands of men, mammoths, and elephants are dead on the battlefield. Aten wonders if he will be thrown in a ditch when it is all said and done.

The fifth gate is about to fall and Aten will not retreat. The Atlantean Emperor has fewer men to protect the last barrier to his homeland. Aten knows he will die right here; he considers everything he will miss while in the afterlife: the love of a woman, the affection of his sons, and the devotion of his men. He is proud of his men. He believes that if his men can die for him, he can die in their honor.

The Atlanteans only have two divisions left to hold the last line of defense. They are the best fighters of Atlantis. The Atlantean elite warriors scream for the chance to die with their emperor. Aten promises to die alongside them.

The Atlanteans open the last gate for an offensive attack. They entice their enemy to fight. Every last Atlantean arrow is bowed and every last projectile is fired from the fifth wall. There is only a trickle of supplies coming to Aten's front. At the bitter end, the Atlanteans have only swords and daggers. Aten gives the last order of his life. He stands on a platform with only thirty-eight thousand men under his command, fighting against seven million enemy warriors.

Aten gets in front of his officers and generals and says, "They will try to take God from our souls. They will take our last breath, but they can't take what we believe. Death is a stepping stone to God. Let us take that step in honor for Atlantis, and God."

The Atlanteans charge at their enemy. Aten stays in the center to lead his men into battle. The enemy arrows miss Aten's forces because of the terrain. The Atlanteans fight for hours. It is up to the last division of Aten's command to give time to Daygun to prepare the Atlantean cities.

In the background of the fight, the Atlantean grandmasters stand at attention to protect the men they made an oath to protect. All thirty-three fighters are ready to die at any given moment for their emperor. The grandmasters have been trained for this. Fighting for their emperor, the grandmasters feel as if they are fighting for God. To the grandmasters, this is the only way they can get to the after life in honor.

The fifth gate is destroyed and the Atlantean offensive starts to lose momentum. The Atlanteans have to retreat, and the Gambuts and Kayouts go through the gates while the Atlanteans have no choice but to fall back.

At this moment, Aten sees the Kayout flag and realizes he has been betrayed. The Atlantean Emperor trusted Melercertis.

The ranks of the Atlanteans fall, and most are slaughtered. There are no more arrows and no more technology for the Atlanteans to fall back on, and they fight for honor and God. Three hours into the fight, the Atlanteans are down to six thousand men. They can no longer withstand the enemy.

In the middle of fighting, an Atlantean General asks Aten to retreat.

Aten yells, "No, I will die here with my division and allow time for my son to prepare! Every second counts for the survival of our civilization."

One general says, "We can send a final message to Atlantis before the bells are taken. What is to be said to your people, sir?"

Aten says, "Tell my sons I love them, and it is time for me to die. Tell the Atlanteans to fight for God. It is up to Daygun to protect the Atlantean Empire. He is the Atlantean Emperor now."

The bells ring across the Atlantean Empire. Kaydence and Daygun receive the message. Even though the fighting is going on at the Great West Wall, Dareous, Quentoris, and Laptos hear the message from their emperor as well. The Atlantean Emperor is telling the Atlanteans not to fear their enemy, or they will take the whole Atlantean Empire.

In the meantime, Aten still stands at the last stronghold ready to die.

The fifth wall is completely destroyed, and the Gambut and Kayout warriors thrust through the walls. Aten scans the battlefield and sees the Kayout are rushing towards him. He now knows his time on earth is very limited. The Great West Wall was never the main thrust. The Atlanteans always thought the Great West Wall would fall first because it has only half the strength of the East. The Atlanteans thought exactly what Ryelyne wanted.

Aten says to one of his generals, "The Great West Wall was merely a diversion. Send a message to my son. Tell him to reinforce Halotropolis and for everyone to stand their ground. Tell him the Kayouts are involved."

The general responds, "Yes, sir."

Aten looks at his messenger and says, "A father has to die to make his sons become a better leader. I will stay here to die with my men. Tell my sons I will see him in the afterlife with God."

The Atlanteans are able to ring the bells one more time, and the whole Atlantean Empire listens to the message that Aten gives to Daygun. Every Atlantean knows their emperor will die. The Atlantean Prince stares at the direction of the bells, wishing they would deliver a different message, but he knows that will not happen.

No Atlantean can believe what they hear. The Atlanteans thought their outer defenses would never be breached. The Great East and West Walls were made to be indestructible.

Soon after, Aten is trapped in a pocket at the end of the mountains. Aten only has a thousand men to fight with him. The Kayouts and Gambuts generals are pushing closer to Aten. The Atlantean Emperor is at a post with his grandmasters. The Atlantean enemy annihilates the Atlantean infantry very quickly. The last fighters with Aten are fighting valiantly. The Gambuts want Aten dead; they want to destroy the Atlantean leader and demoralize the Atlantean's moral.

When the time comes, the Atlantean generals put themselves in front of the enemy to protect their emperor. The Atlantean generals fight and kill but to no avail. The generals stand their ground and die.

The Atlantean Emperor and the grandmasters are the last to fight. The grandmasters use their daggers and swords in close combat. The protectors of the Atlantean Emperor fight in unison. The grandmasters fight and defend each other. As one is about to die, a dagger flies through the air and gives another grandmaster time to regroup and take on another enemy warrior. But they can only withstand so much, and the grandmasters die one by one.

Aten and a few grandmasters are backed into a room inside the mountain. The grandmasters are tired, and cannot fight as they did twenty minutes earlier.

Aten sees a Kayout general and runs to fight him. A circle of Kayout warriors follow the fight. A Kayout general takes the challenge and fights the Atlantean Emperor one on one. The swords fly, and Aten runs his sword through the first general. After the fight, a Kayout archer shoots Aten with an arrow in the right side of his chest. Aten breaks off the arrow, and continues to fight other enemy warriors, killing each one he encounters. The Atlantean Emperor fights another enemy general, but every sword blow makes him weaker.

The wound from the arrow bleeds through Aten's armor, and weakens him. He cannot breathe. He uses every ounce of his remaining strength to fight the enemy general. With one of the sword thrusts from Aten, the enemy general counters and slices Aten's chest right through his armor. The Atlantean Emperor knows this is it. Aten loves every last breath he has left on earth. He tries to remember every breath he has taken, and then he dies.

At the Great East Wall, not a single one of the Atlanteans surrendered, or survived. Twelve divisions have been completely compromised from the Atlantean Army.

Every Gambut general and warrior kicks Aten's body. The hate for the Atlanteans has built up for so long. It is unleashed right here. Hate has filled the room. Aten lies there without honor to his enemy.

Ryelyne walks into the room where the emperor lays dead and he starts to kick the man he loved as a father. Aten's bones are broken and his face is beaten in. Ryelyne knows if he does not do the unthinkable, the Gambut and Kayout warriors will not respect him. They will think Ryelyne is still loyal to his homeland. His mission is still to save the handful of the Atlanteans who will be left after the war. Ryelyne has to do the unthinkable and do what the enemy wants to see.

Ryelyne considers the implications of what has occurred. By sending the Gambuts as the first wave and the Kanis to Atlantean Great West Wall, Ryelyne will have the most powerful army in the world after the war. The Kayout Empire has lost the least amount of warriors in this campaign so far. Thanks to the Atlanteans killing so many Gambut warriors, the Kayouts will most likely be the superpower of the world, and Ryelyne will be their emperor.

Ryelyne assembles the Kanis and Gambut generals to decide how they will continue into Atlantis. He convinces them into making a joint effort to be the first to attack Halotropolis. The hate for the Atlanteans makes the Gambuts agree to be the first, because they want to be remembered as the ones who defeated the Atlanteans' City of God.

After Ryelyne's victory, the Gambut and Kayout warriors will first come upon Halotropolis, but their warriors will not let the City of God fall without a fight. The Atlanteans have a good army and good defenses at Halotropolis. Every man, woman, and child is willing to die to protect their city. The next city is Masaba, and then, if they conquer both cities, they will have a clear path to Atlantis.

Back in Atlantis the next day, a scout comes to the Atlantean Military Council as Daygun is preparing a battle plan to protect his cities.

The scout kneels at Daygun's feet and says, "An Atlantean division is coming from our enemy; they have the colors of Ryelyne's command, and they are marching alone. There isn't a Kayout or Gambut force escorting them."

Daygun replies "Sound the bells and tell Ryelyne's division to stay five miles north of Halotropolis until further orders."

The Halotropolis bells ring and Ryelyne's division stops north of the City of God. Daygun sends a general to Ryelyne's division and asks why they were not killed in battle.

An hour later, the bells ring in emergency military code. An interpreter deciphers the code and says, "Miro says Melercertis didn't want to dishonor a favor from an honorable emperor, but had no choice. The Atlantean division sent to Kayout has been returned unharmed."

Daygun asks the interpreter, "Where is Ryelyne?"

"There was no message of his whereabouts," the interpreter replies.

Daygun has no clue to what to think of this; he does not know where Ryelyne is located. The new Atlantean Emperor wants answers before he allows Ryelyne's division to join the battle. Daygun knows it will be days before the enemy will be able to go forward to Halotropolis.

Six hours later, another messenger approaches Daygun and says, "Ryelyne and Acteon went to Valtear to help in the battle there. There are only a couple of captains in the division we sent to Kayout. Miro is the highest-ranking Atlantean officer. He also brings the Atlantean sword of our people back from Melercertis."

Daygun says, "Tell the division to go to Halotropolis and wait for our enemy, and tell them to bring our sword back to our capital. They are true Atlanteans, and they will defend our fatherland."

Daygun knows the whole world is against him, but he is prepared to die for Atlantis. Daygun is the new Atlantean Emperor and no emperor has ever been in such a complicated situation. Because of the death of his father, the new Atlantean Emperor stays by himself for the next couple of hours trying to ascertain why Ryelyne went to Valtear.

CHAPTER XVI
A YOUNGER BROTHER TAKES CHARGE

Outside the Great West Wall, Dareous, Laptos, and Quentoris, hear the bells, and they cannot believe their ears. The Great East Wall has been taken, and the Great West Wall is on its way. Nextear is catching up with Laptos' army and will intercept them within eight hours. The Atlanteans who fought at Bardia and won are now surrounded. Laptos' army has nowhere to run. He has no choice but to attack the enemy at the Great West Wall.

In the distance, Laptos' army can see the fighting against their homeland. From on top of a hill, he can see the Atlantean defenses are still intact.

Laptos, Quentoris, Laptos, and Tulles, go into a military tent and they discuss how to best help the warriors stationed at their border. They all feel God gave them the chance to live for a reason. The warriors who fought at Bardia are fatigued. The Atlantean warriors believe they will die right here. They cannot go anymore. The captains are worn down, and they cannot lead as they did days before.

Laptos grows angry about the negative energy, and leads the generals to a map on a table.

Laptos says in stern voice, "We have partial divisions, and we have four complete. We must break through to the walls of Atlantis. We are resupplied, and we have artillery."

Dareous replies, "I agree, but there is an army behind us and in front of us. Our scouts say Nextear's army is only hours away. We cannot take on his army."

158

Tulless says, "We must use the sea to enter Atlantis. We can help reinforce the Great West Wall divisions and not lose lives."

Laptos replies, "It will take days to get our armies transported by sea. There isn't enough time. We must fight and hit our enemy at the Great West Wall. If we take on the enemy here, they won't be able to move into Atlantis. Daygun will only have one army to deal with. If we destroy the enemy at the Great West Wall, it will make them reevaluate their battle plans. The bottleneck of the Great East Wall will slow down the enemy's advancement. The enemy's supplies and men will take days to regroup for an assault on the fatherland."

Quentoris says, "If we fight at the Great West Wall, the Atlantean archers will be able to protect us. If we can get close enough to the walls, we can protect Atlantis on this side of the border. The enemy will be fighting two fronts."

Laptos replies, "It isn't the survival of Atlantis, but the word of God. Our God will be nonexistent if we don't act now. God's name will be extinguished from man's memory forever if we don't act quickly."

Quentoris says, "I agree. Aten's name will die in vain. The emperor gave up his life at the Great East Wall. We will do the same here."

Laptos and the generals leave the tent, and they start to give orders to their men. The Atlantean generals have given themselves a reason to fight, and they go in every direction to prepare their armies for battle. The Atlanteans do not have much time. All generals give orders and are ready to attack their aggressors at the Great West Wall within forty-five minutes. Nextear's army will be able to attack Laptos within six hours.

Laptos, Dareous, Quentoris, and Tulless form their armies as one. Laptos knows they only have one chance at this. The Atlanteans and Valteareans have been training together for months. The armies form into military protocol, and they stand with discipline and honor. The men are ready to die right here to give Atlantis a chance to survive. Laptos and Tulless' military may not defeat the enemy, but they will catch them by surprise.

Laptos' army blows their horns and starts to march towards their invaders at the Great West Wall. The Atlanteans stationed at the Valtearean and Gambut border see Atlanteans warriors coming over the hill.

The language barrier between the Kayouts and Gambuts are hindering them from forming a strong defense from the advancing Atlanteans. Most of the enemy's scouts have already been killed by the Atlantean patrols, and the Gambuts and Kayouts at the Great West Wall underestimate Laptos' numbers. Because Nextear's armies are coming closer, the Atlanteans do not have much time. Laptos orders his men to stop.

Mounted on his horse, Laptos yells towards his men, "This is God's first real battle. No one on this side of the wall believes in God except for us. Our enemy wants to destroy our way of life. I will not let that happen under my command. Because of one name, we must give our lives to Him. Life isn't given to us. It is earned. Fight for God. Fight for me."

Laptos' men cheer for their commander.

Outside the Atlantean Great West Wall, the enemy generals are having difficulty in making formations in time to give a strong enough defense. All of their light and heavy cavalry are at the Great East Wall of Atlantis. The enemy is fortified to protect themselves from the Great West Wall bombardment, but never expected an enemy to attack their flank. The Atlanteans charge towards the enemy as a force never seen before. The advancing Atlanteans are determined to get back to their homeland.

The Atlantean cavalry charge in and create havoc, and opens a hole for Quentoris' infantry. Even though the Atlanteans cavalry is small in numbers, they are like a brick hitting glass, and it shatters the formations of their enemy. Right behind the Atlantean heavy cavalry, the Atlantean infantry led by Quentoris is making a larger hole towards the Great West Wall. The Atlantean elite division pushes back their enemy's reinforcements with ease. Laptos does not care about his own life; he only cares about saving his fatherland.

After forty minutes, the Atlantean infantry pushes the enemy back into the Alber Mountains. But, the Mareth and the Kanis led by Nextear are still moving closer. The Atlanteans are about to get pinched. Laptos' army fights harder. The Atlantean artillery is put in place and starts to bombard the enemy in its stronghold. It took some time for Laptos' artillery to get into position, but it is a huge blow to the enemy. The projectiles are like waves crashing against the shore. It is perfectly timed, and no army can withstand such an onslaught.

Dareous looks at the engagement and yells, "Fire!"

Every Atlantean projectile is fired from their artillery. It pounds the enemy until they have to pull back. The Atlantean infantry can feel the projectiles going over their heads. The projectiles explode seventy yards from where they are fighting. In doing so, the trapped attacking Kayouts and Gambuts have nowhere to run. The Kayouts and Gambuts cannot reinforce their men attacking Laptos' advance. The aggressors to the Great West Wall watch while a quarter of their men are slaughtered by the Atlanteans. Laptos' artillery is pushed forward to attack other positions of their enemy. The sequence of firing is so intense; it confuses the Atlantean enemy even more.

Nextear's army arrives, and is forming its ranks to fight the Atlanteans. The Atlantean artillery personnel, on the Valtearean side, fire their last artillery piece and ride to Quentoris' infantry. Dareous decides to burn and destroy what is left of their artillery.

All of Laptos' army fight towards Atlantis. The Atlantean General in command of the Great West Wall is ordered to open the gate. It only takes an hour for Laptos' army to fight back into their homeland. Laptos' archers run up the walls and reinforce their comrades.

Dareous and the others climb to the walkway of the Great West Wall. The Atlantean generals and Tulles run on top of the main tower and look over the battlefield. They all rest for an hour and say nothing of what just happened. The Atlanteans stationed at the Great West Wall are holding back their enemy. Laptos tells the Atlantean generals he will meet them in the Military Chamber in one hour.

An hour later, the chamber room is silent. Laptos paces back and forth.

Laptos says to Dareous, "We got lucky today. The enemy will regroup with Nextear's reinforcements. There are still millions of men to fight against us here. How many divisions do we have here?"

Dareous replies, "We have the Atlantean youth archers and five other divisions."

Laptos says, "This gives us almost nine divisions, but few munitions. We need something to fire. Send a message to the city of

Masaba and tell them to send us munitions. The enemy will attack with larger strength when they regroup. We need weapons to keep them at bay. If we win here, my brother will only have to face one front at Halotropolis. I need at least six divisions to stand here. I will leave Dareous and Quentoris in command here. I want every bow and arrow on the walls, including our youth archers. The Great West Wall has enough ordnance to withstand the enemy for three more days. With the extra archers, the wall will last two more days. It will take three days to get the munitions from Masaba. On the sixth day, I want you to retreat to Atlantis. I will reinforce Masaba. Fight until you can't and then get out of here."

Quentoris says, "Thank you sir. I will defend the Great West Wall with my life."

Laptos replies, "I want a full division to go to the City of God. I know my brother is building up our defenses there. I want Halotropolis to know we stand behind them. I will go to Masaba and wait for orders from my brother. I believe the city is the key to this war. I need to be close to Atlantis and Halotropolis. I will take two divisions with me."

The bells ring from the Great West Wall and Daygun is alerted of his brother's plan. Daygun then gathers his generals together at the Atlantean Military Hall. The Atlantean generals celebrate the good news of the Great West Wall and do not give up hope. It is a boost to Daygun's morale; he is torn with emotions about his father's death and his brother's being alive. Everyone in the Empire is waiting on what Daygun is going to do next. Everyone is ready to fight. Daygun walks to the center of the Atlantean Military Hall. The Atlantean generals are silent, giving Daygun their undivided attention.

Daygun says, "I am so proud of my brother; he's inside the Great West Wall of Atlantis. I was going to reinforce our Western defense, but my brother has already done that. We have six divisions there holding back our enemy. Because of the terrain of the Alber Mountains, it will take some time before the enemy can take it. If we hold the Great West Wall, the enemy will have to attack Halotropolis first. Our main forces should be there. The City of God is impenetrable to any enemy, but we all said that about the Great East Wall. The enemy wants to destroy our society. The City of God is the place to do that. The enemy has hate toward our people and our God. We will use that hate to our advantage. We will take three divisions from Atlantis and defend the City of God. In total, it will give us thirteen divisions to protect the walls of Halotropolis. This is our land, not our enemy's. I will not lose it to people that do not believe in God. If Halotropolis falters, I want the Great West Wall divisions to retreat here to Atlantis. It will take every man on earth to destroy us, and the enemy has already lost hundreds of thousands of warriors. Yes, our enemy won a victory at the Great East Wall, but at what cost? Hundreds of years from now, our historians will say we won at the Great East Wall. We have destroyed two million enemy warriors at the cost of little life of our own. We will fight to the last Atlantean. If we die, our society will be remembered for the rest of time. If we die as men and fight for God, God will not let us be forgotten."

Daygun nods to his servant to make a large circle with a container of salt. When the circle is finished, Daygun orders it to be washed away. There is nothing but a wet floor and salt scattered outside the circle. Everyone in the room looks at him in puzzlement.

Daygun says, "The water pushed the salt outside the circle. We are brothers of Atlantis. I want every leader of the Atlantean Empire to reenter the circle. In doing so, it will show that we are brothers of war to protect our fatherland. We will make our own circle with our souls and determination. Our enemies may try to wash away our civilization, but it is up to the individual to reenter the circle to make it complete, and bring the circle back together. By coming back in the circle, we will come together as our forefathers did centuries before to defeat our enemy."

Every leader and general reenters the circle. There is no hesitation. This is the way of the land. Daygun stands tall. He knows that everyone is ready to take on the world and is willing to die for Atlantis. What is done on earth is done. The Atlanteans are not going to stand down.

The Atlantean crowd cheers in support of their new Atlantean Emperor. It is time for Daygun to become the man his father envisioned him to be. He knows how to lead and inspire the people around him.

All is done. Laptos goes to Masaba and regroups with the Atlantean divisions there. Laptos knows that the enemy will try to take the City of God. Daygun might need him to out flank their enemy. Laptos also knows the key to the war is Masaba. Masaba is only a three hour march from the Great West Wall, while Halotropolis is a full day's journey.

If the Great West Wall falls, those remaining soldiers will reinforce Atlantis. The enemy will have to take Halotropolis and Masaba to even think of taking Atlantis. Even though the enemy won at the Great East Wall, they will suffer heavy casualties in trying to enter the core of the Atlantean Empire. The enemy has lost over two million men at the Great East Wall and at Bardia. The enemy still has nine million men committed to the campaign to destroy Atlantis.

Back at the Great West Wall, Quentoris reinforces the walls just as the enemy attacks. There are two million enemy men there at the Valtearean border, but the terrain of the mountains help keep the enemy from entering the Atlantean Empire. Only two hundred and fifty thousand enemy men can attack the Great West Wall at any given time. There the Atlantean archers have no trouble killing the soldiers below. Every arrow hits its target without even aiming. It is almost impossible for the enemy to transport their artillery across the rough terrain.

The Atlanteans thought the Great West Wall was weaker, but the Alber Mountains actually make it stronger than the East. The mountain valleys are too small for large artillery like the Kayout tightuses. The Atlanteans hold the upper ground and use their artillery to destroy any small enemy artillery that comes near their gate.

Laptos finally reaches the walls of Masaba. There, he is welcomed by the king. Laptos takes command of the cities' military. In the case of war, the emperor's family takes complete control of all military decisions, and he gives the people of Masaba hope.

When word came back about the battle of Bardia to the Atlantean masses, Laptos instantly became a respected hero. Even though it was Dareous' command at Bardia, Daygun's brother was Supreme Commander of the Mearth Campaign. He defeated the army that attacked Valtear and the Great West Wall. The Atlanteans are in desperate times and need a hero. He has brought one more division with him to Masaba. The city is not as fortified as Halotropolis, but is in good position to defend itself.

There is a little time for rest. Laptos goes to the military room in Masaba, and he cries for his father. He finally accepts his father's death, and knows there is a great deal of pressure on his shoulders. He needs time to reconfigure his emotions and the love for his father. Even though Laptos did not agree with what his father said all the time, he will carry out his father's dream for Atlantis.

The two brothers communicate back and forth from city to city. The whole Atlantean Empire knows Laptos stands behind his brother, and Daygun is in charge. Even though Laptos has a substantial victory under his belt, he knows the Atlanteans needs only one real leader, and Daygun is that person. Laptos has looked up to his brother all of his life, and it will not change now. With them communicating back and forth, the whole Atlantean Empire regains hope and is ready to face their enemy.

Kaydence is stationed in the City of God. She is going over battle plans with the Halotropolean generals and keeps their Senate stable. With more divisions coming to Haylos' city-state, Daygun is also is ready for what is about to come. Woman and children evacuate the city. But there are many who will not leave Halotropolis. They feel they are abandoning God.

The Atlantean enemy is regrouping. Supplies are being brought from their east to the front. It is only days before the enemy has enough resources to go forward. Daygun hears from his scouts, and knows he must put up a stand. The Atlanteans know the enemy will have to go through Halotropolis first to completely take Atlantis. Because of this, Halotropolis has made very good fortifications to reinforce their defenses. If the enemy bypasses Halotropolis, the Atlanteans can take their enemy on both sides and out flank them from three sides. The enemy will try to take Halotropolis first and Masaba second. The enemy knows it will require everything they have to conquer the capital city of Atlantis.

The next day, the bells ring. The Atlantean Great West Wall is not being attacked anymore. The new Atlantean Emperor knows the enemy will go around through the Great East Wall. The enemy leaves five hundred thousand men to keep Dareous and Quentoris from attacking their rear.

In three days, the Mearth and Kanis military will enter through the destroyed Great East Wall. Daygun knows there will be nearly nine million enemy warriors at the walls of Halotropolis. As a leader to his people, he has no true plan. It is overwhelming. Millions of lives are in his hands.

Daygun stands at the palace and wonders why the world is against him. To him, the rest of the world is primitive. Mankind is not ready for what the Atlanteans can give to the world. The Eastern World lives in villages. The average Eastern village has a population of three hundred people. Every one of the small communities lives off the land and does not see technology as being important. The Eastern family is very connected and small. In their world, they are content with very little. The Atlanteans believe in the power of one God, but to the people who live on the continent, they do not understand how one God can do everything. It is incomprehensible to their culture.

Daygun brings all the generals and admirals together at the Atlantean Military Hall; he hates the Eastern World for the death of his father. Atlantean technology helped the people in other empires, but they respond with violence and hatred. The Kayouts tried to show some honor by giving back Ryelyne's division, but the Kayouts still betrayed Daygun's empire. He is furious and wants to destroy his enemy. The main strength of the Atlantean Empire is their navy, and he wants to use it to their advantage. At the Atlantean Military Hall, Daygun points at a large map on the table.

Daygun says, "We haven't been attacked by sea yet. We must scout our waters. It's going to happen. The enemy is waiting for something at the Great East Wall. We need to find out what they are waiting for. If the enemy is close to Halotropolis, their navy will land near their army to resupply them. They will try to reinforce their thrust into our fatherland by sea. Send ships to the northern part of the Eastern Atlantean Sea. We will find every ship of the Eastern World there."

Admiral Ashastonous is Supreme Commander of the Atlantean fleet. He was third in command of all Atlantean generals. He is six feet tall, slender, with a short beard, and was top of his class in military school.

Admiral Ashastonous responds, "How can you be so sure, sir?"

Daygun says, "Our enemy has a great deal of momentum right now. Why did our enemy pause? I don't think the enemy's main supply lines are going to be brought through land. It has to be sent by sea. The enemy armies at the Great West Wall are regrouping with the East. With the numbers of our enemy, they need a great deal of supplies. Because the terrain from the continent to our empire is hard to get the resources needed, I believe a good portion will come by sea. Also, they are going to try to exterminate our people. The only way they can do that is to prevent an escape. If they conquer our cities, the sea will be our only way of escape."

Admiral Ashastonous replies, "I will destroy every ship that comes near our shores."

Daygun says, "Protect both sides. Use our scout ships to find the enemy. You won't have to look very hard."

Admiral Ashastonous replies, "It will take two full days to assemble our fleets together. I will start at once."

Daygun says, "Based on what our spies have told me, the Kayouts and Gambuts will march in about a week. I have a feeling we will be attacked by sea in four days. The next few days are crucial. Our navy is stronger than all navies in the world combined. There is no navy that can defeat us. The Kayouts must have made a strong navy, but they don't know of our battlecruisers. They have been made in total secret."

Ashastonous asks, "What if we are wrong, sir?"

Daygun says, "If I'm wrong, we're all dead. This is the only way they can reinforce their army right now. If not, they would have already attacked Halotropolis. Order every civilian ship to start evacuating the sick and injured warriors from the peninsula to our stronghold at the delta."

Ashastonous goes to the East Atlantean Sea with his Armada, and Vice Admiral Radious takes his main fleet to the West Atlantean Sea just in case.

The enemy from the Great West Wall has moved to the Great East Wall. Daygun knows they are waiting for something, but what?

CHAPTER XVII
THE UNKNOWN HERO

At Vasic, Ashastonous goes to the Atlantean flagship; the most powerful ship in the world. The heavy battlecruiser is the largest of all ships in any navy. The Atlanteans built two heavy battlecruisers. The two flagships are twice as large as the other ten Atlantean cruisers and have twice the artillery. The Atlanteans need a victory at sea, and their sailors are ready to die for their empire.

If Ashastonous loses, or cannot find the enemy before the Kayout Empire can reinforce supplies, the morale of the Atlanteans will lose momentum. Ashastonous believes the key to saving the Atlantean Empire will lie in his hands. Even though the Atlanteans have seen the ships from the East, they do not know their military tactics. When the negotiations between the two superpowers began, Ashastonous saw the enemy ships, but he does not know how many are out there. Are there larger ships? The Atlantean Admiral does not know enough about the enemy. He will go to sea and defend his beaches the best way he can.

At this point, seven new Atlantean destroyers have been built since the negations between Kayouts and Atlanteans. The new Atlantean destroyers are larger, faster and better armed than their counterparts. This gives the Atlantean fleet eighty-five destroyers, ten cruisers and two massive heavy battlecruisers. Almost a hundred Atlantean ships will go against the rest of the world.

The Kanis and Mareth Navies are very weak. The two empires have almost nothing. The Atlantean spies have seen their ships and are not scared of a sea battle coming from the Northern Empires. Because the Mareth and Kanis harbors are so far away, it will take weeks before they can even hit the shores of Atlantis. Ashastonous has sent scout ships to the West Atlantean Sea. He ordered the scouts to go farther out to sea to give ample time to counter any invasion.

Admiral Ashastonous has also assigned all military cargo ships into the effort. Every ship that can hold a catapult or giant crossbow has been given over to their sea effort. In the city of Vasic, every man, woman, and child has been raised to go to sea. Sons work with their fathers on the ships, and they both go into battle together.

Because of the distance, the enemy will be unable to surprise the Atlantean Navy. The Atlantean scouts will spot the enemy days before even getting close to Atlantis. In that amount of time, the whole Atlantean Navy can concentrate their forces to destroy their enemy. The Atlanteans do not think the West Atlantean Sea will be the main thrust of any amphibious attack, so they concentrate their main forces to the East.

Vice Admiral Radious is stationed on the west side of Atlantis, and will use military cargo ships to protect the West Atlantean Sea. Ashastonous gave the Vice Admiral the other heavy battlecruiser because his navy is weak. Because Radious might need speed, the Admiral also gave him the new fleet of seven destroyers.

Over the years, the city of Vasic has stockpiled ship catapults and giant crossbows. Radious prepares his ships for battle. Every woman and child in Vasic helps in the war effort. Children carry arrows to the Western Fleet. The women help in the placement of the navy artillery aboard their ships. The men reinforce the ships with shields, and put rams to the front of the military cargo ships. The ships are not armored as well as the Atlantean destroyers, but are similar in body style. The ships' hulls are thicker, to support the weight of land artillery and cavalry. For speed, the ship's sails are larger to compensate. The converted ships are slow if there is little wind, and the sides are thin. If an enemy catapult throws their projectile at the sides of the military cargo ships, it can inflict heavy damage.

Because the Kayout Empire is so vast, there is no way of knowing how many ships are in their navy. The Atlantean spies have seen some of the dry docks building the Kayout battlecruisers, but the Atlantean planters have not seen every dry dock in Melercertis' empire. The Atlantean planters have heard of such dry docks, but they are only a myth. If it was a secret to be kept from the Atlanteans, the Kayout battlecruisers would have been built hundreds of miles away from any city or population. This is a concern for Ashastonous. He is hoping he can catch the enemy by surprise and strike on his terms. The Admiral of the Eastern Fleet can only count on the discipline and tactics of his men.

The next day, the main Atlantean fleet converges together in the East Atlantean Sea. The fleet is ninety-five miles east of Halotropolis. God's city is thirty miles from the east beach and thirty-five miles southeast from the Great East Wall. Ryelyne's army is ten miles deep into the Atlantean Empire, but their enemy does not move. The enemy that took the Atlantean Great East Wall is waiting for something.

This is where Ashastonous waits. The scout ships report to the flagship, but they have found nothing suspicious. Every twenty minutes, Admiral Ashastonous receives an update. There are many islands in the area; all of them are part of the Atlantean Empire. They are also the eyes for the Eastern Fleet. If anything is sighted, the Atlantean towers will be set on fire. The towers can be seen twenty miles from the islands; any Atlantean scout ship can see the towers and inform their Atlantean Admiral.

The Atlantean planters believe the Kayouts are too organized not to have a powerful navy. Melercertis' empire has also been building up their defenses and taking iron ore and bronze from their neighbors. At the same time, the pride of the Ashastonous' navy makes him feel as if they are invincible. He has worked with his captains and trusts their judgment in battle. Most of the captains are veterans; they know how to fight on water. Only the best officers command the new battlecruisers.

On the other hand, Ashastonous sees the enemy's navy as a herd of wild horses coming towards him. He knows they will not be as organized as his fleet. The Kayouts are too vast and do not have the same training as the Atlanteans, but the unpredictability concerns him. The Atlantean ships will attack as one, and the enemy war ships will escort their supply ships. Ashastonous plans to take out the enemy supply ships first. If he sinks the supply ships, the Kayouts' war machine will quickly crumble. The Kayouts need to supply their warriors on the Atlantean mainland. There are supplies coming from the Continental Alliance, but it is too slow for what they need in this campaign. The enemy needs supplies fast, and in great quantity. The Gambut and Kayout mountains are slowing down supply lines to their front. It will take weeks to move needed resources to the enormous Kayout, and Gambut armies.

That night, Ashastonous looks towards some islands; there is not any sign of the enemy. Nothing is happening yet, but why? Ashastonous looks at the bright full moon and wonders if the enemy is looking at the same moon and waiting for battle.

The Atlantean battlecruiser captains are on board the flagship for a late dinner with the Atlantean Admiral to discuss battle tactics. The dining area can easily accommodate ninety people. The woodwork and craftsmanship is equal to the Kayouts.

No one drinks or eats in gluttony throughout the night. All the captains eat slowly as if this is their last meal. Because no one knows what is out there, the Atlantean captains have no concrete battle plans. The captains are not afraid of how to fight or die; they fear what they do not know.

Ashastonous stands and says, "We are here to fight the enemy, and there is no enemy. But they're out there. Our scout ships see nothing, but gentlemen, our antagonists are coming. We have almost a hundred ships. Tomorrow we might fight a hundred ships, or a thousand. It makes no difference. We will protect our fatherland. We may die tomorrow or grieve for our comrades. You might grieve for me as a brother in war. I look at everyone here, and I know this may be the last time I see your faces. We are Atlanteans, and we are ready to die for our empire. The enemy may defeat us on land, but not at sea. If we all work together and fight together, without the fear of dying, we will be victorious. Each step in life is hard, and each following step is harder than the one before. Life is nothing but challenges. It is the challenge that makes us better. Mark my words; the enemy doesn't know what's going to hit them."

The night goes on. The Atlantean captains have been friends for years, and they talk about everything else but what could happen the next day. No one knows what to expect, but every officer has complete confidence in Ashastonous' leadership. Because the captains have to wake up at daybreak, they all depart before midnight.

The next morning on the other side of the Atlantean Sea, Vice Admiral Radious' scout ships find an enemy fleet coming towards them. The Atlantean Western Fleet has one heavy battlecruiser, seven new destroyers, and forty converted military cargo ships at his disposal. To Vice Admiral Radious, the Kanis and Mareth are planning a landing on the west side of Atlantis as well. The enemy's fleet is only twenty miles northwest of Radious' fleet. An Atlantean scout ship sends word back to the Western Fleet very quickly. A lieutenant of the scout ship goes to Radious and salutes him.

The lieutenant says, "There are fifty-six ships about the size of our destroyers coming towards are fleet. Behind them are ninety-seven troop and supply ships. Surrounding them are ten more war vessels. The fifty-six enemy ships are coming at full speed towards us. What are your orders, sir?"

Radious replies, "We must take out the supply and transport ships to protect our shores. My flagship will break away right before we engage the enemy. I want all destroyers to break left with me and try to lure some of the enemy destroyers to follow my fleet. Half of our converted cargo ships will then engage the fifty-six enemy destroyers. While we are looking as if we are going around after their supply ships, the enemy will try to protect their main supply and transport fleet and follow me and our destroyers. The enemy fleet will split up. This will give our military cargo ships an advantage. Half of our converted cargo ships will engage the main charge from the enemy, and the other half will follow the enemy who follows me. When the enemy is at a safe distance from the main engagement, I will then turn around and meet the divided enemy dead on, and we will take them on two fronts. It won't be easy, but it's the only way we will win. Go lieutenant; tell the rest of the fleet."

The orders spread to the captains, and the Atlantean warriors prepare their artillery for battle.

Looking at the enemy fleet ahead, Radious goes to the front of the ship.

Radious yells, "All ships full ahead."

The sails go higher and the oarsmen pull faster. The waves get louder as the Atlantean fleet gains speed. The enemy comes towards the Atlanteans straight on with fifty-six Kanis and Mearth destroyers. It takes less than an hour for the two fleets to get close. Three miles before the engagement, the Atlantean flagship and destroyers break left as if they are going around the main thrust of the enemy force. Almost half of the enemy ships follow the flagship, just like Radious predicted. The enemy wants the Atlantean heavy battlecruiser as a trophy. They have never seen an Atlantean ship this large before.

Before the engagement, the Kanis and Mearth have heard rumors of the colossal ship, but no enemy has seen one. The Atlantean heavy battlecruiser is a complete surprise to the enemy. The enemy knows they must take out Radious' ship first to eradicate fear among their sailors.

One mile before the main enemy fleets engage the Atlanteans; half of the Atlantean cargo ships break off from the oncoming main attack and follow the enemy pursuing Radious. The military tactic starts to work. Radious will turn around at the right moment and attack the pursuing enemy fleet. Vice Admiral Radious will wait until the enemy is too far to be helped by their main fleet. Radious will destroy one enemy fleet at a time with his new heavy battlecruiser.

Radious goes to the rear of the ship to see the enemy fleet following and the captain slows his speed ready to turn around.

Radious yells, "Keep going; pull the enemy away from the main assault."

Fifteen minutes later, twenty Atlantean cargo ships run against twenty-eight enemy destroyers at the original line of engagement. The main Atlantean sea battle is commanded by Holtair. The engagement starts at one o'clock in the afternoon. Both sides shoot their artillery and ram into each other. The Atlanteans concentrate on the oars and sails of the enemy ships and fire rounds of projectiles at their enemy. The Atlantean projectiles are far superior to those of the Kanis and Mareth ships. Holtair's fleet is able shoot their projectiles twice as fast. Even though the enemy has more artillery aboard their ships, the training and better weapons are in favor of the Atlanteans.

At the main sea battle, Holtair's fleet attacks in teams of two. The Atlanteans target the outer enemy ships first. As soon as one enemy ship is disabled, the Atlanteans prey on the next closest ship. Even when an Atlantean ship is under attack, they do not disengage until the main objective is destroyed or disabled.

During the first engagement, Holtair sees a weakness in the configuration of enemy warships. He sees two enemy ships stationary firing on one of his military cargo ships.

Holtair points at the front of his ship and yells, "Fire dead center of their formation. Concentrate there before we have no choice but to regroup."

Holtair's ship rams the oars of one enemy destroyer and fires his projectiles at another at the same time. Both enemy ships fire back and damage his ship in a crossfire allowing the other Atlantean cargo ship to escape from certain destruction.

In the first round of ship to ship combat, Holtair's ship is somewhat damaged, but is still operational. The Atlanteans and enemy ships regroup quickly, and another battle begins as both fleets gain speed for ramming. The battle goes on for twenty minutes before all ships have to turn around again.

On the second engagement, six of the enemy ships are sinking or on fire, and three of the Atlanteans ships are on their way to the ocean floor.

The enemy supply and transport ships realize their warships are in trouble, and flee to the north.

Holtair sees Davin's ship very close and moves towards him.

Holtair yells from his ship to Davin, "Take your battle group and take out our main objective!"

Davin yells back, "If I leave, it will leave you ten ships against twenty-one. I can't leave. You will be destroyed within thirty minutes!"

Holtair responds, "That is an order!"

Seven Atlantean converted cargo ships leave the main engagement to attack their main objective before the third engagement starts. The Atlantean ships are twice as fast as the enemy supply ships.

Holtair remains at the main sea battle. The enemy supply and support ships are the Atlanteans' main objective. Holtair's ships start their third run. He must keep the twenty-one enemy ships from either going after Radious, or after Commander Davin's small fleet. Davin is going against the wind and his sails are inefficient. The enemy's warships can catch up with Davin's fleet pretty quickly if they disengage Holtair's fleet.

The next engagement goes poorly for the Atlantean. Holtair's loses three ships, and the enemy loses four. The Atlanteans keep fighting on. Radious looks back and sees Holtair's fleet being destroyed, but he cannot do any thing about it.

A lieutenant runs to Radious and looks him in the eye.

The lieutenant says, "We must turn around and help Holtair's fleet."

Radious replies, "If we turn around right now, we will all be destroyed. Holtair is an Atlantean warrior and he will die as one. I will see him in the next life, and I will clap for him as I walk towards him in the afterlife."

On the fourth engagement, the enemy destroys the rest of Holtair's fleet, but the Atlantean Commander does take seven enemy ships out of action. The Atlantean's main fleet is completely disabled or sinking. From the main battle, the rest of the enemy ships limp towards the Atlantean heavy battlecruiser.

What is left of Holtair's fleet tries to save the Atlantean warriors floating in the water, but the Atlanteans have lost at the main engagement. While trying to save his men from the water, Holtair can see Davin's fleet catching up with the enemy supply ships.

Radious goes to his stern and yells at Herous, "Assist our seven ships going after the main supply fleet!"

Herous, the commander of the seven Atlantean destroyers responds, "Yes, sir!"

Because of the distance between the Atlantean destroyers and Davin's fleet, Davin will reach the enemy supply and transport fleet first. Radious knows if even one enemy transport or supply ship is destroyed, it will be one less round of supplies, or one less reinforcement attacking the beaches of his fatherland.

Radious does what he planned. He turns the flagship around to attack the twenty-eight enemy ships pursuing him. He also has ten enemy ships coming towards him from the main sea battle which just destroyed Holtair's fleet. The twenty Atlantean military cargo ships, which broke off the main engagement, commanded by Prowless, attack their enemy from the rear. The twenty-eight enemy ships turn around to attack in response. The enemy ships engage the Atlanteans military cargo ships, and the remaining enemy ships from the main battle are going towards Prowless' fleet.

The Atlantean destroyers break away and sail full speed after the enemy supply fleet. Radious knows Prowless' cargo ships will be destroyed if he cannot reach them in time. The hardest decision has been made. Radious had a choice of either going after the enemy transport fleet or going against the thirty-eight enemy ships which are and will engage Prowless' fleet. He made the choice of helping his own men. It will take the flagship hours to catch up to the enemy supply ships, but Vice Admiral Radious cannot leave his men to die.

The twenty-eight enemy ships, which were following the flagship, are attacking Prowless' fleet, and ten more are on there way from the original battle.

The second sea battle begins with the Atlantean flagship going full speed towards the battle. After the first run, the Atlantean cargo ships disable six enemy ships. At the same time, the Atlanteans lose eight of their own. The Atlantean ships start to sink and hundreds of Atlantean sailors abandon ship. Radious is moving closer to the sea battle, but the Mareth and Kanis ships are preparing for another attack against Prowless' fleet. Radious feels helpless at this point.

Vice Admiral Radious goes to the front of his ship.

Radious yells to the captain, "Get the artillery ready. Fire dead center on our enemy and then fire to our stern to destroy their main thrust."

Right in the middle of the enemy attacking Prowless, Radious' flagship enters the battle. The Atlantean heavy battlecruiser is so large it is able to use its artillery to sink three enemy destroyers before the enemy even knows it. This is the first time the Atlantean heavy battlecruiser has seen combat, and it is better than Vice Admiral Radious expected.

Radious still loses the military cargo ships out of range of their flagship. The enemy destroyers attack the Atlantean cargo ships as if the Atlantean heavy battlecruiser is not even there. Radious keeps sinking enemy ships, but loses more of his own fleet in the meantime. Because there is so much confusion, Prowless' fleet gets divided and unable to go on the offensive.

The Atlantean flagship blasts off artillery and their archers launch arrows onto their enemy ships. The flagship is there as if it is a fort in the sea. The disabled Atlantean cargo ships limp to the flagship for protection and try to repair their vessels. In the background, most of Holtair's cargo ships are sinking, and the Atlantean men do every thing to keep their ships afloat.

After the confusion, Radious sees that there are only eighteen enemy destroyers left. The Kanis and Mareth destroyers regroup for another run. The enemy Admiral has ordered his captains to knock out Prowless' fleet first.

The run begins. The Atlantean cargo ships know they are outgunned, but still attack their adversary. Because the Kanis and Mareth destroyers are concentrating only on Prowless' fleet, the Atlantean heavy battlecruiser destroys ten enemy vessels, but the enemy disables or sinks most of the Atlantean military cargo ships. The ten enemy ships from the main attack reach the sea battle and rains havoc on Prowless' remaining fleet.

After thirty minutes of fighting, the flagship and the severely damaged Prowless' fleet take out their enemy. The Atlantean flagship was able to repel most attackers, but sustains damage itself. Most of Prowless' fleet is sinking and the remainder of his fleet is on rescue operations. There are hundreds of Atlanteans swimming from sinking and burning ships. Radious could not reach his fleet in time. Only Davin's fleet, Herous' destroyers, and the flagship go on; they are the only ships left from the Atlantean fleet to attack the enemy transport and supply ships.

After Radious battle tactic, there are only twelve enemy destroyers left of the second sea battle. The enemy Admiral does not want to go against the Atlantean heavy battlecruiser. The enemy decides to help out their supply feet. The enemy Admiral will try to regroup with their ten destroyers which are inside the supply and transport fleet.

There are hundreds of sailors floating in the sea. The disabled ships, from both sides, pull out their survivors. Some ships are on fire, while others are sinking. The flagship pulls as many Atlantean men out of the water as it can. By this time, the battle has gone on for two and a half hours. The Atlanteans heavy battlecruiser chases after the twelve enemy destroyers.

The seven Atlantean cargo ships that went towards the enemy supply ships are attacking. Commander Davin attacks the troop ships first. The enemy supply ships have some artillery, but are very slow. The Atlanteans attack the enemy's oars, and use their projectiles to set the enemy supply ships on fire. It is a well-executed attack. No Atlantean cargo ship is sunk, but all Atlantean ships take some damage.

During the battle, thousands of arrows are shot at Davin's fleet from the enemy supply vessels. Dozens of Atlanteans warriors are killed because they are on deck. The enemy arrows are even able to seep through the portal of the Atlantean oarsmen. Atlantean officers have to throw out the dead through the portal and take over rowing. Right behind them are Herous' seven Atlantean destroyers. The Atlantean flagship will take forty-five minutes to catch up with the enemy fleet.

During the first run of Davin's attack, six enemy troop ships are damaged and on fire. The ten enemy destroyers are inside their supply fleet. Commander Davin tells the rest of his military cargo ships to attack the enemy destroyers. The Atlanteans use the enemy supply ships as cover and attack the destroyers as a team. In doing so, Davin's fleet disables three enemy destroyers. However, Davin's fleet only has three ships left, and the twelve enemy destroyers that destroyed Prowless' fleet are quickly approaching. Commander Davin decides to retreat and wait for the Atlantean destroyers. They go at an angle so the Atlantean destroyers can see and assist the last of the Atlantean cargo ships.

The Atlantean flagship is drawing closer, but it is going to take some time, and time is something that Davin does not have. The seven Atlantean destroyers are only fifteen minutes away from their enemy's fleet. The flagship is on its way, but it will arrive thirty minutes later.

Davin eludes the enemy long enough for the Atlantean flagship to finally catch up and attacks the enemy supply and troopships.

The enemy destroyers regroup and go full speed to attack the Atlantean military cargo ships. Davin's fleet is outmatched and overwhelmed. Enemy destroyers fire their projectiles. Even though Davin's fleet is damaged, they all take on one more enemy destroyer and cripple it. But eventually, all of the Atlantean military cargo ships are disabled or destroyed. Davin's fleet is sinking, but they fire every last piece of artillery at the four enemy destroyers, destroying one.

The men on the Atlantean destroyers can see Commander Davin using a bow and arrow, firing at the enemy. From the Atlantean destroyers, Davin is not doing this to be a hero; he is doing this out of pure adrenaline. With every thing happening in this war, Davin will go down as the unknown hero of the war. This pumps up the morale of the Atlantean destroyers and they lay right into the enemy, destroying the last of the enemy destroyers. At the same time, the Atlanteans lose four destroyers. The remaining Atlantean destroyers pick up the men from the sinking military cargo ships, and Commander Davin climbs aboard Herous' destroyer. He goes right to an artillery emplacement aboard the ship to continue fighting.

After thirty minutes, the Atlantean destroyers go alongside the flagship and use every artillery piece against the enemy. They knock out thirty-nine troop and supply ships, but the enemy still has fifty-eight ships going towards Atlantis. Because an enemy supply ship rammed into the Atlantean flagship, it is damaged and loses speed. The Atlantean destroyers are also crippled in the water. Because of all the damage, the Atlanteans are unable to keep pace with the enemy fleet, and the enemy escapes. The Atlanteans have fought all day, and have no ammunition. There are still Atlantean men in the water, but they are quickly rescued. The Atlanteans have lost too many ships, but the Atlantean warriors will fight again in another campaign.

Meanwhile, thousands of enemy navy personnel are left in the sea to die, as the enemy goes over the horizon towards Atlantis. Radious sends scouts to the shores of Masaba to inform the military officers of the situation. There are no more Atlantean destroyers in their harbors to be deployed to engage the enemy, and the Atlantean East Fleet cannot reach the enemy troops and supply ships in time. The enemy will hit the beaches in two days. The scout ships will reach the shores of Atlantis in nineteen hours. Once the scout ship reaches the beach, it only gives the Atlanteans twenty-nine hours to prepare and attack.

The Atlantean scout ships rush to their homeland. Radious feels as if he has failed Atlantis. He is helpless without ammunition, and he has damaged ships. If another formidable enemy fleet finds Radious' flagship before the Atlanteans can dock, they will be destroyed. Another scout ships goes to Vasic and tells them to prepare for the flagship to reload with more ammunition and undergo quick repairs.

Despite the shortcomings, Radious still has three destroyers, four Atlantean military cargo ships, and his flagship. They all limp back to Vasic, and expect the journey to take two days.

CHAPTER XVIII
THE ARMADA

The same day Radious engages his enemy, the sun is at its highest point. An Atlantean outpost from the far reaches of their island territories spots the Kayout fleet. It is nothing like the Atlanteans have ever seen before. The Atlanteans climb the tallest hill on the island to see the full vision of the enemy fleet. The island towers burn high, telling the scout ships the urgency of what they are witnessing. A messenger docks at the island and gains the information needed to go to Ashastonous.

Seven hours later, the scout ship reaches the Atlantean East Fleet. The messenger goes aboard the flagship and walks straight to Admiral Ashastonous.

The messenger salutes Ashastonous and says, "The Kayout armada has two hundred and twenty-five destroyers, twenty-five cruisers, and three heavy battlecruisers. There are also over six hundred supply and troop ships coming towards Atlantis. They are going a different path than what we expected. However, we can intercept them mid-day tomorrow."

Ashastonous responds, "Daygun was right about supplies being moved by sea. We now know what we are up against. From our spies, the Gambut, Mearth and the Kanis Empires are the main aggressors on land. The Kayouts are using their navy as their contribution to their coalition. In doing so, their presence on the mainland is limited. I have a feeling the Kayouts are the ones who are dictating this war."

Admiral Ashastonous looks at his captain and says, "Pull the flags for an emergency meeting aboard my flagship. Make it happen quickly."

Within an hour, the captains are aboard the flagship, standing at attention in rows, ready for orders. Ashastonous comes out of his quarters and looks at his men in formation.

Ashastonous says, "The Kayouts have stolen our ship technology. We have found the enemy fleet. There are more ships than we can count. If we were any other empire, I would say we go home. Our enemy has more destroyers and cruisers than we do, and the Kayout fleet has three heavy battlecruisers. We will fight our enemy and let our training take charge. They will have no choice but to fight us. Let us give them the opportunity. I have complete confidence in everyone here. I will say no more. Go to your ships and get ready for battle."

No one stays to ask questions. All captains leave on their personal transport boats back to their ship. The Atlanteans know what they have to do to protect their fatherland. Every ship sets sail to intercept their enemy.

The Atlantean fleet is faster than the Kayout fleet. The hulls of the enemy ships are thicker to absorb damage, but slower than the Atlantean ships. In battle, it can be asset or disadvantage. Admirals on both sides know this. In the battle which is about to take place, both navies will know which way they should have taken in designing their ships; slow with a great deal of protection, or fast with less safeguards.

The next day the two fleets are approaching one another. The Kayouts scout ships found the Atlantean fleet the day before and they went on an intercept course. The Kayouts fleet is coming over the horizon. Ashastonous is on the bridge of his ship with his captain.

Ashastonous looks at his captain and asks, "Are you afraid of what is coming at us?"

The captain responds, "Every captain in our fleet believes in you. If you give us the opportunity, we will give our lives for our empire and your leadership."

Admiral Ashastonous walks to the front of his ship to see the full details of the armada coming towards him. Ashastonous sees the fear in his men's faces as he is turns around.

Ashastonous takes a deep breath and yells, "These ships are about to attack our homeland. We have small numbers compared to what is in front of us. We are Atlanteans and the best navy in the world. We will go forward and destroy our adversary. We will face death or victory. I want everyone to think about something. How can any man have fear of someone who wants to take something away from them?"

His men change their outlook and cheer for the Atlantean Admiral. Everyone goes to their positions. The Atlanteans go forward, despite being outnumbered. The winds are in the Atlanteans' favor. The first round of battle will be on Ashastonous' side. They will have the speed. The enemy navy is so large the Atlanteans will be surrounded after the first initial attack. Ashastonous does not know if all enemy ships will attack or half will stay to slow them down. The enemy supply ships are four miles behind their military escort. Through a spyglass, Ashastonous can see the whole enemy navy coming closer towards his fleet.

Seeing the Atlantean ships about to be surrounded, Ashastonous orders all Atlantean ships to form a circle to make a defensive perimeter. Like clock work, all of the Atlantean fleet goes in position. Within the circle, there are four cruisers and twenty destroyers that will stay protected as reserves. The rest of the fleet will face out, posing a threat in all directions. There are layers within layers of Atlantean ship in the defensive formation. The Kayouts do not know how to attack this kind of configuration. The only way they know how to attack is to push forward with their overwhelming numbers.

Within twenty minutes of the Atlanteans forming their defensive circle, the Kayouts attack. The Atlantean cruisers take on the larger ships, and Atlantean destroyers work as a team striking other ships like a venomous snake. The artillery from Ashastonous' fleet correlates their projectiles for maximum destruction. As the Kayouts attack, the enemy ships catch on fire and go dead in the water. Each Atlantean cruiser fires at their enemy in a crossfire and repeats the same action towards another aggressor. The Atlantean destroyers go in and finish what the cruisers started.

Ashastonous' heavy battlecruiser is dead center of the defensive Atlantean circle. On the flagship there are thirty-six giant crossbows and thirty-six catapults. Each projectile can destroy an enemy destroyer. On the deck of the Atlantean heavy battlecruiser are also six hundred archers for close combat.

On the first initial attack, two enemy heavy battlecruisers

start to break through the Atlantean defensive line. The Atlantean flagship and cruisers are overpowering the rest of the enemy fleet. Because Ashastonous' flagship towers his cruisers, his artillery correlates with his cruisers and concentrates on the two enemy heavy battlecruisers. The training of the Atlanteans is showing against their aggressors.

Within ten minutes, the two enemy heavy battlecruisers are damaged. Two Atlantean cruisers and the flagship get the enemy heavy battlecruisers in a cross fire. The two massive enemy ships have no choice but to go in full retreat from the first engagement. While the enemy heavy battlecruisers are drawing back, Ashastonous' ship fires a large round bolder from its catapult at one of the massive ships. The projectile knocks a large hole in the fleeing ship; it hits the water line and the enemy ship sinks very quickly. All enemy ships break off from attack.

During the first Kayout offensive, the Atlantean flagship damages every enemy ship that comes near her. Some of the Kayout destroyers went on a suicide mission and tried to ram the Atlantean flagship, but they could not penetrate the thick hull. The enemy destroyers did not have the speed or mass to ram the Atlantean flagship.

In the middle of the Atlantean defensive circle, supply ships deliver projectiles to their fleet. It is a dangerous task because each small ship has no protection except from their fleet. Hundreds of small boats dock with their fleet to give more ammunition. Each projectile is raised by rope and carried to the deck of each ship.

Ashastonous' ship drops anchor, simultaneously stabilizing the massive fortress in the water. In doing so, the ship is completely stationary and the artillery will have better accuracy. The Atlantean flagship is stuck in its position. It will take eight minutes before the ship can raise its anchor if they need to move.

Ashastonous goes to his captain.

The Atlantean Admiral says, "Raise our flags to tell our ships to stay in formation and stay on the defensive. Our enemy doesn't know what to do with our formation. We are making our enemy guess. In guessing, they will make a mistake. When that mistake happens, we will destroy our adversary."

The second engagement starts. The Atlantean ships are in a tight formation. The fight goes on for twenty-five minutes, and only eight

Atlantean destroyers are damaged. There is little damage done to the Atlantean cruisers. Ashastonous' fleet is still surrounded, but the Kayouts retreat again to regroup. The Kayout Navy has lost one flagship, six battlecruisers, and forty destroyers in little over two hours.

From the enemy flagship, a white and red striped flag rises. This means the Kayouts want to save their sailors out of sinking ships, and Ashastonous agrees. There will be a ceasefire for thirty minutes. This gives the Atlantean Navy more time to regroup. The sinking Atlantean ships go in the middle of the circle and dump as many munitions as they can onto other ships. The Atlanteans cannot retreat; they are trapped. They cannot be resupplied from Atlantis, and there are no reinforcements to help them.

Ashastonous sees the enemy supply and transport ships anchor in the distance. They are going to wait on their warships for protection. Ashastonous cannot believe the enemy ships will not go forward to Atlantis. Ashastonous feels he has saved Atlantis for a little while longer.

The ceasefire is over. The enemy fleet moves back two miles from the Atlantean fleet and regroups. The enemy's cruisers and two heavy battlecruisers move into formation. The enemy is using their heaviest ships to hit one side of the Atlantean defensive perimeter to make a hole for their destroyers to get inside. Fifteen enemy cruisers are in a spearhead formation going towards the west side of the Atlantean circle.

Ashastonous sees what his enemy is doing and yells to his captain. "Order five cruisers to the west side along side my flagship. Order the most damaged destroyers to build a wall in front of the cruiser to slow their progress."

On the damaged destroyers, the men abandon ship in the center of the circle, and a skeletal crew takes the damaged destroyers out to their positions. The damaged Atlantean ships form a line and anchor for the last time. There are only five Atlantean destroyers, but they will save more than what the Atlantean are about to give up. When the destroyers are in position, the reserves are brought out to form a line with the Atlantean flagship. Every archer and artillery personnel from the cruisers and flagship wait until the enemy is in range.

In using the five damaged destroyers, there are no reserves

to protect the Atlantean rear. If the Kayouts break through, the Atlanteans will lose. Ashastonous sees this as an all or nothing risk. The whole battle will come down to this moment.

The Atlantean flagship turns all their artillery west. Five Atlantean battlecruisers are in position. The bulk of the Atlantean cruisers are highly defended in a ninety-degree angle for maximum firepower from their artillery. The Atlantean cruisers and flagship will fire all of their artillery simultaneously.

The enemy attacks, and hundreds of Atlantean artillery projectiles fly towards their enemy. In the middle of the attack, the Kayouts have to break off from all the bombardment coming from the Atlantean ships. Five enemy cruisers go down within three minutes. The Kayouts look for another weakness in the Atlantean formation, and see the rear is not well protected.

After the enemy battlecruisers sink, Admiral Ashastonous decides to attack and go on the offensive. He decides to take the momentum he has and turn the tide. There is confusion from his enemy and Ashastonous wants to capitalize on it.

When the Atlantean fleet counters, it is the most vital time of the battle. Out of pure adrenaline and experience, the Atlantean Admiral moves his flagship to take on the bulk of the two enemy heavy battlecruisers coming towards him. Ashastonous is going to take them on by himself, leaving his cruisers to take the smaller ships.

The Atlantean Admiral runs to the communication flag post of the ship.

Ashastonous yells, "Raise the flags for our ships to breakout and go on the offensive! The enemy is totally confused."

Four Atlantean battlecruisers and fifteen destroyers leave the circle for a full-scale attack. Two of the Atlantean destroyers sacrifice their ships and ram the two enemy heavy battlecruisers. The two Atlantean warships hit hard, and knock a large hole into the two targets, and one enemy heavy battlecruiser starts to sink. The Atlantean destroyers hit in an angle where the hull of the enemy ships is weakest. The other Atlantean destroyer rams deep into the ships and cannot get loose. The Atlantean ship starts to sink with the massive enemy ship. The weight of the sinking Atlantean destroyer is too much for the enemy's heavy battlecruisers, and it capsizes.

Ashastonous decides to ram the other Atlantean destroyer, which is stuck inside the last enemy heavy battlecruiser. Because the enemy ship is not sinking, Ashastonous rams his own destroyer from its rear, and he hammers the Atlantean destroyer farther into the enemy ship. With the major impact, the men of the Atlantean destroyer start to abandon ship. The flagship archers provide cover and most of them survive. However, the enemy ship is doomed and starts to sink in seconds. The enemy sailors of the heavy cruiser abandon ship, but the archers of Ashastonous' ship do not even give them a chance to reach safety of the sea. One of the people abandoning the rammed enemy ship is the Admiral of the Kayout fleet. He is also hit with an arrow before he can leave his ship and dies instantly. The saved Atlantean sailors climb on board their flagship and grab bows to fight for their empire.

Ashastonous' offensive is succeeding. While the Atlantean destroyers keep their enemy out of the defense circle, the enemies' hope of taking the Atlantean fleet is becoming futile. The enemy cannot penetrate the Atlantean fortification and break their formation. Even the ships at the rear of the Atlantean circle are standing their ground.

Two hours before sunset, the enemy has lost almost all of their cruisers in six hours of fighting. The enemy destroyers are depleted as well. The rest of the damaged enemy cruisers try to retreat to regroup.

Ashastonous yells to his captain, "Order four cruisers to attack the retreating ships. We will destroy their morale right now."

The Atlantean cruisers go after them like a wolf in a winter forest. The Atlanteans sink one damaged enemy ship at a time. The enemy can only watch as their mighty fleet gets destroyed. This is a mighty blow towards the morale to the Kayout Navy. After the Atlantean offensive, the Atlantean ships go back into a defensive formation like nothing ever happened. The enemy regroups for another attack.

The Atlanteans lose a total of nineteen destroyers. Ashastonous has twenty-eight fully operational destroyers left and twelve impaired. Only three Atlantean battlecruisers are damaged. The enemy has seven battlecruisers and one hundred and twenty eight destroyers still in operation.

Before the fourth engagement, the enemy appoints Vice Admiral

Zanteara to take over the battle. Zanteara takes the rest of his battle fleet and attacks the Atlantean Navy any way he can. Hoping to confuse Ashastonous, he will go into his tactics in sea warfare. The newly appointed Kayout admiral cannot return to Melercertis defeated. He orders his supply and transport ships to go forward to Atlantis. Zanteara will slow down the Atlanteans so the supply and transport ships have a head start.

The Atlantean supply ships and scout ships are ordered by Ashastonous to follow the Kayout armada. Because the Atlantean supply ships have little munitions, they are faster than the enemy destroyers and are able to avoid the next conflict. The Atlantean scout ships cannot do any damage, but can keep the enemy in sight for the Atlantean ships to follow.

On the fourth round of attack, the Atlanteans go on a full-scale offensive. They have to intercept the enemy supply ships before they hit the shores of Atlantis. The enemy has about an hour head start, and it will be dark soon. Ashastonous knows there will be a full moon, but it will be hard to find the enemy in the dark, even with his scout ships following. The waves of the sea will hide the enemy. In the middle of the fourth battle, Ashastonous orders his destroyers to pursue the armada. Because so many enemy ships have been sunk, the Atlanteans are able to slip by their enemy.

Two hours into the fight, there are only three Kayout cruisers left to fight the Atlanteans. Zanteara cannot fight anymore. The battle has essentially been decided. The enemy has only twenty fully functional destroyers left, and there are sixty-two others damaged. With another attack, the Atlanteans will knock out the enemy completely. Zanteara stops the attack and orders a retreat. Zanteara has to keep what navy he has left. All the rest of the enemy's warships are at the bottom of the sea or on fire.

Admiral Ashastonous sees the enemy trying to retreat, and he orders his fleet to let them go. The enemy picks up many of their warriors out of the water and goes after the enemy fleet. Ashastonous has to go after the enemy supply ships. In fifteen hours, the enemy armada will reach the Atlantean beaches.

The Atlantean supply ships reach the enemy three hours after sunset. They have little ammunition and only destroy twenty-five enemy ships. Some of the Atlantean supply ships ram the enemy, trying anything to stop them. The rest of the enemy ships continue at full speed towards Atlantis.

The Atlantean destroyers reach the enemy about midnight. By daybreak, the destroyers run out of ammunition. The enemy loses close to three hundred and fifty ships during the night. The Atlantean destroyers go in front of the enemy fleet to slow them down, but the enemy keeps going forward.

The Atlantean warriors aboard the destroyers have been awake for over twenty-four hours, and they are very exhausted. But the Atlantean warriors do not stop. They know their families and fatherland are in jeopardy.

Admiral Ashastonous orders all scout ships to go to the nearest dock for more munitions. It will take some time, but the Admiral tells them to meet him at specific points from their shores of where the enemy may land. In calculating time and distance, Ashastonous has a small window of opportunity.

The next morning, the Atlantean cruisers are catching up with the enemy armada. They use their final ammunitions and sink all but a hundred of the enemy ships. Ashastonous then orders all the cruisers to ram the troop ships. After ramming about twenty ships, the ramming is starting to damage the Atlantean cruisers. The Atlantean Admiral orders all of his fleet to go ahead of the enemy ships, and meet the scout ships, which hopefully have ammunition thirty miles southeast of the armada.

Time is the enemy to the Atlanteans. The enemy supply and transport ships keep pushing forward. Ashastonous orders his men to eat, drink, and sleep. The officers even take an oar, and let their warriors rest.

When the scout ships reach their ports, everyone who can carry ammunition does so and resupplies very quickly. When the scout ships dock, they are stocked with as many munitions as they can hold. After fifteen minutes of docking, the scout ships go back to sea to hopefully to meet the rest of their fleet.

Two hours later, the first of the scout ships meet up with Ashastonous' fleet. The ammunition is going aboard his ship first while the enemy can be seen over the horizon. The Atlantean ships are only half supplied and ordered to go back into the battle. With damaged ships and exhausted sailors, the Atlanteans keep going. There is not enough time to supply the Atlantean ships fully. They have to destroy as many of the enemy armada as they can. Hundreds of Atlantean scout ships meet their fleet. Some of the scout ships, which are supplying the Atlantean fleet, are doing so while their warships are moving. After scrambling for munitions, the Atlantean fleet goes in between the enemy armada and the Atlantean beaches. They wait for an hour. The order from Ashastonous is to go forward as a hunter going after game.

The Atlantean fleet is only six miles from the beach. On land, the Kayout and Gambut armies can see their supply and transport ships in the horizon. The Atlantean ships use their artillery and attack. Some of the supply and troop ships make it through. The Atlantean cruisers and destroyers hit and destroy the enemy quickly, but there are simply too many of them. It only takes minutes to destroy an enemy ship, but seventy-two enemy ships make it through. It is a fraction of what the enemy on land needed, and it is a victory for the Atlanteans.

Ashastonous orders his ships back to Vasic. They are damaged from ramming their enemy. The flagship goes back to the military port. His destroyers are ordered to finish the enemy transport and supply ships that are beached on Atlantean soil. The Atlantean cruisers cannot attack because of the depth of the sea. The Atlantean cruisers are too massive and will bottom out so close to their shores. The Atlantean destroyers are the only ones that can get close to the beaches and destroy their enemy.

After it was all done, over ninety percent of the Kayout Navy is destroyed or damaged. The Atlantean destroyers have done what it is asked of them, and they go back to Vasic feeling good on what has transpired. When the Atlanteans fleet gets back to Vasic, the Atlantean battle scars can be seen from the harbor crews. Over all, the Atlanteans have twenty-three destroyers, five cruisers, and its flagship still in action. It has almost destroyed the entire world's navy in two days. Ashastonous has done his duty as a warrior. The ships of the Kayouts had done their duty as well, but at a very high cost. There will not be any other supplies sailing through sea from the enemy's homeland. Because it will take more time to get more supplies from the Gambut and Kayout Empires by land, it will give the Atlanteans a little more time to set up their defenses.

Ashastonous goes back to Vasic and is declared a hero. The Atlantean Admiral sees his damaged West Fleet. The most powerful navy in the world is crippled. When the Atlantean ships get a couple of days of repairing, they leave and are ordered to Atlantis. Because the Atlantean Admiral is in port at Vasic, the city is not in danger of being taken by sea, and the Atlantean armies leave and go to the capital or Masaba. The threat of a beach front is unlikely, and the warriors of Vasic are needed elsewhere. Vasic is too deep into Atlantean territory to be attacked, and the warriors and sailors from Vasic can help their brothers in different parts of their homeland.

Chapter XIX
Waiting for the Door

It is dawn. The Atlantean scout ship sent by Radious lands at the nearest Atlantean dock west of Masaba. It will take the scout three hours on horseback to reach the city and warn his army about the supply ships heading towards Atlantis. A horse is already at the dock for the Atlantean messenger. The enemy will reach the Atlantean beach in nine hours. This is enough time for the Masabaian cavalry to ride to the beaches and meet their enemy.

The scout reaches his destination at Masaba, and Laptos orders all of the Masaban cavalry to get ready for battle. He leads his military force to the beach as fast as he can. When the Atlanteans arrive, they see the enemy soldiers organizing and unloading supplies. Five thousand enemy troops have landed, and only two hundred light and heavy cavalry are there.

When the enemy runs onto the shore, Laptos comes from over the hill at full speed with all of the Masaban cavalry behind him. The Atlanteans dominate the battle, and Laptos wins this excursion easily. The Atlanteans lose very few military resources, and Laptos is becoming a real leader to the Atlanteans.

After the battle, the Atlanteans take prisoners. The captives tell the Atlanteans nothing they did not know already except for who is leading the Kayouts into battle. The Mearth warriors say Ryelyne is the Supreme Commander of the Continental Alliance. Laptos orders this to be kept secret. This could create panic, and bring down the Atlantean's morale. If the Atlantean population finds out a prince of a city-state is involved, it could put the Masaban King in danger.

Laptos immediately leaves the beach and goes directly to the Atlantean capital to speak with Daygun.

In the meantime, the Atlanteans are holding off their enemy, and they still have only one front to fight. The Continental Alliance has lost more than two million men. As more time passes, the Atlanteans have a better chance of ending this peacefully. The Atlantean enemy no longer has a formidable navy, and the enemy supplies are merely trickling into the peninsula.

Three major Atlantean cities still must be conquered, and none of them will go down without a fight. Except overtaking the Great East Wall, the enemy has little to show for what they have lost. On the other hand, Ryelyne's involvement with the enemy can hinder attempts at peace. Laptos cannot believe the news.

The next day, a messenger tells Daygun that Laptos will be in Atlantis shortly. The new Atlantean Emperor assembles his Military Council together once more. If Laptos is coming to Atlantis, he must have something very important to say. Daygun wonders what can be so important. He knows the enemy still needs to regroup and receive supplies by land. The enemy cannot attack for at least two weeks. Destroying the Kayout fleet bought valuable time for the Atlantean civilization.

Looking back, Daygun wishes he did not send Kaydence to Halotropolis. His wife is in no immediate danger. The enemy is a two day march from the city. Kaydence is protected by the best warriors of the Atlantean military. Four elite divisions are stationed at Halotropolis, and Daygun is sending more men to reinforce the City of God from Vasic.

Back in Atlantis, all Atlantean ships, including warships, are ordered to help evacuate the people out of the fatherland. Daygun instructs his civilians to take supplies, and their ships will take them to safe Atlantean provinces off the peninsula. Because of the distance from the Kayout Empire, the Atlantean civilians will have a better chance at survival. The Atlanteans have mapped the entire world. If peace is reached, the civilians can come back. Even though the Atlanteans have won battles, it still does not look good for the Atlanteans. There are close to ten million enemy warriors pouring into Atlantis and preparing to attack Daygun's empire.

Laptos finally arrives to the Atlantean Military Hall. Laptos salutes his brother. Daygun smiles at his brother in pride. The rest of the generals salute Laptos and cheer for his victories. Two years ago, Daygun would not have thought he would be envisioning his brother as he does now.

Laptos says to the council, "This war has taken a toll on our enemy. Now would be a good time to start negotiating for peace. I think I should be the one who starts the process of amity."

Daygun responds, "You are the only option right now. I think they will respect your victories and listen to what you have to say. I hate putting my own brother in danger, but there is no choice. Something has to be done right now."

Laptos says, "Agreed then. I will send a messenger to our enemy for an assembly. There is other news. The prisoners we captured near the beaches of Masaba say Ryelyne is in charge of the assault against our fatherland. I don't know what to make of it."

Daygun says to the council and Laptos, "I grew up with Ryelyne. It is not in his nature. He must have died on the way to Valtear, and this is a diversion to make us think twice on what to do."

Laptos replies, "It doesn't make since for the prisoners to say such things. How would they know? Why would the prisoners lie? If it is true, Ryelyne will know all weaknesses of Atlantis. We can use this to our advantage, but first we have to find out where he is."

The next day, in the Atlantean Military Hall, Daygun says to his generals, "I want all Atlantean warriors who are stationed on our island territories and provinces to return to the peninsula. This will give us two more divisions, and I want them here to protect our capital. We must have two more elite divisions inside the gates of Halotropolis. We will fight there. We will put the fear into our enemy. From our capital, I want all heavy and light cavalry to camp in the mountains near Halotropolis. If the negotiations with our enemy do not work to our advantage, we must destroy as many enemy warriors as possible. In doing so, the enemy will have to sue for peace. I also want every ship we have docked in Atlantis to move women and children out of our empire. We can fight to the death, but our race and culture must survive. We must protect our bloodline."

Two day later, Laptos goes to the front lines to negotiate for peace. His messenger comes back and says he will be speaking with the Mearth Emperor.

Laptos and an Atlantean garrison go to the summit. Daygun's brother sees the true magnitude of the Continental Alliance. As he is looking over the hill, he sees millions of men ready to destroy his homeland. Laptos goes through the outskirts of the Mearth Army. Daygun's brother and his garrison are guided by Nextear's guards to their destination. As the Atlanteans looks around, they can feel the hate from every enemy warrior around them. Laptos dismounts his horse and goes inside Nextear's tent under an armorist.

Laptos stands ten feet from Nextear and says, "We have lost numerous men on both sides, and I hope we can come to an agreement to end this war."

Nextear responds, "We have hated the Atlanteans for hundreds of years. We have brought every warrior from all over the world to destroy your god. There is no turning back. You have done well in the battles against me and my men. I respect you. In ten days, we will destroy Halotropolis. There will not be any negotiation here. Leave here while you still can."

Laptos asks, "Why did you allow me to come here under a truce?"

Nextear responds, "I wanted to see my enemy before I destroyed him. Now go."

Laptos says, "We don't want to fight anymore against the world. There has already been too much death. We will breathe death in the days to come, and it will contaminate our souls. It will reek so badly our grandchildren will still smell mortality in future generations."

Nextear replies, "I understand your concerns for the death of your people. Your empire has gone too far in trying to take my civilization. Your father signed in blood to never attack another empire. Now, the whole world will take the imperialistic nature of your god from the world forever."

Daygun's brother knows he is not getting anywhere.

Laptos says, "I understand, but consider it. One last question if I may? Do you know anything about our generals Acteon or Ryelyne?"

Nextear looks the other way and says, "No."

Laptos says, "Thank you for honoring the armistice." Daygun's brother turns away and starts to leave. Nextear knows Laptos knows too much about Ryelyne from his own expression. The Mearth Emperor cannot let him return to Atlantis. It will destroy the whole campaign. Suddenly, Nextear orders his guards to kill the small garrison and Laptos.

When Laptos starts to mount his horse, Nextear's guards walk quickly out of the tent with swords drawn. Laptos orders his garrison to dismount their horses.

Laptos sees two Atlanteans still mounted and yells in an urgent voice, "You two ride hard and tell Atlantis what you are seeing here!"

Laptos has no time to tell his men in their retreat about what he assumes about Ryelyne. The two Atlantean warriors start to ride back to Atlantis. The other twelve Atlantean men walk away from their horses and wait to see if any aggression comes from the Mareth guards. The Atlanteans put their hands on their swords.

Mearth guards get very aggressive and Laptos' men draw their swords. The fighting starts and every Atlantean guard try to protect Daygun's brother. All the guards attack Laptos, and the Atlantean Prince puts up a good fight, but within two minutes, Laptos is stabbed in the chest and falls to the ground. The other Atlantean guards fight in anger and inevitably fall to the same fate.

The two Atlantean horsemen look back and see what has happened to Laptos. They ride back as fast as they can to Halotropolis to tell what has happened. In two hours, the bells ring and Daygun finds out his brother is dead. Within a month, Daygun has lost two family members. At the same time, the new Atlantean Emperor feels as if a friend has betrayed his empire.

Dareous is ordered to Masaba to take the place of Laptos. He is the only one strong enough for such a task. Many changes take place in Daygun's military. The Atlanteans have just lost a hero. The new Atlantean Emperor orders another division to the City of God.

Daygun organizes for a counteroffensive at Halotropolis. He will lead the Atlantean light and heavy cavalry to the front of Halotropolis. He orders all of the Atlantean cavalry to wait outside Halotropolis in the mountains. Every creature that can be ridden from Atlantis is headed to Haylos' city-state.

At sea, the Atlanteans are starting to evacuate more people out of the Atlantean Empire. All civilians who cannot fight leave first and many women stay back to fight for their homeland. Because Atlantis is a small empire, everyone has learned the arts of war.

More ships come from Atlantean provinces taking supplies and people away. It will still take months to evacuate everyone out of the empire. Daygun knows every second he holds off his enemy; another Atlantean citizen is saved.

CHAPTER XX
SMALL WINDOW OF OPPORTUNITY

The main goal of the Atlanteans is to reach a peaceful negotiation with their enemy. The Atlanteans cannot win this war, but they are hoping to deplete their enemy enough where they do not have a choice but to sue for peace.

Daygun has lost a brother and father to the Continental Alliance, and he wants revenge. At the same time, Daygun has to have peace for his civilization to survive. He wants to end this war. There is too much death on both sides. Since Laptos died unfairly, this will make the enemy fear Daygun as a general and warrior.

Nextear, on the other hand, hates the Atlanteans so much he can think of nothing but destroying Atlantis. He has turned this into a Holy War to motivate his army to die for gods and the empire.

The enemy has to take Halotropolis to reach Atlantis, but the ones who stayed in God's city will not give it up. Anyone over the age of fifteen is either fighting or contributing in some way in Halotropolis. The women have picked up a sword and a bow to protect their homes. Every beast of the Atlantean capital and Halotropolis are nearby to protect God's city. Many Atlanteans think that God will not let Halotropolis fall. The enemy is fearful of such determination, and knows it will be a hard city to take.

Daygun arrives at the gates of Halotropolis. Men cheer as he enters the city. He will oversee the counterattack. Because he can be in harms way, Kaydence will be asked to leave. Just in case something happens to Daygun, she is the last person to take leadership of the Atlantean government.

Nine million enemy troops and beasts wait twenty miles north of the city. When the breeze hits right, Daygun can smell his enemy. The emperor goes to see his wife. Kaydence is ready to lead and fight for the Holy City. The men of Halotropolis are honored to fight with the leadership she has.

Kaydence is in very good shape. She does not have much muscle, but can run forever without tiring. She takes off her royal dress and slips into Atlantean armor. Her greatest strength is her legs. In hand-to-hand combat, she can kick a three hundred pound man right to the ground.

Daygun asked Kaydence to meet him in the court where Aten once asked him to talk. When Daygun sees her at a distance, tears almost come to his eyes. The emperor is so proud of having such a wife. She can fight like a man, but comforts him like the best of all Atlantean women. Daygun embraces Kaydence.

Kaydence looks up at Daygun and says, "I am ready to die with my husband right here in the City of God."

Daygun shakes his head and replies, "I will fight here. Atlantis cannot take the chance of losing us both. I must lead this fight. If I don't make it, you will be in charge of our government."

Kaydence says, "If I flee, I will be betraying my oath as warriors."

Daygun replies, "No, we are saving it. One of us has to leave to preserve our way of life. Halotropolis needs their emperor here. The city will be destroyed, but with my presence, it still gives them hope. I cannot take hope away from these people."

Kaydence looks down and says, "I understand. Who will take my place here? You are the Atlantean Emperor, and I will do what you say."

Daygun says, "Quentoris is coming from the Great West Wall. He will protect the city to the death. Even though he is a very good friend, I have to put him in harms way."

Quentoris enters the city the next day. He prepares his new army for battle. Before Daygun and Kaydence can leave, the enemy starts to march towards the Holy City.

Daygun hears the bells, and he tells Kaydence to leave the city. Hastily, she refuses.

Kaydence says, "I will not leave our people here in fear of dying.

I cannot go against my oath as a warrior of Atlantis. If we die here, our empire is doomed anyway."

Daygun responds, "My brother told me you were the most stubborn woman in the world. He was right, and this is the reason I married you."

They both smile at one another and run away to get ready for what is to come. Everyone is getting in position to fight their adversary. Kaydence would rather die here than die being afraid of her enemy. In her eyes, it is too late to leave. She takes her position, and Daygun reluctantly runs out of the courtyard and mounts his horse to join his cavalry outside the gates of Halotropolis. On his way out, thousands of people cheer as their emperor rides out of the city. Daygun's main objective was to get his wife to safety. Now, he goes on his own instincts to fight for the Holy City. If Kaydence dies here, so will Daygun. The new Atlantean Emperor is fighting for the love of his wife. The main reason he came to Halotropolis has just changed.

Daygun waits in the mountains. Each of his light and heavy cavalry will do something different. Atlantean mammoths will lead the attack. The Atlanteans have two thousand mammoths which will strike the right flank of the enemy's main formation. The elephants are numbered at three thousand, and they will attack to the left of their enemy. Twenty thousand light cavalry will attack the rear. They will attack when the enemy is trying to climb over the walls of the Holy City.

Quentoris and Kaydence take command in different parts of the city; they will give orders when it is time to put the artillery in full attack mode. Halotropolis will attack with their artillery first and kill as many men as they can before the enemy can take over. If they put up a successful defense, the Atlanteans will try to sue for peace again. Otherwise, everyone knows they are not going to make it out of the city alive.

On the other hand, the enemy has another plan. The Continental Alliance splits up. The Mearth and Kanis Empires will attack Masaba, and the Gambut and Kayouts will stay and take Halotropolis. This will leave six million warriors to attack the City of God. Ryelyne is dividing his armies so Atlantis will have two fronts. Because Masaba will be bogged down, the Atlanteans will be unable to counter with the Masaban Army.

Ryelyne looks at the Halotropolis with Tito and Acteon.

Ryelyne says, "I have to destroy my own people for them to survive. The world will completely be different in generations to come. What are we doing for mankind right now?"

Tito replies, "Everything has unfolded to this point. Man will take a step back without Atlantis and take two steps forward in years to come. Mankind will continuously destroy itself to the end of time."

Ryelyne is there to oversee the campaign. He does not like what is going on, but he has to do it. Even as a kid, he prayed to God in the temples of Halotropolis.

Because of his father, Ryelyne cannot take Masaba. The Continental Alliance understands, and says nothing. Nextear takes charge to keep Masaba from countering. The new Kayout Supreme Commander does not respect his father, but he does not want his father dead either. If it comes down to it, he does not want to be there to kill him. Ryelyne will not kill his own family by his own sword, and he asks Nextear to take them captive.

Ryelyne is torn up inside. The Kayout Supreme Commander did not understand the fullness of his actions and oaths while he was in Kayout. He is starting to regret the decisions he made. Even though he has good intentions for the survival of his race, his love for Palexus and the way Melercertis touched him is still having an effect on his emotions. Ryelyne is only trying to save what will be left of his homeland after the invasion. It is a gamble, but he wants to be known as a hero of Atlantis, not as a destroyer.

If the Atlanteans sue for peace or the Atlanteans win, Ryelyne will go down in history as a traitor. He does not know the final outcome of this war, but he goes on his instincts. The odds are against Atlantis.

The battle begins, and the enemy rushes the City of God. The Atlanteans will defend it to the death. The city is the most important city of Atlantean religion.

The Halotropolean artillery and arrows fly over their walls. The Atlantean infantry is outside their gates. The beasts of the Holy City charge the infiltrators outside the cities walls. The Kayout beasts meet the Halotropolean cavalry. The enemy cavalry outnumbers the Atlanteans twelve to one. The Halotropolean artillery fires a barrage of suppressing fire to help protect their mobile forces outside their walls, but it is not enough. The City of God's cavalry is severely beaten, but draws the Kayouts to the front. The Atlanteans fire artillery at their enemy beasts and put a large dent in their enemy's mammoth formations. The Halotropolean cavalry has to retreat back in their gates, having suffered heavy losses. Within one hour, one third of the Halotropolean cavalry is destroyed, and only a fraction of the enemy's cavalry is lost.

The Kayouts bring out their new weapons which took out the Great East Wall. The tightuses are rolling towards the Holy City in great numbers. The Atlanteans concentrate all their artillery towards the enormous war machines. The Halotropolean warriors have never seen such devices. They heard about them, but it is more than what they expected from the Kayouts. Over one hundred and forty tightuses were assembled at the Great East Wall, and they were built inside the Atlantean Empire.

Ryelyne decides to use all tightuses and only attack one side of Halotropolis. Tito is in charge of the frontal assault against the City of God. Over seventy enemy tightuses are lined up in formation and seventy more are waiting to fill the voids.

Ryelyne gives the order. The tightuses go full speed towards Halotropolis' wall. The majority of the Atlantean infantry rushes to the side of the main assault. Ryelyne counters and charges with his cavalry on the other side of the city. It catches the Atlanteans off guard. Ryelyne's military strategies are working from his new army; he knows the weaknesses and strengths of the Atlanteans. The Kayout Supreme Commander knows how to counter the moves of his former generals. At nightfall of the first battle, both sides stand down and regroup for the next day. The Kayouts have won this battle, and the Atlanteans are hurting.

In the meantime, Daygun waits until the enemy thinks they can take the city completely, and then he will attack. The Atlantean Emperor will wait until the enemy's ego is at its highest.

Two hours into the night, Daygun's cavalry take two Kayout scouts as prisoners. The captives give up information about where Ryelyne is located. They know the exact whereabouts of the Atlantean traitor, and the Atlanteans see it is possible to take him out of the battle.

Daygun gathers his generals together.

Daygun says, "Ryelyne is twelve miles away from here looking over the battlefield. We will go around and take him out. The terrain will hide our massive cavalry. He knows the strengths and weaknesses of our empire. Send me a messenger."

A general responds, "The generals of Halotropolis are waiting on our counteroffensive."

A messenger walks in and Daygun says, "Go through the underground waterway into Halotropolis. It will take you all night to get to the City of God. Tell them of our plan and to correlate accordingly.

The next day, Daygun knows he has no choice but to kill Ryelyne. He hopes the messenger made it through. The Atlantean Emperor orders every one of the Atlantean cavalry to prepare to find the traitor. Daygun has to go the long way to attack his old friend. The Atlantean bells ring. The Halotropolean cavalry starts to take the Kayout cavalry outside their protection of the artillery and archers. Halotropolis goes on the offensive. It is a diversion to allow Daygun a safe passage to find Ryelyne. Halotropolis' cavalry is sacrificing to kill one man. There is no way they can win. If Daygun does not kill Ryelyne, every secret and every battle tactic will be in the hands of the enemy. Atlantis must kill the traitor, and it must be done now.

A whole Halotropolean division is ordered to start an infantry offensive outside the wall to create another distraction for Daygun. As the new Emperor anticipates, the enemy attacks the Atlantean diversionary force.

The tightuses finally reach the Atlantean wall as the Holy City is starting to crumble. The Atlantean infantry is holding the enemy back at the moment, but it is only a matter of time before the city is taken. Kaydence fights amongst the Atlantean men outside the city.

Daygun rides his mammoth as fast as he can, surrounded by his light and heavy cavalry. Six infantrymen ride on top of each mammoth, and four on each elephant. The Atlantean light cavalry stays right behind their mammoths; they are the archers and protectors of the elephants and mammoths.

Daygun is not certain of Ryelyne's exact location. But he goes forward hoping to find him. The new Atlantean Emperor takes the enemy on the outside parts of the massive Kayout Army by complete surprise. The Atlanteans know their lands and knows how to hide behind hills and mountains without being detected. The Atlanteans pounce on the enemy.

Daygun attacks with full force. In the middle of the battle, the Atlanteans take prisoners and interrogate them until they find out where Ryelyne is camped. The Atlanteans secure some information and go forward.

The Kayout infantry is rushing toward Ryelyne. The enemy knows Daygun is going after the Kayout Supreme Commander.

The Atlantean horse cavalry protects their infantrymen who just jumped off from the heavy cavalry. Every Atlantean cavalryman has sixty arrows, a sword, and ten daggers. While the Atlantean infantry attack their enemy, the Atlantean horseman either attacks with a sword, bow or dagger. In close quarters, the light infantrymen use their daggers and swords while they rush their enemy. Thousands of Atlanteans horsemen rush and pull back and let their infantry to do their job. The Atlanteans are killing at a rate of twenty to one, riding deeper into the Kayout Army.

In the middle of the fight, the Atlanteans locate Ryelyne's flag. The Atlantean traitor is on top of a hill looking over the battlefield. The Atlanteans rush to his camp. Ryelyne does not retreat; he feels he is right and Daygun must die for his idea to save Atlantis. The new Atlantean Emperor believes Ryelyne helped kill his father by attacking the Great East Wall. If the Kayout Supreme Commander does not stand his ground against Daygun, he will be known as a coward within his new army.

Ryelyne goes to the battlefront without fear; he believes in his cause and stands by his decision. Three divisions of the Kayout elite come to Ryelyne's aide. The enemy makes some ground and punches a hole into Daygun's offensive. In turn, the Atlanteans start to lose ground. The Atlantean mammoths go forward and make a hole in the enemy lines. The Atlantean light cavalry is right behind Daygun's main thrust and breaks the lines of the Kayouts. Ryelyne tries to reform his infantry lines, but the Atlantean cavalry is too strong. Daygun caught Ryelyne's men off guard. The Atlantean Emperor can see where the enemy lines are trying to be reinforced and charges to break it again.

In the middle of the battle, Daygun and Ryelyne see each other. The chances of them seeing each other on this battlefield are one in a million, but it happens. Daygun is furious. Because of the heat of battle, he blames the Kayout Supreme Commander for his father and brother's deaths. Daygun desires nothing more than to kill his former best friend. At this point, Ryelyne is surrounded with Atlanteans. He cannot retreat back to the safety of his army.

Daygun dismounts his mammoth and approaches Ryelyne. Daygun feels betrayed; he cannot believe that his best friend would do something of this magnitude. Every Kayout inside the Atlantean perimeter are losing their lives. More Kayouts come to fight the Atlanteans, but Daygun's offensive has the advantage of terrain, and they repel their enemy. Most of all, the Continental Alliance cavalry is on the front lines attacking Halotropolis.

Ryelyne imagines Palexus, and fears he will die having made the wrong decision.

Daygun approaches Ryelyne and pulls out his sword. The Kayout Supreme Commander does the same. In the background, Ryelyne's men are starting to gain ground. The Atlantean Emperor knows he has a small window of opportunity to fight without interruption.

The bells ring from Halotropolis. It tells the new Atlantean Emperor a wall is being compromised inside the Holy City. Daygun is six miles away from the city and seven miles from the breach. The window just got smaller for the Atlantean Emperor. He has to get back to Halotropolis. Daygun must destroy Ryelyne quickly. It has to be the two which fight one another without interference. The Atlantean mammoths are keeping all of the Kayout infantry at a standstill at Ryelyne's camp, but no one would dare intercede in this fight.

Daygun and Ryelyne meet with their swords. All of the Atlantean and Kayout warriors stay out of their way. Ryelyne strikes first against Daygun. They go back and forth with blows of their swords. The Atlantean Emperor does not have time to waste, and he is very aggressive. During the attack, the Kayout Supreme Commander counters every move. One minute into the fight, Daygun opens himself up to Ryelyne, giving him the opportunity of a fast victory, but it catches the traitor off guard. Daygun capitalizes on the Kayout Supreme Commander's mistake and slices him in his upper back. It is not a sudden fatal wound, but disables Ryelyne. The Kayout Supreme Commander falls to his knees covered in blood and the

Atlantean Emperor stabs Ryelyne in the back just like the Atlantean traitor did to his own people.

Ryelyne falls and says, "I'm sorry it came to this, Daygun. I am not what you think. In the afterlife, you will see me as a brother again, and God will let you see my true heart towards our civilization."

Daygun replies, "I have lost my father and brother. Now, I had to kill by best friend. I still love you as a brother. I will see you in the afterlife and we will talk. I need to understand. Be ready for me, and I will hug you as a brother in years to come."

Ryelyne grabs Daygun's arm and dies at his feet. Every Atlantean warrior cheers for their new emperor. The whole Kayout Army is stunned by Ryelyne's death. Acteon sees his commander killed and he is caught off guard. He loses focus while fighting and is killed by an Atlantean arrow. The Kayouts back off from trying to rescue their dead Supreme Commander. The enemy knows they are defeated on this ground. The Atlanteans have cavalry, archers, terrain, and surprise on their side, but Daygun cannot go forward without high casualties.

Daygun orders a full retreat. The Atlantean cavalry has lost very little in this battle and conquered their main objective. The Atlantean infantry lost seven thousand men out of sixteen thousand. Now, the Atlantean cavalry is worrying about the City of God. Daygun is thinking of Kaydence and to take her out of the city.

CHAPTER XXI
THE HOLY CITY

Daygun's cavalry takes the longer route and goes towards the compromised Halotropolean wall. Because most of the Kayout cavalry is attacking the Holy City, Daygun's cavalry has no opposition in killing enemy pockets outside the Continental Alliance's main army.

The only way Daygun can help Halotropolis is to get to the gates. The Atlantean Emperor goes around the rocky terrain. He looks with his cavalry over the hill. They see the full extent of bloodshed at the Holy City.

Daygun points at the battlefield and says to his generals, "Most of the enemies' cavalry is on the other side. This is where we need to charge. This is where our enemy is weakest. We will have to fight a mile and a half to get under the protection of the Halotropolean archers. Blow the horn for a full scale attack."

The horns blow and the Halotropolean warriors see their emperor coming. Every mammoth and elephant goes full speed to the aide of Halotropolis. Daygun's cavalry has to fight their way through the Gambuts and Kayouts. The Atlantean cavalry charging towards God's city is destroying their adversary's infantry with ease. The Atlantean enemy does not have the military resources to fight back Daygun's offensive. Most of the enemies' artillery and cavalry is on the other side of the city.

A mile deep into the enemy, Daygun pulls back from the fight. He looks at his light cavalry commander and says, "Take seven thousand light cavalry and fight alongside the Halotropolean walls. Reinforce the Halotropolean infantry outside their gates. Take a strike force under the protection of our archers in Halotropolis and push back our enemy which is taking our weakest point of the city."

Within twenty minutes, Quentoris sees Daygun's cavalry fighting outside the walls and says, "Protect Daygun's light cavalry. Concentrate our artillery ahead of their thrust."

The artillery fires and gives Daygun's light cavalry a chance. The archers fire ahead of the light cavalry, and they are able to break through.

Inside the Holy City, the enemy starts to break through other walls. Thousands of Atlantean men and women fall back to other defenses. The Atlanteans have to give up parts of their city in order to regroup. The Holy City's inner fortifications are not as strong as the outside walls, and it becomes easier for the enemy to take over the Halotropolean defenses.

Daygun's light cavalry arrives at the weakest point of the city and is able to take back what they lost. Luckily, the enemy is still being destroyed by the Atlantean's artillery outside the gates. It makes it easier for the Atlantean light cavalry to destroy their enemy. The Gambuts and Kayouts cannot organize a strong enough counteroffensive to take what they are losing.

Never the less, Quentoris know the city will eventually be sacked. The Atlantean bells ring and what is left of the Atlantean light cavalry gives up the ground they just took. They go in full retreat to the safety of their gates. Daygun knows the only way to save his people is to take them outside the city and retreat back to the capital.

Outside the city, Daygun's heavy cavalry is starting to lose momentum and cannot hold out much longer. The enemy's cavalry starts to counter the Atlantean offensive. Daygun has to retreat into the gates of Halotropolis as well.

Quentoris and Kaydence are there waiting for Daygun to enter the gates. Crammed with mammoths inside the courtyard, Kaydence goes to the gate. She waits for the Atlantean Emperor.

Daygun arrives inside Halotropolis and he jumps off his mammoth and runs to Kaydence.

Daygun looks at Quentoris and Kaydence and says, "We are getting out of here. Order what is left of our heavy and light cavalry to the rear of the city. Quentoris take command of our walls and create a barrage of arrows outside Halotropolis. Let the enemy have the rest of the city. Kaydence, get your men and hold off our attackers inside the city. Get the civilian population out of here. We will explode with our cavalry and allow our archers a safe haven to fight outside the city. This is the only way we are going to survive."

What is left of the Halotropolean cavalry goes to the rear of the city where the outside enemy is weakest. Quentoris' men fight hard and establish a perimeter around the rear gates so the Atlanteans can retreat. Quentoris' infantry fights hard to build up a perimeter outside the city. The Halotropolean archers fire at the rear of the city and concentrate their fire to allow the Atlantean cavalry to spearhead out of the gates.

The Halotropolean gates open. Twelve hundred mammoths and eight hundred twenty elephants push forward through the massive gates. Right behind them is their infantry fighting alongside their cavalry. Once the Atlantean spearhead makes an open circle, their Halotropolean archers come out of the gates and fire their arrows deeper into their enemy, allowing their cavalry and infantry to go forward. The circle gets larger and the Halotropolean civilians help. Over a hundred and twenty-five thousand Atlantean warriors are outside the walls fighting and gaining ground.

Back in the City of God, Kaydence is still fighting to allow more civilians to be saved. The Atlantean civilians are fighting alongside their military. Daygun gives the order to evacuate the city. Some Atlanteans will not retreat and fight their enemy until they have sacrificed their lives. Some inhabitants of Halotropolis do not want God to see them retreating and run away from their fears.

In the middle of the last stronghold inside the city, Daygun is trying to find his wife. An Atlantean warrior tells him Kaydence is inside fighting to help protect a segment of the City of God. The Atlantean archers are protecting her infantry as arrows are going over her head. She is growing tired, but she is giving every breath so more people can get out of Halotropolis.

Daygun goes towards the location, He screams her name. Finally, he sees her. Kaydence cannot hear him and fights on. The Atlantean Emperor runs to her in the middle of a fight. Daygun fights on her side for a couple of minutes and pulls her out of harms way. She screams out in frustration while she sees her army fighting in front of her.

Back at the rear gates, it is growing dark. Most of the Halotropolean civilians are outside the gates under the protection of their military. Daygun orders the archers to fire a barrage of arrows for the next ten minutes while the last of Atlantean infantry flees the city. The Atlantean spearhead is a complete success. The Atlantean Emperor orders Quentoris to lead the last of Atlantean infantry outside Halotropolis.

Daygun leads Kaydence out of the City of God. Some of the archers give up their lives for their emperor to be able to escape. The Atlanteans' infantry is trying to fight their way out of their enemy which has surrounded them. The Continent Alliance cannot get an overwhelming force of archers or cavalry to break the Atlantean's lines.

Inside the city, there are little pockets of Atlantean fighters, but they die quickly. In one of the pockets, Haylos, King of Halotropolis, dies with his men. Now, three of the most important Atlantean political figures are dead. King Haylos joins Emperor Aten and Laptos in the casualties of this war.

In their retreat, the Atlanteans lose more than two thirds of their military from Halotropolis. The rest escape as fast as they can. Daygun's cavalry picks up as many survivors as possible during the escape. The enemy follows them until nightfall. The Kayouts and Gambuts cannot put their forces together fast enough to attack the Atlanteans when Daygun gets four miles outside the city. Because of the terrain around Halotropolis, it gives the Atlantean archers the advantage. The Atlantean cavalry stays to the rear to keep their people safe. The Atlanteans know the terrain, and the enemy knows they will walk into a trap if they try to attack at night.

After losing at sea and the Great West Wall, the Kayouts and Gambuts have a much-needed victory. With the taking of Halotropolis, the momentum shifts back to the enemy. The Kayouts and Gambuts let the Atlanteans escape, and the enemy regroups in Halotropolis. Even though Halotropolis is damaged pretty badly, the city is now a stronghold for Melercertis.

In the middle of night with the moon in the background, Kaydence and Daygun ride alongside one another with their retreating Atlantean warriors. Every citizen and warrior of the City of God has been ordered to Atlantis. Out of three hundred thousand Atlantean citizens, only seventy thousand survived. Since the citizens of Halotropolis fought so well for their fatherland, Daygun promises them the first bids to evacuate the Empire. They have already done their duty as warriors. The formal citizens of Halotropolis have proven themselves.

Melercertis does not know how to tell Palexus that her husband has been killed in battle. The Kayout Emperor gives Ryelyne a hero's death ceremony. He regroups his men and tells every army of the continent to go to Masaba and wait to attack their enemy. There are still many Atlantean soldiers at the Great West Wall and at Masaba. Melercertis has to destroy Masaba and the Atlantean Great West Wall before he can launch the final attack on the Atlantean capital. If Melercertis does not take Masaba first, he could be attacked on two fronts. He is comforted in knowing that the Atlanteans are losing the war very quickly. His forces still have more than eight million men and more cavalry than the Atlanteans. If Melercertis can take the two cities, he will have control of the world.

In the meantime, Daygun orders Quentoris to take charge of the military at Masaba. The odds keep stacking up against Quentoris to make it through this war alive. He is a warrior and will do whatever the Atlantean Emperor asks of him without question. Daygun knows his friend has gone through a great deal already, but he is the best man qualified to take on the enemy at Masaba. The enemy has to go through rough terrain to get to Masaba, but Quentoris knows a shorter route. In using the passage, he will beat the Kanis and Mearth Army.

CHAPTER XXII
THE ULTIMATE SACRIFICE

Daygun receives word from his scouts that the Continental Alliance is almost at Masaba. Dareous is ordered back to Atlantis, and Quentoris will be the Supreme Commander of the Masaban forces. The Atlantean capital will not be attacked until Masaba is taken. The Atlantean Emperor orders all Atlantean warriors stationed at the Great West Wall back to Atlantis. The Great West Wall warriors are ordered to let the walls fall. They are ordered to go around Masaba and go towards Vasic. After Vasic, they are to veer off and then go to Atlantis. They are ordered to avoid the enemy at all cost.

The Masaban warriors know they will have to sacrifice their lives for their empire. The Atlanteans need more time to evacuate their capital. There are ten divisions in Masaba, and the Masaban King does not want to let it go. Mantis knows his son, Ryelyne, is dead. Ryelyne knew the weaknesses of the Great East Wall leading into Atlantis. He believes the enemy is much weaker without his son's guidance. The main concern for the Masaban King is his civilian population. He cannot let what happened to the Halotropolean population happen to his.

Mantis wants revenge for his son's death. He wonders what the enemy could have done to make his son become a traitor. Ultimately, he blames the enemy for his son's decision to turn his back on Atlantis.

Daygun wishes he could order the Masaban Army to retreat to save lives, but the city has to be sacrificed for the majority of Atlanteans to retreat off the peninsula. The Atlanteans need more time, and that time can only be bought with Atlantean lives. Mantis knows the enemy will not be able to take the city quickly. Daygun needs as much time as possible to save his race from totally being wiped off the face of the earth. There is still the possibility to sue for peace, but the Atlantean Emperor knows freedom from strife is probably a false hope.

The Atlantean capital is the strongest city in the Atlantean Empire. It is twice as strong as the other two cities combined. The capital has more warriors coming from the Great West Wall. Every piece of artillery, munitions, and food is being stockpiled in the capital. The Atlanteans are also setting up even harder defensive parameters outside the city to keep the enemy from using their tightuses. Daygun is learning the enemy's tactics. The enemy does not have the advantages as they had in previous battles. However, Masaba is stranded on its own.

Mantis wants to be the one to defeat the enemy. The Masaban King believes in his men and is counting on their loyalty. Right before the city is surrounded; Quentoris arrives and goes straight to Mantis.

Quentoris says, "I have an executive order from Daygun to take command."

Mantis responds, "It is yours and so are my men."

Quentoris says, "It will be my last command. There will be over eight million warriors at your kingdom's walls. There is no way to escape. You and I will die as warriors for our empire."

The Masaban horns blow and Quentoris and Mantis run up to the tallest tower in the city, they see Nextear's first wave of soldiers approaching. The Continental Alliance is fifteen miles away. He knows the enemy will wait for the rest of their army before they attack. Mantis wants to destroy the enemy which sacked the City of God. The Masaban King is filled with rage and hatred; he wants to kill every enemy warrior with his own blade.

Quentoris examines the battlefield and wishes nothing but death to his enemy. Daygun's messenger has ordered his warriors to stay and fight. If Quentoris can somehow escape when the city is sacked, he has been ordered to return to Atlantis. The Masaban Supreme Commander knows this is a suicide mission. He sends one last message to his family to tell them he will see them in the afterlife.

At the tower, Quentoris says to Mantis, "Three of our leaders of the peninsula are dead. I can't let you be the fourth. I want you to retreat back to Atlantis. I will lead this battle."

Mantis responds, "My son is the one who betrayed our empire. I take full responsibility as a father. I feel somehow as if I save my people here, I am making things right. I have ten divisions here and two hundred thousand civilians willing to give their lives for the Atlantean Empire. If they have a chance to survive, I can't let them die."

Quentoris asks, "What are you getting at?"

Mantis says, "Three hundred years ago, we found iron ore right at our doorstep. The ore was not even a mile away from our city. The mining was done at the mountains south east of here; we extracted rich veins of iron ore. In doing so we tunneled straight to my city. The mining tunnel is right underneath our feet. It is large enough for our heavy cavalry to pass through. On the other side of the mountain range is a passage to a valley. Get my civilian population out of here."

Quentoris responds, "I am responsible here. It should be you who leads your people to safety. Why was I not notified about this?"

Mantis says, "It was lost in time. Quentoris, my son destroyed my family's name. In three days our enemy will take my city. We are subjected to Atlantis, but let me take command of the battle here. You will become a hero when Daygun finds out you saved tens of thousands of lives and more divisions brought back to Atlantis. The message from Daygun said if you can make it out alive to retreat back to Atlantis; the tunnel is that opportunity."

Quentoris says, "I will get your people to safety. We will stay for the initial attack. The enemy needs to see men on the walls fighting them back. If they see only a hundred thousand men on the walls fighting, they will take the city in a day. We need them to think there are hundreds and thousands of men here. We will fight hard until they start to take the city's second line of defense."

Mantis asks, "Would you like to see the tunnel?"

Quentoris replies, "Let's do this quickly. We need to go over how to keep the enemy here as long as possible."

The two leaders go in the tunnel and there are miles of channels going every direction. They all lead to the valley below. Tens of thousands of people can fit comfortably inside. Quentoris is amazed at what he sees. He knows he has a fighting chance to get home to Atlantis.

Outside the city, Melercertis and Nextear regroup their men for battle. The enemy moves the tightuses onto the battlefield. The tightuses are aligned to face the east side of Masaba. Because the Atlanteans have little cavalry, they have to compensate with artillery. The city has more artillery than Halotropolis. The enemy will attack from every side to confuse the Masaban city. Melercertis does not know the weaknesses of the city and decides to attack every direction at the same time. The cavalry of the Gambut, Kanis, Kayouts, and Mareth, are on each side of Masaba to attack the gates. It will not take long before the enemy is inside Masaba.

Mantis looks outside his chambers and sees the enemy advancing. He hears his enemy chanting and yelling death to the Atlanteans. The Atlanteans do the same.

At the Great West Wall, the army commander is Cregnikias; he took the place of Dareous when he was assigned to Masaba. His men are marching to Atlantis and can hear the roar of the enemy from twenty miles away. The warriors of the Great West Wall can hear the hate and determination of their enemy. Cregnikias' men look straight while they march and show no emotion from what they hear. There are some Great West Wall officers wanting to help, but all respect their orders. They believe in Daygun and obey him, even though their fellow countrymen are about to die.

Melercertis looks upon Masaba and orders his army to attack. The Atlanteans fire all of their artillery. At this point, the enemy is not yet in range of the Atlantean archers. This time the Atlantean infantry is staying inside. There are more archers than what the Atlanteans had in Halotropolis. The Masaban artillery will destroy anything on the battlefield, but eventually Masaba will run out of munitions. The Atlanteans made more artillery pieces when the war began, but they have to resort to crude artillery pieces for this battle. The Masaban archers have over three hundred arrows apiece. The Atlantean blacksmiths worked twenty-four hours a day to get the numbers. Masaba has the firepower to destroy an entire empire, but not the world.

The battle begins, and the Atlantean artillery fires in fast increments. The Masaban artillery fires at will. It is a desperate time, and the Atlanteans know it. They hit the enemy no matter where they point their artillery, but there are simply too many soldiers to defeat. Some artillery positions focus their firepower on the tightuses. With random firing from the Atlanteans, Melercertis' men are confused. They do not know where to attack or regroup. The enemy's language barriers are not helping much either.

Melercertis sees a weak spot in the ranks of the Masaban artillery and orders the tightuses to attack the east and north wing of the city. There is some concentration of fire from the Masaban artillery, but not enough to repel the number of tightuses. If the tightuses reach the Atlantean walls, there is nothing the Atlantean's artillery can do.

The Masaban artillery is fixated and cannot move. The artillery is on turrets, but cannot move from one end of the city to the other. The main objective of the Atlantean artillery is to take out the tightuses before they reach the walls. The enemy has tens of thousands of men dying on the battlefield, but there are millions to take their place.

At first, the Atlanteans seem to beat back the enemy advances. Due to the steady stream of Atlantean firepower, the enemy becomes scattered and cannot concentrate on one area of Masaba. The Atlantean's giant crossbows are destroying anything that is coming close to the walls. There are two hundred giant crossbows firing on the battlefield and the artillery personnel are able to fire every two minutes. When the enemy infantry comes into range of the Atlantean archers, a barrage of arrows flies through the sky and kills anything in its path.

The Atlantean catapults fire out two hundred pound circular boulders and mow down the ranks of their enemy. On the other hand, the enemy's catapults are not in range to do any damage to Masaba. Because the enemy's projectiles lose momentum from the long distance, some enemy catapults hit the Masaban walls and bounce right off. None of the enemy catapult's boulders go over the walls. The Masaban defenses are taller and thicker than those of Halotropolis. The tightuses finally reach their objective on two sides of Masaba. There is confusion as to where to send the Atlantean infantry inside their city.

The Atlantean infantry and archers meet the tightuses. The Atlanteans infantry goes where the enemy swordsman are debarking into the city from the covered chariots. Because the Masaban walls are so tall, only the men on the top levels of the Kayout towers are able to come over the Masaban defenses. The Atlantean infantry fights back the enemy coming out of the tightuses, but more enemy tightuses hit the walls. Thousands of Kayouts and Gambut jump onto the walls of Masaba.

The Atlantean infantry strikes the enemy inside their city, and the Atlantean archers are backing them up. The Kayouts use the tightus' rams, and smashes all four sides of Masaba's gates at the same time. The Atlanteans take out three tightuses before the fourth tightus finally tears down the Masaban north gate. The Atlantean infantry compensates and engages the infringed area of the city.

At the Masaban north gate, Mantis leads his men into battle, but he wants to die. The King of Masaba feels guilty about Ryelyne's decision to attack his own people. As a father, he feels he could have had done something different. Mantis draws his sword and fight besides his men. The Masaban King has so much hatred for the enemy that his anger keeps him going forward. He puts himself in harms way because of his anger. He kills ten men without falling short of breath.

At the eastern side of Masaba, Quentoris is in dire need of reinforcements. He rushes to the nearest tightus, which is trying to breach the wall. He sees a Masaban general fighting with his infantry and decides to assist. He knows it is a matter of time before the enemy has complete control of the wall.

Near Quentoris, his Atlantean archers are quickly running out of arrows. They take every arrow out of enemy soldiers and use them again. The women rush to bring more arrows to the front, but many women die in the process. The Atlantean artillery has only enough munitions for another hour. The enemy's main objective is to take the Masaban artillery out of action. They start to succeed, and less artillery is firing at their army beyond the walls of Masaba.

Quentoris orders the Atlantean military inside the secondary wall of the city where the tunnel is located. There are more archer munitions ready for the next fight. The Atlantean infantry stays at the first wall to fight back their enemy.

Thirty minutes pass, and the Atlanteans start to lose ground again at the first line of defense. More tightuses breach over the walls. The defenses of the city are crumbling.

Back at the Masaban north gate, Mantis is losing men very quickly and does not have reinforcements. Mantis continues to fight on, and he does not care if he dies. After a while, he becomes exhausted, and it becomes harder for him to fight. Because the Masaban King is fatigued, the enemy turns towards him. The enemy acts like a pack of lions, and can see weakness in the Masaban King.

Soon, Mantis is surrounded. The Masaban King looks at his city and orders one more charge. Mantis fights back his enemy, but a young Gambut warrior slices Mantis through the thigh in the middle of a fight. It is not a fatal wound, but slows him even more. Another enemy archer sees this and puts an arrow right in Mantis' back. Shortly afterwards the gate is taken, and the enemy has full control of the city's north gate. The Atlanteans cannot take it back. There are not enough Atlanteans to retake it. Mantis dies in seconds from the arrow, and the father of a traitor is dead.

On the other side of the city, Quentoris has tens of thousands of civilians already in the mining tunnels. The channels have good ventilation for the people inside. It has hundreds of torches for light. The tunnel is very crowded. The Atlanteans have over twenty thousand archers, seven hundred heavy cavalry, seventy thousand infantry, and twelve thousand light cavalry ready to break through the wooden doorway to the valley below. The doorway is hidden from the other side by a thin layer of rock. Quentoris runs to the doorway towards the valley.

Quentoris yells inside the tunnel, "Do it now!"

The mammoths push forward and knock down the doorway. Everyone starts to remove the rocks in front of the doorway, and the heavy cavalry is able to move easily out of the mouth of the tunnel. There is no enemy to be found. It was not expected for anyone to be here. Melercertis' main objective was the city, not the area where the Atlanteans are fleeing.

Back in Masaba, fifty thousand Masaban warriors stayed behind to give a chance for their civilians to live. The tunnel is ordered for the walls to collapse inside. Hundreds of boulders fall, and no one can enter the tunnel. It seals the fate of the people still inside Masaba. The tunnel was the only way out.

The bells ring in an older Atlantean code. Most of the officers were taught the code in military college. It tells the rest of Atlantean

Empire what Quentoris is doing and what he has planned. He knows the enemy will follow. He does not know if his message will be transmitted to the next Atlantean bell post because it may have been abandoned. Over seventy thousand civilians from Masaba are on their way to Atlantis.

Three hours later, the city is taken. Melercertis is inside the city and sees the tunnel. He orders his men to investigate. Thirty minutes later a scout goes to Melercertis.

The scout says, "We found where the tunnel leads. It is a shortcut we can't get to; we will have to go around. We see the Atlanteans in the horizon fleeing."

Melercertis responds, "Send ten divisions to take them. The Atlanteans are cowards after all."

The Atlanteans from the Great West Wall, who are on their way to capital, can hear the bells ringing and are only twenty-five miles from Quentoris. Cregnikias orders his cavalry and youth archers to Quentoris' aid. The Great West Wall commander tells a messenger on horseback to go to the bell post and instruct Quentoris to meet them north of the Campiton Gorge. It will take the messenger an hour and a half just to reach the bell post. This is half way. Cregnikias is disobeying Daygun's orders.

Cregnikias gathers his generals together and says, "I am going against Daygun's direct orders. You have the right to relieve me of my command. Do you have any objections?"

A general responds, "I don't agree with disobeying orders, but it would be too late to ask the Atlantean Emperor from this distance. I know Daygun would want us to help. It is no longer your responsibility to ask for forgiveness. It is all of ours. We are with you."

The Atlantean messenger from the Great West Wall finally arrives at the bell post and sends the message to Quentoris. During this time, Cregnikias' archer youth and cavalry are running very quickly to the Campion Gorge. Because they are so young, they do not tire while running. Cregnikias takes his men and runs to the gorge as well. The Great West Wall general has over ninety-five thousand men. The main thing Quentoris needs is heavy and light cavalry.

Quentoris knows the enemy cavalry will come after him. The enemy cavalry has to go the long way around the hills and mountains, but there are only two ways out of the mountain range. The Atlantean generals only have an hour and a half before the enemy cavalry can reach them.

In the middle of the people from Masaba trying to reach the Campion Gorge, the enemy finally reaches Quentoris' men. While running, Quentoris tells the men to set up for battle. He is still fifty minutes from the gorge where they are to meet the army from the Great West Wall. Quentoris gives the order to turn around and meet the enemy dead on. The Atlanteans cannot run anymore. Quentoris does not know exactly where the Great West Wall army is located, and the Kayout and Gambut cavalry are right behind them. He sends a messenger to the gorge to tell the men from the Great West Wall where they are located. Quentoris does not know the strength of Cregnikias' men. He just hopes they can help in some way.

About twenty minutes from the gorge, Quentoris' messenger sees light and heavy cavalry coming towards him. The messenger does not know if they are Atlanteans or his enemy. He stops his horse and waits to see if it is the Great West Wall army. Moments later, the messenger sees that they are Atlanteans. The messenger hurriedly tells the Great West Wall cavalry where Quentoris is located. Eight hundred Atlantean cavalrymen rush to Quentoris' defensive perimeter. Right behind them is the Atlantean youth, and they run at full speed toward the battle. Cregnikias' warriors have been looking for Quentoris' army. They went to the gorge and did not see them there; they know Quentoris is in trouble and go towards Masaba.

At this time, the enemy's heavy and light cavalry catches up with the last survivors of Masaba. Quentoris' men try to fight them off, but are losing. His archers are running out of arrows, and they are outmatched against the enemy's light cavalry. The Atlanteans have to use the arrows in close quarters to protect their infantry. With little cavalry, Quentoris is doomed with what he has to fight with.

The enemy is destroying the left flank of the Atlantean warriors. Quentoris sends his infantry to compensate. Then, out of nowhere, Cregnikias' light and heavy cavalry charge into the Kayouts and Gambuts offensive, precisely where reinforcements are needed most.

The enemy generals see that Cregnikias' cavalry starts to make good ground. The enemy reinforcements stop a half-mile away from Quentoris' defense. The enemy watches their cavalry start to lose ground, but they cannot do anything about it. The enemy finally gives the order for their reinforcements to help their comrades. They charge at full speed and Quentoris braces for the impact.

At the last minute, Quentoris counters with his army. The Masaban Supreme Commander knows his men are in better shape, and the enemy has been running to catch up with them. Unfortunately, Quentoris' archers run out of arrows. They cannot help their infantry with their bows. The Atlantean archers draw their swords and fight with their infantry. The Great West Wall cavalry is starting to lose beasts. The enemy cavalry overwhelms the Atlanteans' cavalry.

The Atlantean youth finally reach the battlefield and form a line to fire at their adversary. The enemy is being attacked on two fronts. The enemy cavalry attacks the youth archers, and the young archers fight back their attackers. After the Atlantean youth take an enemy stronghold, they charge forward into the battle.

Later, the Atlantean's two armies converge with each other. The Atlantean youth help resupply Quentoris' archers and they fight as one. In two hours, the enemy is taken out completely. There is no retreat from their enemy. The Atlanteans are tired of losing, and this is the first time the odds are in the Atlantean's favor. The Atlanteans take pride in killing their adversary. When the enemy first attacked, the Atlantean were destined to lose. Now, they are taking the battlefield. For the Atlanteans, it does not take long to take out two hundred fifty thousand enemy men.

After the battle, Quentoris wants to attack the whole Kayout Army back at Masaba. If they take the enemy by surprise, they can cripple the enemy before the attack Atlantis. The Atlanteans only lost fifteen thousand men. Quentoris and Cregnikias meet at the gorge. The Masaban Supreme Commander talks to the Atlantean generals from his army and the Great West Wall and asks for their advice. Even though Quentoris is the highest-ranking officer, the Great West Wall generals convince Quentoris they need to regroup in the capital. Daygun orders the Great West Wall to the city of Atlantis, and the Masaban Supreme Commander should do the same.

Quentoris orders a messenger to go to the Atlantean bell post to seek orders from the Atlantean Emperor. He believes they could inflict serious damage by attacking the enemy at night, but he does nothing until he has orders from Daygun. Quentoris knows he can take the enemy and he wants it bad. At the same time, he is a loyal and obedient to his emperor.

The orders come back to continue to Atlantis. Quentoris is angry. He knows it is only a matter of time before he will die, and he wants it now on his own terms and conditions. He would rather go down as a hero than try to flee to the Atlantean capital, and he feels cowardly for retreating.

Quentoris can no longer feel pain. He is dead inside. Before, the general had compassion on the men he led. Almost ninety percent of those who Quentoris has led into battle are dead, and he feels he should have died with his men. On the way back to Atlantis, Quentoris sees a badly wounded warrior who fought with him at Bardia. He was stationed at the Great West Wall after the fight. He picks him up and carries him on his horse all the way back to the capital. There is so much death in Quentoris' heart to love anything but his own men. The only thing holding him together is honor and loyalty to the new Atlantean Empire.

Chapter XXIII
The Last Battle of Atlantis

The Atlanteans had a very good victory at the Campion Gorge. Overall, the Atlanteans destroyed more than a million and a half enemy warriors at Masaba and the gorge. No one who fought in Masaba thought they would be alive to fight another day. Their survival was due to the leadership of Quentoris, but he is returning to the capital a broken man. The war has changed him. He is mentally exhausted. He does not even know what he is fighting for anymore except to save what is left of his civilization. The two cities which helped Atlantis become a strong empire are destroyed, and no one in the Atlantean Empire will ever be the same.

Two days after the battle of Campion Gorge, Quentoris' soldiers reach Atlantis. He has seen nothing but death and destruction. The general marches into his capital and he is greeted as a hero. The warriors from Masaba can barely march into their capital. After the Atlanteans arrive into the city, the injured are ordered towards their hospitals and they are the first ones to be evacuated out of the city by ship.

Outside the gates of the Atlantean capital, battle artillery is being prepared, but Atlantis is always set up as if a war would happen the next day.

The enemy has only seven and a half million soldiers left out of twelve million. The Atlantean capital will be harder to take than the Atlantean Great East Wall. Nevertheless, the Atlanteans are backed into a corner.

Due to the valiant efforts of those at Masaba, Daygun had some time to make more artillery and munitions. Atlantis is the last stronghold of the empire. Daygun has less than half of his military left. The Atlantean Emperor has lost good generals, but they have men ready to protect their capital. The city has more artillery than the Atlantean Great East Wall and Halotropolis combined. The only weakness of the capital is its large size. The capital has more ground to cover. Every piece of food in the Atlantean Empire has been transferred to the city just in case of a long battle.

The capital is still being evacuated. Daygun feels he can take the enemy here and sue for peace if the city holds out long enough. The enemy is very deep inside Atlantis and their supply lines are very long. Daygun is glad to know that Quentoris and Dareous are still alive. Since Quentoris has entered the capital, Daygun has noticed he is acting differently than he did in the past. He looks at his people and looks right past them. He still functions as a general, but he is void of emotions.

Quentoris' main tactical strength is with artillery. Dareous is from Halotropolis, his strength is with the sword and infantry fighting. Daygun is from Atlantis, and his major attribute is the bow. All of them will work as a team in the battle to come, and they must trust one another's judgment in the heat of battle.

The Atlanteans are ready. The Continental Alliance sets up camp four miles north of the city outside Atlantis. The enemy waits until they have all their men to attack as one. It is all or nothing. The enemy soldiers do not even consider the long lasting effects of the world losing so many men. They only know that they cannot stop now.

The Atlantean ships have had more time to evacuate civilians and wounded soldiers. The enemy will not spread out their men on an expedition to find the Atlanteans which are fleeing right now. Melercertis, Borealeous, and Nextear know if the Atlanteans fall here, finding and destroying their adversary will take time. It will take time to rebuild a navy to find the Atlanteans, but they are confident in destroying the whole civilization. The Atlanteans have land all over the world. The Continental Alliance will have to take their enemy out one location at a time.

The Atlantean capital has always been the key in destroying the Atlantean civilization. Without a capital, the Atlanteans cannot grow. One of the Kayouts' main goals is to destroy the libraries inside the Atlantean capital. In doing so, the Atlantean technology will be hindered, and God's word will be destroyed.

On the second day of being surrounded, the Atlantean generals assemble to make a plan. Quentoris, Dareous, and Daygun look at a map on a table and Daygun looks up at Quentoris.

Daygun says, "We are on the verge of losing this war. We have almost fifty thousand archers ready to fight. Each of them has close to two hundred arrows a piece."

Quentoris adds, "Our artillery is ready and at your disposal. In the last month, we have produced seventy catapults and forty-five giant cross bows. We have cut down every molless tree in our empire. This puts us at four hundred catapults and three hundred giant crossbows. Each of the giant crossbows has sixty pieces of ammunitions. We only have three walls to protect. The enemy cannot attack our harbor. The Continental Alliance will try to take our city, but it's going to be at high price."

Dareous says, "Our infantry is ready."

Daygun replies, "This is the last battle of Atlantis. Either we win or lose. No matter what we do, we have to leave Atlantis. Our scientists say there is too much death here. There is a very good possibility of a grand epidemic from diseased drinking water. The whole world could die from such a plague. Over a hundred years ago, the same things happened in Garsha. At first, there were fifty thousand deaths, and then hundreds of thousand of people died from the decaying bodies left over from the war. The whole world is in trouble. The enemy will kill themselves. We can try to explain this to the enemy in a way to sue for peace, but they will not understand. The enemy will think that we are just trying anything to get out of this war intact. Because of their ignorance, they will kill more of their own people than what we will do here. We have to leave Atlantis and not come back for years. We have to leave and stop all interaction with the rest of the world. This is going to be hard. We will have to isolate ourselves."

Dareous questions, "Where will we go?"

Daygun replies, "There are whole continents which are isolated from the rest of the world. There is also the Iteru River which flows backward from the sea. The people there are isolated from most of the world. It can help us to survive. About three thousand miles away, there is a land inhabited only by primitive tribes. They have little technology in tools or weapons. They will not be a threat to us there. It is a long journey, but our population needs to reside far from this destruction. We must scatter out to insure the survival of our race."

Quentoris says, "What about the rest of the world?"

Daygun replies, "We can't think about the rest of the world right now. The only people we should be concerned about are Atlanteans. We can dodge the epidemic. The rest of the world will die. This will help our race to survive in the far future."

Quentoris says, "What if there isn't an epidemic this time around? What if the disease doesn't exist or is eradicated? What if mankind became immune to this disease?"

Daygun replies, "We will regroup and conquer our land in the next couple of years when we are ready. I have put every piece of iron ore in reserve to build swords for future wars. There are six military cargo ships which survived from the Mareth and Kanis sea battle, and they are on route to Mancater to start on production of our swords."

Dareous says, "That is over three thousand miles away. This is the storm season and the chance of them making it is slim. With that kind of weight, the ships cannot make it through a heavy storm."

Daygun says, "I had to put our iron ore at a safe place where the enemy cannot take it or destroy the facilities we are going to build there. All iron ore is on board our ships. Ashastonous is on the important journey. If I can't trust my Admiral in doing this, who can I trust? He knows every way of the seas and oceans."

Quentoris stands up and says, "As for the matter at hand, we must destroy the enemy here. We must deplete the numbers of our enemy where they will not want to find us."

Daygun replies, "In the last month, the heroes of our empire have become clear. There will be more to come. The ones who gave their lives to God and our empire are the heroes. They will never be forgotten. I have lost a brother and a father. They are heroes to me and our people. I will mourn for them after this war. Now, I can't be angry or depressed. I have to govern my emotions for the greater good. I have a whole empire to save."

Nothing happens at Atlantis for a couple of days. More ships come in and out of the harbor. Everyday the capital is less crowded. The food stores are three fourths full. People try to save everything they can before Atlantis is conquered. Many inhabitants of Atlantis do not want to leave, and want to defend their empire to the death.

The Atlantean battlecruisers and destroyers are repaired from the damage suffered during the sea battles. The warships are used to evacuate people as well. The battlecruisers are to be used to transport food. The men of the ships are to reinforce Atlantis in their last stand. The sailors on the warships feel as if they have been trapped aboard their ships and are ready to fight the enemy on land.

Kaydence helps in the Atlantean hospitals taking care of the children and the elderly that were wounded in Masaba and Halotropolis. She is also prepared for battle. She loves her husband and obeys him, but at the same time, she is ready to fight to the last man. She is also tired of fleeing. Kaydence is worshiped by all Atlanteans. She is the perfect role model to her people. Because Kaydence loves Atlantis so much, she makes sure she is seen doing things in her community. She wants people to know royalty is equal to the rest of the population. She is humble, but she also knows the Atlanteans need to see their leaders taking charge. It brings hope to the people of Atlantis.

The Atlanteans are ready to fight, and they have also noticed more activity from their enemy. The tightuses are on the front line. It is time for last battle of Atlantis. The Atlanteans are prepared and so is their enemy. The Atlanteans are tired of waiting to die. They will face their destiny head on.

Melercertis and Tito stands on a hill looking towards the Atlantean capital.

Melercertis says, "What has the world done? We are about to destroy the most technological empire of the world. The world has taken religion and twisted it. On this side of the battlefield, man is using our gods as an excuse to destroy an entire race. Who is to say our religion is the right one?"

Tito replies, "If we don't do this, our religion will destroy us back home, and the rest of the world will see us as being weak. You are leader of the world. We will lose everything if we don't go forward."

Melercertis says, "You're right. There is no other way. Send in the assault. It is time."

The Kayouts start their attack. The crossbows of the tightuses start to move into range. Over two hundred tightuses go straight up towards the northern gate of Atlantis. The rear of Atlantis is covered by sea. The capital only has three sides of land to protect. The east and west side of Atlantis is covered by hills, and it is hard for the enemy infantry and cavalry to attack in significant numbers. The only flat area outside Atlantis is the northern side, and the Atlantean artillery positions are heaviest there. The Atlanteans start to fire their artillery. The bombardment is concentrated on the battlefield for maximum efficiency. Every spot outside the Atlantean defenses is covered in fire. The only things moving on the battlefield are the tightuses. In the middle of the first attack, every invader is either dead or on fire. Within an hour, over a hundred thousand enemy men have lost their lives. The tightuses stop at the front of Atlantean capital and cannot go forward. Because of the bombardment from the Atlantean's giant crossbows, some of the tightuses catch on fire, but the Kayouts extinguish the fires and continue to go forward.

The tightuses roll closer to the wall of Atlantis. The Atlantean's giant crossbows try to compensate, but they can do little. It takes a while to change the tilt of the Atlantean giant crossbows. They are the most powerful pieces of artillery on earth, but their weakness is changing the angle to fire quickly.

The Atlantean catapults are easier to maneuver than the crossbows and do what they can to fight the tightuses. Nevertheless, some tightuses hit the first Atlantean wall. The enemy men come outside the tightuses and into the Atlantean capital. The archers of the Atlantean secondary wall fire on everyone who comes out of the giant covered chariots. Not a single one of the enemy soldiers makes it out alive. Dead men pile on top of each other. The men of the tightuses have to pull their dead out just to stay on the offensive.

While the Atlanteans are preoccupied with the tightuses, the Continental Alliance's artillery moves forward. The enemy catapults fire on the walls of Atlantis. The Atlantean's giant crossbows change their tilt and return fire to the enemy catapults. Some of the Atlantean walls are already damaged badly, and the enemy infantry cannot go forward until a wall is totally breached. The Atlantean archer emplacements are firing out upon their enemy. Atlantis has more archers and more arrows than they did in the previous two cities. The Atlanteans can fire for hours without running out of arrows. In the last month, every person that knew how to make an arrow did so for this battle.

Daygun orders what is left of the Atlantean heavy cavalry to gather outside their gates. The Atlantean cavalry goes towards the tightuses. The Atlantean mammoths ram right into the enemy armored protected chariots. During the Atlantean offensive, many tightuses are destroyed. The mammoths correlate their attack to hit the Kayout war machines at the same time. Because the tightuses are top heavy, the large covered chariots tumble over and kill the enemy inside. The tightuses retreat to regroup. It took a month to build such structures for the sole purpose of destroying the walls of Atlantis, and they are now being wiped out on the first run.

While the tightuses' retreat, the enemy's heavy cavalry charges the Atlantean heavy cavalry. They go head to head towards each other. The Atlanteans are outnumbered, but fare well against their enemy. In the background, the horns blow from Atlantis and the Atlantean cavalry returns into the gates. Daygun cannot afford the total destruction of his cavalry at this point.

There have been heavy causalities on both sides, but it becomes a stalemate. The enemy lost a quarter of their heavy cavalry, but most of all, the enemy is losing too many of their tightuses.

Daygun climbs onto the first wall and cheers for his men. Because Daygun starts to cheer, the rest of the Atlanteans cheer in the aftermath of the battle. Even though it was a gridlock on both sides, it seems the Atlanteans won.

Within thirty minutes, the tightuses go forward again with their heavy cavalry. The Atlanteans fire on the enemy heavy cavalry and wreak havoc. The enemy has no choice but to fall back. The enemy tries to remove their dead from the battlefield, but the Atlanteans kill those who do. There is no ceasefire. This war is to the death. There will be no prisoners taken on either side. At this point in the war, there is so much hate; no one sees each other as human beings anymore. Each person on each side is an enemy without a soul.

A constant stream of ships is coming in and out of the harbor. Each ship leaves twenty minutes after docking. Men, women, children, and supplies are thrown onto the ships. Supplies are stowed below deck after embarking. There is no time for detail.

The Atlantean flagships take a little longer to transfer supplies on board. The Atlantean flagships are so massive that twenty minutes is not enough time. It takes an hour to load the heavy battlecruisers to capacity. In turn, some Atlantean ships have to wait.

At this time, only thirty-two percent of the Atlantean population has evacuated. There are not enough ships for the task. The men and women are trapped in their city and they are preparing to fight to the death.

Daygun's heavy and light cavalry will soon be ordered for another offensive. He is waiting for the enemy's heavy cavalry to come out. The Atlanteans will be outnumbered twenty to one in cavalry, but the Atlanteans are still better trained. The Atlantean heavy cavalry is not afraid, and they are ready to fight to the death.

Out of nowhere, the tightuses come towards the city again. The enemy's heavy cavalry is right behind. The gates open and the Atlanteans come out full speed. The Atlantean cavalry hits the right side of the enemy. It seems the Atlantean mammoths are enraged. The Atlantean beasts have never fought as hard as they do now. The enemy animals almost retreat as the Atlantean beasts go forward. The Atlantean heavy cavalry destroys nine to one on the battlefield. The Atlantean archers and artillery destroys the rest. After an hour, there is almost not an enemy beast to fight back against the Atlanteans. The Atlanteans almost kill every mammoth and elephant in the enemy's arsenal.

The enemy archers come forward to the battlefield and fire on the Atlantean heavy cavalry. The Atlantean heavy cavalry is trapped and destroyed. It seems every mammoth on earth is dead in the Atlantean Empire. Two months ago, there were tens of thousand mammoths in the world. Now, they are almost extinct, and those still living are used to move the tightuses. The Atlantean archers stop the advancement of their enemy.

The next couple of days, the enemy keeps trying to attack the Atlantean northern wall, but the Atlanteans keep them in check. The enemy tries to take on the west northern side of the Atlantean capital. The Atlanteans change the direction of their artillery to compensate for the threat. Daygun is a little concerned because the artillery to the left side of the city cannot reach the enemy. This is something the Atlanteans never thought to be possible. This is the weakest wall of the Atlantean capital. The Atlanteans counted on their natural barriers to keep the enemy from attacking.

On the fifth day of the attack on Atlantis, there are very

few Atlantean cavalry to attack in an offensive. The Atlantean infantry will be destroyed if they decide to go beyond their archers' protection. The enemy catapults and tightuses focus on the Atlantean archer emplacements and the defenders of the Atlantean capital are massacred. The Atlantean archer and artillery emplacements are being destroyed one by one, and it is allowing more enemy warriors inside the Atlantean capital.

The tightuses go towards Atlantis and are able to slam right into the weakest part of the wall. The Atlanteans do destroy the majority of the enemy tightuses, but they cannot take them all. The Atlantean archers do not have a good angle on the enemy due to the configuration of their walls.

From the tightuses, the enemy pours into Atlantis. It is a massive attack. The Atlantean infantry is sent in to defend the holes. Dareous takes charge and keeps the enemy at bay, but at high cost. It almost becomes a pushing match between armies. The Atlanteans kill the enemy in the city's alleyways, but the Atlanteans have to give up the first wall. This makes the Atlanteans go backwards towards the next stronghold.

When it is all over, the enemy has taken the first barrier into Atlantis. The enemy tries to take the second wall quickly, but the Atlanteans defend it with everything they have. The enemy has to regroup, and try to think of another way to take the second defensive Atlantean wall.

Daygun, Quentoris, and Dareous gather to form a new strategy. It is only a matter of time before the enemy takes the city completely. The Atlantean ships are still evacuating people out of the capital, but the majority of the civilian population is still in the city, and there is not enough time to save them. There are still ninety thousand children under the age of sixteen inside their city. All are being transferred out first. Daygun is trying to buy time. The wounded have been transferred to Malserta; it is an island city fifty miles from the Atlantean Empire.

Daygun says, "What can we do? We can't defeat them. We don't have the resources. It is suicide."

Quentoris replies, "Most of our men are already dead. We might as well die with honor."

Dareous says austerely, "The race will survive. We must use every last Atlantean warrior to fight. We must buy a little more time. We gave an oath to our empire to protect it. We must kill as many of our enemy as we can. If we do, they won't be able to pursue the ones we are trying to protect. The enemy will go back home. We will not be forgotten after they take our capital. If some Atlanteans live to tell what has happened here, we will spread the word of God. One day man will be ready for His guidance. Man is too primitive for such wonderment as God. Thousands of years from now, mankind will understand what we see in Him, and want to take His hand."

Quentoris replies, "Daygun, we will all die here except you. You are needed to create order. We will all go to heaven because we are protecting God's children. I am dying for God and the children of Atlantis. You are the key holder to His word when man is ready. As Atlanteans, we must carry the word of God to the end of man's existence."

Daygun says, "I should die here in honor. I will not leave as a coward."

Dareous replies, "You're not going to be a coward. You will fight on for Atlanteans after we are dead, and the continued name of God will rest on your shoulders. You sir, are the basis of our culture. If you die here, our culture will die with you. You must live to help our culture survive."

Daygun says, "I agree with you all. I have never had better friends here, and no other emperor will have more loyal and braver men. I will go to my grave knowing I had to run to protect our race. I have to honor your bravery and what you believe in. Remembering you will help me fight my struggles in the years to come. You are the true leaders here. Nevertheless, I need you outside Atlantis."

Quentoris says, "I will stand to protect you no matter what. I will do what I can. If the timing is right, I will board the last ship. In doing so, I will be your protector in our lands abroad."

Dareous says, "I will do the same. I will do what I can, but you are the most important thing to me and my empire. I am the first to fight and the last to live."

Daygun hugs Quentoris and Dareous as brothers and salutes them as warriors. They all leave the room and go to their positions to prepare for the final fight. Quentoris and Dareous stay at their post for twenty-four hours without sleep. The archers fire on the enemy to show them that there is not a weakness in the ranks of the Atlanteans.

After forty-eight hours, the enemy makes a final push and takes the second wall. The Atlanteans have killed over two million men at this point in the battle. The Atlanteans fire upon their own buildings with artillery. The Atlanteans do not want to give the city to the Continental Alliance. They do not want to leave anything behind that can be useful for the Kayouts or Gambuts. From the top of the highest tower in the capital, the Atlantean warriors can see fires all over the Atlantean Empire. At a distance, Masaba and Halotropolis have very thick smoke rising from their walls.

Quentoris orders half of his infantry to fight between the second and third wall. Every man, woman, and child is fighting side by side for God and honor. The children will even die for the belief in their empire. Honor has been instilled in every Atlantean. The Atlanteans kill tens of thousands of men, but at a high cost. Still, the men would rather die on an offensive than wait to die.

On another Atlantean offensive, the enemy counters with their own offensive. The Atlanteans are pushed against the wall of the third barrier. The Atlantean archers give cover for their infantry, but the Atlanteans are trapped and slaughtered. The enemy reaches the harbor gate and tries to takes it. It is the final barrier to the Atlantean enemy.

Dareous and Quentoris are there to oversee the defense and go aboard the ship with their emperor. There is so much fighting and the enemy is advancing too quickly. From a distance, the two generals shake their heads at one another and run toward each other.

Dareous says, "We need one more push from our infantry to hold them back."

Quentoris responds, "The only way we can do this is with leadership from you and me."

Dareous says, "We have fought this far in battle to die here."

Quentoris responds, "God gave this time to save our civilization. It is time to die in honor. We gave an oath to protect our empire and Daygun."

Quentoris' infantry meets the Continent Alliance head on. Dareous' archers go to their position and fire down into the city. Explosions of fire are hitting the enemy inside Atlantis. The whole city is ablaze, except inside the harbor. Women and children fight for their lives, but they cannot escape. There are still pockets of fighting where Atlantean children are holding their positions.

Kaydence and Daygun are advised to board the flagship. Some soldiers have stayed near the ships to protect the emperor. They all know they are going to die. Three and half million enemy warriors are in and outside the Atlantean capital. The Atlanteans blaze the rest of their city.

Daygun and Kaydence start to leave on the last ship. A battlecruiser was the last ship that is allowed inside the harbor. The Atlanteans cannot take anything else from the city. The Atlanteans have to leave most of their books and technology behind; they know it will be burned, and all Atlantean's history will be destroyed as well.

On the way out, Kaydence and Daygun have to fight off enemy warriors who have made it to the harbor. Daygun has to use all of his daggers from his vest just to protect Kaydence. The archers of the Atlantean battlecruiser fire their arrows, allowing Daygun to escape. Kaydence saves her husband from a Kayout who was going to stab her husband in the back.

Finally, the last of the royalty boards the ship. There is a long road to the harbor and nothing but buildings on each side. It is the last bottleneck of the Atlantean city. Dareous and Quentoris are there to defend it. They give their lives for the safety of their emperor. When the ship shoves off, the enemy infiltrates Quentoris' and Dareous' last stronghold inside the capital. The Atlantean enemy pours into the last bottleneck of the city.

Daygun and Kaydence watch with sadness as Dareous and Quentoris' army is taken over. The Atlantean Emperor thinks of what he has left behind, and wishes he could have died with his countrymen. Kaydence and Daygun think of the children who gave up their lives just to save the few who escaped. The whole capital is on fire. Daygun looks at Kaydence and holds her hand for his own comfort. The Atlantean Emperor left his friends to die; he is really disturbed about his men. They were not just loyal to him. Quentoris and Dareous were loyal to God and the Atlantean Empire.

Everyone on board the ship looks at the city of Atlantis for the last time. Daygun is the leader of his people, but he does not know where to start from here. The Atlantean Emperor will do what is needed for his race to survive. The Atlantean Emperor asks to speak. He goes to the highest part of the ship.

Daygun addresses his people, "We have lost our city and our land. The only way we are going to survive is if we distribute our population all over the world and not say a word of who we are. We will go to all stretches of the world where the enemy can't find us. I will set up a colony where Orion ruled and help make our empire great. He was one of the forefathers of our beliefs. But we all can't go there. If we conglomerate together, they will find us and destroy us all. We will go to every continent in the world. We will still stay in contact and trade with one another. We must divide to survive. We will blend in with the rest of the world. We must learn the language of the lands we reside in and always remember that we are Atlanteans. The rest of the world believes in multiple gods. The world isn't ready to believe in the one true God. We must remember Him and spread his word. We must keep Him in our hearts. We have a journey with God. Let Him guide us. Our race may die, but God will not let us be forgotten. As long as we believe in Him, Atlanteans will be in the hearts of man forever."

The ship goes toward the sea, and the Atlanteans do not say anything, but accept their fate with honor and courage.

Chapter XXIV
The History That Has Never Been Written

Duncan, the archeologist, floats in his subliminal mind and overlooks the devastation of Atlantis. He sees the giant burning pillars in Atlantis' harbor. The archeologist understands the columns are important in today's world. His conscious mind is battling his subconscious. He sees the Atlantean women and children dead with a sword or bow in their hands. Everyone on the peninsula died in honor for their empire.

Duncan floats like a feather to where Dareous and Quentoris died for their beliefs. The archeologist cries in his mind for their deaths. He stays there hovering over their bodies like a balloon and says a prayer for their souls. He sees the dead Atlantean warriors as friends and countrymen.

After witnessing the devastation of Atlantis, Duncan goes forward in time. The archeologist sees things as if he is looking inside a crystal ball. He sees millions of men dead on both sides of the battlefield.

Duncan sees the Kayouts and Gambuts leaving Atlantis. As Daygun's scientists predicted, disease strikes mankind and man almost becomes extinct. Most of the world dies from the microorganisms which infect most of the population after the Great War. The dead bodies on the battlefield started an epidemic. After the war, Duncan sees the plague killing over eighty percent of the world's population. No one is able to avoid the sickness. In his thoughts, all technologies of the world were forgotten, and mankind had to start all over with a clean slate.

A little while later, Duncan can sees a civilization creating the sphinx in Egypt. He is not sure if it is the work of the Atlanteans, but he can feel their presence. He sees a woman's face on the Sphinx, rather than what man sees today.

The archeologist goes in darkness and moves quickly to sees where he excavated the mountain city in Spain and how it looks in its prime. He sees the Atlanteans making the city inside and the battle which took place when the inhabitants were slaughtered.

At the entrance of the Atlantean Great East Wall, he can see a barricade to keep people out of the old Atlantean Empire. The Continental Alliance sees the peninsula as where evil is created. The peninsula is capped off from the rest of the world. To the population on the continent, the two statues of God at the Atlantean Great East Wall are considered malevolent.

Duncan is becoming more aware of his surroundings and feels as if ants are all over his body. He feels as if his soul is going into a tornado. He sees the Atlanteans all over the world in small villages. They keep to their beliefs and their children learn of their heritage. The children are told to keep silent of their identity to the rest of the world. The Atlanteans adapt to the cultures they encounter.

Duncan starts to go forward five hundred years, and sees the Atlantean buildings being empty and a large tidal wave destroying the whole Empire of Atlantis. The earth's Tectonic plates shift, putting the Atlantean domain under the ocean. Duncan gets cold and sees the whole peninsula going into the sea and sinking. Even the East and Great West Walls are submerged. Every aspect of Atlantis is wiped off the face of the earth. In the far off lands, Duncan sees the Atlanteans praying to God, and teachers still teaching the ways of their culture.

All of a sudden, he wakes up. Duncan is in a hospital in France. It is hard to move because his muscles have not moved for some time.

Duncan tries to move and asks the doctor, "How long was I was out?"

The doctor replies, "Almost six weeks."

Duncan asks, "What happened?"

The doctor replies, "We don't know exactly. Because of your kidney stones, you were dehydrated. From the pain, you became unconscious, but that would not have put you in a coma. Your brain activity was high the entire time you were under. It is like nothing we have ever seen before."

The next day Rachel and Kyle come to see Duncan. They were flown in by helicopter by Mr. Callaway. They tell him of the finds of the excavation. Rachel says she is starting to work on the alphabet of the writings inside the mountain. She cannot make sentences of it yet, but she thinks it will only take a couple of months to decipher. Duncan reveals what he saw in his unconscious travels. He asks them to keep it secret.

Three months later, Duncan is feeling better and goes back home to recuperate. He rests in a small city in Texas. He is asked to give a speech to a group of student archeologists in the state. He goes to a university in Texas and goes to a pedestal. He thinks on what to say. The whole crowd is silent. Behind Duncan is a large screen showing pictures of the city inside the mountain. The story of his finding has become famous across the world. He clears his throat.

Duncan says, "I have found a civilization which has been lost in time. In mankind's past, the inhabitants were strong and powerful. After evaluating our findings, my team and I realized that they had to be from a far away land. So far, we have found no reason for this civilization to even be there. I believe they were there in hiding. The cultures around the time didn't have the same levels of technology. The civilizations of the city were far more advanced than any other culture of their time period. Due to our discoveries of their military technology, it is apparent that these people were imperialistic."

Duncan clears his throat again and says, "Now, we as a nation think we can't be conquered, but we can. No nation or empire should think they are the best in the world. Rome was brought down. The Greek states were destroyed. In our recent history, Hitler thought Germany would rule the world for a thousand years. Where does it stop? In our own past, we have been imperialistic, and we still are. Past empires and nations take other nations for their resources. Today, we do the same with oil, and play the wrong politics to acquire it. We manipulate the world to get what we want. Our mistakes will haunt us in the future. We as a nation should be better heroes and leaders to the world, or we will end up like the people we just found. I think the city inside the mountain is a reminder to us of how we can be destroyed by our brothers from other nations. We need to go to the next step of evolution in making mankind better. The site we found is not a discovery as archeologists know it. It is a reminder to mankind of what can happen."

The whole crowd is stunned by Duncan's comments. The crowd stands and claps for the archeologist, not because of his find, but because of his perspective. Duncan knows the story of Atlantis will happen again, but he wonders when? Through his discovery, he hopes he can bring man together. The archeologist does not know if what he saw was simply his dream, or what the Atlanteans wanted him to see.

To Be Continued